Other People's Marriages

Rosie Thomas is the author of a number of celebrated novels, including *Bad Girls, Good Women, A Simple Life* and the Top Ten bestsellers *Every Woman Knows a Secret, Moon Island, White* and *The Potter's House*. She lives in north London, and when not writing fiction spends her time travelling and mountaineering.

Acclaim for Rosie Thomas

'Rosie Thomas writes with beautiful effortless prose, and shows a rare compassion and a real understanding of the nature of love'
The Times

'Compelling . . . a master storyteller'
Cosmopolitan

'A story full of passion . . . will keep you reading long after bedtime'
New Woman

'Honest and absorbing, Rosie Thomas mixes the bitter and the hopeful with the knowledge that the human heart is far more complicated than any rule suggests'
Mail on Sunday

'A special talent'
The Times

Other People's Marriages

Rosie Thomas

arrow books

Reissued by Arrow Books in 2003

1 3 5 7 9 10 8 6 4 2

First published in the United Kingdom in 1993 by Michael Joseph

Arrow Books
The Random House Group Limited
20 Vauxhall Bridge Road, London, SW1V 2SA

Random House Australia (Pty) Limited
20 Alfred Street, Milsons Point, Sydney,
New South Wales 2061, Australia

Random House New Zealand Limited
18 Poland Road, Glenfield
Auckland 10, New Zealand

Random House (Pty) Limited
Endulini, 5a Jubilee Road, Parktown 2193, South Africa

The Random House Group Limited Reg. No. 954009

www.randomhouse.co.uk

A CIP catalogue record for this book
is available from the British Library

ISBN 0 09 946247 8

Typeset by SX Composing DTP, Rayleigh, Essex
Printed and bound in Denmark by
Nørhaven Paperback A/S, Viborg

For Charlie and Flora

Grateful thanks for their advice and help during the writing of his book are due to Nicholas and Angelica Browne, Huw Alban-Davies, Helen Powers and other friends, Lindsay Thomas, Beatrice Gehr, Susie Orbach, Stephen Amiel and Sally Berry, Tony Lacey, and to the best editor, Susan Watt.

One

It was the end of October. As London receded and the motor-way bisected open country they saw the flamboyant colours of the trees. Autumn in the city was a decorous affair of fading plane trees and horse chestnuts, just one more seasonal window display, but here the leaves made fires against the brown fields and silvery sky.

'Look at it,' Nina said. 'There's no elegant restraint out here, is there? That's real countryside. Where I belong now. How does the poem go?'

She knew it perfectly well, but she shifted cautiously through the layers of her memory that contained it. Memory could still play tricks on her, bringing her up against some scene or a view or simply some remembered words that would make her cry. She had cried more than enough for now.

' "Season of mists and mellow fruitfulness," ' Patrick supplied for her.

'Yes, that's it.'

The poem brought to mind completion, or rather the conclusion of some important cycle, and the slow but inevitable stilling of the blood and consequent decay that must come after it.

Nina turned her head and stared out of the rear window as if she hoped to catch a last glimpse of London. There was nothing to be seen except the road, and the traffic, and the unreticent scenery. She had left London, and had not yet arrived anywhere else. It was as if the expansive world she had unthinkingly occupied had shrunk until it was contained within Patrick's car. 'It's how I feel, rather.'

'You are not particularly mellow.'

She laughed, then. 'Nor fruitful.'

'You have your work, that's fruit. And you are only thirty-five.'

And so even though she was a widow there was still time for her to meet and marry another man, and to mother a brood of children if she should wish to do so. Not much time, but enough. In his kindly way Patrick did not want her to lose sight of this, although he was too tactful to say it aloud. She was grateful for his consideration, but with another part of herself Nina also wished that her loving friends would stop being so careful now. She thought that she needed someone to shout at her:

Your husband is dead but YOU are ALIVE and you must bloody GET ON with it.

It was what she was trying to shout at herself. Going to Grafton, coming to Grafton, rather, now that they were on the road and more than halfway there, was part of getting on with it.

Nina reached out one hand and put it on Patrick's leg, above the knee, and felt the solid warmth of him caught in the thickness of his clothes. He didn't shrink, didn't even move, but Nina quickly lifted her hand and settled it back with the rest of herself, where it belonged. She felt, as she quite often did nowadays, that Richard's death had removed her from the corporeal world just as conclusively as it had removed him. Widows didn't touch. They accepted unspeaking hugs and silent pats on the shoulder and strokings of their cold hands, but they didn't reach out themselves for the reassurances of the flesh.

'Thank you for driving me all this way.'

He took his eyes off the road for a single second to look at her. Patrick was a careful driver, as his car proclaimed. It was a sensible estate model, armoured with heavy bumpers and crumple zones. Today the rear seats were folded down and the most precious and valuable of Nina's belongings were packed inside. The rest of her things were in the removal van, somewhere on the same road.

'I wanted to drive you. I want to see you properly settled in the house.'

He returned his eyes to the road. A German tour bus swelled in the rear window, and he moved aside at once to let it pass. Richard would have stamped down hard on the accelerator and sent his frivolous car swirling ahead. Nina peered up at the faces behind the skin of glass. They were elderly couples, on a good holiday, intent on enjoyment together. She pinched on the blister of her own sadness before it could pointlessly inflate.

'Do you want to stop off somewhere for a cup of tea?' Patrick asked her.

'No, not unless you do. Let's just get there.'

There was a basket in the back of the car in which she had packed the kettle, cups and tea for themselves and the removal crew, as an article on moving house in a homemaking magazine had advised her to do. In the days before the move Nina had become a paragon of organization. She had made dozens of lists, adding and crossing off, defining and redefining her intentions. She would not be caught out in the small issues, at least. Every box and carton and piece of furniture was labelled with its eventual destination in the new house, she had measured and checked every dimension twice, she knew the whereabouts of every necessary key and switch and security code.

It was the large issues that were more problematic, like whether she was right to be moving, or whether she was insane to do it, as most of her loving friends certainly suspected.

'Are you okay?' Patrick asked.

She smiled sideways at him. 'Fine.'

The countryside unscrolled alongside them. In an hour, more or less, they would be in Grafton.

The great twin towers of the cathedral were visible first. They stood with the town drawn around them in the quiet and fertile fields enclosed by a rim of little grey hills. It was a perfectly

English prospect. The pilgrims who came to Grafton five hundred years before would have had the same view as they wound their way down from the chalk uplands.

The town had grown some ugly outskirts since Nina's childhood. Coming from the London road they did not go by the new business park set in its landscaped gardens. Instead, on this eastern side, there was a huge red-brick supermarket, an estate of miniature red-brick houses shuffled close together, a pair of petrol stations confronting one another across a stream of cars, and a Little Chef. The road became a maze of roundabouts and traffic lights, and litter whirled up in the wind.

'Drive straight through,' Nina said, wanting to apologize for this modern mess. Patrick pointed the car towards the cathedral towers.

Once they had crossed the river by the Old Bridge, they were in the old town where the medieval streets curled in their protective pattern towards the cathedral and the close. It was four o'clock in the afternoon, the traffic was curdled and there were crowds of shoppers on the pavements, mothers with buggies and schoolchildren and pensioners outside Boots, but the sight of the place made Nina happy. The superficial look of it had changed, but the bones of it were the same as they had been when she was growing up, the same as they had been for hundreds of years, and the bones were beautiful.

The pale limestone of the buildings was butter-soft in the late sun. The curves of the streets, Southgate and Coign Street and Drovers, were graceful, and the proportions of the houses and the lines of their roofs were intimate and pleasing. There was a glimpse of a cobbled square through an archway, and the grey front of a Norman church.

'Where now?' Patrick asked.

'That way.'

Nina pointed. There was a narrow entry, just wide enough for the car, where the stone of the old walls was pocked and darkened with the rubbing of countless shoulders.

They passed through the entry and came out into the glory at the heart of Grafton, the cathedral green with the close to one side behind high walls and the great west front of the cathedral itself.

Patrick looked up at the wide tiers of golden stone, the carved companies of faceless saints and archangels in their niches, ranked upwards and rising between the exuberance of columns and piers, to the vast darkened eye of the west window and the height of the Gothic pinnacles towering above.

'I had forgotten how very grand it is,' he murmured at last.

Nina was pleased, possessive.

'I forget, too. Every time it amazes me. There's my house.'

To one side of the green, forming its northern border, there was a terrace of fine Georgian houses. There were four wide steps with iron railings leading up to each front door, and the balconies to the tall first-floor windows were an intricate tracery of wrought-iron leaves. Nina's new house was in the middle of the row, looking directly out over the mulberry tree in the centre of the green.

As she climbed out of Patrick's car, stretching her legs and easing her shoulders after the confinement of the long drive, she stopped for a moment to gaze up at her own blank windows.

'When I was a little girl I always said that I wanted to live in Dean's Row. My mother used to laugh. "Why settle for that?" she used to say. "Why not the Bishop's Palace itself?" The answer was always that I didn't want to marry the Bishop because he had funny teeth.'

Patrick came to stand beside her.

'And now here you are.'

She heard the silent rider, *Maybe it isn't such a half-arsed scheme to come and live down here*, as clearly as if he had enunciated it.

'Have you got the keys?'

Nina took the heavy bunch out of her bag and held it up. 'Yale, Chubb and burglar alarm.'

Patrick waited beside his car and let her go alone up the four steps to unlock the door.

*

She liked the house empty, like this. She could see and admire the ribs and joints of it. In the drawing room the oak floorboards were two handspans broad, smooth and glowing with age. The window shutters folded into their own recesses in the panelling with seductive precision, and the thin glazing bars divided the glass and the late afternoon light into eighths, sixteenths, tidy fractions. Over her head in the hallway the curving wrought-ironwork of the stair rails sprang up from each stone tread and drew her upwards through the centre of the house. The bedrooms were square, well-proportioned, each with its iron grate and painted overmantel. The house was much too big for her, but that did not matter particularly. Richard had left her wealthy. The memory of that, the surprising figures contained in his will, could still catch her off-balance.

At the top of the house the previous owners had created a studio. The slope of the pitched roof, concealed by a low parapet from the green and the cathedral's west porch, was a sheet of glass. There were the Gothic pinnacles, seeming to float above Nina's head in the breadth of the sky.

It was here that she would work. Her plan chests and her drawing board and her desk would be installed, neat and complete, with her boxes of paints and coloured ranks of inks and pencils. Nina was an illustrator of children's books, her work much admired.

'Nina?'

Patrick's voice rose from a long way beneath her.

'I'm coming.'

He was standing outside the drawing room. The door stood ajar behind him, to admit a view of the mulberry tree and of the saints and archangels in their stone niches.

'What do you think?'

'It's wonderful. A beautiful house.'

She put her arms around him and hugged him. Again she felt the resistance – not rejection, but containment – that told her he didn't know what to do with her. It wasn't that she expected anything. Patrick was gay. She had known that for all

6

the ten years they had been friends. But his awkwardness emphasized that her bereavement and the sympathy which followed it had set her apart. She was separate. She was to be treated with care, when in reality her grief and her needs made her long to be pulled in, peremptorily handled, to be loved so roughly that the memories were obliterated. Nina longed for it, bled for it.

'Shall we go down to the kitchen and have some tea?'

Patrick patted her shoulder. 'Excellent.'

He had unloaded the boxes from the back of his estate car and stacked them inside the front door.

'You should have waited for me to help you carry that in.'

'Nina, darling, if I can't manhandle a few packing cases, who can?'

Patrick dealt in antiques, singlehandedly and rather discriminatingly, from his house in Spitalfields. His speciality was early English oak.

Nina said quickly, 'I'm grateful for everything you've done. Not just today, but ever since Richard died.'

Patrick had come to her directly, on that first afternoon, after the telephone call from the house in Norfolk.

'It's okay,' Patrick said. 'You know where I am if you need me.'

She did know, but she was also convinced, with a sudden lift of her spirits, that she had done the right thing to sell the houses and the cars, to put Richard's modern art collection in store, and come to Grafton. She couldn't remake herself in London except as Richard Cort's widow. Here, she was free to make herself what she would.

'Tea.'

The kitchen was in the basement. There were Smallbone cupboards, painted teal blue, expanses of brick and slate. French windows looked out on a small paved yard at the back of the house. Nina took the kettle out of the basket, filled it, plugged it in and set out the cups and saucers. Patrick prowled behind her, opening the doors into the larder and the utility room, inspecting empty cupboards and wine bins and sliding drawers in and out on their smooth runners.

Nina did not much care for this kitchen. The opulent rusticity of it was not to her taste. In London, with Richard and for their friends, she had cooked in a functional space of stainless steel and black granite. But she did not plan to change this place, because it would not be the centre of this house as her old kitchen had been in the last one. She would cook for herself, as quickly as possible, and that would be all.

She poured out the tea and handed Patrick his cup. For the lack of anywhere else to sit they hoisted themselves up and perched side by side on one of the worktops. Patrick gave his characteristic short snuffle of amusement.

'Look at these dinky cut-outs and finials. I'm surprised there are no stencilled flowers.'

'I could paint some in. You're right, though. Richard wouldn't have liked it, would he?'

In London they had also lived in a Georgian house. But Richard's architect had gutted the interior. He had made it a series of huge, light spaces and they had furnished it sparsely. Richard had also owned a modern apartment, where he set out the growing collection of paintings and sculpture and where they sometimes gave parties, and then there had been the house near the sea in Norfolk, stone-floored and thick-walled. These solid, geometric places had contained their life together, and after his death Nina had been unable to contemplate their emptiness. She had sold them, and added even more money to his startling legacy. Richard had been a lawyer, who had also bought and converted and sold property. The mid-eighties had made him rich, although it was not until after he died that Nina realized exactly how rich.

Patrick drank his tea and regarded her. Nina sat with her shoulders hunched forward, her fingers laced around her cup. She looked composed, quite well able to make her own decisions and order her life, as she had always done. He admired her, and her strength. He had witnessed other deaths recently and

8

observed their effects on those who were left behind, and Nina's levelness impressed him,

He asked, 'Is that why you've come here?'

'Because a cathedral close, a little place like Grafton, and this house are so much not Richard's kind of thing?'

'Yes.'

'Partly so. Also I like the feeling that I belong here. There is a sense of being rooted. That's important, isn't it?'

Patrick, who had grown up in Ilford, let it pass.

'Don't you know anyone here any more?'

'Not a soul.'

Nina was an only child. She had spent her childhood and youth in Grafton, but she had left to go to art school when she was eighteen. Her parents had moved away less than a year later, and both of them were dead now. Her remaining links with the town had long ago broken. She laughed suddenly.

'I'll be able to recreate myself entirely, with no one looking over my shoulder. Don't you envy me the chance to get rid of those tiresome labels that people attach to one over the years? *Nina doesn't like curry, knows nothing about music, always cries in those sentimental French films.*'

He nodded, agreeing with her. '*Patrick drives like an old lady, is such a coffee snob, will never learn to ski.*'

They were both laughing now, with affection.

'Don't make yourself too different. All your friends who love you like you are will miss you.'

'I won't.' Nina was thinking, If I start again, away from the places we knew together, I won't feel left behind. Is that a naive expectation?

Upstairs there was a heavy double thump on the door knocker. The men had arrived with the van.

Patrick directed the unloading. The job took less time than he had expected, because Nina had brought so little with her. There were a few pieces that he remembered from the London house, a Queen Anne chest on chest, some Beidermeier that would look

9

well in the plain, square rooms, sofas and chairs, and a French bateau lit. Within two hours the van was emptied and the men were on their way home again.

After they had gone Nina and Patrick had a drink in the drawing room. It was furnished so sparsely that their voices faintly echoed. The illuminated cathedral front swam in the darkness beyond the windows.

'Will you be comfortable enough?' Patrick asked at length.

'I wanted to bring as little as possible.' She was not sure, now. She remembered how the storage people had come to wrap the pictures and modern pieces in burlap and polythene before carrying them away.

'This will be fine for the time being. I can always add more things.'

Different things, she meant, not the old ones.

'Would you like me to stay? I could take you out to dinner somewhere.'

'Thank you, that's nice of you. But it's a long drive back. And I should unpack a bit, I suppose.'

Patrick understood that she wanted him to go, to leave her alone to confront whatever it was she intended. He drank a second glass of wine, reluctant to leave her, and then stood up. Nina went down the stairs with him, and out to the green where his car was parked. They made arrangements for a weekend and promised to telephone one another. Then Patrick kissed her on both cheeks, climbed into his car and drove away.

Nina went back into the house and shut the door. She walked slowly up the stairs to her bedroom and stood at the foot of the bed, her fingertips resting on the high, smooth scroll of polished wood. Richard had bought the French bed for her as a wedding present.

On their wedding night he had held her in his arms, rocked her and told her to imagine that they were in a real boat adrift on a benign ocean. She had smiled at him, drowsy with happiness and sex, and the sea of contentment had seemed boundless.

Nina wrapped her arms around herself now, digging her nails into the flesh of her shoulders to feel the confirmation of pain.

'*Why* did you leave me?' she asked the empty air. 'I can't bear it without you.'

To have come home to Grafton seemed a pointless gesture. Even if she sold everything she and Richard had jointly owned, shedding the possessions of a shared life, his absence would still come at her out of the mundane actions of each successive day.

Nina began to cry, noisily, into the silence of her new house.

TWO

Janice Frost and Marcelle Wickham were the first to notice Nina. They were in the big supermarket and in the distance, as if the perspective lines of the shelves held her vividly spotlit just before the vanishing point, they saw a tall, thin woman in a long black skirt. Her red hair was pinned up in an untidy nest on the top of her head and her mouth was painted the same colour, over-bright in her white face.

'Who is that?' Janice wondered. Janice knew everybody interesting in town, at least by sight.

Marcelle looked. As they watched, the woman moved away with her empty wire basket and disappeared.

Marcelle lifted a giant box of detergent into her trolley and squared it up alongside the cereals and tetrapacks of apple juice.

'Haven't a clue. Some visitor, I suppose. Crazy hair.'

They worked their way methodically up one side of the aisle and down the other, and then up and down the succeeding avenues as they always did, but they didn't catch sight of the red-haired woman again.

Nina paid for her purchases, sandwiching them precisely on the conveyor belt between two metal bars labelled 'Next Customer Please', all the time disliking the frugal appearance of the single portions of meat, vegetables and fish. She loved to cook, but could find no pleasure in it as a solitary pursuit.

She had no car in Grafton. She had sold the Alfa Romeo that Richard had bought her, along with his Bentley coupé, in the grief-fuelled rejection of their possessions immediately after his death. To take her back into the centre of town there was a round-nosed shuttle bus that reminded her of a child's toy. She squeezed inside it with the pensioners and young mothers with their folding pushchairs, and balanced her light load of shopping against her hip. The bus swung out of the car park immediately in front of Janice and Marcelle in Janice's Volvo.

The next person to see Nina was Andrew Frost, Janice's husband. Andrew did recognize her.

Nina had been working. She was painting the face of a tiger peering out of the leaves of a jungle, part of an alphabet book. For a long morning she had been able to lose herself behind the creature's striped mask and in the green depths of the foliage. She worked steadily, loading the tip of her tiny brush with points of gold and emerald and jade, but then she looked up and saw blue sky over her head.

It was time to eat lunch, but she could find no enthusiasm for preparing even the simplest meal. Instead she took a bright red jacket off a peg and went out to walk on the green.

Andrew had left his offices intending to go to an organ recital in the cathedral. He was walking over the grass towards the west porch, pleased with the prospect of an hour's music and freedom from meetings and telephones. He saw a red-haired woman in a crimson jacket crossing diagonally in front of him, and knew at once who she was. She had worn a costume in the same shade of red to play Beatrice.

He quickened his pace to intercept her.

'It's Nina Strange, isn't it?'

Nina stopped. She turned to see a square man with thinning fair hair, a man in a suit who carried a raincoat even though the sky was blue.

'You don't remember me,' the man said equably.

A thread of recollection snagged in her head.

'Yes, yes I do. Wait a minute . . .'

' "When I said I would die a bachelor, I did not think I should live till I were married." '

'Oh, God, I *do* remember! It's Andrew, isn't it?'

'Andrew Frost. Benedick to your elegant Beatrice.'

'Don't try to remind me of how long ago.' Nina held out her hand and shook his. She was laughing and her face was suddenly bright. She remembered the plump teenaged boy who had played opposite her in the joint Shakespeare production of their respective grammar schools.

'You were very good. I was dreadful,' he said.

'No, you weren't. And your calves were excellent in Elizabethan stockings.'

Andrew beamed at her. 'I was going to hear some music, but why don't we go across to the Eagle instead? Have you had lunch?'

Nina hesitated.

Small fragments of memory were rapidly coalescing and strengthening, swimming into focus in front of her like the images in a developing Polaroid snapshot. She could see the boy now, inside this grown man, and as she looked harder at him the boy's features grew more pronounced until it seemed that it was the man who was the memory. The sight of the young face brought back to her the long hours of rehearsal in the school hall smelling of floor polish and musty costumes, the miniature and tearful dramas of adolescence, the voices of teachers and friends. It was disorientating to find herself standing on the green again, almost within the shade of the mulberry tree, but clothed in the body of a middle-aged woman instead of a schoolgirl's.

'I can't. I really shouldn't today. I'm working. I've only come out for five minutes' fresh air.'

It was three days since she had spoken more than half a dozen words to anyone. She didn't want the questions to start in the saloon bar of the Eagle. She was afraid that if she was given a chance she would let too many words come pouring out, and she didn't want Andrew Frost to hear them.

'Working? Are you staying in Grafton?' He was standing with one hand in his pocket, the other hitching his raincoat over his shoulder. He was friendly and relaxed, no more than naturally curious.

'I . . . I've come back to live. I bought a house, in Dean's Row.'

Andrew pursed his mouth in a soundless whistle, 'Did you, now?'

Nina asked quickly, 'What about you? Did you follow on from Benedick and find your Beatrice?' There was a gold wedding ring on his finger.

'I married Janice Bell. Do you remember her?' Nina shook her head.

'Perhaps she came after your time.'

Nina wanted to move on. It was reassuring to have made this small contact, but she needed a space to adjust Andrew Frost in her mind. She pointed to the cathedral porch.

'You can still get into the recital. Perhaps we can have lunch together another day?'

Andrew took a business card out of his wallet and wrote on the reverse. When he handed it to her she read the inscription 'Frost Ransome, Consulting Engineers', with Andrew's name beneath followed by a string of letters. Nina pursed her lips to whistle too, mimicking his gesture.

The boy's face was swallowed up again now by the fleshier man's.

'We're having a party, at home, on Thursday evening. That's the address. It's Hallowe'en,' he added, as if some explanation was necessary.

'So it is.'

'Spook costumes are not obligatory. But come, won't you? Janice'll like to meet you.'

'Thank you. I'm not sure . . . I'll try.'

'Who do you know in Grafton these days?' He was looking at her with his head on one side.

'Not a soul.'

'Then you must come. No argument.' He reached out and shook her hand, concluding a deal. 'Thursday.'

Nina would have prevaricated, but he was already walking

away towards the cathedral. She went back to her desk and bent over her tiger painting with renewed attention.

She had not intended to go. She had thought that when Thursday came she would telephone Andrew's office and leave an apology with his secretary. But when the morning and half the afternoon passed and she had still not made the call, she recognized with surprise that her real intention must be the opposite.

Nina finished her painting and carefully masked it with an overlay before placing it with the others in a drawer of the plan chest. She was pleased with the work she had done so far. The new studio suited her, and she was making faster progress than she and the publishers had estimated. She would go to the Frosts' party, because there was no reason for not doing so. Quickly, as if to forestall her own second thoughts, she looked in the telephone directory for the number of a minicab company and ordered a car to collect her at eight-thirty.

Marcelle Wickham was a professional cook, and she was spending the afternoon at Janice's to help her to make the food for the party. The two of them worked comfortably, to a background murmur of radio music.

Janice admired the rows of tiny golden croustades as they came out of the oven, taking one hot and popping it into her mouth.

'Delicious. You are a doll to do this, Mar, do you know that?'

'Pass me the piping bag.' Marcelle wiped her hands on her apron. The logo of the cookery school at which she worked as a demonstrator was printed on the bib.

'I like doing it. I like the' – she gestured in the air with her fingers – 'the pinching and the peeling, all the textures, mixing them together.' Her face relaxed into a smile, elastic, like dough. 'I love it, really. I always have, from when I was a little girl. And I love seeing the finished thing, and the pleasure it gives.'

Janice sighed. 'You're lucky.'

Marcelle filled the piping bag with aubergine purée and began to squeeze immaculate rosettes into pastry shells.

'I read somewhere that cooking is one of the three human activities that occupy the exact middle ground between nature and art.'

'What are the others?'

'Gardening.'

'Ha.' Janice glanced out of her kitchen window. Her large, unkempt garden functioned mainly as a football ground for her two boys.

'And sex.'

'Ha, ha!'

They glanced at one another over the baking sheets. There was the wry, unspoken acknowledgement, of the kind familiar to long-married women who know each other well, of the humdrum realities of tired husbands, demanding children and sex that becomes a matter of domestic habit rather than passion. They also silently affirmed that within their own bodies, and notwithstanding everything else that might contradict them, they still felt like girls, springy and full of sap.

'Perhaps I'll concentrate on flower arranging,' Janice said, and they both laughed.

'So exactly who is coming tonight?'

'The usual faces. Roses, Cleggs, Ransomes.'

These, with the Frosts and the Wickhams, were the five families. They ate and relaxed and gossiped in each other's houses, and made weekend arrangements for their children to play together because all of them, except for the Roses, had young children and in various permutations they made up pairs or groups for games and sport, and went on summer holidays together. There were other couples and other families amongst their friends, of course, and Janice listed some of their names now, but these five were the inner circle.

'Five points of a glittering star in the Grafton firmament,' Darcy Clegg had called them once, half-drunk and half-serious, as he surveyed them gathered around his dining table. They had drunk a toast to themselves and to the Grafton Star in Darcy's good wine.

'That's about fifty altogether, isn't it? No one you don't know, I think,' Janice concluded. 'Except some woman Andrew was at school with, who he bumped into on the green the other day.'

'Oh well, there's always Jimmy.'

Again there was the flicker of amused acknowledgement between them. All the wives liked Jimmy Rose. He danced with them, and flirted at parties. It was his special talent to make each of them feel that whilst he paid an obligatory amount of attention to the others, she was the special one, the one who really interested him.

'What are you wearing?'

Janice made a face. 'My best black. It's witchy enough. And I've got too fat for anything else. Oh, God. Look at the time. They'll be in in half an hour.'

The children arrived at four o'clock. Vicky Ransome, the wife of Andrew's partner, had offered to do the school run even though it was not her day and she was eight and a half months pregnant. Janice's boys ran yelling into the kitchen with Vicky and Marcelle's children following behind them. The Frost boys were eleven and nine. They were large, sturdy children with their father's fair hair and square chin. The elder one, Toby, whipped a Hallowe'en mask from inside his school blazer and covered his face with it. He turned on Marcelle's seven-year-old with a banshee wail, and the little girl screamed and ran to hide behind her mother.

'Don't be such a baby, Daisy,' Marcelle ordered. 'It's only Toby. Hello, Vicky.'

The boys ran out again, taking Marcelle's son with them. Daisy and Vicky's daughter clung around the mothers, weepily sheltering from the boys. Vicky's second daughter, only four, was asleep outside in the car.

Vicky leaned wearily against the worktop. 'They fought all the way home, girls against boys, boys definitely winning.'

Janice lifted a stool behind her. 'You poor thing. Here. And there's some tea.'

The boys thundered back again, clamouring for food. Janice dispensed drinks, bread and honey, slices of chocolate cake. The noise and skirmishing temporarily subsided and the mothers' conversation went on in its practised way over the children's heads.

'How are you feeling?' Marcelle asked Vicky.

'Like John Hurt in *Alien*, if you really want to know.'

'Oh, gross,' Toby Frost shouted from across the kitchen table.

Vicky shifted her weight uncomfortably on the stool. She spread the palms of her hands on either side of her stomach and massaged her bulk. Her hair was clipped back from her face with a barrette, and her cheeks were shiny and pink. With one hand she reached out for a slice of the chocolate cake and went on rubbing with the other.

'And I can't stop eating. Crisps, chocolate, Jaffa cakes. Rice pudding out of a tin. I'm huge. It wasn't like this with either of the others.'

'Not much longer,' Janice consoled her.

'And never again, amen,' Vicky prayed.

The relative peace of the tea interval did not last long. Once the food had been demolished there was a clamour of demands for help with pumpkin lanterns and ghost costumes. William Frost had already spiked his hair up into green points with luminous gel, and Daisy Wickham, her fears momentarily forgotten, was squirming into a skeleton suit. Andrew had promised to take his own children and the Wickhams trick-or-treating for an hour before the adults' party.

'I'll leave you to it,' Vicky said, bearing away her six-year-old Mary who screamed at being removed from the fun. 'See you later. I'll be wearing my white thing. You can distinguish me from Moby Dick by my scarlet face.'

After she had gone Marcelle frowned. 'Vicky's not so good this time, is she?'

Janice was preoccupied. 'She'll be okay once it's born. Look at the *time*. Toby, will you get out of here? Please God Andrew gets himself home soon.'

'Shouldn't bank on it,' Marcelle said cheerfully.

Nina chose her clothes with care. She was not sure what Andrew had meant when he said that fancy dress was not obligatory. Did that mean that only half of the guests would be trailing about in white bedsheets?

In the end she opted for an asymmetric column of greenish silk wound about with pointed panels of sea-coloured chiffon. The dress had cost the earth, and when she first wore it Richard had remarked that it made her look like a Victorian medium rigged out for a seance.

And as she remembered it, the exact cadence of his voice came back to her as clearly as if he were standing at her shoulder.

She stood still for a moment and rested her face against the cold glass of her bathroom mirror. Then, when the spasm had passed, she managed to fix her attention on the application of paint to her eyes. At eight-thirty exactly her car arrived.

The Frosts' house was at the end of a quiet cul-de-sac on the good, rural side of the town. From what was visible of the dark frame to the blazing windows, Nina registered that the house was large, pre-war, with a jumble of gables and tall chimneys. There were pumpkin lanterns grinning on the gateposts, and a bunch of silver helium balloons rattling and whipping in the wind. Nina's high heels crunched on the gravel.

When the door was opened to her she had a momentary impression of a babel of noise, crashing music, and a horde of over-excited children running up and down the stairs. Something in a red suit, with horns and a tail, whisked out of her sight. She stopped dead, and then focused on the woman who had opened the door. She was dark, with well-defined eyes and a wide mouth, and was dressed in a good black frock that probably hid some excess weight. On her head she wore a wire-brimmed witch's hat with the point tipsily drooping to one side. She looked hard at Nina, and then smiled.

'You must be Andrew's friend? Nina, isn't it? Come on in, and welcome.'

The door opened hospitably wide. Once she was inside, Nina realized that Andrew's wife had spoken in a pleasant, low voice. The noise wasn't nearly as loud as it had at first seemed, and there were only four children visible. Nina understood that it was simply that she had undergone a week's solitude, and was unused to any noise except her own thoughts.

'I'm Janice,' Janice said.

'Nina Cort. Used to be Nina Strange, when Andrew knew me. I'm sorry I haven't come in fancy dress.'

Janice waved her glass. 'Your dress is beautiful. I only put this hat on at the last minute, and Andrew is defiantly wearing his penguin suit.' Her mouth pouted in disparagement, but her eyes revealed her pride in him. 'Come on, come with me and I'll get you a drink and introduce you to everyone.'

Nina followed her down the hallway towards the back of the house. The man in the devil suit was sitting at the foot of the stairs, and he glanced up at her as she passed. His eyebrows rose in triangular points.

Andrew Frost kissed her in welcome, and gave her a glass of champagne. Nina drank it gratefully, quickly, and accepted another.

She was launched into a succession of conversations, but felt as if she was bobbing on a rip tide of unfamiliar faces. The effect was surreal, heightened by the fact that some of the faces were ghoulishly made up, swaying above ghost costumes or witches' robes, while others sprouted conventionally painted from cocktail dresses or naked and pink from the necks of dress shirts constricted by black ties. The man in the devil suit prowled the room, flicking his arrow-headed tail. A delectably pretty girl of about eighteen threaded through the crowd offering a tray of canapés and the devil man capered behind her, grinning.

Nina loved parties, but for a long time Richard had been there for her like a buoy to which she could hitch herself if she found she was drifting away too fast. Now she was cut loose, and the swirl of the current alarmed her.

The room was hot, and confusingly scented with a dozen different perfumes. There was a woman in a long white dress, majestically pregnant, and another, younger, in a shimmering outfit that exposed two-thirds of her creamy white breasts. There was a dark man with a beaky profile, two more men who talked about a golf tournament, a thin woman with a reflective expression who did not smile when Nina was introduced to her.

Nina finished her third glass of champagne. She had been talking very quickly, animatedly, moving her hands like fish and laughing too readily. She realized that she had been afraid of coming alone to this house of strangers. Now she was only afraid that she might be going to faint.

She wanted to hold on to someone. She wanted it so badly that her hands balled into fists.

She held up her head and walked slowly through the chattering groups. It was only a party, like a hundred others she had been to, perhaps a little rowdier because these people seemed to know each other so well. Grafton was a small place.

The kitchen was ahead of her, more brightly lit than the other rooms. There were people gathered in here too, only fewer of them. In the middle of them was Janice, without her hat, and another woman in an apron. They were laying out more food on a long table.

'Can I help?' Nina asked politely.

'No, but come and talk,' Janice answered at once. 'Have you met Marcelle? This is Marcelle Wickham.'

The woman in the apron held out her hand and Nina shook it. It was small and warm and dry, like a child's.

'Hi. We saw you in the supermarket, Jan and I. Did she tell you?'

'I've hardly had a chance to speak to her. I'm sorry, Nina. I'm just going to tell everyone that the food's ready . . .' Janice pushed her hair off her damp forehead with the back of her hand.

'We wondered who you were,' Marcelle explained.

Nina's hands moved again. 'Just me.'

'Who, exactly?' a man's voice asked behind her.

'Look after her for me, Darcy, will you?' Janice begged as she hurried past. The man inclined his head obediently and passed a high stool to Nina. She sat down in the place that Vicky Ransome had occupied earlier.

'I'm Darcy Clegg,' the man said.

He was older than most of the Frosts' other friends, perhaps in his early fifties. He had a well-fleshed, handsome face and grey eyes with heavy lids. He was wearing what looked like a Gaultier dinner jacket, conventionally and expensively cut except for a line of black fringing across the back and over the upper arms and breast, like a cowboy suit. He had a glass and his own bottle of whisky at one elbow.

'That is a spectacular dress,' Darcy Clegg drawled.

Nina liked men who noticed clothes, and bothered to comment on them.

'How long have you been in Grafton?' he asked.

Sitting upright, in the kitchen light, Nina sensed that the inquisition was about to begin.

She explained, as bloodlessly as she could, who she was and what she was doing. Darcy listened, turning his whisky glass round and round in his fingers, occasionally taking a long gulp. This new woman with her green eyes and extraordinary hair was interesting, although evidently as neurotic as hell. There was some strange, strong current emanating from her. Her fingers kept moving as if she wanted to grab hold of something. Darcy wondered what she would be like in bed. One of those hot-skinned, clawing women who emitted throaty cries. Nothing like Hannah.

'And has your husband come down here with you?' Darcy asked. Nina still wore Richard's rings.

'He died nearly six months ago. Of an asthma attack, at our house in the country. He was there alone.'

'I'm very sorry,' Darcy murmured. A recollection stirred in him, troubling although he couldn't identify a reason for it, and he made a half-hearted effort to pursue it. Who had told him a similar tragic story? When the connection continued to elude him Darcy shrugged it away. In many trivial ways he was a lazy man, although he was tenacious in others.

'What about you? Do you live in Grafton?' Nina felt that it was her turn.

'Outside. About three miles away, towards Pendlebury.'

'And are you married?'

Darcy turned his grey eyes on her and he smiled, acknowledging the question. 'Yes. My wife's name is Hannah. In the silver décolleté.'

Of course. The luscious blonde with the bare breasts. Nina was beginning to fit the couples together, pairing the unfamiliar smiling faces two by two.

'And the girl handing round the canapés is Cathy, one of my daughters. By my first wife.' The smile again, showing his good teeth. Darcy Clegg was attractive, Nina was now fully aware. Politely he filled her glass and they began to talk about how Grafton had changed since Nina's schooldays.

More guests filtered into the kitchen, following the scent of Marcelle's cooking, and the noise swelled around Nina once more.

Gordon Ransome brought his wife a plate of food and a knife and fork wrapped in a napkin. Vicky was sitting in a low chair in a corner of the drawing room, where a side lamp shone on the top of her head. He glanced down at her for an instant and saw the vulnerable pallor of her scalp where her hair parted. He had not noticed before that it grew in exactly the same way as their daughters', and he felt a spasm of exasperated tenderness. She had collapsed into a chair that was too low for her, and she would need help to struggle to her feet again. The voluminous white folds of her dress emphasized her bulge.

When she looked up he saw also that there were dark circles under her eyes and her face was small, and sharp-pointed.

Vicky took the plate and hoisted herself awkwardly upright,

wincing as she did so. She began to eat, ravenously, even though she knew that after half a dozen mouthfuls the burning would begin under her breastbone. She was made more uncomfortable by Gordon looming impatiently above her.

'We mustn't be too late,' she said. Alice had a cough and their sitter was only fifteen.

'I don't want to go yet,' Gordon snapped. 'We've only just got here.' He swung away with his hands in his pockets, feeling immediately ashamed of his bad temper. But he often felt that his helplessly pregnant wife and his little daughters were like tender obstacles that he had to skirt around, day by day, walking softly lest somebody should start to cry. He loved them all, but they took so much of his care.

Darcy Clegg came to Vicky with a cushion for her back.

Later the dancing began in another room that extended sideways from the main part of the house. There was a wood-block floor in here, and tall windows in one of the gable ends that looked out across a swimming pool covered over for the winter. Andrew had hired a mobile disco, a boy with two turntables and a set of speakers who had set up some lights that made globs of colour revolve softly in the beamed recess of the roof. The young DJ quickly sized up his audience and opted for an opening medley of pounding sixties rock. The innocent exuberance of lights and music and jigging couples were suddenly so powerfully reminiscent of the student parties of fifteen years ago that Nina found herself laughing to see it. It also made her want to leap up and dance.

Gordon watched the dancers too. He was trying to identify exactly what it was that he wanted, on top of several glasses of champagne and a malt whisky he had swallowed quickly, in the kitchen, with Jimmy Rose. There was Cathy Clegg in some tiny stretchy tube of a skirt that showed off her thighs and small bottom, or Hannah, with her expanse of white breast and her habit of biting her cushiony bottom lip between her little white teeth. Darcy's women, of course. Not either of those.

He did want a woman, Gordon recognized. In the hot, impatient way he had done when he was much younger. He had to be so careful with Vicky now. Her fugitive sleep, her cramps, her tiredness.

Gordon liked Stella Rose, Jimmy's wife, who everyone called Star. He enjoyed dancing with her at the Grafton parties, and talking to her too. She had a quick, acerbic intelligence that challenged him and a tight-knit bony body that did the same. To single out Star also made some kind of retort to Jimmy, who was always whispering to and cuddling other men's wives. But he did not feel drawn to Star tonight. She had been drinking hard, as she sometimes did, and he had last seen her in the kitchen, haranguing kindly Marcelle about something, with dark patches of smudged mascara under her eyes.

There were others, amongst the wider group, but Gordon did not move on to search for any of them. Instead, deliberately, he let his consideration circle back to the new woman in the look-at-me dress. He had met her briefly at the beginning of the evening, what seemed like many hours ago now. She had been polite, but slightly remote. He thought she was aloof, probably considering this party of the Frosts' to be dully provincial. Then, a while later, she had slipped past in a knot of people and her exotic draperies had fluttered against him.

He noticed that she was standing on her own, apart, and apparently laughing to herself. One of the discs of revolving light, a blue one, passed slowly over her face and then over her hair. It turned a rich purple, like a light in a stained-glass window, and faded as soon as he had seen it. Gordon felt a tightening in his throat.

'Would you like to dance?'

Nina, that was her name. It came to him, once he had asked her.

'Thank you.'

She let him take her hand, quite easily and naturally, and lead her into the throng of people. They began to dance. He saw how she let herself be absorbed into the music, as if she was relieved to forget herself for a moment. Some of the stiffness faded out of her face, and left her looking merely pretty instead of taut and imperious.

'Do the Frosts often give parties like this?'

'Often. And always exactly like this.'

The flip of his fingers, she saw, acknowledged the combination of sophistication and hearty enthusiasm, champagne and student disco, fancy dress and cocktail frock, that she herself had found so beguiling. Nina had forgotten this man's name, but she felt an upward beat of pure pleasure to find herself here, dancing, amongst these people who knew nothing about her.

Darcy was lounging in the doorway, observing the dancers, with Jimmy beside him. Jimmy had pulled off the red hood of his devil suit and had then raked his fingers through his hair so that it stood up on top of his head in a crest.

Jimmy murmured to his companion, 'Who is La Belle Dame Sans Merci? Nobody will introduce me.'

Nina and Gordon were on the far side of the room, absorbed in their dance.

Mick Jagger sang out of the speakers, *Pleased to meet you, hope you guessed my name* . . . and all the couples in their thirties obligingly sang back, *Whhoo hoo* . . .

'Perhaps she doesn't want to meet the Devil,' Darcy suavely answered. 'But her name is Nina something, and she has bought the house in Dean's Row where the Collinses used to live. She is a widow, apparently.'

'La Belle Veuve, then,' Jimmy said. And then he added with relish, 'I smell trouble, oh yes I do.'

Nina had arranged for the car to come back for her at twelve-thirty, and she was ready for it when the time came.

Her dancing partner had been claimed by his rosy, pregnant wife. The little Irish devil man had made a surprising pair with the tall woman with the reflective face. Andrew and Janice had come to the door together, to see Nina off, and had stood shoulder to shoulder, smiling and waving.

In the taxi Nina leaned her head back and closed her eyes.

Two by two, the people swam up in her mind's eye out of the swirl of the party. She could recall all the faces, not so many of the names. Somebody and somebody, somebody and somebody else. It seemed that everyone was half of a pair. The whole world was populated by handsome, smiling couples, and behind them, behind the secure doors of their houses, were the unseen but equally happy ranks of their children.

Nina's loneliness descended on her again. It was like a gag, tearing the soft tissues of her mouth, stifling her.

'Dean's Row, miss,' the driver called over his shoulder.

Inside her house, the silence felt thick enough to touch. Nina poured herself a last drink and took it upstairs to the drawing room. She stood at the window, without turning on the lights behind her. The floodlights that illuminated the west front were doused at midnight, but Nina felt the eternal presence of the saints and archangels in their niches more closely than if they had been visible.

She rolled her tumbler against the side of her face, letting the ice cool her cheek.

To her surprise, she realized that the pressure of her solitude had eased a little, as if the statues provided the company she needed. Or perhaps it was the party that had done it.

It was a good evening, and she had met interesting people. They were nothing like her London friends, these Grafton couples, but she was glad that she had met them.

'And so, good night,' Nina said dryly to the saints and archangels.

28

Three

Vicky stooped down, lowering herself from the knees because it was weeks since she had been able to bend from the waist. She held on to the banisters with one hand and with the other gathered up the trail of Lego blocks that Alice had left scattered along the landing. The effort made her breathless and she had to wait for a few seconds before making the journey into the bedroom to put the blocks away.

The girls' room was messy, heaped with discarded clothes and a jumble of toys, and Vicky wearily pushed her hair back from her face as she surveyed it. She had no strength left to do anything more than sleepwalk through these last days, and she turned away and closed the door, feeling guilty as she did so. She was not particularly houseproud, but she did not like the threads of her domestic organization to unravel completely because she was too exhausted to hold them firm.

Across the landing was the room prepared for the baby, and on her slow way downstairs again she stopped for a moment on the threshold. The cot had done duty for Mary and Alice and the white paint was chipped, but there were new curtains and a new cover on the daybed and the drawers of the chest were layered with tiny clothes. The Moses basket with its folded white blankets lay ready for Gordon to bring to the hospital so they could carry the baby home in it together.

Vicky thought about how in a few days' time she would be here again with her new child. She would sit in this room in the silence of the night to feed it, watching the play of muscles in its face as it blindly sucked, feeling the steady flow of her milk. Her breasts ached now, and there was a pain low in her back that made her lean awkwardly backwards to try to ease it.

Downstairs, Alice was sitting on the sofa watching afternoon television. She had her bed blanket with her, and her thumb and one corner of the blanket were poked into her mouth. Alice was at nursery school only in the mornings. Vicky plodded across to her and the child made room without taking her eyes off the screen.

'Tired Mummy,' Alice remarked automatically.

'That's right.'

Vicky lowered herself, letting out a gasp of breath, and Alice snuggled up against her. Vicky put an arm around her shoulders and they settled down to watch together.

The child's bare arm was round and smooth, still with a babyish ring in the flesh around her wrist. There was plasticine under the sticky fingernails and a faint smell of damp hay emanated from her hair.

'That man is silly,' Alice said, pointing to the television screen.

'Is he?'

Vicky was thinking vaguely of the business of her children growing, the invisible multiplication of their busy cells, and the branching of veins and laying down of bone to support more growth, upwards and away from Gordon and herself, so that one day their present adult functions would become Mary and Alice's own. She imagined under her daughter's fine hair and the armour of her skull the eye of her brain restlessly moving, photographing the infinitesimal details of her world and storing them, creating a miraculous index that would enable her to occupy the enlarging shell of her body with ease and confidence.

The small shape resting against her seemed charged with an almost unbearable perfection.

Vicky had always felt an intense physical pleasure in her children's bodies, a pleasure that was almost but not quite erotic, from the moment after Mary's birth when the midwife had hoisted the baby into her arms and her womb had contracted with an amazed spasm of love and tenderness. She remembered how when Mary was tiny, six years ago, Gordon used to carry her into their bed in the early mornings and they would lean over her naked folded limbs and serrated face to feast on this embodiment and extension of their love.

Six years ago, not now: Vicky smiled at the contrast. Gordon's practice was much busier these days and his hours were longer, and the mornings were a scramble to dispatch him and the girls to their separate destinations. There was too little time to spare, but she knew that all parents of young children suffered from that. There would be time again, she was sure of it. She shifted her position, her thoughts sliding away in another direction, to the pain in her back.

Then she said suddenly, 'Alice, will you run into the kitchen and fetch me a towel from the big cupboard?'

Alice ran, unquestioning for once, because of the sharp note in her mother's voice. Vicky's waters had broken.

Gordon drove home from the office. He had telephoned Vicky's mother and she was already on her way to collect the girls, and Marcelle Wickham would pick Mary up from school and stay at home with the two of them until their grandmother arrived. He concentrated on the road and the swirl of the traffic, frowning, trying to channel his attention down a single avenue directed towards reaching the house and conveying Vicky to hospital. He had been called out of a meeting and fragments of the discussion and the points he had been intending to make collided in his head.

There was a long queue of cars snaking up to the roundabout at the city bypass, but he calculated rapidly that it would be quicker to wait in the line than to turn back and take a less direct route. As the car inched forward his thoughts ran on the hours ahead in the labour room, and then jumped backwards to the births of Mary and Alice. He could remember the contractions reflected in Vicky's face, the way her mouth pinched in at the corners as she struggled to ride them, her cries and wails, and her final triumph and the emergence of the wet, black heads, like a conjuring trick. Each time, he recalled, he had been amazed by the appearance of a baby at the climax of it. It was as if the months of preparations and anticipation and ante-natal classes had been academic for him, or theoretical, with no particular end in view. And then there had been the extraordinary emergence of a third and completely other individual from what had once been only himself and Vicky. Now it was about to happen yet again, and there would be a new person around whom they would rearrange the formulae of their lives. Gordon wished that it might be a boy. He had begun to feel, lately, that he might be overpowered by the collusion of women in his house.

The car had almost reached the roundabout. In the middle of a November afternoon the fading light drew a greenish halo around the buildings and bridges, but some of the autumn trees were still bright. The burning colours made him think of the new woman, the one who had come to Andrew's party, and the splashes of coloured light roving over her hair. Gordon circled the roundabout and saw the dual carriageway ahead of him. He accelerated hard towards home.

Janice had arrived to wait with Vicky while Marcelle had taken Alice with her on the school run. The two women were sitting on upright chairs in the kitchen. Vicky's chin was tucked into her chest as she concentrated on her breathing, but she looked up as soon as she heard Gordon come in. He saw her relief at the sight of him and the way her hair fell childishly straight on either side of her cheeks. He wanted to lift her up, as he might lift Alice, and at the same time to shake her back into herself, to remake the Vicky she had once been out of the Vicky and mother she had become. He took hold of her hand and smiled at her.

'It's all right, I'm here now.' He spoke to her, too, as he might have done to the children. 'Are you having contractions?'

'Not very big ones yet. But they're coming quite often. The hospital says to go in now.'

32

He could see that it was an effort for her to talk. 'Come on, then,' he said calmly.

'Her bag is in the hall,' Janice told him. 'Everything's in it. Here's her coat.' They draped it around her shoulders and helped her to her feet.

'Don't worry about the girls,' Janice said to Vicky when they had shuffled to the car. 'Away you go, both of you.'

She stood in the driveway and waved them off, as if they were departing on holiday.

It was only fifteen minutes' drive to the hospital, but by the time they reached it Vicky felt afraid. A porter and a nurse saw them arriving and came out with a wheelchair. Vicky saw their faces through a fog of pain and confusion.

As the days passed, Nina began to establish a pattern by which to live. She went upstairs to her studio early in the mornings and worked, and by the middle of the day she had completed enough of a painting to satisfy herself. Then, in the hollow afternoons, she went for long walks. It soothed her to have a routine with which to parcel out her time; she found that by observing it she could still some of her restlessness. Sometimes her walks took her through the town, and she observed the new façades of shops and restaurants pasted on to the old buildings, and the faces of the people as they criss-crossed the liver-coloured paving blocks of the pedestrian shopping precinct. At other times she headed in the opposite direction, through one of the new estates at the city margin and out through a no-man's land of half-made rutted tracks that led to windy fields marked out for development, and on into the open country. She walked quickly, with her hands in the pockets of her coat, observing the dips and folds of the mild landscape and the pencil lines of plough furrows and now leafless trees. Back at home in the evenings she read, and telephoned her friends in London, assuring Patrick and the others that she was neither lonely nor going mad.

She did not, either, spend quite all of her time alone. She

found herself beginning to be included in the circle of women that quietly revolved within the group of smiling couples.

It was Janice Frost who made the first overture. She telephoned Nina one morning and invited her to lunch, and Nina had accepted before she could think of any particular reason to refuse. She walked out to the Frosts' this time, and when she reached their neighbourhood she looked with interest at the big houses set back in their gardens. She had once had a schoolfriend who lived in one of these turnings, and it seemed that nothing much had changed since those days. There were perhaps more cars, wives' runabouts, parked in the sloping driveways. The roads were quiet, and a stillness hung over the roofs and tree tops, but it seemed to Nina that she could actually hear the sonorous bass note of prosperity humming away. If she had stayed in Grafton, she wondered, would she have married and come to rest in one of these solid houses?

She had already turned in at the Frosts' gateway when a car braked and stopped on the gravel behind her. Nina turned and saw a BMW driven by Darcy Clegg's wife. The two women reached Janice's front door together.

'Hi,' Hannah said breathlessly. 'Jan just called me and asked me to come on over for lunch with the two of you. I left Mandy in charge of the shop.'

Nina wondered if she was supposed to know anything about the shop or Mandy. Janice opened the door to them. She was wearing jeans and a loose shirt, but her eyes were made up and she appeared younger than she had done on the night of her party. She kissed Hannah and waved her inside, and drew Nina after her. The kitchen was warm and scented with food, and the table was properly laid for three with linen napkins and wine glasses. Nina had been feeling a prickle of impatience, but it subsided now. She accepted a glass of white wine and leant against one of Janice's worktops. Janice began to chop herbs beside her. There was a view of garden and fruit trees and a football goal from the window.

Janice said, 'I'm glad you could come. I didn't have a chance to speak to you the other night, it was such a scramble. I realized afterwards how unfriendly it must have seemed.'

'No. I remember what it's like, giving a party.'

'The Frosts are wildly hospitable. Without them none of us in Grafton would ever see each other.'

Hannah had perched on a stool with her legs crossed. She was wearing suede trousers and a light cashmere sweater, and her pale blonde hair was half pinned up to show her soft neck. Quite soon she would have crossed the dividing line between voluptuous and fat, but for now she was luscious with her pearly skin and plump mouth. Nina thought that she looked cream-fed, sated. Darcy must be attentive in bed. Her own singleness made her feel dry and angular by comparison, with creases in her skin and a sour ache between her shoulder blades from the effort of keeping her head held up.

'I like it. I need to have people around. I'm the only one of us who doesn't have a proper job,' Janice explained to Nina. 'I wanted Marcelle to come to lunch too but she's demonstrating today. She teaches cookery at the Pond School, you know.'

Hannah laughed. 'Nina, Janice may not have a job, but she does everything else. She sits on every committee in Grafton, Friends of the Cathedral, PTA, you name it. She works for at least three different charities, and if anyone wants something done they invariably ask Mrs Frost first. Her energy exhausts us all.'

Nina smiled too. She began to see a more rounded version of this hospitable Janice, with her neat dark hair and faintly domineering manner, and she liked what she saw.

'Let's eat while we're talking,' Janice said briskly, and moved them to the table.

There was a warm salad with wild mushrooms, and a vegetable pie. Hannah drank steadily and Janice kept their glasses filled. Nina had been intending to work that afternoon but she drank more wine and ate hungrily, out of the pleasure of having good food cooked and laid in front of her. She abandoned the idea of work, without regret. It was pleasant to sit here in the kitchen glow talking to the women.

It came to Nina suddenly that she had been stiff, lately, with the effort of containing herself within the bounds of polite behaviour. She could feel the petrifaction in her face and along the rigid links of her spine.

Then there was a surprising blurred moment when the wine and the women's unforced friendliness seemed to dissolve the bounds, and she felt that she could be as she really was instead of pretending otherwise. Hannah said something, although Nina immediately forgot what it was. Something about how the house in Dean's Row must seem big and quiet.

Nina began to cry.

She cried when she was alone, too often, but she had not broken down in front of other people, strangers, since the first weeks after Richard's death. It was both a shock and a relief to find the tears running down her face.

The two women came round the table to her. They stooped on either side of Nina's chair. Hannah touched her shoulder.

'Is it what I said about your house? I'm so sorry if it is. I didn't think.'

Nina took a tissue that Janice held out to her and blew her nose.

'It's all right. It's not you. It just happens. I'll stop in a minute.'

They knew, both of them. She had told Darcy Clegg at the party that Richard was dead. It had been absurd of her to imagine that she could come here and recreate herself as a different person. There was always and for ever the same old self to live with, with the same dull catalogue of griefs and anxieties. The thought made her mouth twist in resignation. Now she must explain some part of what she felt to these friendly women with their unvoiced curiosity.

Nina took a breath. 'My husband died, earlier this year. I came back to live here because I thought it would be easier than staying in London where there were so many more things to remind me of him. Sometimes it *is* easier. Then I remember all over again that he's gone, and I think for a minute that I can't bear it. But I can, of course. That's all it is. I'm sorry to be embarrassing when I hardly know you.'

'You aren't embarrassing.' Hannah was indignant. 'I am, if anyone is.'

Janice nodded. 'And you do know us. You can talk to us, if you want to. Or forget about it, if you'd rather.'

The moment was over. Nina was grateful to the two of them, but more grateful still to have regained her own self-control.

'I would rather,' she said softly.

The women went back to their places. Janice took another bottle of wine out of the rack opposite Nina and raked at the capsule with a corkscrew. More wine glinted into their glasses.

Nina turned to Hannah.

'Tell me about your shop.'

It seemed important to go on talking about something else, anything else. She was touched by their concern, but she felt too raw to accept it. She wanted to show them that she was not receding, only that she couldn't advance any further towards them.

Hannah was anxious to make amends for her own apparent clumsiness.

'It's a dress shop. La Couture. Darcy bought it for me not long after we were married because he thought I needed something to keep me amused. I surprised him, rather, by making a bit of a success of it.'

Janice chipped in, pleased that Nina was recovering herself, 'You should go in and have a look. It's in Southgate, opposite the bookshop. I don't go because I can't afford it. Can I, Hannah? There isn't a thing in there under ninety quid.'

Hannah ignored her.

'It became a success because there's plenty of money in Grafton.' She rubbed her thumb and forefinger together. 'And people like to dress up and show it off once in a while. At Jan's parties, for instance. Or at least they did. They're not so sure, now there's this recession. I think they've still got the money, most of them, but they're not convinced they should wave it around for all to see.'

You and Darcy wouldn't worry, Nina thought. And she also thought of Richard's money, wedged behind her like some invisible wall. She saw that Janice's dark eyebrows had risen a fraction. There was some puritan disapproval of Hannah in her, and of Hannah's cheerful vulgarity. Nina wondered how these two women and their partners properly fitted together. Did they like one another, in truth? The friendliness that had warmed her earlier presented itself with chillier undertones.

Nina finished her wine, and held her hand over her glass when Janice inquiringly lifted the second bottle. They began a laughing exchange of Grafton gossip, the three of them relieved that they had safely negotiated the moment of Nina's tears.

'I'll give you a lift back,' Hannah said, when it was time to leave. 'I'm probably over the limit, but I'm going to risk it. I usually do, don't I, Jan?' There was something about Hannah's gurgling laugh and the confiding lift of her shoulders that made Nina wonder what other risks Hannah habitually took, and whether Hannah had intended to arouse the speculation. Janice made no comment. She came out to the car with them, and put her hand lightly on Nina's arm.

'You know where we are,' she said, without emphasis.

'Yes,' Nina answered, liking her again.

Hannah drove fast and carelessly, and deposited Nina at the entry to the cathedral green.

'Come and see me in the shop?' she asked.

'Yes, of course I will.'

'I'm sorry I'm stupid. Darcy's the only person who doesn't really bother about it.' Hannah drove away, revving the engine too hard, leaving Nina on the kerb.

Vicky Ransome's baby was delivered by Caesarean section six hours after she had been admitted to the labour ward. Her obstetrician had been inclined to let her labour on for a while, as he explained to Gordon, because she had already achieved two normal deliveries. But then the monitors had indicated that the baby was becoming distressed and an examination revealed that it had turned in the birth canal and was now presenting the left shoulder instead of the head. Vicky herself was exhausted and growing panicky.

'I won't try to turn it again. I think we'll just whip her in next door,' the doctor said. Gordon was given a mask and a green gown to cover his business suit, and followed the trolley carrying his wife into the theatre. There was a calm flurry of surgical procedures. He watched, aware of his own helpless detachment even though he held Vicky's hand and whispered encouragement to her. He waited, and then beyond the screen that protected Vicky he saw the baby lifted out from her sliced belly like a marine creature being wrested from a viscous crimson sea.

'A beautiful little girl,' the medical team told him.

'A girl?' Vicky repeated.

The baby cried, and after they had handled its tiny body and wrapped it for him Gordon was given it to hold. Then they were busy with Vicky, with the white and crimson folds of flesh and fat and muscle, stitching the flopping bag of her body back into place. Gordon was cold and shivers of nausea fluttered under his breastbone, but he made himself breathe in and exhale steady gulps of medicated air. He bent his stiff neck and looked down into the baby's opaque black eyes.

'I'm sorry,' Vicky said later. They had sponged her face and put her into bed in the ward, and the flowery curtains had been closed around them. The baby was with the paediatricians, but they had been assured that everything was quite normal.

'Why sorry?' Gordon felt jerky with tiredness. He had been briefly hungry but his appetite had left him even though he had eaten nothing. His mouth was slimed with hospital tea, and he could smell his wife's blood thickly in the back of his nose.

'Not to do it properly. Was it horrible? It's just a blur, to me.'

'No, it wasn't horrible. How could it be? It was beautiful.' He lied half-heartedly, wishing that he could command sincerity. He was sure that there must be some formula of words that would reassure her, and would light her face from beneath the skin in the way that it had been lit after the births of the other two babies, but the formula evaded him and he heard himself disappointing her.

'I know you wanted a boy.'

They were whispering. The ward lights had been turned off for the night, and they were artificially held together in a small circle of light directed downwards from over Vicky's head. Vicky had gone past tiredness, and she looked bright, with the skin stretched taut over her cheekbones. He knew that she needed to talk, although the ward sister had warned him he must only stay to see her settled. He thought of their bed at home, and the silence of the empty house. The girls were safely with their grandparents.

'I don't mind what it is, so long as it has everything intact and you are safe. You know that.' He bent his head and kissed her folded hands.

'She. *She* has everything intact. She's a girl.'

Vicky was becoming querulous. He knew she was near to tears and he wanted to leave so she could close her eyes on the tears and drift away into sleep.

'A beautiful girl. A little sister,' he reassured her.

'Helen. We are going to call her Helen, aren't we?'

It was one of the names they had discussed. Gordon preferred Olivia, and for a boy he had wanted Oliver. But he whispered, 'If that's what you would like. Yes, of course.'

It was like soothing the children at bedtime, so they could turn inwards to sleep with the day's wrinkles straightened behind them. Vicky and he had lovingly argued the merits of Mary against Alice when the first one was born, and it was Vicky who had capitulated then.

'Mr Ransome?'

The white paper turret of a nurse's cap appeared around the curtain. Gordon stood up at once, and pressed his mouth against his wife's forehead.

'Sleep,' he said. 'I'll come in as soon as I can tomorrow.'

He left her and the leather soles of his shoes squeaking on the linoleum floor faded into the night-time murmurs of the ward.

The cathedral was almost empty. The last of the thin trickle of tourists brought out by a winter's day had drifted away to the coach and car parks, and the medieval quire stalls with their famous carvings were not yet occupied by choristers fidgeting before evening choir practice. There were circles of light at the chancel steps and over the pulpit, but the nave and the side chapels were almost in darkness. A verger passed down the central aisle with a pile of hymn books in his hands. Someone began softly to play the organ, and the quiet mass of the great building took up the notes and dispersed them, letting them filter down again seemingly charged with the whispers and echoes of its own voice.

Gordon sat at the back of the nave, with his briefcase and a file of papers relating to the cathedral works on the wooden seat beside him. His head was tilted back as he tried to discern the familiar outlines of the Gothic vaulting above him, and at the same time he reflected on the slow weathering and decay of the limestone that was the concern of the Conservation Committee. It seemed that the organ notes as they seeped through the arches and between the huge pillars, fading and falling away into silence, eloquently expressed the crumbling of the stone through the silences of seven hundred years.

When the twelfth-century stonemasons had completed their work on the cathedral, the artists followed them to glorify their creation with the brilliance of gilding and the exuberance of primitive colours. Every wall and screen was painted, pattern on vibrant colour, and the paint and gilt lay over the stone like a skin, protecting it from the air's abrasion. Only then, over the centuries, the custodians of the cathedral lived and died and changed, and the raucous hues of the original decorations were slowly stripped away. They were replaced by pale classical colours, or by nothing at all, leaving the grey-gold limestone naked and exposed to the onslaught of sulphur dioxide.

Gordon had worked with the rest of the Grafton Cathedral Conservation Advisory Committee for more than two years in preparation for this week. Over the next few days the scaffolders would arrive with their poles and planks to erect a membrane around the cathedral within which the restoration of the sickened stone could begin. He had just come from another meeting of the committee, at which the conservationist dean had announced that the Preservation Trust, with the Prince of Wales as its Patron, had raised a further million pounds which would enable a second stage of restoration to follow on from the first. The work would take years, but the contemplation of its beginning gave Gordon a firm sense of professional achievement. This solid spur stuck up from the sea of his personal confusion like the ridged back of an island.

He stood up and gathered his belongings. He was not quite sure where he was going. The house was empty and he was disinclined to go back to it. Vicky would be in hospital for several more days, and his daughters were still with his parents-in-law. He had no obligations, except for his work and the daily visits to Vicky and the baby. This brief interval of freedom was liberating, but it was also disconcerting. He found himself moving cautiously, as if testing for invisible barriers. He received the telephone calls and the invitations of the Grafton couples one by one, and politely refused them.

Gordon went out of the side door, closing it behind him on the organ music and the echoes. It was not yet dark, but the green was rainy and windswept, an expanse of wet grass and fugitive leaves. He hesitated, with the massed ranks of saints and prophets soaring in their blackened niches behind him. Then he began to walk. He was halfway down the length of Dean's Row when he met the woman. At first she was just a face, possessing the kind of unknown familiarity that might have sprung out of a dream. Then she took on a more solid shape. She was wearing a waxed jacket, boots and an emerald green scarf, and her red hair was pulled haphazardly back and tied at the nape of her neck. Her face was shiny, as if she had walked a long way in the open air. They were almost past each other, but they stopped and then looked back, momentarily unsure of the social ground between them.

'I'm Gordon Ransome,' he reminded her. 'We met at the Frosts'. We danced together.'

'I remember.' Nina had reached the steps that led to her front door. She stood one step up, and with this advantage she could look down at him. He was pale, and the rims of his eyes were reddened and sore. 'I heard about the baby. Congratulations.'

'Thank you.'

Gordon wanted to keep her where she was, to hold her shining face in front of him, and he wondered clumsily what he might say next. But it was Nina who asked him, 'Are you busy? Would you like to come in and have a cup of tea?'

They sat in the kitchen together. They made the conventional exchanges about the house and its position and Nina's removal to Grafton, and all the time Gordon watched her as she opened cupboard doors, reached up to take cups from a shelf, placed the filled teapot on a tray. She was tall, with long bones and faintly awkward limbs. He could imagine her white feet, the spaces between her toes, and the curved chain of her spine, nape to coccyx, as clearly as if they were exposed to his eyes. She was smooth and clean, like her surroundings. The kitchen was very tidy, the surfaces bare and gleaming, and this orderly place contrasted sharply with Vicky's arrangements. Vicky believed that the children's happiness and creativity counted for more than clean tiles, and so the floors silted up with toys and the walls sprouted drawings and crayoned messages.

'How is Vicky?' Nina was asking.

'Not as fit as after the other two. It takes longer to recover from a Caesarean, obviously. She might be there for a week. But she will be fine, and there are no problems with the baby. She's feeding well, doing the right things. Vicky's a natural mother.'

'Is she?'

'She always has been, even before we had our own. She has an extraordinary affinity with children. Partly to do with her

43

work. She's a psychotherapist, working with children in difficulties, at a special unit we have here. She has only been able to do it part-time, recently, of course. But I'm told she is very, very good.'

Gordon heard himself heaping up this praise of his wife as if he was pushing sand into a channel against the incoming tide.

Nina paused, holding the tray of tea things. 'We could take this upstairs, and sit more comfortably. Only the fire isn't lit, I'm afraid.'

'I could do that.'

He took the tray from her and followed her up the stairs from the basement. In the room overlooking the green the shutters were open on to the oblique view of the cathedral front.

'What will Vicky do?'

The question startled him at first, but then he realized that Nina meant her career, now that they had Helen also.

'She will be able to work in the mornings once she's back on her feet, I should think. There's a woman who lives locally, her own children are grown up and she comes in sometimes to take over when Vicky's at the unit. She's very reliable, completely trustworthy.'

'That's good,' Nina answered, conscious of the surface neutrality of this exchange. Her ears strained to hear some barely audible subtext. It was there, but she could not yet decipher it.

There was a basket of kindling and logs next to the hearth. Gordon knelt down and made a thick twist of newspaper, then flicked a match to it. He made a pyramid of kindling over the flames in the grate, deftly supplementing it with thicker pieces of wood as the fire crackled and caught. He rested on his heels for a moment, watching its progress with his back to Nina. The yellow light changed the bare room, softening and warming it.

For Nina it was like being given a present, to have the luxury of company, to have Gordon kneeling in front of the hearth making a fire for her with casual masculine efficiency. Her own efforts more often led to a blackened mound of fuel and nothing more than a wisp of acrid smoke, so quite often she did not even

44

bother to try. Nina half smiled at the blatancy of this stereotyping. She would have liked to imagine that she could light a fire as well as any boy scout, but the truth was that she could not. She had made many such discoveries since Richard's death.

Gordon turned round. He saw the glimmer of her amusement, and wondered at it. He thought perhaps she was laughing at his firelighting.

'Don't you have any bigger logs than these?'

'Come and have your tea,' Nina said. 'I haven't found out where to get logs, not yet. I don't suppose it's too difficult.'

'I can arrange a delivery for you, if that would help.'

As he moved, leaving the fire and coming to sit down opposite her, Nina became aware that she was attracted to him. The realization delivered itself to her fully formed, with all the physical manifestations. A thick heat spread like a slow current pumping through her veins. She shifted in her place, glancing behind her as if her burning skin might mark the cushions where she sat. Gordon's cup rattled in its saucer as she passed it across to him.

'Perhaps,' she said. 'Yes, that would be kind.'

The man wasn't looking at her. She was grateful and also disappointed. There was a confused image of his wife behind him in the full sail of pregnancy and the faces of his children like cherubs that might have floated out of the stained glass in the cathedral. Gordon's head was turned away to the windows.

'You have a wonderful view from here.'

The sun had set, and the lights illuminating the west front had come on while they were watching the fire.

'It makes me and my belongings seem rather dim by comparison.'

'I don't think so,' he said quietly. And then, 'Do you know what's about to happen?'

She put her cup down, slowly. Gordon stared at her hands, with the wedding ring and a diamond on her left one. She pushed her fingers through her hair, and he remembered the

45

revolving lights settling on her head and changing its colour and then circling on.

'What is about to happen?'

'A huge conservation programme. To restore the exterior first and then, eventually, the interior. Do you see how the statues are eroded?'

He beckoned to her, and they went and stood at the window. In the floodlights the stone figures shone out in their ascending tiers.

'Look at the faces, and the hands.'

They were worn, chewed away almost to featurelessness. Noses and fingers and in places feet and whole heads had been lost. The stone was blackened and pitted.

'They are very old,' Nina said softly, to defend them.

'They are so old and fragile that if we don't do something to preserve them they will crumble away altogether. Luckily something can be done. Tomorrow the first scaffolding crews arrive. That portion of the front will be covered' – he gestured with his hand, close to her shoulder – 'so the work can begin.'

'Is it your work?' she asked.

'I'm an engineer, not a conservationist. But we are part of the restoration team, yes.'

Nina gazed at the inscrutable faces. 'How can they be repaired?'

'The damage has been done by sulphate crystals building up on the stone. The rain dissolves the salts and washes them into the tiny cracks, and then the wind and sun dry them and harden them into crusts that split and flake the stone away. The treatment is to apply a coat of lime, like a poultice.'

Gordon wanted to talk about this. The prospect of the ancient fabric being regenerated was an affirmation of some greater good that he was anxious to acknowledge, and he was also fascinated by the mechanical and chemical techniques commanded by the conservationists. But he did not want to bore the woman by ploughing unstoppably on about stone and scaffolding.

'That won't bring the faces back, will it?' Nina asked.

He said, 'There is a way of rebuilding them.'

'How?'

She was interested. He could tell by her voice and her expression. He felt a charge of pleasure.

'They soak lengths of hessian in baths of the lime wash, and then they wrap the statues in the hessian. The wash sucks out the dirt, the blackness that you can see, and at the same time feeds natural lime into the stone.'

'Giving it back its strength.'

'Exactly. And the missing features, noses or fingers or even whole heads, can be rebuilt with mortar.'

Nina imagined the companies of prophets and angels reawakening, intact again, and shining out once their shrouds of limed cloth had fallen away.

'It will be like a little Judgement Day,' she said, more to herself than to Gordon.

'Yes. I thought that, too.'

'Only that would be to deify the Conservation Committee, wouldn't it?' She smiled sidelong at him.

'No, we are only the instrument of a higher authority, of course,' Gordon answered.

They stood in silence for a moment, contemplating the scale of the work that was about to begin. There was perhaps a foot of empty air between them, but it was as if their skins touched.

'How many statues are there?'

'Three hundred and twelve, from the Madonna and Child to the martyrs in the topmost row.'

'I shall enjoy watching the work,' Nina said at length.

'There won't be a great deal to see. You will lose your splendid view to an expanse of tarpaulin, I'm afraid.'

'I shan't mind,' Nina told him.

Gordon looked at his watch. It took him a moment to register what time it was. He had been in Nina's house much longer than he would have guessed, and it was time he went to the hospital to see Vicky and the baby. He found himself gazing at Nina's hair and wondering what would happen if he picked up a strand to wind between his fingers. He cleared his throat, sounding in his own ears like an over-eager schoolboy.

'If you are interested, I could take you around the interior of the cathedral to show you what the long-term conservation plans are.'

'Yes, I would like that. Very much.'

She was facing him now. They would be silhouetted in the uncurtained window, for the invisible passers-by on the green.

Gordon moved away towards the door, saying quickly, 'I'll call tomorrow afternoon, at about the same time, and we can go across there together.'

Nina agreed. She would wait for him, and then they would go out to the cathedral and look at Gothic arches and fan vaulting.

When he was gone, and she was alone again, she missed him in the spaces of the house.

Four

Through the glass partition at the end of his office Gordon could see his partner at his desk.

Andrew was working with his head bent over a sheaf of estimates and a calculator. He had been sitting in the same position for perhaps an hour, during which time Gordon shifted the papers on his own desk into revised heaps.

Andrew's calm absorption irritated him; he felt the irritation as sandpaper patches caught between the hard plates and the tender lining of his skull. He had plenty of his own work to do. He had spent the first hour of his day out on a site on the other side of the county, and had gone from there to a meeting with the county planners who were proposing to build a sports complex on the site. He was supposed to be writing a report that would accompany the Frost Ransome tender for the structural engineering works, but he had not yet even looked at his notes. He had thought of nothing but the day's progress towards four o'clock, and his visit with Nina to the cathedral.

The private line rang on his desk. He picked it up, wondering if she could somehow have discovered this number, and found that it was Vicky.

'Yes. Yes, love, of course I am. Just busy. How are *you*?'

'Stitches are a bit sore, and I'm quite tired. The ward was very noisy last night, two new arrivals. One woman with twins.'

He heard the quiver in her voice. She wanted his sympathy, but did not want to admit to it. This tremulous mixture of vulnerability and stoicism worked again at the sandpaper patches within his head.

'Poor Vicky. And poor woman. How's Helen today?'

Much more wide awake. I've just fed her, and she's lying here with her eyes open, staring at me.'

He felt a jolt of protective love for both of them that went awkwardly but inevitably in tandem with his irritation. 'Take care of yourselves until I come in this evening.'

'Talk to me for five minutes. Tell me some news. It's so boring and lonely in here.'

She was about to cry. It was the complicated measure of post-natal hormones, Gordon reasoned for her. Was the rush of anxious sadness the same after a Caesarean birth as after a normal one? It must be. Perhaps even more intense. He must try to have a word with the ward sister while he was at the hospital this evening.

'Gordon?'

He told her about the morning's work, about the site visit and the report waiting to be written, parcelling up and delivering the small subjects and avoiding the big one that he felt like a thick layer of felted wool between them.

'Darling, I have to get on with some work now,' he said at the end. 'I'll see you later.'

'Love you,' Vicky said in a small voice.

'Love you too.'

He picked up his pen and made himself pitch into the dreary depths of his morning's notes as if they were a cold sea. At the end of twenty minutes he had written an acceptable draft report. He looked at his watch and saw that it was three forty.

In the corridor, as he struggled into his coat in his hurry to leave the building, he met Andrew. Andrew's blue shirt was as crisp as it had been at the beginning of the day, but the knot of his blue and lilac paisley tie was loosened to indicate that he was in full-tilt mode.

'Are you going to the hospital?' Andrew asked mildly. He was interested, properly concerned, without giving out even a breath of criticism of his partner's unscheduled early departure.

'Yes. Dropping in at the cathedral for something first, actually.'

Andrew was less interested in the restoration project than Gordon was.

'Ah. See you in the morning, then, about the supermarket drawings?'

'Yes. Yes, I'll be in by half eight,' Gordon called over his shoulder. His car was parked in its initialled slot at the back of the building. Behind the wheel, on the short drive into town, he felt as if he had made some thrilling and ingenious escape.

He found that he was laughing with pleasure and exhilaration, at his freedom and at the prospect of seeing Nina.

Nina was already in the cathedral. In the last days she had begun to feel comfortable in Grafton, as if she was settled in her own place rather than crouching in hiding, and this new feeling of being at ease had grown with the welcome that the women had given her.

But since yesterday afternoon, since watching Gordon lighting the fire in her drawing room, her perspectives had shifted again. She had been excited and fearful, and so she had left her house early and walked the short way over the green, certain that Gordon would find her. She sat at the back of the nave, at the end of the last row of wooden chairs, staring at the darkening glory of the east window.

Gordon had to cross the green from the opposite side, and so when he passed the west door he made the small detour under the bare ribs of the newly erected scaffolding and in through the inner door, as if to check that the interior was all that it should be before he brought her here. He saw her at once, sitting with her back to him, with her long limbs folded and seeming more elegant in repose. He was overtaken by gratitude and happiness that she should be here, in the great dim space, quietly waiting for him. He went to her and put his hand on her shoulder, not lifting it when she turned her face up to look at him.

'I'm glad to see you,' he told her, offering her the truth without any varnish of social nicety.

'And I you.'

The quiet solemnity of her response pleased him too.

She stood, and her height and the heels of her shoes put her eyes on a level with his.

'Show me,' Nina said.

He said, trying to sound light, 'Now you have asked for it.'

He took her on a slow tour of the aisles and side chapels. She listened gravely as he explained the projected works, asking an occasional question but mostly remaining silent as he talked.

'It takes a long time to assess the effects of stone conservation work,' Gordon said. 'Perhaps a hundred years, or even more. The Victorians saw what was happening here, and tried to reverse it by painting over the stone with a kind of impervious varnish. It was the favoured technique of the time, the best available to them. But the outer coat hardened further with years of exposure to the air, and underneath it the stone softened and crumbled away. Do you see this?'

They had passed through a Gothic doorway on the south side of the chancel into a pillared hallway. Ahead of them an exuberant flight of stone steps curved upwards under an intricately vaulted ceiling. Nina paused at the bottom step. It was hollowed and worn shiny, but as the springing geometry of the stairs drew her eyes upwards she also saw the black flakes of stone that were breaking away to reveal the paler crust beneath. The thirteenth-century magnificence had come to look sickly, diseased. Gordon stooped beside her, with one hand splayed over the base of a pillar. He rubbed with the tips of his fingers into a stone hollow the size of his fist, and then withdrew his hand to show her that it was gritty with dust.

'Can it be put right?' Nina asked.

'We can try. Using the best methods at *our* disposal, and hoping to be more successful than the Victorians. Some of these pillars will have to be replaced.'

52

Nina put her head back, following the jets of stone with her eyes, imagining the scale of the work.

'The rest will be treated in the same way as the exterior, with lime wash coloured with stone dust and skimmed milk to match the old stone as closely as possible. The coating protects the stone, but lets it breathe at the same time. In a hundred years or so, the cathedral's conservators will know whether we have been successful or not.'

Nina liked the absence from his meticulous explanation of both arrogance and the assumption of omnipotence, but she was also warmed by the underlying optimism of what he described. It was satisfying to contemplate the endurance of the cathedral, this medieval glory of branching pillars and mouldings decorated with ball flowers, solid and cared for and beloved, at the heart of the other careless Grafton with its car parks and chain stores and shopping precinct. She thought of the perpetual counterpoise that underlay this urban contrast, between spiritual endurance and material desire, and was pleased to find it so neatly summarized around her.

Somewhere out of sight beyond the curve of the stairs a door opened, and the dim air was filled with chattering voices. Around the corner appeared a stream of boy choristers dressed in ruffs and white surplices over plum-coloured robes. They swept past Nina and Gordon, jostling amongst themselves and covertly laughing, and descended into the cathedral. Behind them came the choirmaster and a line of senior choristers, and then a chaplain with a heavy bunch of keys. Gordon nodded to most of the men as they passed and held up his hand in greeting to the priest. It was time for Evensong.

Nina and Gordon followed behind them, and then turned down the length of the nave to the west door again.

'Thank you,' Nina said when they reached the door. Inside her head there was a rich collage of decorated stone and candlelight and fluttering surplices.

'I hope I didn't bore you,' Gordon said stiffly. He was suddenly aware that he had talked, and she had barely spoken.

'No.' Nina smiled at him. The choir had begun to rehearse a *Te Deum*. The boys' voices climbed up, and higher, as invincible in their harmony as the soaring steps they had just come scuffling down.

Outside it was dark. Gordon wondered disconnectedly where he should offer to take her, trying to calculate how much time was left to him. Could they go to the Eagle? Across to the Dean's Row house again? He couldn't bear the idea that he must lose sight of her, but he knew he would soon have to go to the hospital and somewhere within himself find the buoyancy to lift Vicky out of her depression.

Nina was still smiling. The splendour of the cathedral, and the singing, and the startling pleasure she felt in Gordon's company had lapped together with the images of regeneration in the conservation work to produce a high, curling wave of happiness. She knew that since Richard's death she had been walking inside a blank-walled box and had been unable to raise her head to look beyond it. She understood in the same moment that she was afraid of what Gordon Ransome threatened, of the edge they were balanced upon, but at the same time she longed to pitch herself over it, for the affirmation of physical response, as a release from the steady and monotonous solitary confinement of her days. The directions forward seemed to multiply entrancingly ahead of her.

She thought that Gordon was going to reach out and touch her. She stepped away, containing herself.

'I should get back now. I have some work to finish,' she muttered.

Her immediate need was for solitude. She had no doubt that there would be tomorrow for Gordon and herself, tomorrow and other days. This confidence surprised her, but she did not question it.

Gordon found that he almost ran after her, like a boy. He dodged to stand in front of her, cutting off her line of retreat.

'Shall we meet again? Perhaps I could buy you lunch tomorrow?'

No, not lunch, he remembered. He was committed to lunch with Andrew and a pair of retailing entrepreneurs for whom they did a great deal of work.

'Or dinner, rather? Could you manage that? It would have to be late, perhaps, after the hospital . . .'

He heard her cutting short his bluster.

'Dinner would be fine. Thank you.'

'I'll pick you up at about half past eight.' He had to call after her. Her heels clicked musically on the cobbles as she swung away from him. Gordon was happy as he went to retrieve his car from the malodorous recesses of the multistorey park.

He was early for visiting. Vicky looked up in pleased surprise as he edged around the floral curtain protecting her bed. Helen was in her arms, a white bundle of hospital cellular blanket, and Marcelle Wickham was sitting in the single armchair next to her.

'Hello, darling, is everything all right?' Vicky asked him. He acknowledged silently that it was a matter for concern nowadays if he arrived anywhere before the last minute.

'Of course it is. I wanted to see you both, that's all.' He kissed her overheated forehead and laid one finger against the baby's cheek. He kissed Marcelle, too, noticing her perfume, reminded by it of dancing with her at parties. Then he glanced around for somewhere to sit. The curtained space was full of bunches of flowers, fading fast in the heat. The flowers pushed into inappropriate vases that were mostly too small looked as uncomfortable as he felt. There was a faint but distinct smell of vomit in the ward, underlying the perfume and flower scents. Gordon put his coat down on the end of Vicky's bed and loosened the knot of his tie.

'Sit here, Gordon. I'm on my way back to pick up the kids from nativity play rehearsal.' Marcelle stood.

'No, Marcelle, you don't have to rush away because Gordon's arrived.'

'Stay a bit longer. I haven't seen you for weeks.' They spoke in unison, unwilling to have the buffer removed from between them.

'This baby is gorgeous.' Marcelle bent over to admire her once more. 'You are so lucky.'

Her face was drawn with sadness. Gordon wondered if she wanted another baby herself, and if dour Michael Wickham wouldn't agree to it. He remembered how one summer barbecue afternoon, with his tongue loosened by beer, Michael had complained to him, 'Bloody kids. They're like vampires, aren't they? They take every hour of the day and every ounce of your energy, and your wife's and they still want more. Why do we do it?'

They had been surrounded by the children of the various families, by the noise of a rounders game, and the cries of 'It's not fair' and 'He hurt me'. Gordon couldn't remember what he had said in response.

Marcelle had gone. Gordon sat down in the chair and Vicky gave the baby to him. He gazed down at the little face, seeing Mary and Alice in the compressed features. The same, each time, but different. He held this tenacious fragment of optimistically combined genes for a moment, and then laid her in the crib beside the bed.

'Marcelle brought me a picnic from the school. I was hungry,' Vicky explained. There was a white box on the bed table, and when he looked into it he saw the remnants of some savoury pie and two brandy snaps. Vicky had a sweet tooth. He felt criticized, because he had not thought to bring her anything to eat himself, although he knew the hospital food was poor. He took her hand and wound his fingers through hers. Her fingers had swollen up at the end of the pregnancy, and she had had to take off her rings.

'Are you still feeling blue?'

'Not too bad.' Vicky hoisted herself up against the pillows, making a face at the discomfort as she did so. 'It's only the stitches, really.'

Gordon had not seen the wound since he had watched the delivery itself. He imagined the line of stitching above the curling hair where he had liked to kiss her. It would be like a closed mouth, he thought. The scar would fade to a faint white line. The doctors had told them that.

'You'll be better soon.'

'I know. It's okay. Have you had a busy day?'

Very clearly, he heard the tonelessness of their questions and the other, unspoken dialogue concerning their separate and irreconcilable needs.

'Not particularly. I came here straight from the cathedral. The scaffolding is going up.'

Vicky was even less interested in the conservation work than Andrew was. 'It'll be up for ever, I suppose. What a shame it has to be done now.'

Now or in a hundred years, Gordon mused. I might have missed seeing it. He felt privileged to be part of this regeneration, and the thought of seeing it with Nina made him falter, on a dancing beat of pleasure, so that he had to lean sideways, twitching at a parched flower that hung out of a vase to hide his joy from Vicky.

Visiting time was in full flood. The ward hummed with camcorders, and with the noise of older siblings who slid on the polished floor and swung on the high ends of the beds.

'I called the girls this afternoon after I spoke to you,' Vicky said, with her eyes on the other mothers' children.

'Is everything okay?'

'Mum says they're both a bit weepy and anxious. Alice wet her bed last night.' She hesitated, and then said without looking at him, 'I wondered if it might be a good idea for you to bring them back early? They could have the weekend at home with you, and come in to see the baby before we bring her back.'

It was a challenge to him, like an unorthodox move in a chess game. Vicky was giving him an opening to show his concern for his children's well-being by removing them from their grand-parents and attending to them himself through a winter weekend. Like a drowning man, Gordon glimpsed a series of flickering images of two days of freedom. He saw Nina in her green scarf, and the squared lights and shadows that divided the ceiling of her cool, bare drawing room.

'I have a mound of paperwork to do, love. If I clear it while you are in here I'll have more time once you do get home. And I think it'll be more unsettling for the girls to whisk them back again when they are expecting to stay longer with Marjorie and Alec. They'll think something is wrong.'

Vicky pleated the white sheet between her fingers. Her stomach still made a noticeable mound under the covers.

'It was just a thought.'

He put his hand over hers. 'Mary and Alice are fine. How could they not be, with a mother like you?'

'And a father like you.' There were a dozen edges to her words.

Gordon felt the stubborn base rock of his resistance when he smiled back at her. 'We'll be okay. You rest and get your strength back.'

It was almost the end of visiting time. He leant over Vicky and kissed her as he had done when he arrived, but she would not look at him. Gordon's queasy swell of tenderness and rancour was spiked with premonitory guilt.

'See you tomorrow.'

'Yes. Gordon?'

'What is it?'

'Is everything all right?' The bland formula of a searching question, repeated. It delivered her fears up to him, a package that he should unwrap.

'Of course it is. I want you to come home, that's all.' Bland and tidy lies, also, putting aside the parcel.

'Only two or three more days.' She leaned back against the pillows, relinquishing him.

On his way out Gordon found the ward sister in her office. He mentioned Vicky's depression as if she might offer some potion to dispel it.

'Nothing to worry about,' she reassured him. 'Mums with two or three children already at home often worry if they will be able to cope with the new one, you know. It can seem a daunting prospect, especially after the physical stress of a Caesar.'

The sister seemed young for a position of responsibility. She had a round face and short hair under her cap. Gordon noted her attractiveness, automatically, without further speculation.

'Vicky will cope,' he said. It was the rampart of maternal competence that she had erected that made him feel excluded, or at best edged out on to the margins of their female-strong family. The petulant thought eased his guilt a little.

'With the right back-up,' the sister said. Gordon caught the suggestion of a rebuke, but now that he was almost free he was ready to ignore it.

'Naturally.' He smiled at her.

He made his way down the corridors with the stream of departing visitors and out to his car.

The quiet house soothed him. Gordon walked through the rooms with a tumbler of whisky in his hand. He didn't want anything to eat and in any case the spirit tasted much better than food, good and fiery in the back of his throat.

He went upstairs and into the children's bedroom, and knelt beside Alice's bed to bury his face in her pillow. He smelt the ghost of her in the sheets, and in her nightgown pushed under the quilt. The absence of his daughters' antiphonal breathing, of the hot exhalations of childish dreams, made him long for them to be home again. But at the same time he savoured this brief isolation in his own house. He listened to the sounds of it, to the boiler firing and the swill of water in the pipes, with a freshly attuned ear.

Gordon stood up again and smoothed Alice's pillow to remove the imprint of his face. He went through into the big bedroom and made a slow circuit of the bed. He had made it this morning but he could never make the white cover lie in the right folds, as Vicky did. The bed seemed lumpy, dishevelled, as if it was concealing something. Gordon picked up an ornate perfume bottle from the dressing table, and put it down again

59

without sniffing at it. He moved the boxes and photographs, seeing the prints of them left in a faint film of dust. One of the top drawers was slightly open. He drew it out further, and looked in at the satiny straps and bones and folds of Vicky's underwear.

He turned away and sat down heavily on his side of the bed. He picked up the bedside telephone and sat with it on his lap while he groped on a lower shelf for the directory. When he found it he flipped impatiently through the pages, searching for the name of the couple who had owned the Dean's Row house before Nina. He found it quickly, and then dialled the number beside it without waiting to think.

She answered after two rings, saying her name rather than hello. Her voice sounded amused, as if she was smiling into the mouthpiece.

'Nina, it's Gordon. Gordon Ransome.'

'Yes.'

It was a statement, not a question, making him think that she had even been expecting his call.

'I wanted to talk to you.'

It was much easier to say it over the telephone. He felt suddenly that he might confess anything, and that she would listen with sympathy. 'I couldn't wait until tomorrow evening.'

He had crossed a divide. He couldn't go back and pretend just to be a friendly conservationist. There was a new pressure within himself, like an inflating balloon, and he realized that it was happiness.

'I'm glad you called. I wanted to talk, too. I thought you might be a friend of mine, Patrick, from London.'

Gordon was fired with jealousy of this unknown man.

'Are you disappointed that it isn't?'

Nina laughed then. 'No. Not disappointed at all.'

Gordon felt this first avowal like a thread between them, stretching through the air from the well-worn territory of his house away into the darkness to some new terrain that was lying in wait for him to discover.

'What are you doing?' he asked.

'Sitting in my kitchen. Looking at all these doors and cupboards with nothing much behind them.'

She had not wanted to sit in the upstairs drawing room because the view, and the ashes of the fire he had lit lying in the grate seemed too closely connected with him. She was as eager as a girl, and also fearful of whatever manoeuvres tomorrow evening would bring.

Gordon recalled the bareness of her house. 'You are travelling light.'

'It seemed the easiest way.'

He knew this was an acknowledgement of her reason for coming to Grafton and of the attendant truths that she would reveal to him in time, in their own shared time. He imagined these truths peeling away, like layers of fine tissue, each layer matched by a discarded layer of his own, until they knew each other entirely.

The vision made him confident and he asked, 'Would you like me to come over now?'

After a fractional pause she answered, 'No. Let's meet tomorrow, as we arranged.'

It was illogical, but she felt the need to preserve some propriety, in case it became necessary to defend herself against him. She also wanted to give herself the pleasure of anticipation. It seemed a long time since she had looked forward to anything. She tried to imagine Gordon at the other end of the line, in some orderly domestic setting like Janice Frost's, amidst children's toys and family-dented furniture. A black wing shadowed her for an instant and then flew on.

'Gordon?'

'I'm still here.'

'Is everything all right?'

The same question that Vicky had asked, meriting an altogether different answer.

'Yes,' he said simply, knowing that it was, and that if it was not they would make it so between them.

'Good night, then,' Nina whispered.

'Good night. I will be there tomorrow.'

The dinner was not a success. Gordon chose the restaurant because it was some miles away from Grafton and not much frequented by anyone he knew. When he arrived with Nina they found they were almost the only people in the over-frilled dining room. They sat facing each other across a daunting table, feeling themselves under the scrutiny of the tiptoeing waitresses. The food was pretentious and poor, and soupy music washed over them as they ate.

Gordon was angry with himself for his bad choice, and as embarrassed as an adolescent on a disastrous first date. He dissected the food on his plate, chewing and tasting nothing, while Nina barely touched hers. Gordon was made more uncomfortable by his conviction that Nina and her husband would have been familiars in whichever London restaurants were the fashion of the week, and that she must be judging this provincial disaster with a cold eye. Gordon did not know London well, and he was mistrustful of city gloss. He understood himself well enough to be aware that he was a success in a small place, and to have been satisfied with that, until he contemplated his distance from Nina.

Their talk was stilted. They made openings and waited for one another to respond, but the beginnings were not bold enough to overcome the music and the eavesdroppers, and they faltered and dried up one by one. In the end they discussed their work and the cathedral project and Grafton, and the achievements of Gordon's daughters, like the strangers they were. Nina was wearing a scarlet jacket braided and frogged with black silk, and with her pale face Gordon thought she looked like some androgynous, doomed hussar. He wanted to hold her, shielding her from the cavalry, instead of sitting over tepid food and talking about education provisions. Gordon wondered if yesterday's intimacy had been a hallucination.

At last the meal was over. He paid for it without totalling the bill and they went out into the cold air. He held open the door of his car for her and she sat in the passenger seat, composedly arranging her limbs and her large hands and feet and then keeping still in the way that he now recognized, with a helpless wash of admiration.

They drove in silence for a while. Then Gordon said, because he thought that he must say something or they would drive all the way to Grafton without speaking, 'Sorry. That was bloody awful.'

'It doesn't matter.'

She said it as a statement of fact. He realized that she was telling him the truth. She was not judging him or the restaurant, or adopting a faint air of martyrdom over a disappointing evening as Vicky would have done. The meal had not been important, whether it was magnificent or mediocre; it was simply a rite that they were enacting together.

'I wanted to take you somewhere special, that you would remember,' he explained. The intimacy had not disappeared. He felt the softness of it between them, in this leathery space dimly illuminated by the dashboard lights.

'I will remember.'

To his amazement she reached out and took his hand, lifting it off the wheel so that he drove one-handed, and then she linked her fingers through his. She held both their hands tight against her warm thigh. In his happiness and gratitude Gordon wanted to close his eyes and rest his head in her lap.

'Let's go home,' Nina said.

They reached Grafton and Gordon parked his inconspicuous car in an inconspicuous corner a short distance from the cathedral. They walked quickly through the narrow entry that gave access to the green where a street lamp shone on them and made them hurry, not looking at one another, on and out to the relative darkness of the green itself. The cathedral was a black perpendicular to their left. They turned right down Dean's Row, passing the secure doors and curtained windows of Nina's neighbours. Gordon thought fleetingly of the families behind them, within their domestic defences. He knew that he was about to leave his own married castle with its moat and battlements behind him, and that he was doing it gladly.

They reached Nina's front door. She unlocked it and turned off the alarm and let him into her house.

They stood in the hallway, with the street door secured behind them. There was a light burning over their heads in a plain glass lantern, too bright for their eyes. Gordon watched her as she unbuttoned her coat and put her bag aside.

It was such a pleasure to be here in this safe place after the prissy constraints of the restaurant. They were both smiling, sidelong, not yet confronting one another.

Then she turned to him and he caught her by the elbows and held her against him. She turned her face up and he kissed her. Her mouth opened at once and he tasted her tongue, and suddenly both of them were full of hot confusion, rubbing their faces together and panting a little. He pushed her backwards so that she was caught against the wall. His fingers fumbled with the frogging of her jacket until somehow it opened and he found a silky layer underneath it with lace and straps, and into his head swam the memory of Vicky's drawer filled with the same female things. Only they were not the same, and his surprise and pleasure at the difference shot through him like a scalding wire, burning him, so that he closed his eyes and knotted his fingers in her hair while their mouths sucked greedily together.

The light was very bright. When he looked again he saw Nina's eyes staring into his, with the reflections in the black pupils receding to a point beyond his reach. She wriggled sideways and slipped out of his grasp. With the same movement she shrugged off her coat and left it hanging over the banister rail. The open front of her jacket showed a black slip and some black lace over white skin faintly marked with tea-coloured freckles.

'Come upstairs,' she said in her clear voice.

She held her hand out to lead him but he followed at once, watching the swing of her hips and the tightening of her calf muscles as she climbed the stairs.

Her bedroom was on the second floor, above the drawing

room, with the same view of the cathedral front. Nina released the shutters from their wooden recesses and folded them across the windows, securing them neatly with the old catches. Gordon waited at the foot of the bed, watching her. She switched on a lamp on a low table and he saw a scrolled wooden headboard and a plain white cover. There were none of the lace-edged pillows or ancestral teddy bears favoured by Vicky.

Nina took off her red jacket and put it aside. She stepped out of her skirt and he saw that she was wearing stockings with lace tops, and ribbon suspenders. Vicky always wore tights, and he recalled how the mesh paled over the half-moons of her buttocks when she bent down in the closed space of their bedroom.

He stumbled to Nina, reaching for her, his mouth dry. But she evaded him, smiling a little, and he was left standing while she bent and stretched to pull her short slip over her head by the lacy hem. Then she raised first one foot and then the other on to a chair to unhook her stockings from the ribbon tongues. He saw the bunching of the gluteal muscles as she peeled the nylon skin down the freckled whiteness of her thighs.

Nina watched him watching her, evidently gauging the impact of this half-ironic sketch of a striptease.

She shook out the wisps of stocking and laid them tidily across her folded skirt and slip. Then she stood upright, in her black knickers and brassiere, with one arm folded across her chest and the other over her belly.

'It's a long time since I undressed in front of a man.'

A man not her husband, Gordon translated, a man not connected to her by the daily familiarity of body textures and scents, sweet or stale, in the uncritical and mundane condition of marriage.

'You are lovely,' he said, although he had not yet arranged his impressions into an opinion. 'Let me look at you.'

Wanting to match her, he unbuckled his belt and undid the trousers of his second-best suit, navy blue with a faint pinstripe. Vicky called it his Tory suit because she thought it made him look like the Home Secretary. He put the trousers over the back of another chair and faced her in his socks and shirt-tails, with his erection tenting the white cotton in front of him. Nina unwound her arms and slid against him, quickly, so he only glimpsed her white belly and the blue shadow between the lace cups of her bra. She unbuttoned his shirt and slid her hands inside it, over the lateral muscles and the collar of flesh around his midriff.

'Getting fat,' he whispered with his mouth against her hair.

'Merely acquiring some solidity.'

Her head was bent. She seemed smaller without her high heels, and more fine-boned. Her shoulders were narrow and marked by bigger freckles, almost blotches. She was looking down, sliding her hand under the elastic waistband of his shorts. Her fingers grasped him. Gordon lifted his hands over his head, like a boxer in victory, to give her the freedom to do what she wanted. He tore open his cuffs and dropped his shirt on the floor. She stretched the elastic ribbing and pulled it down over his hips, to expose him. Her mouth was slightly open, her lower lip protruding. It made her appear solemn, judicious. She moved her fist up and down, so that the head of his penis was shrouded and then revealed again. While they looked at it a tear of moisture bled from the open eye.

It was odd, this slow motion, Gordon thought. He could not remember when he had last felt so avid, but at the same time he was held aside from the burning in his balls and the threatened kick at the base of his spine by the woman's dreamy detachment.

'You make my dick stand up and touch my chin,' he said.

That was better. He saw the fastidious twist at the corner of her mouth, but at the same time there was a drooping and thickening of her eyelids, as if a surge of blood had puffed them out, that made him think she liked to hear him say it.

Nina held him in her hand, weighing his balls. She put her thumb under his shaft and ran it upwards, to the tip, feeling the shiver it drew out of him.

The man rocked on his feet, spreading his toes on her polished floorboards, leaving faint, moist prints. Richard had never used words like 'dick'. His lovemaking had been tender, affectionate rather than headlong. But this man was not Richard, nor was he anything like Richard. That was a good thing.

She knelt down, gazing at him for a moment, at the thick mat of hair that tapered upwards to the umbilicus, the solid thighs and broad slab of belly. Then, using her fingers to guide it to the right place, she took his penis in her mouth. She ran her tongue around the constricted neck, tasting the salt and iron. Gordon cupped his hands at the back of her skull, bracing his legs apart and arching his back so she could attend to him.

He let himself think of staying like that, swelling into her mouth until he came, but it was no more than an idea, an acknowledgement.

'Let me look at you,' he repeated.

He tilted her head back so that he saw her foggy eyes, and then lifted her up. He unhooked her bra and drew the straps off her shoulders, then put his mouth against the red chafe line that changed the colour of the freckles from tea to rust. Her breasts were small with bumpy brown nipples, and they pointed downwards and outwards like unripe fruit. He rubbed the nipples in turn between his fingers as she wound her arm around his neck. She drew him backwards, in an awkward dance step, until the side of the bed caught her behind the knees and they fell on to the white cover. Nina bumped her hips up against him, pushing and trying to guide him with her hands, greedy now. Her eyes were closed, turned inwards into her head. Her breasts fell aside, no longer elastic, and revealed the tender knobs of her breastbone.

Gordon held himself over her for an instant, enjoying this moment of dominance. He splayed his hands over her belly, and then crooked his arm under her hips so he could lift her. He took off her pants and knelt with his knees beneath her buttocks. She had a sparse lick of sandy hair, and a surprisingly tight, flat stomach like a boy's. Her hip bones jutted prominently on either side. Vicky's belly was rounded and generous, like the pillows on her bed, even between her pregnancies.

He bent his head over Nina, kneading her skin with the heels of his hands.

'Not a single stretch mark,' he marvelled, meaning only to convey his admiration. Vicky's skin between her navel and the points of her hips was marked with two fans of fine, silvery lines.

'Not a single pregnancy either.'

'I'm sorry. That was clumsy of me.'

'It's all right. We were happy as we were.'

He did not want to think of her husband at this minute, or of Nina's past life that he had no knowledge of, nor did he want to remember Vicky and everything else he knew too well. He lowered Nina's hips and slid away, over the side of the bed, to kneel in front of her. He put his tongue to the wet gingery hair and parted the lips and worked at her until he heard her sigh.

Gordon lifted his head. Her hair was wound across her face like a veil. He moved again to lean over her, big and dark, and she opened her eyes to contemplate his face.

'I want to fuck you now,' Gordon said.

Richard had not used words like 'fuck' in bed.

'Yes,' Nina said.

He pushed her legs wider, excited and made rough by her apparent submission, but she put her hands in the way to stop him.

'Shouldn't you use something?'

'I've got some in my jacket pocket.'

After his lunch with Andrew and the retailers he had made an excuse before going back to the office and had hurried into the big Boots in the precinct. He made sure he didn't know the girl at the checkout, and he had bundled his purchase through with some toothpaste and dental floss. In spite of his fore-thought, now that the time had come he didn't want to use one of the things.

'But I had a medical check-up a month ago, for insurance. A full blood test, everything negative.'

Her eyes were very close to his. The proximity made her appear cross-eyed, greedy.

'I trust you, then. And I haven't been with anyone since Richard died. I was always faithful to him before that.'

He didn't want to hear about this fidelity, a tribute paid to love that was locked and sealed away from him. For answer he moved her hand out of the way and spread her open with his fingers. As he came into her she asked,

'Are you faithful to Vicky?'

He made the first thrust. 'Not as of this minute.'

She was hot, and pleasingly tight around him. His entering her seemed to have released some catch. Her face changed and softened. She wound her legs around him and as he found his rhythm her fingers raked over his back and worked his buttocks, pulling him into her. They rolled over, and over again, with their mouths covering each other's eyes and cheeks and throats.

She was good, Gordon thought. She was responsive and he liked that and he liked the whistle of her breath and the way she came on top of him and worked up and down so her bumpy little breasts hung over his chest with a sheen of sweat gleaming between them. They fitted together, hand in glove.

'Turn over,' he whispered. 'I want to see your backside.' He saw the concupiscent thickening of her eyelids again. Perhaps her husband hadn't talked to her in bed.

She did as she was told, turning her head to one side with her mouth open so that a wet patch of saliva formed on the pillow.

He came into her from behind and she stretched out her arms over the coiled sheets, clenching and opening her fists in alternating submission and aggression. Gordon licked her shoulders and rubbed them until the white skin flushed a dull pink, and then they rolled again and she twisted her legs around his waist, trapping him.

'Now you are mine,' she said fiercely. She held his wrists too.

'Is that what you want?' he whispered. Her hair had fallen back and he could see her face. The skin was loosening over her cheekbones and under her eyes and the recognition of her imperfections, and of his own, filled him with sympathy and compassion for them both.

'I do *now*,' Nina said.

'I am here now.'

Her mouth looked sore. She bit her lower lip and he kissed it where the teeth marks showed for an instant in the chafed skin. He freed his hands and stroked her face as she tilted her hips upwards, to reach for him. Carnality seemed interleaved with tenderness and he knew that she felt this too because her face had changed again. It had become clear and he could see directly into it, as if the cross-hatched skin had become transparent.

She said 'Oh,' seemingly surprised.

He knew she would come soon and he worked at her, both of them panting. When she did come it was with a series of small inhuman yelps that made him think of a nocturnal animal caught in the undergrowth. Her fingers dug into the thick muscles of his back, and her head fell blindly back to offer him the taut white cords of her throat.

Afterwards she was breathless and she laughed, as if still surprised, and held herself against him, rocking them both.

After a while she said, 'You now. Do you know what I would like?'

'What would you like?'

She had grown more confident, he noticed, made secure by their success so far and by her own satisfaction. Her eyes were bright and her tongue showed between her teeth.

'I'd like to drink you.'

Gordon's breath caught. It had been his first thought when she knelt in front of him, and the suggestion offered so coolly made him stiffen as he had done at the very beginning.

'Do, then.'

She knelt between his legs and tucked her hair behind her ears with a prim gesture before lowering her mouth to him.

'Vicky doesn't like it. She says it makes her feel she is going to choke,' he betrayed her,

Nina lifted her head for a second. 'Braggart.' Her coolness struck him with a jolt of lust.

He came quickly, feeling her mouth hard and soft, with a spasm that seemed to wring his heart.

She moved to lie beside him, her lips shiny, and he tasted the juice of himself when he kissed her.

'Thank you,' he offered bathetically, but she moved to stop him. She put her arms around him, motherly now, and rearranged the crumpled coil of the quilt around their shoulders.

Nina lay quietly, looking up at the contours of the shuttered windows and the ceiling over her head. The room seemed to have changed its dimensions. It was enlarged, made to seem a light space full of humming air by her unexpected happiness. She wanted to lock her arms more tightly around the man, holding him to her so as to preserve this minute, but she made herself stay still. She would not think of what would happen next, only of what had just happened.

'It seems very simple, doesn't it?'

Gordon had drifted almost into sleep. He had slept badly the night before, in intermittent snatches disturbed by dreams. For a second he was surprised by where he was, and by Nina's voice. He roused himself with an effort.

'Sex? Or else as complicated as . . . molecular biology. Or astrophysics.'

'It starts off simple.' She meant between the two of them, new as they were now, before they had to make further reckonings. She wanted to have that acknowledged, to exonerate themselves for the time being.

'I know what you mean,' he helped her, 'But I don't agree. Every time you take someone new to bed, after the first person, it is a process of re-creating yourself through a new pair of eyes, a different set of sensors. Each attempt at re-creation has to refer to all the successes and failures that have gone before.'

His hand had rested in the hollow of her waist. He lifted it and settled it higher, over the convex span of her ribs, and she felt the two hand-shaped patches of skin cooling and warming by exchange.

'It becomes more complicated with each renewal, because each of you brings to bed more history under the skin and behind the eyes.'

71

He had been thinking of Vicky, and home, and super-imposing this woman and her bedroom over the other, noting where the images overlapped and where the differences lay, shadowy outlines like an improperly registered colour print.

Nina said, 'That sounds . . . intensely narcissistic.'

Gordon laughed. 'I am sure you are right. But not simple.'

He intended it as an oblique tribute, wanting her not to think that he had just fucked her out of blind lust. But he was also wary as he lay with her arms round him and her bedcovers heaped over them. He was not sure what expectations she might have. He thought of their separate histories, skipping connections in his head that led him to ask, more abruptly than he might otherwise have done,

'What was your husband like?'

'In bed?'

'I didn't mean particularly in bed.'

'He was very gentle.'

Nina turned away a little, stretching out on her back. The happiness was still with her. It did not threaten to become dislodged and float away.

'Can you stay? Stay the night, I mean?'

Gordon thought. The idea was tempting, and the alternative was not. If he got up early enough in the morning, he could drive quietly home to feed the cats and change his shirt and be in the office by eight-thirty.

'If I may.'

He saw that she was pleased. She turned back again, cuddling up to him as Vicky did. He was more awake now. The images of there and here did not overlap or blur together any longer. They stood apart, sharp in their differences. He let himself savour them.

'We had a very nice life,' Nina said slowly. 'We had a lot of friends, we did all kinds of things, but really we were doing them just the two of us, on our own together.' She wanted to tell Gordon about what it had been like, but she chose deliberately colourless words, thinking to spare them both.

'Go on,' he said. He settled her head against his shoulder to encourage her.

'We had a house in London, and a house in Norfolk not far from the sea. Richard was a weekend painter, and he liked the sky. We used to walk on the beach, and bring back driftwood. There was an open fire, and there was always a debate about which pieces to burn and which to put on the shelf to admire.'

Gordon relaxed. His body weight seemed to increase, sinking downwards into a comfortable place.

'Go on,' he said again.

'When he died, at first I only felt angry. For a long time, it felt like a terribly long time, I was so angry with him for breaking our contract.'

'What happened?'

'He was in Norfolk, on his own. It was midweek and I was in London because my agent and I were meeting an American publisher. Richard sometimes went there alone to work, using the fax and the telephone. He liked the peace and the isolation. On the morning he died he had been working in the garden. The wheelbarrow was on the path, and there was a rake and a spade beside it. He had a severe asthma attack. A neighbour found him, lying between the wheelbarrow and the kitchen door.'

Gordon said nothing, but he held her and stroked her hair.

'I should have been there. He shouldn't have been doing anything strenuous without his inhaler. He needn't have died.'

When Nina had reached the house with Patrick Richard had already been taken away, but she could see him lying on the path under the crab apple tree, twisted over his defeated lungs. Dry-eyed and with a stiff face she had made the neighbour describe exactly what she had seen.

'Are you still angry?'

Nina told him, 'No. It's six months ago, now.'

But he could feel her loneliness. The hunger it generated in her was magnetic, and also faintly repellent. He felt a weight of sympathy coupling with his liking for her, and a tinge of alarm.

73

The alarm concentrated under his diaphragm like the onset of indigestion.

'Go on talking,' he said. Nina settled more comfortably against him. As he listened to her Gordon was conscious of the planes and angles of her house around them, an unknown place with the potential to become familiar. He felt already that he knew this room, and would remember the details of it if he never saw it again.

Nina told him about Richard and their life before his death. She told him small things that made pictures of ordinary days and he liked the way she did this for him, filling in a domestic background as a painter at a canvas. She described the house in London, and he remembered reading about the conversion in an architecture magazine and was impressed. He felt his perceptions of her changing all the time. He was sleepy again, and although he struggled against it he dropped into a doze for a few seconds. When he woke up again it was with the momentary impression that he knew her very well, better than he knew Vicky.

Nina realized that he was almost asleep. She watched him as she talked, and saw the involuntary flickers of his facial muscles, and the relaxation of his jaw that left his mouth a little open as his breathing steadied and deepened. She switched off the light and turned in the darkness to curl herself against him. In his sleep he put his heavy arm over her hip, and she knew this was how he must lie with Vicky.

When Nina woke up in the morning the feeling of lightness was still with her. It was dark in the room behind the heavy shutters, but she could make out the shape of Gordon's features as he slept. She remembered the night and the happiness from it was secure, even though she knew they must now face the day. She lay, memorizing the outlines of his mouth and eyes so she would be able to recall them when he had gone. At last, her stare penetrated his sleep and he stirred and opened his eyes to see her. Almost at once he was looking for his watch.

'Twenty past seven,' Nina told him. It was early to her.

He sat up. 'Is it? As late as that? I must go.'

'Do you have to?'

She had imagined they would have breakfast together. She had even planned how she would lay a tray and bring it up.

'Yes. I have to be in by eight-thirty.' He was thinking of the way home, a hot shower and turning the car round again for the office. He put his hand out to touch her cheek. 'I'm sorry. Perhaps I should have gone home last night.'

'I'm glad you didn't.' She knew that he was about to get out of bed and leave her. 'I'm glad you were here. I was happy when I woke up. I lay and looked at your face. You made me feel happy.' She knew it was too much to tell him but she smiled anyway.

'That's good. I'm just sorry I have to go,' he repeated.

He leaned across to kiss her and then moved quickly out of the bed. He went across the landing to the bathroom and lifted the wooden seat of the lavatory. There were jars of cosmetics and coloured bottles on the glass shelves, and he looked at them as he emptied his bladder. He avoided even a glance at himself in the mirror.

Nina had propped herself against the pillows. He retrieved his clothes and dressed himself. He felt clumsy in his socks and underclothes with her watching him. When he was ready to leave he went to the end of the bed, feeling scratchy and constricted in his creased Tory suit. She swung her legs out from under the quilt. When she stood up he saw her body and remembered it, and at once he wanted to push her back into the nest of heat and strawy scents they had made. Nina wrapped herself in a striped bathrobe and tied the belt. She came and stood close to him and he put his arms round her, letting her warmth seep into him.

'Thank you,' he said.

There was a movement of her shoulders, not quite a shrug. She did not want thanks, but reassurance.

'I'll call you,' Gordon said, evading her need.

Nina nodded. 'Yes.'

He kissed her forehead, and then let her go. She watched him to the door of her bedroom and made no attempt to follow him down the stairs. Gordon descended through the dark house and let himself out into the street.

It was only just light, and Dean's Row was deserted. Across the green he saw the scaffolders' wagon arriving with a load of poles and planking. Quickly he turned the corner into the narrow alley. It was a relief to shut himself into the sanctuary of his car.

He drove around the perimeter road, through the first wave of commuter traffic, passing the turning that led to the hospital. He did not think he had been seen by anyone who knew him; he was safe if he could reach home. He listened to the weather and traffic reports without taking any note of them. Memories and impressions of the night were beginning to sort themselves inside his head. When the traffic summary was replaced by rock music he found that he was smiling, and drumming his fingers on the wheel.

There was one more risky point. When he turned into his road he craned down the length of it, but there was no one about. His neighbours' new Mercedes was parked in their driveway where it could be properly admired, and the upstairs and downstairs curtains were closed. No one else was likely to have noticed that he had been out all night. Gordon swung into the drive of his solid, Victorian house. Everything was secure. He locked the car and went quietly round the side of the house, past the conservatory, to let himself in through the back door.

The kitchen was warm and silent. He heard a rattle and a bang beside him as Alice's cat slid in through its flap. The animal came to rub itself against his legs, purring mechanically. Gordon rubbed his chin with the tips of his fingers. He had fifteen minutes: time for a shave and a shower, and even a cup of coffee. He was whistling softly as he put the kettle on.

Gordon was glad to find his home quiet and safe, as if the night had never happened.

But for all his sense of relief and reprieve, he knew already that he could not bear the thought of not taking Nina to bed again.

Five

Nina waited all of that same day for Gordon Ransome to telephone her. She went up to her studio and sat at her drawing board, automatically dipping the tip of the fine brush into her paints, but she was only pretending to work.

She felt loose in her joints, and as languid and sleepy as if she had eaten a heavy meal. Sometimes she found herself smiling when she remembered some detail of the night's intimacy. She tried to manufacture irritation with this new hypnotized condition, but there was only a stubborn satisfaction. She began to imagine what certain of her women friends would say if she told them, and their various shades of scepticism or envy.

At first she was happy, with an edge of anticipation warmed by certainty when she looked at the telephone beside her. But then, as the hours crept by, she grew colder and less confident. She thought more often of Vicky full-blown in her pregnancy, and the new baby, and of her own thoughtless capitulation to a man she hardly knew. The night they had shared seemed to change its significance, losing its recollected warmth and becoming merely sordid, shameful. From longing to hear his voice she swung to embarrassment at the thought of ever having to encounter him again.

The telephone rang only once, at five o'clock, and she snatched it up immediately, betraying herself. It was Janice Frost.

'Nina? Andrew and I wondered if you'd like to come over and have supper on Sunday. Nothing elaborate, just the Cleggs and the Roses after golf, and probably Gordon Ransome before Vicky comes home on Monday. Not the Wickhams, because they're busy.'

Nina said at once, 'That sounds nice.'

Then she became flustered at the thought of facing Gordon under the scrutiny of the smiling couples and lied hastily, 'But . . . I had thought of going to London for the weekend. I don't know if I'd be back in time . . .'

'Don't worry,' Janice said easily. 'It's only a kitchen supper. Come along by eight if you're back, and if you feel like it. Have a good weekend. Bye.'

At last, at seven o'clock, Nina could bear the silence no longer. She had made no plans for the weekend, but she ran down to her bedroom and crammed some clothes into a bag and then telephoned Patrick. It would be better to leave Grafton, to make herself unavailable. That would be the right statement to make. As she walked through the wintry rain to the station, Nina wished for the first time since leaving London for the freedom of a car.

Patrick's panelled rooms in the Spitalfields house were reassuringly the same as always. He had lit candles in the old black iron sconces, and there was a smell of melted wax and wood smoke.

'What has happened?' he asked Nina.

Nina tilted her wine, looking at the pinhead bubbles faintly distorted and rainbowed by Patrick's handblown Venetian glass. Small details of the physical world seemed suddenly to have become very clear; there were the tiny stitches in a tapestry cushion beneath her elbow, a faint smear of wood ash on the oak table, the whispered scratch of nylon mesh as her calves rubbed together.

'Happened?'

'Yes. Is it a man?'

There was a different look to her. He had noticed it as soon as she arrived.

Nina laughed. 'Clever you.'

'Not especially. It's plain to see.'

Patrick stood up and put another log on the fire. The half-burned ones were mantled in white ash seamed with glowing scarlet threads. Watching him, and seeing his economical, faintly old-maidish movements as he tidied the stone hearth, Nina thought how much she loved him, and also loved this room where everything had been chosen for its beauty and placed with care and attention. It drew her back to Richard's world and made a contrast with the Grafton houses that she had visited, bursting with children and haphazard furniture and colour supplement chintzes. This small piece of superiority distanced her from Gordon who had filled her mind through the train journey. The recognition of their differences reassured her.

'It's nothing. One night, that's all. He's married, with about a dozen children. But it *was* very nice, just for the one night.'

Patrick did not give any sign of approval. He was wary and tentative in his own relationships, and celibate now. He had shared the months of Nina's grieving for her husband and he was glad to see her sudden brightness, but the circumstances were not what he would have wished for her.

'Be careful,' he said, knowing that he sounded joyless.

She nodded her head to acknowledge the warning, moral and emotional and physical.

'I was. I shall be.'

But she felt wonderful, sitting and drinking her wine and watching the fire in Patrick's company. It was wonderful to have given and received love again, however briefly. The shame had faded away, leaving her with clear eyes to admire the miniature perfections of the ordinary world. Her head teemed with ideas, silently drifting like thick snowflakes. She began to think of her alphabet paintings, and it came to her that she might paint a rainbow in the bowl of a glass, like Patrick's, with a medieval room reflected in it like a jewel.

'Nina? What would you like to do? We could go to a late film, if there is anything you want to see.'

Patrick watched her.

'I don't want to go out. Unless you do.'

He could remember the precise mixture of dreaminess and sharp awareness, although he had not felt it himself for a long time. The contemplation of it made him both envious and sad.

'Are you hungry? Shall I cook something?'

Nina uncrossed her legs and stood up, going to Patrick and putting her arms around him. There was a tiny hole at the shoulder seam of his vicuna sweater, and the fairish hair at the neat shaved line beside his ear glittered with silver. When they hugged each other she felt that he stood solid and there was no longer an involuntary recoil from the old crudity of her grief. She patted his shoulder gently, like a mother, and released him.

'Let's cook something together. It's ages since I made a proper meal.'

She was hungry, she realized.

Nina followed Patrick into his austere kitchen. She opened the door of his refrigerator and looked in at the neat single portions of food. She had not been expected, of course.

They were both lonely. The various modes and varieties of loneliness confronted her like the meat and vegetables on the white racks. She remembered the Grafton couples with their big warm kitchens and pine tables and easy hospitality, and the façades of smiles.

Her first judgement of them had been a simplification. It had been born out of envy, and the over-awareness of her own solitude. Last night with Gordon Ransome she had glimpsed confusion behind the smooth faces, and now she felt a beat of gratitude for the past happiness of her own marriage.

She held the refrigerator door open wider.

'What shall we make?' she asked Patrick.

At seven-thirty, after a day of meetings and a distant site visit, and after he had been to the hospital and come home at last, Gordon dialled Nina's number. There was no answer, not even the bland invitation of an answering machine. He held the receiver for a long time, listening to the hollow ringing tone.

He tried again and again, through the slow weekend until the digits were imprinted in his head like a mantra, but there was never any reply.

For Nina it was a London weekend like many others she had known. The form of it was both familiar and already consigned to history. She went with Patrick to the theatre to see a play by a new feminist writer, and to Blooms for dinner with Patrick's friends. On Sunday morning they went to Brick Lane market to rummage for treasures amongst the faded bric-à-brac, and then to Hampstead for a lengthy lunch with more old friends who only noted with pleasure that Nina looked well, almost herself again.

At the lunch there was an architect, recently divorced, whom she had not met before, although he claimed to have known Richard. After they had eaten they went out to walk on the heath amongst the Sunday crowds of dog-exercisers and kite-flyers and children on tricycles. The architect walked beside Nina, and after a little way he asked her if she would like to have dinner with him one evening.

Nina's hands were in the pockets of her coat. She rubbed the residue of crumbs and fluff between her fingers, and looked ahead at the silhouettes of walkers against the greenish sky on the crest of Parliament Hill. This afternoon was perfectly familiar to her, like the wider axis that contained it, and she had felt herself growing impatient with it as the hours passed. She was thinking about Grafton, and wanting to hurry back there.

She smiled at the architect. 'I can't, but thank you. I don't live in London any longer. I moved away to the country and I have to go back this evening.'

'Next time you are in town then, perhaps,' the man said, observing the conventions.

It was getting dark, with the rapid sinking into gloom of a December afternoon. The party broke up as one couple with their children turned at an angle across the heath towards their own house.

'I should get back to Grafton,' Nina said to Patrick. She calculated that if she caught the six o'clock train she could be at the Frosts' house by not long after eight. She did not let herself reckon beyond that. Patrick heard the note of urgency in her voice.

'I'll drive you to Paddington,' he offered.

At the station Nina hugged him again. He made a surprised face, to indicate that he was unused to such an abundance of affection.

'Next time, will you come down to stay with me?' she asked. Her face was bright. She had discovered something, some seam of happiness, and she wanted to share it with him or to have him admire it. 'There are nice people. I'd like you to meet them.'

He accepted that she was being generous. 'Of course I will come.'

'Good. Maybe I'll give a party.' There had been lots of parties before Richard died.

'Be careful, won't you?' Patrick repeated.

'Certainly.' She laughed, and again he found himself envying her abandonment to whatever would come. He stood on the platform and waved as the train pulled away, and then drove slowly back to Spitalfields through the Sunday blackness of the City.

All the way back to Grafton Nina willed the train to go faster, like a schoolgirl longing for the hour of a crucial party.

Jimmy Rose held up the television remote control, aiming it at the screen as if he wanted to shoot and kill. He made the circuit of the channels and discovered what he already knew, that there was nothing he wanted to watch. He depressed the volume control and watched Harry Secombe's face swell to fill the screen, silently mouthing.

Stella was upstairs somewhere. The Roses lived in a small modern house and without the noise from the television Jimmy could hear the creaks that she made, crossing the bedroom floor to open a cupboard, and then the metallic rasp as she set up the ironing board.

Jimmy stretched his legs in front of him and drank the remains of a beer from the can. It was dark outside, but he had not yet drawn the curtains across the big window that looked into the garden. He could see himself fishily reflected in the black glass.

Usually Jimmy enjoyed Sundays. He made it a rule not to do any work, nor even to think about work if that was feasible, and to concentrate on pleasing himself. It was a matter of satisfaction to him that he and Star had long ago come to a comfortable agreement about this. Star liked to garden on Sundays, or to sit quietly and read, whereas Jimmy was not interested in the garden and he read only occasional thrillers or sports biographies. Jimmy's preference was to stay late in bed, to go off to play squash or golf with one or more of the Grafton men, and afterwards to drink with them in the bar or the clubhouse. Sometimes Star and the other wives would join them for the drinking part, although he preferred it when they did not. Sunday evenings, if they were not entertaining or invited out anywhere, were a pleasantly hazy slide towards bedtime and the jolt of Monday morning.

This Sunday, however, had not been one of the best. Darcy Clegg was Jimmy's usual golf partner, but today Darcy had proposed a swap. Darcy himself had partnered a regular golfer called Francis Kelly, and Jimmy had ended up with Michael Wickham. Michael had hardly spoken to Jimmy or anyone else throughout the round, and he seemed to take a grim satisfaction in playing extremely badly. He had hooked most of his drives into the rough halfway along the fairway, and putted as if he were using a yard broom,

Through Jimmy's efforts they had managed to hold level as far as the short fifteenth hole, but they lost that one and the next three in succession. By the time they reached the clubhouse bar Jimmy was in as bad a mood as Michael himself. He did not like to lose at any game, and he particularly disliked losing to Darcy.

The clubroom was crowded with golfers, most of them men, although not many of the members had braved the wintry fairways beforehand. The bar was a popular Sunday drinking place for the prosperous and established Grafton set who considered the Eagle on the cathedral green to cater only for tourists, and the other city pubs to be spoiled by kids and electronic games and loud music. Francis and Jimmy edged through the knots of convivial drinkers, with Michael frowning in their wake.

'A man could die of thirst,' Jimmy said, eyeing the press at the bar.

The other three had had to shoulder their way forward, but Darcy did not. A way opened into the groups in front of him as heads turned and hands reached out in greeting. Satisfaction was perceptible, as if the drinkers were now reassured that they were in the right and proper place because Darcy had arrived.

'Darcy Clegg, the man himself.'

'You haven't been out there this morning, Darcy? It's much more comfortable in here with a glass in your hand, I can tell you.'

Darcy nodded his big head, smiling a faint but amiable smile and bestowing a word here and there. He reached the bar, and held up a finger to the sweating barman.

'Morning, Mr Clegg. What'll it be?'

'Four pints, Gerry, and whatever you are having.'

Darcy did not ask his companions what they were drinking, nor did anyone question his right to buy the first round. He handled the exchange adroitly, as he did everything else, but his expression indicated that he was part of this only so far as he wanted to be, and also somewhat above it.

The clubroom was unusually crowded, and once their drinks were served they had to perch on stools around one of the low tables in the main body of the room because there was no space at the bar.

'What's up, Michael?' Jimmy drank, and tiny wings of froth were left at the corners of his mouth. He added, 'Apart from your golf, that is.'

Michael shrugged. 'Nothing's up. Sorry to lose you the game.'

He turned his glass on the table. He was a dark, lean man with crisp hair turning grey. He had doctorly hands, faintly reddened and with prominent wristbones. He was never forthcoming, but his moroseness this morning was beginning to affect everyone.

Jimmy felt almost physically pained that this precious and pleasant Sunday time should be spoiled. Darcy's big frame seemed uncomfortable on the small stool, and he was already glancing over Francis Kelly's shoulder to the noisy crowd at the bar. In a minute, Jimmy knew, he would get up and go to join them. Jimmy's response to this, for which he disliked himself, was to talk too much, clowning for the benefit of the three other men. He told a story about events at a recent conference his small company had organized, but he did it too hurriedly and with too much false comic emphasis. Darcy looked at him with his eyebrows slightly lifted, and only Francis laughed.

When Jimmy saw Hannah Clegg in the doorway he was relieved. Normally he would not have been pleased to have this Sunday session disrupted, although in most other circumstances he liked Hannah as well as admiring her appearance. But today she was welcome. Now, at least, Darcy would not stroll away in search of better company.

Hannah came across to their table trailing appreciative glances. She was wearing a sleeveless suede jerkin over a cream sweater, and cream knitted trousers that showed the vee between her thighs. She kissed the four of them in turn, Darcy last.

'I thought I'd catch you in here,' she said gaily. 'Just a small gin and tonic for me, Darcy. I'm on my way to pick up Freddie.'

'Is he all right now?' Michael asked, looking up from his beer.

'Yes, thanks, Michael, he's fine. A lot of fuss about nothing, as it turned out.'

Freddie was the Cleggs' six-year-old. Hannah explained to Francis and Jimmy that the little boy had developed a startlingly high temperature a few days before, when Darcy was away on business, and their GP had been slow to arrive. In a panic Hannah had telephoned Michael, who was at least a doctor although his field was orthopaedic surgery not paediatrics. Michael had driven round to the Cleggs' mansion to examine the boy and reassure Hannah.

Jimmy and Francis listened to this recital without much interest. Hannah was inclined to talk at length about her children. She put her hand out and touched Michael's shoulder. Her fingers with elongated pale pink nails rested lightly for a moment.

'Thank you,' she said again.

Michael's body skewed sideways as he tried unobtrusively to lean away from her, but his manner lost some of its stiffness.

'It was nothing. I said so at the time. I was glad to do what I could, which was not much.'

'Just the same, thank you.'

Hannah's soft face was pink, and her lower lip jutted out to reveal the darker pink tissue within. Michael looked full at her, unnoticed by the others, and then dropped his gaze back to his drink. Hannah settled comfortably at the table. She told Jimmy that they would be meeting later at the Frosts, and that Nina Cort would be there, and then she turned away to talk to Michael.

Jimmy bought another round and concentrated on drinking steadily, hoping to recapture some of the sense of Sunday camaraderie that stayed with him like a blessing through the following week. He loved the way the men were friendly and informal at these times, but were yet held together by unwritten rules. It offended him when someone failed to obey the rules, as Michael had done this morning.

Hannah showed no sign of leaving. She accepted Jimmy's offer of a second gin and tonic, and when the drinks had been consumed Darcy checked his watch and announced that they must go. Hannah made no protest, and five minutes after they had left Michael followed them. Finally Francis also drifted away.

Jimmy went to the bar and drank a quick whisky, wondering if he should join another group, but the day was already spoiled. He went home and found the house empty. Star had told him she was going out somewhere, although he had forgotten exactly where. He made himself a sandwich and fell asleep in front of the television, and then woke up with a headache when Star came back.

He heard her coming downstairs now, and then clicking across the woodblock floor of the hall.

'Why are you sitting with the curtains open?' she asked when she saw him.

'Why not? Nobody can see in.'

Star went across and closed them. She was wearing a shirt cut like a man's, but made of peacock-blue silk, and a pair of tight trousers in some elasticated material that showed the lines of her good legs. She did not usually take so much trouble with her appearance for a Sunday supper at the Frosts'.

'You look nice,' Jimmy said lazily. He held out a hand. 'Come over here.'

She came and stood in front of him for a moment. Jimmy reached up and put his hands on her hips, kneading the flesh over her long bones and then sliding his palms inwards over the slight protuberance of her stomach so that the smooth silk slithered under his fingers.

'I like this shirt. Is tonight something special?'

He was looking forward to it, he realized, after the fiasco of the day. He liked well-upholstered Janice and her dark eyes as much as he liked Hannah Clegg, and his ears had sharpened at the news that Nina Cort was also coming, although he had not betrayed his interest to Hannah.

'Special? No, I don't think so. Aren't you going to change?'

He stood up. Star was two inches taller than he was, and with him in his socks the difference seemed greater than that. He had always liked it, ever since they had first met, this feeling of being overreached by her. He pressed his face forward and with his mouth found her neck, warm inside the collar of her shirt.

'Mmm. You smell lovely.'

'Aren't you going to change?' Star repeated.

Jimmy sighed. His mood had completely altered. He felt light-hearted and optimistic.

'If I must.' He made his eyebrows into beguiling peaks as he looked at her. 'Won't you come up?'

'It's a quarter to eight.' She had turned away and bent down to straighten the sofa cushions behind him.

Jimmy sighed again, more theatrically. 'A quarter of an hour used to be plenty,' he cajoled.

She seemed not to hear what he was saying. Jimmy hesitated, and then shrugged and went whistling upstairs in his good humour to change out of his golf clothes.

Nina was the last to arrive at the Frosts'. As she paid off her taxi at the gate she saw Gordon's car parked further along the road. She rang the doorbell, remembering the night of Hallowe'en, and Andrew came to open the door. Instead of a dinner suit he was wearing a patterned jumper that proclaimed Sunday.

The Frosts' other guests were sitting in the room where they had danced at the party. Nina remembered that there had been coloured lights revolving overhead, and she had felt a premonitory beat of happiness to find herself momentarily set free from her grief, dancing amongst people who knew nothing about her.

Now she saw Darcy Clegg's handsome, heavy face, and Hannah with her hair pinned up in a sleek chignon, and Star in a bright blue shirt. To her left, a dark shape in an armchair, was Gordon. Nina could not look directly at him.

Of the three women only Star greeted her with friendly attention. Janice distractedly offered her cheek to be kissed, and Hannah waved her ringed fingers from the other side of the room. There was a cool edge to the atmosphere, Nina thought, or perhaps she was beginning to distinguish these people more clearly.

She found her way to a place on the sofa beside Darcy. Andrew put a glass into her hand and she cupped her hands around the slippery bowl of it. There were soft cushions behind her, and when she tasted the wine there were the complicated flavours on her tongue. The physical world took on sharp significance again.

'You've just come back from London?' Darcy asked. He too was wearing the Sunday uniform of a sweater and corduroys, but the trousers were Italian and the sweater was cashmere.

'Yes. I went up to stay with an old friend of Richard's and mine, to see a play and have lunch with some people.'

She offered this simple account to Gordon, without glancing in his direction, and she knew that he listened to her.

Darcy had read the reviews of the play in the Sunday papers, and they began to talk about what Nina had thought of it. The conversations elsewhere in the room started up again, although Nina did not hear Gordon speak. Someone was describing a disastrous round of golf, and generating a good deal of brittle laughter. It was Jimmy Rose, of course. Each of Nina's senses, not only her hearing, seemed abnormally sharpened. She could hear the unspoken words underlying the bantering talk. Jimmy had been upset and disappointed to lose the game. The clarity of her perceptions made her feel strong and lively.

Darcy was watching her from beneath the shield of his thick eyelids. There was a faint flush over her cheekbones and her fingers fluttered up and down the stem of her glass.

And then, without warning, the recollection that had stirred in him when they were first introduced delivered itself to him, almost complete. Somebody had described the circumstances of Richard Cort's death, and then had made an allegation that did not particularly interest him at the time. But he remembered it now, with a sharpening of curiosity. It was a woman who had told him the story, a woman he knew quite well, at a useful party in London a few months before.

The theatre conversation continued while Darcy idly speculated.

'Did you see the Arthur Miller?' he asked, and Nina offered her response still with the faint colour in her face. Across the room Jimmy Rose was grinning at them, although neither Darcy nor Nina paid him any attention.

The elder Frost boy, Toby, came in. His hair was shaved close at the nape of his neck and a long hank at the front fell forward over his eyes. He was wearing a loose top with a hood and enormous shoes.

'Hi, all.'

With this generalized greeting he seated himself on the edge of the low table that filled the middle of the room. With one hand he swept back the lock of hair that immediately fell forward again. Nina noticed with interest that he was perfectly at ease, and thought that at the same age both she and Toby's father would have been paralysed with shyness in the unlikely event of being asked to confront a roomful of their parents' friends.

I'm getting old, she thought, amused.

'Have you done your homework, Toby?' Andrew demanded.

'Yeah, Dad, it's okay,' the boy answered, raking at his hair again.

'I hear you played well yesterday,' Darcy offered.

'Not too badly.'

They began to talk about a school football match. Nina had nothing to contribute, and in any case she did not know how to talk to twelve-year-old boys. Under the cover of momentary invisibility she let herself glance across at Gordon. His eyes met hers.

She was shaken at once by a sense of intense familiarity.

Her knowledge of his shape and of the lines of his face was so intimate and tender that it seemed shocking to contemplate it in the midst of this neutral gathering of friends.

She felt that she knew this man so well that it was as if Richard was here, sitting in an armchair in Andrew Frost's den. The room would certainly be called the den. Nina's mouth curved and she saw her smile answered in Gordon's eyes. They looked at each other with amazed pleasure for another two seconds, and then Nina turned her head away.

It was inconceivable that the conversation around them had not stopped, that everyone else in the room had not fallen into silence as they took stock of what must be blindingly obvious. But they were all still talking, and no one had even glanced at them. Nina's heart was knocking irregularly and her mouth seemed full of sand.

She took a long gulp of her wine and at once she felt drunk, her head and limbs seeming to drift an alarming distance apart.

Janice leaned forward with her hand on her son's shoulder.

'Is Will ready for bed? And if you've finished your work, Toby, you could think of an early night as well.'

'Oh, *Mum*.'

'Do as your mother says,' Andrew told him.

There was no real protest in the boy's response, or reprimand in Andrew's. With her sharpened perceptions Nina understood that they were playing the roles of parents and child in the ordinary loving Frost family for the benefit of the rest of them. Hannah Clegg was nodding and smiling. Façades, Nina thought, and remembered the handsome, happy couples as she had first seen them. The sense that she was beginning to look beyond the obvious came sharply back to her. Her eyes met Gordon's again, guiltily, greedily.

'I'll go up to check on Will, and then we can eat,' Janice was saying. The boy gave his hair a last shake and wished them a languid goodnight.

A moment later there was a general move. Darcy escorted Nina, with the fingers of one hand just touching the small of her back. She knew that Gordon followed behind her, but her legs functioned well enough to carry her through to the kitchen.

Janice was in her apron, behind the kitchen counter. 'I told you it was only a family supper,' she apologized to Nina. 'If we eat in the dining room it seems rather formal and serious, like entertaining clients.'

Andrew passed behind her and patted her bottom. 'I prefer the dining room, myself.'

'Stay home in the morning to do the extra clearing up then,' she answered coolly. 'Nina doesn't mind. Do you, Nina?'

'Of course not.'

'Sit where you like, everyone. *Not* next to your partners, please.'

Nina found herself placed between Darcy and Jimmy Rose. Gordon was on Jimmy's other side, out of her sight. The table was elaborately laid with linen napkins, heavy silver cutlery and thickets of polished glasses, contradicting Janice's insistence that this was a casual evening. Evidently perfectly at home, Darcy walked behind the chairs pouring white Alsace into a glass at each place.

'Toast,' Hannah declared loudly, when everyone's glass had been filled. With her luxuriant hair pinned up she looked different, and older, as if her eyes and mouth were drawn upwards by tiny, taut threads.

'To friendship.'

'To loving friendship.'

Surprisingly, it was Star who amended it. From her place opposite she nodded her grave head at Nina. There was a moment's silence around the table, until Jimmy satirically echoed his wife.

'To loving friendship.'

They all drank, except for Janice who was busy behind her kitchen counter.

She brought an oval dish to the table. Resting in a bed of green salad leaves was a terrine of vegetables, in which tiny batons of carrot and courgette and flowers of broccoli floated in a clear golden jelly amidst a rain of green peppercorns. Nina knew how long such things took to concoct, and wondered again about the protestations of simplicity. This was competitive cooking.

'Oh, Janice, look at this. It's so *pretty*,' Hannah said.

Janice pursed her lips. 'Have you ever seen Marcelle's version? This is a pale imitation. Hers just *glows* with goodness.' She added, for Nina's benefit, 'Marcelle is a wonderful cook.'

'I remember, from your Hallowe'en party,' Nina said. Then she heard Gordon's quiet voice, only it seemed to set currents stirring in the air between them.

'Michael is a lucky man.'

'*Is* he, would you say?' Jimmy Rose smirked.

Janice took her place at the end of the table opposite to Andrew. She was pleased by the reception of her terrine. Raising her glass, she said, '*I* want to drink the toast, too. To loving friendship, Star. That's what it's all for, isn't it? The hard work and the risks and the planning and the worrying, all the difficult things each of us does, to make the lives we have and to keep hold of them . . . It's so we can enjoy the pleasure of evenings like this, with our friends around us. Good friends, loving friends. We're missing Vicky, but she'll be home tomorrow, and at the same time we're welcoming Nina.' She looked earnestly around the table. 'This is what counts, isn't it? Us being here together, for food and wine and talk?' Janice's cheeks were crimson.

'Of course it is, darling,' Andrew murmured.

'Eloquently put, Janice,' Darcy said, and she gave him a defiantly grateful smile.

'Well, I don't care. You know I'm not particularly clever, and you may think I'm sentimental. But I love you all, and this is my favourite way to spend a Sunday evening.' She emptied her glass with a flourish.

Hannah clapped her hands. 'Hear, hear,' she called. 'May there be many more evenings like this one.'

'Darling, there will be. Exactly like this,' Darcy said softly. 'Why should there not?'

Nina listened more than she talked.

It occurred to her that the edge of uneasiness lay within the partnerships themselves, and not between the couples. The couples clung together in their group, to affirm themselves and their partnerships.

The voices rose around her and wove themselves in and out of the clink of cutlery and glasses and she chose to pick out one voice at a time and follow it through the twists of the conversation like a coloured thread through fabric. She heard Star, and the way that she spun her words so fluently and punctured Jimmy's nonsensical chatter, and then she heard Darcy who pronounced and knew that his lazy drawl would be listened to, and Hannah's cries and giggles, and Janice's gossip that grew less coherent as the wine influenced her and Jimmy distracted her by grinningly stroking her bare forearm. Andrew directed the turns of the conversation from the head of the table, and through it she strained to hear Gordon's low, unemphatic comments although he spoke almost as little as she did herself.

Nina tried to yoke the couples together in her mind, making Hannah's trills counterpoint Darcy's bass, setting Star's sarcastic wit against Jimmy's sly Irish loquacity and Andrew's faint pomposity against Janice's tipsy skittishness. But now they resisted her efforts to pair them and so to eavesdrop on them as couples. They split away into individuals, and then coalesced again into a group of friends, a group whose homogeneity in the end surprised her.

Andrew filled another set of the good glasses, this time with second-growth claret. Janice brought beef Wellington to the table and covered the plates with overlapping circles of rosy meat rimmed with golden pastry. There were immaculate vegetables in white and gold dishes, and Janice was praised again for the excellence of her dinner.

'You're not a very great talker,' Jimmy said to Nina as they ate their beef.

The conversation had turned from ski-ing to cars. Hannah was resting her chin in her hands as she sighed, 'I love my little 325. It's *soooo* sexy.'

'I don't know much about cars,' Nina answered neutrally.

'But are you not interested in what they tell you about their owners?'

She thought, I can't remember Gordon's. She had spent more than an hour sitting in it, but she had no idea what variety it was. Something grey and solid. Not like him. That's a stupid game.

'What would you guess Darcy drives?' Jimmy pursued.

'Let me think. I know, a red Porsche.'

'Wrong,' he scoffed. 'That's what *I* would choose, if I could afford it. No, Darcy has a Maserati. Obviously. And a Range Rover for the mud and when he mixes with the county. Which are usually one and the same thing.'

'Quite true,' Darcy said equably from her other side. 'Jimmy is only jealous, of course.'

Nina found herself laughing. Jimmy Rose was amusing, in his sharp way.

'Who would not be jealous of the man who possesses Wilton Manor, a Maserati *and* Hannah?'

'I thought I might buy myself a car,' Nina heard herself saying.

'Haven't you got one? No heavenly chariot?' Jimmy's eyebrows peaked.

Quickly she said, 'I used to have an Alfa Romeo Spyder, but I sold it.'

'Beautiful machines,' Andrew pronounced.

'Sexy machines,' Jimmy added.

'You must buy another glamorous car because you are a glamorous person,' Hannah told her with slightly drunken assertiveness, and Nina found herself smiling across the table at Star. Even though Star had talked and laughed almost as much as the others her voice was cool, and Nina had the impression that she had held herself aloof from the mood of the party. Perhaps it was her intention to act as an antidote to Jimmy, who had made more noise than anyone else.

'Then you will have to advise me, Hannah.'

Andrew had cleared away the dinner plates and now there were individual chocolate souffles, with cocoa-brown crusts puffed high above the white rims of their dishes. There was another chorus of admiration.

'The person to ask is Gordon.' Hannah waggled her spoon at him. 'Gordon knows the most, Gordon is an *engine* expert even more than Andrew, even though he's staying pretty buttoned up tonight. What's the matter, Gordon? Post-natal depression?'

Janice stood up, not very steadily. 'Coffee for everyone? Andrew, what else have we got for people to drink?'

He sighed, 'She'll have a headache all day tomorrow, you know.'

'So long as she doesn't have one tonight.' Jimmy winked.

Nina slipped out of her chair. Jimmy hopped to his feet and drew it back for her with a flourish. Janice waved a hand.

'Use my bathroom, Nina. First on the left up the stairs. The downstairs one is probably full of trainers and rugby shorts. The boys never pick up a thing.'

It was a relief to escape the hot room and the smoke from Darcy's cigar. The hall was cool and dark. Nina went slowly up the stairs, peering in the dimness at the gilt-framed pictures on the walls. She opened a door and saw the Frosts' bedroom, with a light on in the bathroom beyond it. There was a thick carpet sculpted into patterns, and a long wall of mirrored cupboards. Janice's negligee was laid out across one corner of the plump bed. Nina tiptoed like an intruder. On a tallboy there was a silver-framed photograph of a slimmer Janice in her wedding dress, one hand holding back a billow of net veiling. Nina picked it up, and the breath of her curiosity fogged the polished silver. She replaced the picture hastily and went on into the bathroom.

There were more mirrors in here, and polished chrome rails with neatly folded towels. The towels were cream with satiny flowers appliqued in the corners. Nina wondered if Andrew and Janice liked to admire themselves in their mirrors when they made love in here or in the bedroom, watching the reflections of their coupling receding into infinity.

She sat down without locking the door.

Gordon had left the table. He could think of nothing but finding Nina, and securing a few seconds of her for himself, away from the intolerable repetitive babble of the dinner party.

He opened the bathroom door and saw her. She looked up at him, shocked, like a scared little girl with her tights twisted around her knees and her ankles crossed.

'What are you doing here?'

He was touched by her anger and shame at being caught in the act of peeing.

'I wanted to see you. There's nothing to hide.'

She finished, then dried herself and straightened her clothes with the neat womanly movements that he loved.

'They'll notice we're both missing.'

'No, they won't. They'll think I'm downstairs with the rugby shorts.'

They moved together, and after they had kissed he held her face between his hands and examined it intently.

'I called you. I called you all weekend.'

'I ran away,' she told him simply.

'Don't run away again.'

'There's nowhere to go.'

'I'd find you anyway.'

He was pushing against her and Nina put her arm up to one of the mirrors to support herself. As he turned his head Gordon saw the reflection of her, and the way the loose sleeve of her blouse fell back to reveal the bluish-white, egg-shaped hollow of her armpit. He was swept by a wave of tenderness that contradicted and intensified his need for her.

'Nina, Nina. Can I see you again? When can I see you?'

'Yes. I don't know when.'

'Yes is enough for now.' He kissed her again, wanting to fuse himself to her but she slipped away from him.

'We must go back downstairs. You first.'

He loved her carefulness and self-control. 'I wish we didn't have to. It's a particularly silly evening.' He wanted to apologize for its deficiencies.

'No it isn't,' she argued. 'It's warm and friendly, like Janice said. You must go now, or they'll guess what's happening.'

He kissed her again, his mouth scraping hers. Then he went, and Nina was left staring in the mirror into her own anxious eyes.

Jimmy and Janice were the only ones left in the kitchen. Jimmy cleared the table and Janice haphazardly loaded plates into the dishwasher. He brought a stacked tray round to her and put it to one side while she bent over the wire racks.

'God, Janice, look at you. You know you've got a great arse on you.'

Jimmy said it half-jokingly, as he always did, but there was enough wistful sincerity in his voice. Janice straightened up at once. Her face was damp and flushed and wisps of dark hair stuck to her cheeks. Her hostess manner of the early evening had evaporated.

'Great's the word. Half of it would be plenty. Don't be an idiot, Jimmy.'

He had reached out and with the tips of his fingers lifted one of the strands of hair. She was alarmed and almost eager. Jimmy twisted the coil of hair, his face flat.

'An eejit, that's what I am.' Gently he withdrew his hand.

They contemplated each other for a minute more, their eyes on a level. Then Janice frowned, groping for something through her sudden tiredness and the effects of the wine.

'Are you and Star all right?'

His smile came back as quickly as it had vanished, with the associated repertoire of eyebrow contortions.

'As right as rain. As right as ever. Shall I carry through the coffee tray for you, madam?'

When Nina came back to the den she found that someone had put on some slow music, and Janice and Jimmy and Hannah and Andrew were dancing in the space in front of the fire. Hannah rested her head on Andrew's shoulder. Gordon and Star were sitting apart talking intently together. Nina sat down beside Darcy.

'Would you care to dance?'

She felt the full weight of his disconcerting charm. He was very handsome although there were pads of flesh almost obliterating the strong bones of his face. Even after the drink he had taken in his eyes remained sharp under the puffy lids.

She smiled. 'I think I would rather sit.'

Nina was tired now. She wanted to go back to the peace of her own house, but she did not know how to go away from Gordon.

'Let's sit, then,' Darcy said. After a moment in which they watched the two couples slowly gyrating he leaned closer to her, with an effective intimacy that closed off the rest of the room. Nina smelled cigars and cologne, and whisky on his breath.

'Tell me,' he invited, 'what do you think of our provincial little world?'

'What do I think of Grafton? I grew up here, remember.'

'Yes, I remember that. I meant, do you ever regret exchanging everything in London for this?'

He nodded at the dancers.

Nina realized that he was trying to set the two of them apart, at a sophisticated, metropolitan distance from the others, even Hannah. He wanted her to conspire with him in noticing the ways that Janice's furniture and food and even their shared friends fell short of their London counterparts.

Nina felt dislike of Darcy instantly flare up inside her, in defence of Gordon and the evening's warmth. She tried to resist the impulse, but her eyes slid across the room to where Gordon was sitting with Star. Star's head was bent and she was shading her eyes with her fingers. She looked as if she was trying not to cry.

'I don't regret the exchange at all,' Nina answered sharply, trying to focus her attention on Darcy. 'I'm very happy to be here. Besides, the advantages of living in Grafton far outweigh the disadvantages. There is the way I have been made to feel welcome, for instance. I probably wouldn't have encountered anything like it if I had made the move in the opposite direction.'

Some of her dislike was for herself. She had noticed the details of the Frosts' hospitality that would have told her immediately, even if she had known nothing else, that these were not London people. She had probably noted them with an eye just as sharp as Darcy Clegg's. But that did not mean that she wanted to collude with him.

Darcy's intentions seemed to change at once, with alcoholic unpredictability.

'*I* miss it,' he said. 'More than I am usually prepared to admit. More than most people would guess, given everything I have here.'

'I wouldn't have guessed,' Nina said. Her dislike of him

melted away again. She had drunk her share of the wine too, she remembered.

Darcy added, 'But we provincials have to find our challenges and diversions where we can.'

She had no idea what he meant. He lifted his hands with his fingers bunched, as if he were holding strings. She had the impression suddenly that he was the puppet master of the group, and the others, tired and more or less drunk as they were at the end of the evening, were the puppets who danced for him. Her skin prickled down the length of her spine. At the same moment she became aware that Jimmy Rose was watching the two of them over Janice's lolling head.

Across in their corner, Star said softly to Gordon, 'It isn't just tonight. It's every night. I think to myself that I don't mind, that I don't care what he does, but I do. I care for myself, for being humiliated in front of my friends. I'm sorry, Gordon. I've drunk too much. Not for the first time, eh?'

Gordon was vividly aware that Nina had looked at them, then looked away again. What was Darcy whispering to her about?

Star reached out her hand, and reluctantly he took it.

'If he makes you unhappy, why don't you leave him?' he asked her.

Star raised her head. 'Will *you* have me, if I do?'

It was a joke, and not a joke.

'Star, how could I?'

'You couldn't, of course. But you know it's you I'd have, if I could.' She smiled at him then, a lopsided smile of self-mockery.

The record ended and Hannah stepped back from Andrew, making an elaborate curtsey of thanks. He put his arm around her waist and steered her back towards Darcy.

Nina saw that Star was on her feet, apparently quite composed. It was clear that the evening was over.

The three women went away with Janice to find their coats, and Gordon and Andrew murmured together about some business that they needed to attend to in the morning. Jimmy and Darcy found themselves standing together by the front door.

'Well then,' Jimmy said softly. 'It's La Belle Veuve, is it?'

'What do you mean?' It pleased Darcy to appear not to catch his meaning.

'She likes you.'

'Does she?' He accepted Jimmy's tribute without betraying any interest in it, although he felt a flicker of satisfaction that was strengthened by his certainty that he felt no reciprocal liking for Nina Cort. Such aloof, contained women had never attracted him.

Jimmy laughed, and having sown the idea was subtle enough to leave it to germinate alone.

'What was the matter with Mike Wickham today, do you think?'

Darcy shrugged. 'How would I know? Time of the month, probably.'

Jimmy laughed again. 'Just the same, I'd prefer not to be landed with him next week.'

Darcy dropped his heavy arm around Jimmy's shoulder and patted it reassuringly. 'Back to the usual set-up on Sunday, then. That way we can be sure of winning.'

The women came in a group down the stairs. Jimmy allowed himself a moment's luxurious contemplation of their separate possibilities, abundant Hannah and tawny, mysterious Nina, juicy unobtainable Janice and Star, his own.

He called cheerfully to Nina, 'We'll give you a ride home, since we're the nearest to you.'

'Thank you. Star kindly offered already,' Nina said.

They reached the door in a flurry of thanks and good nights. Nina was caught up with the Roses and swept out, away from Gordon, and she was only aware that he watched her going and wanted to hold her back. The evening was finally over.

When everyone had gone Janice leant against the banisters.

'Have I drunk a lot?'

Her eyes were smudged, as if they were melting into the frail surrounding skin, and the rosy pencil line with which she had outlined her lips at the beginning of the evening had turned brown as it faded. When she had been drinking and came to the end of an evening's high Janice's confidence sometimes collapsed, leaving her confused and vulnerable, and vividly reminding Andrew of the much more tentative girl he had married.

'You have,' he told her. She followed him when he went back into the kitchen.

'Not badly too much?'

'No. You were enjoying yourself. It was a good evening.'

Andrew opened the window and a draught of cold air tasting of earth and rain penetrated the smoke and perfume that hung in the room. He peered inside the dishwasher and began to rearrange the dirty plates in the proper sequence. Behind him Janice asked, 'We do give good evenings, don't we?'

Andrew straightened up. The dish that had held the beef contained a layer of congealed fat, and the butcher's string made a greasy curl on the countertop. He wanted to tidy the kitchen and then to spend a few minutes in the dark and silence of the garden before bed. But Janice stumbled towards him, needing reassurance, and he gave it.

'We do. Thanks to you. You do the arranging and the shopping and the cooking. All I do is open the wine.' He referred to what was an old joke between them, a joke that had worn thin and shiny with time.

'No, you do such a lot more than that.' She reached out and caught his hand. 'You are a very good husband.' She groped for the words, mistily now. 'You are, very good to me. We all love you. I love you.'

Andrew hugged her, feeling her weight in his arms. Her hair smelt of the cooking she had done, the afternoon spent chopping and sautéeing. Without knowing that he did it he leaned slightly away from her towards the washing up that still waited to be done. It was the understanding between them on these evenings that Janice prepared and he cleared away.

'I love you too.' The formal exchange. It was not an untruth, not exactly, rather a truth that had changed its colouring.

Andrew closed off the thought. He did not want to pursue it.

'Jimmy was very lively tonight,' Janice began. She wanted to make amends in case her flirtatiousness had disturbed him.

'Jimmy is Jimmy.'

'I know that,' she sighed. Andrew heard a whisper of regret in her admission, but he let this second thought follow the first into limbo.

'I'll help you finish here,' Janice said after a moment. 'It won't take a minute.' She had regained some of her briskness.

They worked side by side, stepping around each other in the familiar space. Janice imagined the pattern of their footsteps on the tiled floor, like the intricate movements of some domestic dance.

The unaccustomed whimsy of the idea made her smile.

Sometimes Andrew's footsteps would diverge, leaping to work and away from them all, whilst hers would lay down more regular loops, to school and to other houses. But still the centre of the pattern would be printed here on the kitchen tiles. It was a comforting notion.

The kitchen was tidy enough to satisfy them both. Andrew wiped the top of the units with a cloth, sweeping the crumbs and remnants carefully into the cup of his hand. He had always been neater around the house than Janice.

'I'm going to bed,' Janice said, giving a little yawn like a cat's.

'I'll be with you in a minute. Five minutes' fresh air, and then I'll lock up.'

It had been raining, but now the sky was partially clear. There was a ribbon of thick cloud overhead, marked by a paler rim, and beyond it in the west a few stars were visible.

Andrew made a slow circuit of the garden. It was too dark to see much and he made each step carefully, testing his familiarity with the ground against the confusion of darkness. He ducked his head under the branches of a cherry tree that overhung the path, and then found a bench set back between the bare twigs of dogwoods. He sat down, feeling the damp grainy wood under his fingers. The small noises of the garden were magnified, much greater in importance than the low note of distant traffic on the bypass.

Andrew let his head fall back against the seat. His eyes closed and the damp air sealed them like a compress. He had also drunk a good deal. The voices of the evening sounded briefly within his skull, and then he dismissed them. The silence was sweet.

When he looked again with dark-adjusted eyes he saw the irregular bulk of the house and the loose composition of trees that framed it. One corner of the trellis that supported a wisteria against a wall had come loose, he recalled. He would have to fix it on Saturday, bringing out his toolbox and a ladder from the garage.

With the domestic certainty of the intention he felt unexpected happiness lifting and ballooning within him. There was this house and its gardens, and the solid, inarticulate love he had for his sons, and there was Janice. He remembered her blurred glance at him this evening when she brought up Jimmy's behaviour, and her need for love and reassurance, and the kitchen smell in her hair.

The happiness was as taut as a drum beneath his rib-cage.

As he got up and walked back towards the house he was thinking that it was not an audacious life, but it was round, sufficient. It was what he had. Upstairs in the silence of the house Janice was already asleep. Andrew undressed and got into bed beside her, warming himself against the generous curve of her back.

Six

Forty excited children seethed under the magnificent fan-vaulted roof of the cathedral's chapter house and leapt on and off the ancient stone seats that lined the walls, unawed by their surroundings. It was the first full rehearsal for the annual Grafton nativity play.

Marcelle Wickham sat on a folding chair with a list and a clipboard, and a wicker hamper beside her. Daisy Wickham had been chosen to be one of the angel chorus. It was an honour but it was a double-edged one, because with the invitation had come a suggestion that Daisy's mother might like to help with the costumes. Marcelle had sighed, and then for Daisy's sake agreed that she would be glad to do it. Now, with three weeks before the first performance, sixteen of the children were still uncostumed, including the ox and the ass.

Marcelle looked up from her list to see Nina standing beside her.

Nina was wearing her bright red jacket and her hair frizzed out over her shoulders, reminding Marcelle of her first glimpse of her in the supermarket. She shone like a beacon against the austere stone backdrop of the chapter house.

'Thanks for coming,' Marcelle said.

The director was calling his cast to order. Marcelle and Nina lowered their voices.

'The ones I've finished are in here.' Marcelle lifted the lid of her wicker hamper.

Nina unfolded an angel's robe. The fabric was the cheapest

plain white cotton but the garment was beautifully cut, with a yoke and falling folds of sleeve.

'No tinsel haloes?' she asked.

'*No* tinsel haloes. To Daisy's great disappointment.'

'So what would you like me to do?'

She had heard Marcelle talking about the cathedral play, and about the sewing that remained to be done, and had diffidently offered to help her. In the last weeks Nina had felt the cathedral beckoning her, so that her steps continually returned to it. The creamy stone of the great pillars and arches and the pieced-together miracle of the medieval glass thrilled her as they had always done, but now she was as much affected by its place at the heart of Grafton. The towers and pinnacles seemed to gather the streets inwards, anchoring and interpreting them, and connecting the lives beyond them.

Once she would have dismissed the idea as fanciful, but she was convinced that the cathedral and its works were the secular as well as the spiritual heart of Grafton. The business park and the shopping precinct and the closes and avenues of new houses were only peripheral, the bright green leaves, whereas the cathedral was the roots and more than the roots, the black earth itself. Nina had never experienced any religious feeling and she did not know if what she was experiencing was religious, but she loved the sense of continuity, of the daily services that were offered up whether the people came or not, and the rhythms of the chapter and the close beyond her windows.

Marcelle said, apologetically, 'It's the animals, really. The ox and the ass, and the lambs. I know it's a cheek, asking a professional artist like you, but I thought perhaps some painted masks . . .'

Nina cut her short. 'I can do masks, if that's what you would like. Or I can do more representational heads, if you would rather. Not fibreglass or anything too ambitious but papier-mâché needn't be as tacky as it sounds.'

'*Could* you?'

'Easily.'

'I *think* masks. The children are quite small, especially the lambs. Those are the two, at the front.'

A pair of six-year-olds, one with a head of tight brassy curls, squirmed at the front of the group of children.

The angel choir had shuffled to its feet, Daisy Wickham amongst them. They were joined by the twelve boy choristers from the Cathedral School and their musical director raised his hand.

The children began to sing the Coventry Carol.

Nina's eyes and throat were stung by the sweetness of it. Her parents had brought her to the cathedral every Christmas to see the nativity play and to hear the carols. She was swept back to childhood and the memories of hard wooden seats and the faint smell of cough sweets and fir boughs.

Daisy Wickham peered sideways to make sure her mother was watching, and then made an embarrassed face at her.

From the four rows of children Nina picked out another face she knew, or thought she recognized. He was amongst the choristers, a boy of about nine. He had a cap of fair hair cut in a square fringe above his eyebrows, and a round, sweet, rather stolid face.

'That must be a little Frost, surely, the one at the front on the left?'

'Yes. It's William, the younger one.'

He was like his brother, but his features were still girlish and pretty. Nina watched the boy as the carol ended, and reflected on the slow changes that would transmute him into the glowering adolescent and then, at last, into a version of Andrew Frost.

For the first time in many months she wished for a child of her own, to see her growing and unfolding in the way that William Frost would do.

The rehearsal ended at eight. By the time it was over Marcelle and Nina had divided the outstanding cutting and sewing between them, and Nina had promised to bring roughs of her masks to the next rehearsal.

'I'm so grateful,' Marcelle said. She was, in truth, because she was sure that whatever Nina undertook to do would be done well.

They said their good nights and separated. Nina walked away across the green, thinking of Vicky at home with her husband and her new baby, and of the choir of angels, other women's children, rehearsing their carols.

Marcelle drove across town with Daisy in the back. She was a good driver and she felt comfortable, in this brief interlude, within the insulated box of her car. She liked the soft greenish glow of the instrument panel and the slow burr of the heater, and the way the lights outside licked over her face and then receded behind her. She would have been happy if home had been much further away; if she could have driven on, suspended like this, with the traffic blinking past on the opposite side of the road.

When she reached the house, Marcelle noted that a light was on behind the drawn curtains in Michael's upstairs study. The tranquillity induced by the night drive was slipping away from her. Her mouth tightened, she felt it, and felt the vertical lines marking her cheeks.

'Here we are, home again,' she said brightly to Daisy. Michael's car was in the garage. She left hers on the sloping drive, and carried Daisy's music case up to the front door as the tired child shuffled behind her.

The house was quiet, except for the distant sound of the television. Marcelle let her bag and Daisy's music drop on to the hall floor.

The air seemed heavy and stale with the taint of Sunday's unresolved quarrel.

It had been a terrible argument, the more frightening because it had swelled out of almost nothing, out of an ordinary weekend disagreement about whether Michael devoted enough time to his children. He had come into the kitchen, dressed for golf.

Marcelle had demanded, 'Are you going out again? What about Jon and Daisy, don't you think they might like to see their father on a Sunday? They don't see you all week, do they?'

'Yes, I am going out. I'm going to play golf. I work hard and I need time away from there' – he meant the concrete and glass slabs of the hospital '– and from here as well.' Michael had made a gesture with his hand as if to push back the walls of their house.

The resolute coldness in him had scared her, and then it had made her angry. She stared back at him over the chopping board, the kitchen table, the basket of ironing waiting to be folded.

'I work hard, too, Michael. What about me?'

His anger had answered hers, and then exceeded it.

'Everything here is about you. Your standards, your ideals. You want to be the perfect mother with the perfect family, you want your job, you want your house just so. It's all to do with what *you* want. You want it, you have it, but don't expect me to conform to the design.'

'It isn't a design. I do it out of love for you all.'

Marcelle had begun to shout. Her fear was intensifying but it became fear of herself, because she never shouted, never made scenes.

'It doesn't come across as love.'

'I can't help that, Michael. Perhaps you can't accept what you won't give.'

'It's always me, isn't it? What I can't or won't do? I support you, don't I? You have your children, your hobbies, your sewing and cooking. It doesn't seem to me that you have a bad bargain.'

'Cooking isn't a hobby, it's my job. I make my contribution, as far as I can, with two children to care for as well.'

The argument had grown, sloughing and bouncing between the two of them and gathering momentum until it became an avalanche of unleashed resentment. Reason and consideration had seemed to stand up like sticks in its path, only to be snapped and swept away.

'Perhaps the truth is that you don't love me any longer,' Marcelle said.

'Perhaps,' Michael agreed coldly.

The avalanche had run out of impetus, with no more ground

to consume. Hot-mouthed, they regarded each other across the bleak murrain.

Marcelle had become aware of the heavy silence spreading through the house. She knew that the children were crouching upstairs in their bedrooms, listening to their parents' ranting voices. She had felt pinched with shame, for herself and for them.

A moment later Jonathan had appeared pale-faced at the head of the stairs.

'Don't argue,' he had shouted. 'Stop arguing.'

'Adults do argue,' Michael told him sharply. 'That's something for you to learn.'

He had gone out, then, with his golf bag slung over his shoulder.

Jonathan's homework books were spread on the kitchen table now, but Jonathan was in the next room watching television. Michael had collected him from a late evening at school. The boy glanced up at his mother and sister.

'Hello, Ma, Daze.'

'Hello, Jon. Had a good day? Where's Daddy?'

Marcelle asked the question although she knew the answer already.

Jonathan shrugged. His eyes had returned to the television screen. 'Upstairs, working.'

Marcelle ran Daisy's bath and saw her into it. Then she went along the landing to Michael's study and opened the door. He was sitting at his desk, surrounded by papers and files and medical journals. He had been staring at a research paper, but he had taken in none of the information it contained. Instead, since Marcelle had come in, he had been listening to the sounds of the house. There had been a quickening of the air, and the joists and timbers had seemed to creak under the pressure of her briskness. He heard her feet on the stairs, and the sound of water running, and the children following her directions. This was so familiar to him that he had to concentrate to extract the idea of his wife, separate in herself, from the fug of domesticity. He was frowning when she opened the door.

'Had a good day?' he asked, taking off his reading glasses and rubbing the bridge of his nose.

Marcelle saw the frown. 'Yes, not bad. Nina's going to help me with the costumes for the play.'

'That's good.'

'I'll see Daisy into bed, then I'll make some supper.'

'Fine. I'll be down before too long.'

Marcelle hesitated, running her fingers around the smooth circumference of the doorknob. She was reassured to see him, here in his place, because she was half afraid that there would come an evening when he would not return home. But her relief was immediately soured by her resentment of him, and the two sensations made a sickly brew inside her. Struggling with herself she went and stood beside his chair. When she looked down she could see the patch of thin hair on his crown, and the fine network of thread veins on the nearest cheek.

In a distant voice she offered, 'If what happened on Sunday was my fault, I'm sorry for it.'

It was the first time it had been mentioned since Michael's return on Sunday afternoon.

After a moment, he said, 'I am sorry, too.'

He did not make any move to touch her, even to take her hand, as he once would have done. Marcelle waited, staring at the work on his desk. It was a report on the orthopaedic rehabilitation of geriatric patients after hip replacement operations.

'Will you come down and have a drink?' she asked, wanting to find a warmer voice than the small, cold one that came out of her.

'I won't be too long,' he repeated.

She left him to his work, and went to see the children into their beds.

Gradually the baby's mouth went slack and the drowsy sucking stopped completely. Her head fell back as her gums released the breast. Vicky held her still for a minute, gazing at the tiny dark crescents of her eyelashes and the whitish pad of tissue on her upper lip, rimmed with milk. This baby was like Mary and Alice had been but she was also different, more beautiful and more precious, because she would be the last one. There was no doubt about that. Gordon would never agree to a third try for a boy.

Vicky rocked the baby in her arms, softly humming. She had already forgotten the painful labour and her stitches and the depression that had assailed her in hospital. She had come home and her life had closed around her again. The girls were pleased with their new sister, and Gordon was being assiduous in his efforts to help. Helen slept, and fed, and slept again. The house enclosed them all, like a warm cocoon.

When she was quite sure that the baby was asleep, Vicky lifted her up and walked softly into the next room. She wrapped her in her white blanket and laid her down in the Moses basket.

It was the middle of the morning. This was the time that always seemed to Vicky to be the brightest and safest of the whole day. It was an optimistic interim of radio music and kettles and vacuum cleaners, before the day tipped over into the more ambivalent stretches of the afternoon. When she was at work, at the clinic, she liked to see child patients at this innocent time.

There was no need to think about work yet, she reflected. The remaining weeks of her maternity leave stretched ahead of her.

Vicky went into the kitchen and leaned against the sink, looking out into the wintry garden. There was an inverted pyramid of baby clothes hanging on the tree of the rotary clothes-line. It was a day of thin sunshine and the shafts of light struck horizontally through the windows. Dust motes swirled like light particles in the solid-seeming bars of brightness. She felt dreamy, almost dazed by the colourless sunlight falling on her face.

When the telephone rang on the wall beside her she lifted it absently and murmured, 'Hello?'

There was the momentary weightless silence that signalled Gordon on his car telephone.

'Darling? Is that you? You sound funny. Are you all right?'

'Yes, I'm fine. Helen has just gone to sleep. Isn't it a lovely day?'

'What? Yes, beautiful. I wanted to make sure you were okay. I'm going to be on site for most of the rest of the day, and it'll be difficult to reach me.'

'Don't worry. We're perfect here, Helen and me.'

'I'll ring you later, then. You'll call Janice or someone, if you need anything?'

'Of course I will. I don't need anything. Thanks, anyway. Gordon?'

'Yes?'

'I love you.' She cradled the receiver against her shoulder, still looking out at the garden and the clothes gently rotating on the line.

'Love you too. I won't be late,' Gordon said.

Vicky hung up. Moving slowly, luxuriating in the light, she filled the kettle and admired the diamond flashes in the water as it splashed in the sink.

Gordon drove back the way he had just come, this time with Nina beside him. The interior of the car seemed full of the scent of her, and the ends of her hair and the soft points of wool that stood up from her clothes gave off a crackle of static electricity. He wanted to touch her, rubbing her to discharge the sparks and then to press his mouth against her and drink her in.

'Where are we going?'

He was watching the road, but he was pricklingly aware of the pull of the muscles around her mouth, the sheen of her skin and the bloom of tiny hairs revealed by the oblique sunlight. It was no less than miraculous that he had achieved this expedition with her, at the cost of nothing more than a small lie to Vicky and a penetrating glance from Andrew as he had eased himself out of the office.

'You know where we are going,' he answered. 'To buy you a car.'

Teasingly, Nina had repeated Hannah's suggestion to him, and he had responded to it in full seriousness. She had been touched.

'Yes, I know that, and it's very kind of you to take me.'

'*Kind?*'

'Certainly. But *where* are we going to buy me a car?'

'To a Mercedes dealership I know. Near Bristol.'

'Ah. Do I definitely need a Mercedes? Wouldn't it be more sensible to settle for something utilitarian and Japanese?'

'There is a Nissan place right opposite the Merc showroom, if you need to make a comparison. But it was you who mentioned a Mercedes in the first place.'

'I know. I have always rather liked the idea.'

His hand left the wheel and reached for hers. Their hands locked together but they looked ahead, at the road signs that loomed and then whirled past rather than venture a glance at each other.

'A Mercedes is a sensible car. Solid, reliable, immaculately engineered.'

Nina laughed at his earnestness. 'If you say so.'

'And sexy. If you choose the right model.'

'Sexier than . . .' Nina pursed her lips. 'Hannah's BMW, say?'

'Much.' He did look at her then, and she was surprised and then caught undefended by the heat in him. Their linked hands rested against her thigh. Nina heard the rasp of her own breathing.

'Just as you are sexier than Hannah herself.'

'I don't think so.'

'Oh, but you are. Hannah is obvious, whereas you are subtle. Hannah is a hot day at the beach and you, you are . . . a forest path in the moonlight. A matter of shadows and suggestions, and sudden clear patches of pure silver.'

This poetic flight from a man so unpoetical touched her again. She felt a kindling of affection that was separate from the welter of her other confused sensations.

Nina stared ahead of her again. A sign swept towards them. Bristol, 20m. Gordon disengaged his hand from hers as he overtook a Volvo the same colour as Janice's. Lightheartedly, but also out of a secret kind of retrospective jealousy, she asked him, 'Which of the other wives do you like? If not Hannah?'

114

Gordon shrugged. 'I don't know. Star, perhaps.'

Nina remembered the impression of her weeping at the Frosts' on Sunday evening.

'Is she unhappy?'

'Who knows? No unhappier than anyone else would be, I imagine, married to Jimmy Rose.'

It was a deliberate deflection and Nina silently accepted it.

The Mercedes showroom was a sleek affair of plate-glass windows and shining bodywork by the side of a busy road amongst a network of more busy roads. There was indeed a Nissan garage directly opposite to it, a much brasher looking place with a border of snapping flags flying from tall white poles.

Nina and Gordon stepped out from Gordon's car into a world of steel-blue reflections in glass and long, polished bonnets and cold sun striking darts from mirrors and chrome. Even the specks of mica underfoot twinkled up at them. They walked shyly to the doors of the showroom, half-dazzled by the light and pleased to find themselves as a couple in this adventure, as if they had emerged into a surprise holiday.

Once they were inside a salesman in a blue suit came briskly to meet them.

'Good morning, sir, madam. Can I help you?' He had a mouth overful of teeth, all of them bared in a smile.

'Madam is looking for a car,' Gordon said.

Nina was seized by an urge to giggle, and to dig him in the ribs with her elbow. Controlling herself she said seriously, pointing to the nearest blur of shining metal. 'Something like this one, perhaps.'

'Ah, yes. The 190E. That particular car is two years old, but covered by our full warranty, of course. The mileage is a *shade* higher than average, which is reflected in the price, naturally. The metallic jade is very popular. And the smoke grey interior.'

'What else is there?'

'What are you looking for, exactly? Is it the 190, or something larger? A new car, or a previously owned model?'

Nina blinked. 'I'm not sure.' And then seeing the man's smile patronizingly widen she improvised, 'A saloon car, not too big. It doesn't have to be new.'

Gordon, her lifeline, had wandered away. She saw him amongst the curves and planes of metal, appraising the machines. It made her think romantically of his business, translating spidery plans into airy structures of glittering tensile steel. She followed him towards the back of the showroom, with the salesman beside her.

Gordon stopped alongside a red car. It was the colour of audacious lipstick, and it had a black hood and wheels of silver spokes and the air of being inappropriately corralled here amongst the humbler models.

'What about this?' Gordon murmured.

'*This* one?' Nina touched the long nose of it. Her fingertip left a tiny smudge on the sheen of scarlet.

The salesman was there at once. 'The 500SL. Power hood, thirty-two valve engine, the top of the range. A very nice car. This one is a year old, twelve thousand miles, one gentleman owner, fully serviced by us from new.'

He jingled with the ignition key and pressed a switch to the right of the gear lever. The hood began to glide upwards and backwards, and then slowly furled itself like some fantastical umbrella. Inside there were black leather seats, a walnut fascia and a little leather-rimmed steering wheel.

'It is very pretty,' Nina said.

'Top speed of 155 m.p.h. Not that that is much use to us here, but dead handy on the Continent. The car's capable of more, but the governor cuts in at that point. Nought to sixty in six point five seconds, so you won't be finding many of the boy racers in XR3s cutting you up at the lights.'

'Very impressive.'

Behind the salesman's shoulder Gordon silently mouthed at her, '*Very sexy.*'

Nina kept her face straight.

'Would you like to test drive it at all?'

The car gleamed at her in its bright red glory. She could see her face reflected in the voluptuous curve of the wing, her hair reddened to a blaze. This wasn't the sober saloon she had envisaged.

'Why not?'

There was at once a clicking of fingers and opening of tall doors behind her. The salesman sprang into the black leather seat and switched on the engine. A soft purr with a threatening, throaty undertone rose like bubbles through champagne. Smiling like truant children, Gordon and Nina followed the car outside. The salesman climbed out and held the driver's door open for Nina.

'But there are only two seats,' she said.

Gordon bowed. 'I'll wait. Enjoy the drive.'

Nina slid into the car and braced her hands experimentally on the wheel. She looked down the nose of it to the gun-sight of the three-pointed star on the end, and gently touched her foot to the accelerator.

'Left around the building, and then right into the main road,' the salesman encouraged her. As she eased the Mercedes away Nina distinctly heard Gordon's wolf-whistle.

At first she was nervous, and then she was exhilarated. The purr modulated to a noise like tearing silk and the car shot forward. She swung the wheel too hard and had to jerk it back again, and they sailed out into the stream of traffic.

'Power steering,' the salesman reminded her.

It was very fast. The road opened up and the bunch of dull cars in their wake dwindled to dots in her mirror. She braced her arms and felt the car respond to the lightest touch on the wheel. The glossy bonnet in front of her shimmered like a stretched satin ribbon, and the grey road temptingly unwound ahead.

The salesman had been reciting the selling points, but now he had gone quiet. Nina glanced at his face, and then at the speedometer. She was doing a hundred and five miles an hour. She lifted her foot, and the scenery caught up with her again.

'Quite a quick motor,' the man said. 'I can see you like that.'

'I do, rather,' Nina said, surprised by herself.

But she knew that she had been entirely seduced. The more she drove the car, the more she wanted to drive it. The speedometer crept up again, and her head fell back, and she wanted to turn on the radio and sing and drive straight on for ever into the winter sun.

'We could make a turn just ahead,' the salesman ventured.

Reluctantly she did as she was told.

When they swooped back to the showroom and Nina saw Gordon innocently lounging with hands in pockets beside his own unremarkable family saloon she muttered a mock curse under her breath. It cost her a pang to climb out of the black leather seat and abandon her bright red seducer, even temporarily.

Gordon strolled over to meet them. 'How was it?'

The salesman fanned himself with his clipboard.

'I liked it,' Nina said demurely.

'Shall we go across there and have a look?' Gordon nodded at the busy flags over the lines of Nissans.

Nina turned her back on them and stretched her fingers out again to the red shine. There was nothing so vulgar as a price ticket anywhere in sight.

'How much is it?'

The man consulted a list on his clipboard. 'Sixty-two nine fifty, this particular car.'

She was opening her mouth, amazingly, to say *I'll take it*, when she felt Gordon's hand descend very firmly on her arm.

'We'll just take a walk, and think about it.'

Then they were outside again in the cold sunshine. A stronger wind had begun to blow, and there was a fringe of cloud away to the east.

'I loved it. It isn't at all what I intended to buy, and now I can't bear to think of settling for anything less.'

Her cheeks were hot. Gordon's arm and shoulder felt very warm on one side and the chill on the other sliced into her. She realized that her blood was racing, and that she was excited, for the car and for the bright day and for Gordon himself. He lowered his head and kissed her, open-mouthed. His hand slid inside her coat.

'Can you afford it?'

She thought of the money that Richard had left her, dead weights of it invisibly stored up in banks and securities, and of Richard himself, as she had never seen him, lying on the path under the branches of the trees. He was gone, and he would never come back.

'Yes, I can pay cash.'

His eyes widened a fraction, and the palm of his hand grazed her nipple under the layers of clothes.

Speed, and money, and sex, Nina thought giddily. The old cliché. But it was none the less exciting for that.

'Then let me do the deal for you,' Gordon said.

They went back to the showroom together, and he began to negotiate.

From the salesman's face, Nina knew that he was jealous of them both. He was jealous of her for her car and her money, and of Gordon for his possession of her. The atmosphere in the mock-plush side office was as tense as a drawn wire.

'I can't go any lower than that. That's shaved our profit right down to a couple of points,' the man complained.

'Then we'll go along to Forshaw's and see what they can offer us,' Gordon said simply. Nina was awed.

After half an hour, she had her red car for exactly fifty-five thousand pounds, and the salesman was wiping his forehead with a folded handkerchief.

'I'll come in with a banker's draft the day after tomorrow,' Nina said and smiled.

They shook hands, at last.

Outside again, Nina put her arm through Gordon's.

'You were terrible. The poor little man.'

'Poor nothing. He doesn't sell many of those in a week.'

'My beautiful new car. Thank you.'

On the forecourt, faced off by the lines of Nissans, they kissed again. Nina shivered with his arms around her.

'Get in,' Gordon said, and held the door for her. They drove away in silence, aware of their own breathing and the fog of one another's breath on the cold air. When they reached the motorway Nina slyly put her hand out, reaching for him with the images of smooth red wings and the glitter of chrome in her mind.

'It's a long way home,' she whispered.

He knew that she had been turned on by the car, and by the whole secret, frivolous expedition they had made together, and that seemed to him delightful and also erotic.

'I can't wait that long,' Gordon said roughly.

Ahead of them was a sign for a motorway rest area, and amongst the blue and white symbols innocently offering themselves there was a bed. It had a head and foot and a neatly turned-down white sheet.

Nina heard the tick-tick of the indicator, and they swung left in a line of drivers leaving the motorway. The Travelodge at the far side of the enclave was deserted at this time of day, the double row of windows masked by net curtains. There were no other cars in the motel's parking area.

'Wait here for me,' Gordon said.

After he had gone through a door at the end of the block marked 'Reception', Nina felt suddenly conspicuous sitting alone in his car. She sank lower into her seat, drawing the collar of her coat up around her neck, and then dismissed her fears as absurd and sat upright again. A moment later Gordon came back and took his place behind the wheel once more. Then he opened his hand to show her a key with a plastic number tag. They both stared at it.

'Do you want to do this?' he asked her. 'In a motel room, with me?'

She gazed out at the windswept tarmac and the tossing branches of trees that had been planted to break the noise of the road.

Gordon said, 'The other night was happenstance. We can dismiss that, if you like. You were lonely, I stepped out of line, Vicky was in hospital.'

The second time, she supplied for him, was different. It was a matter of volition, and if the act was repeated they would have to make the necessary reckonings afterwards. Her own husband was dead; this man, with his direct language and appetite, was another woman's husband. She knew the weight of her own loneliness, and remembered how Gordon had lightened it, and understood equally well that he would not and could not entirely dissolve it for her.

But even as Nina pondered the equation, with her eyes fixed on the trees, she was forced to acknowledge that she did want him again. More than that, it was inconceivable that she would find the strength of will to deny that she did. This mundane place, the breeze-block outline of the motel, and the key in his hand, were invested with significance because of their association with him. She did not understand how this had happened, only that it had happened and she could not now escape whatever was to follow.

She took the key from his hand, and metal and plastic jingled together.

'I do want to,' she told him.

He kissed her, forcing her head back against the headrest, and his mouth grazed her skin. They left the car, and walked unsteadily towards the motel room.

It was a small rectangular box, with a hollowed bed flanked by cheap drawers faced in brown plastic veneer. A bathroom walled into one corner revealed pink tiles and a floral curtain.

Gordon tossed the key on to the bedcover.

'I'm sorry. This is horrible.'

He was thinking of the pale, dignified spaces of her house in Dean's Row. He remembered her bedroom as clearly as if he was looking at a photograph of it. But he had wanted this second time, if it was to happen, to be in a neutral place that was neither hers nor his.

'It isn't horrible or beautiful. It's nowhere,' Nina said gently.

He was grateful to her for this reading of his needs. But now they faced each other in the perfunctory approximation of a bedroom, a place that was occupied without affection by hurried businessmen and travellers and illicit lovers like themselves, he saw their condition more clearly, stripped of its romantic glow. He saw a middle-aged man, made weary of his good wife by the repetition of too many days. He had brought Nina here – and in this clear light he knew that she was not the wild girl he had conjured up the other night but a sad widow, also no longer young, with fine lines in her face – to commit an act of adultery.

A memory of the cathedral on the night he had shown it to her came back to him. He had been intent on Nina, but he also remembered the organ music and the singing of the choir at practice. He was not a conventionally religious man, and he had married Vicky in a register office, but he had a confused sense of a simple and faithful life, established and approved by a higher authority, that might have been lived along lines that were parallel to but infinitely distant from the tangle and heat and disillusion of his real existence.

'What is it?' Nina asked him.

He tried to say 'nothing' but at the same time he half turned away from her, looking through the net curtains to where his car was parked between oblique white lines.

'Guilt. And fear, and a belated desire not to hurt anyone.'

She went to him and put her arms around his waist, under the shelter of his jacket, and held him as if he were a child, or an old friend.

'Yes,' Nina said. 'I understand.'

Because of the simplicity of her response, and also because he did see her face so clearly and close up with the marks of time and grief in it, he felt his doubts gather together and lift and swing away from him. He was left with pure conviction.

'I love you,' he said. 'I loved you the other night, at Andrew's. In that bathroom.'

He also wanted her, more insistently than he had ever wanted Vicky or any of the women he had ever known.

She put her hand up to his mouth, to stop him, but he caught it and held it.

'I love you,' he repeated. 'I don't know how this has happened. I didn't ask for it, but it's here and I don't want it to go away. I don't want you to go away, never, never.'

He was whispering to her, with his lips against her face. All the perspectives had changed. The room had become a sanctuary, benign and familiar and precious for that, and the horizons beyond it had vanished as if a thick, kindly mist had descended.

'You don't love me. You can't love me because you don't know me,' Nina told him. Richard had known her, after their years together.

'I do know you. What more do I need to learn?'

He undid her clothes and peeled them off her tea-freckled shoulders. He kissed her skin and tasted the warm saltiness of it, and pushed her back until they lay in the bed's hollow and gazed into the reflections in each other's eyes.

'Take off your clothes too,' she ordered him.

He clawed at the buttons and buckles, discarding the business carapace. Her knuckles clashed against his as their hands worked. Then, when he knelt above her, she stared up at him and her lips and eyelids were thickened with lust. He remembered how she had looked the first time, in her unornamented bedroom.

Nina's hand descended on him, and she watched the effect through half-closed eyes. A moment later they were tangled together, mouths and hands and limbs. Her narrow hips insinuated themselves beneath him, snakily lifting, not offering herself but commanding him. She was different from Vicky, who waited to be led. Vicky was not submissive, not exactly, but there was an understanding that she preferred to bestow rather than to demand. There was a moment's pure confusion as the woman beneath him receded and then merged with the familiar images of his wife, and then split away to resume her own identity, utterly strange to him.

The marriage of strangeness with intimacy was like a chemical entering his bloodstream, sending such a narcotic kick through his body that he was afraid he would come now, too soon, like a boy.

'Tell me what you think. What you feel,' she demanded when he came into her. And then, 'Oh, I *want* you.'

'You've got me. Nina, Nina. I think you are extraordinary, unmatchable. I feel like fucking you for ever.'

He wanted to bury himself, to shoot himself into a milky galaxy of stars inside her. He wanted to become timeless and fathomless, as if he had died and turned into a star, as his mother had long ago promised he would do.

Instead, their coupling in the motel room was quick, and feverish. The carnality of it startled them both. There was no time, as they had felt there was time the first night. They longed to reclaim one another after the separation. There were the Frosts' dinner party and London and the days in between to be obliterated, and the car showroom and the salesman and the motel itself. They went at each other blindly, as if it was the last thing they would ever do.

Afterwards, lying with Nina's hair spread over his eyes and her weight on top of him, Gordon imagined the noise they had made penetrating the stud walls into the mirror boxes on either side of them, and into the ones beyond those, and he prayed fervently that they were empty.

When his breathing became even again he stroked her hair away and peered upwards, trying to see her face. She was staring at the woodchip wallpaper. He was at once intensely jealous of whatever it was that held her attention away from him.

'I meant it, you know.'

'Meant?'

'I love you.'

'Hush.'

Her face, the skin over the bone, and the rest of her body, had now become irrelevant, although he loved them also with a kind of detached affection. He was much more vividly aware of the internal spark, the invisible imp, that animated her. He wanted to catch hold of it, and wondered at his own possessiveness.

'Tell me more about Richard.'

'I was thinking about him just then. How did you know?'

'A guess. Not a particularly inspired one.'

She leaned over him, her small bumpy breasts falling against his chest.

'I'm sorry, I didn't mean that I had withdrawn from you. I think of him often. It's very odd when someone who is quite young and apparently fit dies suddenly, like Richard did. One minute the person is there, filling your life, and then in a day, in an hour, he is completely gone and will never come back.'

'What do you feel now?'

'I'm not sure. Grateful, usually. For what we had, you know.'

He digested that for a moment.

'What do you want from me?'

He heard himself asking, like a petulant boy, for reassurance, compliments, approval.

Nina propped her head on one elbow, looking down at him. She appeared to be amused, and he was momentarily irritated by her.

'I mean, I'm only a simple bloody engineer. I'm not rich or smart or clever. I don't know the right restaurants in London, I can't even fix the right restaurant here. I'm married, I've got three kids, too much work to do . . .'

She cut him short. 'I don't want anything from you.'

Then she indicated the room. He examined the MDF fittings and plyboard wardrobe with plastic knobs, the wall-mounted mirror and the round tin tray bearing a kettle and a sugar bowl filled with teabags, sachets of coffee and milk powder.

'Just this,' she said. And with a touch of coquetry she ran the flat of her hand up his flank, over the thickening flesh at his waist to rest on his chest. Under her hand, it seemed to Gordon that she had it in her power to make the drab place beautiful, and to invest him with more significance than he could ever truly possess. He felt a lick of undiluted happiness.

'Are you afraid of it? Of me?' Nina demanded.

'No. Not a bit. I can't believe my luck, that's all.'

'Or I mine,' she told him softly.

He saw that she was cold and he drew the covers around her

shoulders. She settled herself comfortably against him and they lay in silence for a minute.

'I won't try to take you away from Vicky.'

It was a promise she felt obliged to make, although she was not sure she would be able to keep it. It was hard enough to accept that she must relinquish him in an hour, as she would have to.

'I know that. Thank you.'

He felt a separate, invincible tenderness now for his wife and daughters. It was important that they should not be hurt, whatever came.

Gordon was full of optimism. He kissed the top of Nina's head. 'Come and get into the bath with me.'

They went into the windowless pink cell and ran the water, and Nina emptied the contents of all the complimentary sachets into it so that bubbles mounted to engulf the taps, and steam obliterated the mirrors. They lay down in the foam, folding their limbs to accommodate themselves, and sickly scented water slopped over the edge of the bath and puddled the tiles.

They talked through the steam, exchanging simple details about their lives. It seemed important that they should know if the other had sisters or not, had travelled and how far, could speak French if not German, had read Updike, disliked John Major.

When the water was cold, Gordon said, 'I must go back now.'

They dried each other, gently like children, and disentangled their clothes.

When they were ready to leave they stood in the doorway, gazing back at the bed and the tea tray and the surfaces of plastic veneer. Then Gordon closed the door, with affection, as if he was sealing into the room a portion of their history.

They drove quietly back to Grafton. The weather was changing; the sky was clouded and a bruised light looked as if it might be the herald of snow.

Seven

It was a cold December, and the fields and hills beyond the city were stilled and drained of their colours by night after night of hard frost. A Christmas tree was put up on the cathedral green, exactly as Nina remembered from her childhood. Looking out at it from her windows she thought that even the strings of coloured bulbs that twisted through the branches were the same.

Darcy and Hannah Clegg sent out elaborate printed invitations for their Christmas Eve party. It was to be the fifth successive year that they had held the party, and it had long been established as the social centrepiece of the couples' year.

Nina put the Cleggs' invitation on the mantelpiece in her drawing room, from where Gordon picked it out from amongst the Christmas cards. He had called to see her after a visit to the cathedral. The whole of the west front was now masked with scaffolding and protective sheeting.

'Are you going to this?'

'Yes, I am. Why not, really?'

They were edgy with each other today, although she had run downstairs at the sound of his knock and when the door was closed they had fallen back against it in a rush of eagerness for one another.

'I can only stay for a few minutes,' he had whispered, while his fingers were already busy with the buttons of her shirt.

Afterwards they had pulled their clothes together again, and stood uneasily in the drawing room in front of the cold afternoon hearth. Gordon had refused her offer of tea, explaining that Andrew was waiting for him at the office.

Nina was galled by what she interpreted as a suggestion that she should stay away from the party. It would be the first time Gordon would have to face her with Vicky beside him.

'I didn't mean that you shouldn't come,' he said at once, taking her hands. 'I want to see you, every possible time, wherever it is. I'm only afraid that I won't be able to hide how much I do want it.'

'You will be able to. It will be like at the Frosts'. Easier than that, because Vicky will be there.'

'It isn't easy.'

His answer was so simple, so heartfelt, that Nina saw she was unreasonable. It was no more than the unpalatable truth that she would be jealous of Vicky, and it was also true that she would have to learn to swallow her jealousy and digest it, because there was nothing else to be done.

'I'm sorry,' she said at once.

They held on to each other as if they could keep everything else at bay with the tenderness between them. Their separate identities miraculously melted together, and they were convinced that they understood each other entirely. So it was that they swung in a moment from distance to delight.

To Gordon, the spare Georgian house across from the cathedral was both a sanctuary and a snare. When he was away from it he thought of it constantly, yet when he came into it he moved cautiously, always reckoning the time he could spare in minutes and replaying in his head the evasions he had made in order to reach it.

Today Andrew had been clearly impatient when he had announced that he must make another visit to the cathedral. Had he only imagined it was the dawn of suspicion? There had been several half-explained absences lately. Yet Gordon could not bear to think of staying away from Dean's Row. Nina filled his head and his imaginings. He believed that he now knew how a compulsive gambler or an addict felt, and at the same time was repelled by his connection of Nina with such things.

He asked her, with his mouth moving against her forehead, 'When can we meet again?'

He felt the small movement of her shoulders, a gesture of impotence rather than carelessness.

'When you next can spare an hour.'

That was how it had been since the day of buying Nina's car. They had met four or five times, always hurriedly, always with a sense of the rest of the world lying in wait for them.

The minutes of an hour added up for Gordon now. He could almost hear them ticking, like a bomb. It was a long time; it was hardly time to draw breath.

'I'm sorry,' he offered in his turn. 'That is just how it is. I'd spend every hour with you, if I could.'

Nina nodded, and then lifted her head. He could see the tiny whorls and knots of colour in her irises, and the black pupils fractionally dilating. He imagined the pull of the ciliary muscles on the tiny lens within her eyes, and the twin inverted images of himself laid on the retina only to be righted again by the brain's conviction.

That was the brain's power, he thought, to make logic out of what it saw clearly to be the wrong way up.

'I'm going to drive to Bristol tomorrow. I want to give the car a proper trial,' Nina said.

Since she had taken delivery of the red Mercedes it had spent almost all its time in the garage of the cobbled mews behind Dean's Row.

She added, 'I need to buy some materials for Marcelle's nativity costumes.'

'I'll come with you,' Gordon said, obliterating with a grandiose stroke the next day's obligations. Her pleasure immediately rewarded him.

'Will you?'

'Somehow,' he promised, already ambushed by his own anxiety.

*

129

Marcelle was driving to work at the Pond School. She was currently teaching on one of the college's best money-spinners, a twelve-week intensive course designed to bring novices up to the standard where they might look for work as ski-chalet cooks. Her current set included Cathy Clegg, one of Darcy's nineteen-year-old twins, who was a perfect example of the Pond's introductory cooking student. Cathy's only real interest in food was in how much or how little of it she could consume before a millimetre of surplus flesh appeared on her miniskirted hips.

As she drove Marcelle was reflecting on the lack of enthusiasm from her class, and in another compartment of her mind she was running through the afternoon's demonstration. She would be showing the students how to make ciabatta bread, and enlarging on some techniques associated with bread and dough preparation before the next morning's practical session.

Her attention was fully engaged and she drove the familiar route automatically, almost unseeingly.

Marcelle had taken a roundabout way via the outer bypass instead of facing the morning's traffic through the middle of the town. By this route she would cross a branch of the main railway line that ran out to the west of Grafton. The fading echo of mainline expresses heard from the cathedral green was supposed to mean that rain was coming.

The branch line was not much used, but today, as she looked ahead over the flat crowns of the hawthorn hedges, Marcelle saw the red and white arms of the level-crossing barrier begin to descend. When she rounded a bend and could see the crossing itself, the gates were already down and the red warning lights were flashing to indicate that a train was coming. Marcelle muttered, 'Damn' and slowed to a stop in front of the gate.

On her own side of the line hers was the only waiting car. At first, because she was busy with her thoughts, she registered only that there was another vehicle drawing up on the far side beyond the tracks.

Then, after two or three seconds, some recollection of shine and redness made her look again.

Immediately she recognized Nina's new Mercedes. The flashness of the car had given rise to some wry remarks amongst the Grafton wives. Marcelle saw that it was Nina at the wheel of the red car, and that there was a passenger with her.

The train was approaching. She could hear the rumble of it, and out of the corner of her eye she saw a blur of movement as the dark shape rolled around a bend towards the crossing.

In that moment Marcelle realized that Nina and her passenger were laughing together, and that there was a shiver of intimacy between them that she couldn't have described, or accounted for by their expressions or postures. She was only certain that it was there, and that the couple had not seen her, and that the man was Gordon Ransome.

A second later the engine of the train hid them from her sight. It was a heavy diesel pulling a line of clanking goods wagons. Marcelle counted them as they went by, sixteen in all, and then the swaying brown box of the guard's van at the end. In the minute that it took the train to pass she collected her thoughts, and began to compose the simple explanations that would account for Gordon and Nina laughing together, alone in her car on a weekday morning, enjoying a closeness that seemed to exclude the rest of the world.

The guard's van swept by, reopening her view like a curtain being drawn back.

Marcelle saw Nina's hands still braced on the wheel, two small white patches. She also saw that the two heads were slowly drawing apart, and she knew for certain, as surely as she also knew who the two people were, that they had kissed while they were waiting for the train to pass by.

The red lights at the side of the barrier stopped flashing. In a moment the gates would automatically swing upwards once again. But while the two cars waited, separated by the rails and the red and white bars, Gordon and Nina saw Marcelle watching them.

In her turn, Marcelle saw how their faces turned into stiff ovals pocked with the dark holes of shock.

The rear of the train had disappeared. The gates silently lifted, moving through an invisible arc until the twin arms pointed upwards and the way was left clear.

Both drivers eased their cars into gear and they crept towards each other over the wooden ramp. Marcelle lifted her hand in a wave and Gordon and Nina both smiled back at her. Even as they passed each other Marcelle recognized what it took for them to overlay their expressions of alarm with smiles of conventional greeting.

Then the Mercedes was gone, dwindling in her rear view mirror and vanishing around the bend in the road.

Marcelle drove on towards the Pond School, trying to lay straight in her mind the implications of what she had seen. Two miles further on, while she was still thinking of Vicky with Helen strapped to her front in a baby sling, she caught a glimpse of Gordon's grey Peugeot. He had left it in a corner of the car park belonging to a roadside restaurant.

'Did she see you?' Nina gasped. 'Did she recognize you?'

'Of course she did.'

Pale-faced, Gordon stared ahead at the road as he tried to work out the significance of what had happened.

'She couldn't have seen us kiss. The train was in the way,' Nina said.

'I think she must have seen enough.'

How could they, he wondered, have imagined that they were invisible and impregnable, just because they were so happy to be together?

They were both shaking. Their instinct was to pull off the road and find comfort and reassurance in touching each other, but to do so where they could be seen would be to compound their absurd mistake. Gordon was asking himself, even now, *Where can we go in future? Where will we be safe?*

'There could be a perfectly ordinary explanation. Your car could have broken down. I was giving you a lift. I just passed by. Gordon?'

She was seeking his reassurance, and he tried to give it.

'Yes. Maybe.'

'What shall we do, then?'

He couldn't think of anything in particular. It seemed now inevitable that someone would have seen them, and he was amazed by his preceding carelessness. 'Nothing. I don't believe there is anything we can do, except brazen it out if we have to with a breakdown story.'

'Do you think Marcelle will say anything to Vicky?'

He thought about it. 'No, I don't suppose so. Not directly. Perhaps she'll try to warn her in some more oblique way. I don't know. What do women say to each other in these circumstances?'

'I have never been in these circumstances before.'

The edginess came back again as they veered from complicity to opposition.

They drove for a little way in silence. Gordon was trying to work out what would happen if he told Nina now that it must end, before anything else happened. But it was only a distant speculation. They had already come too far to imagine retracing their steps.

They came to a crossroads, and a sign indicating that they were only a few miles from the motorway. Nina lifted her hands from the wheel for an instant.

'What do you want to do? Shall we go on?'

He answered at once, 'Yes. Let's get as far away from here as we can, if only for a few hours.'

His certainty won her back again, and her spirits lifted. Their story would be believed, there was no reason why it should not be. It had been a warning; they would be more careful in the future.

She put her foot down and the Mercedes shot forward.

In the demonstration kitchen Marcelle went through the motions of mixing and kneading her bread dough while a dozen students lounging on the benches in front of her yawned and whispered and made notes. Cathy Clegg sat at the front, with her long legs in thick black tights negligently propped up on the dais.

She twined an escaped strand of streaky blonde hair through her fingers as she gazed out of the window.

Marcelle had given the lesson often enough to be able to do it on auto-pilot. As she worked and talked a segment of her mind slid over the morning's conundrum and then away from it, to wonder about the other Grafton couples.

What she had seen made her feel precarious. She had not confessed even to Janice that she was afraid her own marriage was faltering; her communications even with her closest friend about this were always on the level of wry jokes, jokes that turned on the helplessness and childishness of their men. They were never to do with their own loneliness, or disappointment, and even so Janice sometimes shrank from this comic half-truth-telling to reaffirm her own contentment.

'But they aren't so bad, the two of them, are they, Mar? They could be much worse, after all.'

She would wrinkle her nose in the pretty way she had, and smooth the loose folds of her skirt over her hips.

Their men could be drunks, or womanizers, Marcelle supplied for her. Or violent, or cruel or criminal – but those were the traits of men in other places, weren't they? Husbands in television documentaries, newspaper articles. They were nothing to do with the steady couples and the security of Grafton, with its golf club and good schools and with the golden cathedral at its heart.

Marcelle had assumed it was only her own marriage that was dying away into silence, and that it must be doing so through some fault of her own. If she could be better in some way, she reasoned, then Michael would warm to her again. In the meantime she would not admit that she was afraid, even to Janice. She didn't want to betray too much, to admit that there was so much darkness beneath the smooth, shining surface of their lives.

This morning's glimpse of Gordon with Nina had not troubled her merely for Vicky's sake, although that did concern her also. It was more as if in the moment at the level crossing some stretched-taut piece of insulating fabric had been pierced, and now the pinprick was tearing apart to become a gaping hole. Through the hole came a cold and threatening draught of suspicion that blew all around her. It was not just her own life that was in difficulties. The placid and normal world that she struggled to maintain had become as precarious as a conjuring trick. What was the reality in Grafton, Marcelle wondered, and what was the illusion?

The oven pinger interrupted her thoughts.

'Mrs Wickham? The bread?' a student helpfully reminded her.

'Thank you, Emma.'

There had been a time when Marcelle had found it definitely uplifting to cook good food for lovers and friends, although for some reason it had seemed not quite acceptable to admit as much. The young were less worried about such things now. But in the last years – for how long had she felt it? – cooking had become a matter of work, and of repetitive family duty.

Art and nature, Marcelle thought, remembering one of her oblique conversations with Janice. Gardening, and cooking, and sex. Where had the subtle and diverse pleasures gone to?

It was four o'clock. She could hear the clatter of other students in the corridor outside.

'That's all for today,' she told her students.

She left the class and went quickly to the staff room to collect her coat, avoiding the tea-drinking gaggle of other teachers, and emerged from the front door. Immediately she caught sight of Cathy ahead of her, who must have skipped out without doing her share of the clearing. Cathy ran down the steps towards a young man who had just clambered out of an illegally parked Golf. Loud music issued from the wound-down window.

Cathy shouted, 'Barney!'

Marcelle paused at the top of the steps, wrapping her arms around her chest to keep out the cold. Her breath clouded in front of her.

Barney Clegg greeted his sister with a double feint to her head, and then a bear-hug.

'Hey, I'm home, are you pleased? Good day's cooking?'

'Great. The cooking was okay. Here, have some bread, you're always hungry.'

He took the chunk that she produced for him and gnawed enthusiastically at it.

'This is great. Did you make it?'

'Don't be a dope. Marcelle did. She'd be thrilled if I had. Wouldn't you, Marcelle?'

She had come quietly down the steps behind Cathy. The two Cleggs turned their smiles on her. They both had long upper lips, and very white, perfectly even teeth that proclaimed expensive orthodontistry. Marcelle could see their joint resemblance, presumably to their mother, whom she had never met.

'You could, Cathy, if you felt like it.' She knew she sounded like a schoolmistress, not the bestower of culinary inspiration to last a lifetime. The realization depressed her. 'Hello, Barney. Are you home for Christmas?'

Darcy's eldest child was away studying at agricultural college.

'Yup. Come to liven the old place up a bit.' He grinned engagingly at her, displaying his father's charm and what would turn into the same creases at the corners of his eyes. Barney was over six feet tall, broad-shouldered and blond-haired, with a healthy aura that suggested he spent much of his time in the fresh air. In his trainers and American baseball jacket with white leather sleeves he seemed huge, towering over Marcelle like some benevolent if not very intelligent giant.

'So, how're you, Marcelle? Apart from having to teach Cathy, that is? And the family?'

Cathy swiped at him with her black leather rucksack. They were like healthy animal cubs, Marcelle thought, playing outside the nest. She smiled up at Barney.

'Very well, thank you. But I must go and pick them up from Janice's, or they'll be wondering where I am. Have a happy holiday, won't you?'

As Marcelle crossed the road to the car park the two Cleggs piled into the Golf and slammed the doors, calling their goodbyes to her. The car accelerated away in a diminishing blast of noise and music.

It was Janice's day for the school run. When Marcelle reached the Frosts' house the winter daylight had all but gone and the street lights made the sky look thick and black. Janice's car was already in the driveway. The children were in the kitchen, and so was Vicky Ransome with her baby and the two little girls.

Marcelle took the mug of tea that Janice handed her and gave her children the attention they needed. Jonathan had scored a goal in a football game, and Daisy was anxious about the evening's singing rehearsal.

'Well done, Jon. There's plenty of time, Daisy. We'll have supper and then go to the cathedral. Look, William isn't worried, is he?'

William didn't take his eyes from the television screen.

Marcelle sat down at the table with her mug of tea, facing Vicky.

Vicky's open blouse showed the strong stalk of her neck, and her head nodded tenderly over the contented baby. While she watched Vicky Marcelle became sure that she could not possibly say anything about what she had seen. Her anxiety about what it meant together with the responsibility for keeping silent pressed heavily on her. She wondered if there were other secrets, secrets that she could not guess at, inhabiting the room and separating the three of them.

'How are you?' she heard herself asking Vicky.

Vicky looked up. Her wings of hair swung back to expose her cheeks and the collar of flesh, not yet dissolved, that pregnancy had laid down around her jawline.

'It's tiring, with three of them. Alice wakes up often at night, always when this one has just gone off. I spend a lot of time creaking across the landing from one bedroom to the other, hurrying to stifle the cries. And then sitting in the baby's room, feeding her, imagining we are the only people in the world who are awake. There is that particular silence in the small hours that seems unbreakable.'

'I remember.'

'But Gordon is being very good. Better by far than he was with the other two.'

Marcelle could well imagine that Gordon would come home and guiltily try to compensate for what he did elsewhere. She felt hot shivers of indignation directed at him, and at Nina.

'That's nice,' she said pointlessly, seeing the red car again and the two bewitched profiles sliding apart from each other.

Later the same evening Vicky was watching television. She was sitting in her usual chair with her feet curled up beneath her and her hands wrapped around a mug of hot milk. It was only the reminder that the milk must not be spilt that kept her from dozing off. She was tired, but there was no point in going to bed to sleep before Helen had woken for her last feed. The baby lay in her basket on the sofa. Vicky drank some of her milk, and the skin that had formed on the surface of it caught on her top lip. The act of rubbing it away reminded her strongly of being a little girl, sitting in her dressing gown ready for bed while her mother listened to *The Archers*. The comforting childhood feeling of being secure and in the right place pervaded the present, too, falling around her and enclosing the children and Gordon in its warmth.

In the kitchen Gordon tidied up after their dinner, a Marks & Spencer curried chicken dish that he was not particularly fond of. There was a milk-rimed saucepan filled with tepid water on the draining board, and Vicky had stood a bunch of dirty cutlery in it to soak. Yellow-crusted eggshells and toast fragments left from the children's tea had fallen out of a bent tinfoil dish on the worktop, and there was a high water mark of tea leaves and whitish scum clinging to the sides of the sink. Next to the tinfoil dish was the clear polycarbonate sterilizing drum for Helen's feeding equipment. The bottles and teats floated murkily inside it.

Gordon set about tidying up. Vicky was not a fastidious housekeeper, and he preferred domestic order and cleanliness. For a long time, they had tried not to let this difference be a source of irritation between them.

As he worked, Gordon thought deliberately about Nina. He set himself the test of recalling the shape of her hands and fingernails, the way her hair grew back from her forehead, the exact timbre of her voice. The details came to him without effort, but invested with clear importance that was separate from the jumble of everything else that made up his life. He knew that he was in love with her.

When he was satisfied with the order of the kitchen he went through to the living room to find Vicky. When she saw him she pushed out her jaw in a yawn that turned into a lazy smile, and stretched her arms with the fingers bent inwards at the knuckles in a way that made him think of a cat.

'Vicky?'

He was exhausted with the weight of having to keep the truth from her, and by the opposing need to tell her, to blurt out what was happening and share the bewilderment of it with her.

'Mmm?'

I've fallen in love with Nina. I want to live with her. I don't know how not to be with her all the time. How can I explain that to you?

'Did you see Marcelle today?'

She saw us at the level crossing. I know what she saw, and therefore what she knows.

'Yes. She came to pick the kids up from Janice's while I was over there this afternoon. Why?'

Marcelle had said nothing, then. Not yet.

'No reason, really. It seems a while since we saw the Wickhams. I passed her in the car this morning, which made me think of it.'

The room seemed to shiver around him, with all its accumulated weight of familiarity, curtains and covers chosen, books collected, photographs and mementoes and worn patches accumulated over the years lived through together. It shivered with the precarious balance of the necessary truth against his merciful deception.

Vicky sighed. 'We should have an evening, I know. But, to be honest, I don't think I've got the energy to do it. Perhaps we could have some people in over Christmas?'

He put his hand on her shoulder. There was a pad of flesh there, and he felt the dent where the broad strap of her nursing bra bit into it. He knew her so well; he saw her set in her separate place like a fly in amber, or a fish held fast in the winter ice, and himself beside her, a way apart. The two of them no longer flowed together, they didn't blur and coalesce and give off energy by their combination as they once had done.

'You don't have to bother about anything like that. We'll only do it if you want to.'

Vicky stretched herself again, luxuriating in his concern for her.

'All right. Only if we both feel like it. Is that Helen waking up? Have a look for me.'

He leaned over the basket. The baby's eyes were open. They were very deep and dark in her tiny red face, and they stared straight up into his.

'Yes, she is awake. Do you want her?'

Vicky undid her front buttons in answer to him. He saw the armoury of her underclothes, and then the veined blue-whiteness of the overfull breast when she released it. The loose flesh of her belly swelled up in another curve below it. There was a tissue pad in her bra cup that gave off a stale-milk smell. He thought of Nina's spare, freckled body and its touching knobs of bone.

Gordon lifted the baby carefully out of the basket. Her heavy head wobbled against him and he cupped it in his hand, noticing how the silky skin wrinkled over the hard, fragile skull. As he held her with her tiny face against his cheek he felt a rising up of pain inside him that made him want to cry out. He breathed in the scent from the downy head and the pain grew so acute that he did not know how he could contain it.

Then Vicky held her empty arms out for the baby, and he handed his daughter over to her.

The evening before the dress rehearsal for the nativity play Marcelle and Nina met at the Wickhams' house. The two women had not seen each other since the morning of the level crossing. Nina brought with her the animal masks that she had made in her studio over the last few days. She had taken a lot of trouble with them, as if doing so would somehow atone for everything else.

In Marcelle's dining room Nina took the masks one by one out of their wrappings and laid them out for her approval. They were very light and simple, stylized suggestions of animal faces rather than attempts at realism, but Marcelle could see at once how effective they would be.

'They are good,' she said, picking up one of the lambs to examine it more closely. She held it to her face, and regarded Nina through the oval, slanting eye holes. Then she lowered the mask again and the two women looked straight at each other.

'Are you sure they are what you wanted?' Nina asked.

'Yes. Really, they're perfect. I could never have made anything half so good.'

Marcelle wrapped them carefully and put them aside. There were play costumes all round the room, arranged on hangers hooked to the picture rail, everything labelled and pressed ready for the dress rehearsal.

There was a moment's silence.

Marcelle wondered what she should say, whether there was some word of caution or advice or admonition for Vicky's sake that she might offer. Nothing came into her head, and she saw Nina twisting her wedding ring round and round her finger. The ring appeared too loose for her. She felt sad, and sorry for Nina as well as Vicky.

Nina also waited. She didn't know Marcelle well enough, but she wished she could confide in her. Could she plead with her now, *Don't judge us too harshly. Don't assume it is only what you think, a bald and commonplace act of adultery.*

But then, how else could she explain what it was to Vicky's friend? By emphasizing her own need, or Gordon's, or the happiness that they generated for each other when they were together?

There was nothing, she realized, that she could say to excuse herself or Gordon. The weight of dislike and mistrust coming from Marcelle was no more than she should expect.

Neither of them spoke, and the silence lengthened into awkwardness. It was Marcelle who broke it, at last.

'Thank you for helping me out. It must have taken hours of your time.'

Now they could not mention what they both knew because the moment for it had slipped past. Marcelle was angry with herself, and at the two of them for placing her in this dilemma.

'It didn't take that long,' Nina lied. 'I'm glad there was something useful I could do.'

Marcelle would not tell anyone, Nina was finally sure of that. We must be careful from now on, she thought, experiencing a surprising surge of relief and gratitude that made her almost lightheaded.

Michael Wickham looked in to the dining room. It was after eight, but he was formally dressed as if he had only just come in from the hospital. Nina had the impression that he was irritated by the sight of them hovering with their masks and by the clutter of costumes, but he made the offer of a drink politely enough.

'Yes, do stay and have a drink,' Marcelle echoed. 'A drink, at least. I feel that I ought to be offering you dinner, after all you have done.'

'Is there any dinner?' Michael dryly interrupted.

'Yes. In half an hour.'

Gordon had promised Nina that he would telephone this evening. Vicky would be out of the house for two hours, after the children were asleep. She said quickly, 'I can't stay even for a drink, but thank you anyway. If there's anything else last-minute I can do . . .'

142

Marcelle did not suggest anything. Nina said good night to the Wickhams and drove back to Dean's Row.

'Did Marcelle say anything?' Gordon asked. He was sitting on the edge of the double bed, looking out beyond the undrawn bedroom curtains to the grape-black sky. There were toys and baby clothes on the floor by his feet.

'No.'

It was one of their flat, melancholy telephone conversations. Sometimes they could forget the distance and talk as if they were touching each other, but tonight everything they said seemed to convey less than they meant. They both wondered what they were doing, begging questions, making these banal offerings of words into thin, humming space.

'When can I see you again?' Nina asked. She twisted the spiral cord of the telephone around her little finger.

'I don't know. I'm not sure, it's not a good week. And Andrew made some crack this evening about my disappearing acts.'

Nina wondered why he should have to account for himself to Andrew, but she only said, 'Does that make it difficult? I'm sorry.'

'There's no reason for you to be sorry.' With an effort, wanting to change the direction, he said, 'I love you.'

'I know,' Nina answered soberly.

It was plain that the mood would not change, and neither could offer the other any comfort. Gordon tried to imagine how it would be if he left the house and the children and drove straight to her.

'I'll call you soon,' he promised.

'Yes. Please call.'

She hung up, wanting to sever the connection for herself.

The night of the nativity play came.

Nina had imagined that she would not go, but when it was time she found herself drawn across the cathedral green to join the people who gathered together in convivial groups at the west door. After all, she told herself, she could not hide in her house for ever.

The chapter house was packed. Nina slipped quietly around the octagonal margin, looking for an empty place on one of the benches. She nodded to the handful of familiar faces in the crowd as she passed by. At length she found a single seat, removed from anyone she knew, and sat down with her hands folded in her lap.

Marcelle and Michael sat near the front, with Jonathan fidgeting in between them. Marcelle felt a flutter of nerves for Daisy's sake. Stella Rose sat on the other side of Marcelle. Her face was calm as she gazed intently upwards at the geometrical tracery of the windows. Jimmy Rose was a Catholic. He very rarely chose to accompany his wife to the great barn, as he called the cathedral.

The Frosts and Toby, nagged into a dark blazer for the occasion, sat two rows behind them. By tradition, they would join the Wickhams later for a drink. Andrew always jovially referred to this occasion as the Christmas kick-off. Janice knew and greeted almost everybody in the Grafton audience.

Nina saw the Cleggs come in. Hannah was wearing ankle-length dark mink, her blonde hair in striking contrast to the smooth fur. Hannah held Laura's hand and Darcy guided Freddie. The two small children were dressed in double-breasted dark blue coats with velvet collars. Behind their father came Cathy and Lucy, attracting their due of covertly or openly admiring glances. Following the twins was a big, blond young man Nina had never seen before. When he turned sideways to ease between the benches she saw his profile, and recognized the family resemblance.

She had been looking at the Clegg boy, and then her glance travelled away, drawn along a valley between the row of heads. With the shock that was now becoming familiar, she saw Gordon. His two little girls sat between him and Vicky. Vicky was on the end of a row, with a white bundle in her arms. Her hair had been cut into a neat, shiny bob. All four of them were staring straight ahead, a model family, quietly waiting for the play to begin.

There was a movement to Nina's right, at the great double doors of the chapter house. Then there was an organ chord and the cathedral choristers came slowly forward, two by two, in their cassocks and snow-white surplices.

They were singing, and the chapter house fell silent.

Once in Royal David's city, the choir sang.

William Frost sang a solo verse. His voice was perfect, rounded and strong and pure, and it rose as effortlessly as a hawk riding an air thermal. Under the square-cut fringe of fair hair the boy's mouth made an innocent secondary oval within the choirboy oval of his face.

Through the doors of the chapter house came two children dressed as Joseph and Mary. There was the Mary-blue robe that Nina had last seen hanging from the picture rail in Marcelle's dining room. Mary, awed and solemn-faced, was leaning on a third child who paced between them. This boy was wearing a plain grey leotard with a dark cross etched on the back from shoulder to hip, and his face was covered by Nina's donkey mask.

Nina and Star Rose and the Grafton couples and their children sat with the other people under the great fan vaults of the chapter house roof and watched the unfolding of the nativity play.

The shepherds in their rough coats and the kings in their magnificent robes came to offer their gifts to the Christ child, the lessons from the Gospels were read and the carefully memorized lines were clearly spoken. The Holy Family and the white-robed angels and the animals in their masks gathered around the crib. Daisy Wickham and the schools choir and William and the other choristers sang their carols, and the children's solemn faces reflected the renewed wonder of the Christmas message.

The play was both simple and grand.

Nina was moved, and she felt the collective emotion of the people around her, the rows of heads with their hidden thoughts made momentarily clear. She felt that she was gathered in with

145

the rest, and made safe, as she had not done in the cathedral since she was a young girl.

Almost at the end, Helen began to cry. Vicky tried to quiet her, and through the valley of seats Nina saw Gordon's face as he inclined his head towards his wife. He looked different, like someone else, like any one of these other husbands and fathers, not like a man who was her lover.

Vicky slipped out with Helen in her arms. She drew a soft wake of smiles after her as the double doors opened to let her out. Her cheeks were pink, and she held her head up.

For the last carol the audience stood up to sing with the choirs. The familiar words and music drew Nina backwards into herself as a child, standing between her parents in the same place to sing the same carol. And as if she was contemplating it with the imperfect, simplified judgement of a child it seemed sad that there was no continuity beyond her, that she had no child of her own to bring in her turn.

When the play was over Nina sat amongst the flurry of leavings until almost everyone else had filed away. Gordon went by without seeing her, with Andrew and Janice. The Cleggs waved as they passed, and the tall boy who must be Darcy's son nodded as if he believed he should know her. When she was sure that everyone must have gone far enough ahead she followed them through the double doors and down the steps into the nave. She gazed upwards, to the compound shafts of the pillars and the Gothic arches that sprang from them. It was here that Gordon's tour of the restoration work had begun for her benefit.

She did not want to leave by the west door, because she was sure that the Grafton couples would be gathering on the green beside the Christmas tree, ready to begin their season's celebrations. If anyone looked for her, they would assume that she had slipped out by the north side.

Nina sat down in the shadows of the nave. The organist was playing a Handel voluntary. She could see the shaft of light behind the curtain up in the loft.

She wondered if she should pray, but she could not think how she might expiate herself.

At last, after a long time, one of the vergers came to stand beside her. He was a very tall young man in a black cassock that was too short for him.

'I'm afraid the Cathedral is closing now.'

There was no one left in the aisles or in the rows of wooden seats.

Nina smiled. 'I'm going home,' she told him.

Eight

On Christmas Eve Wilton Manor was lit up like a cruise ship at anchor in a sea of parked cars.

Michael and Marcelle Wickham walked the short distance to the house in silence, but as soon as the door opened to them they found their smiles and went into the party together.

Marcelle glimpsed Jimmy's crest of sandy hair, and the Clegg twins, one in ankle-length and the other in thigh-high black Lycra, and Gordon Ransome's narrow, handsome head politely inclined as he listened to something Hannah was whispering to him. Hannah was wearing a tight sheath of gold that seemed barely to contain her.

Marcelle took a glass of champagne from the tray someone held out and drank half of it. Now that she had escaped her own house she was eager for company and conversation and the comfort of a drink. As if the pressure in her ears was suddenly equalized the hubbub of the party broke in on her. She heard music, and raised voices, and the chorus of greetings. Her spirits lifted in response.

'Marcelle, Michael, at last!'

Darcy's cowboy-fringed arm descended around her shoulders.

'Merry Christmas, Darcy.'

'Have you got a drink? Hey, that's only half a drink. Let me fill it up for you.'

More champagne foamed into her glass. She was aware that Michael had moved away from her side. She could see Janice, and the Kellys, and a dozen other familiar faces in the hallway under the Christmas tree and amongst the crowd of people in the drawing room. She let herself be carried forward to meet them, to the kisses and the greetings and the gossip, her fingers curled firmly around the glass in her hand.

Gordon watched her go. Then, involuntarily, he searched out Nina. She looked pale, thinner than usual, in a simple black dress that revealed the bony wings beneath her throat. Their eyes met, and then jerked away again.

The manor house was polished and scented, elaborately decorated with great silvered garlands of pine and holly, and warmed with log fires in all the wide grates. Hannah and her stepchildren had overseen the preparations, because Darcy was unusually preoccupied with his work. The little Clegg children had stayed up to greet the first guests and were now asleep upstairs, with their name-appliqued stockings hung over the ends of their beds, but Darcy's three grown-up children were a noticeable presence at this year's party.

Lucy, Cathy and Barney had invited a contingent of their own friends, and these younger people with their different haircuts and impromptu clothes wove a contrasting thread through the fabric of the party. They asked the disc jockey behind his turntables in the conservatory to play unfamiliar music in place of the sixties and seventies hits, and they danced differently, waving their arms in loose groups instead of two by two.

The Grafton parents, whose own visiting mothers and fathers were mostly at home watching over their grandchildren, were made suddenly aware that there was another generation crowding up behind them.

Michael and Darcy stood shoulder to shoulder in their dinner jackets, watching the young. Michael had refused champagne and was drinking whisky from a tumbler.

He said to Darcy, over the rim of the glass, 'Did you ever believe you would grow old? We children of the sixties always knew we had it, whatever it was, the big secret, the elixir of life. We always thought we'd hold on to it, too. It makes it doubly hard to accept that it's already gone, spent, inherited by this lot.'

He tilted his glass towards them, not quite sober by this time, and the whisky slopped.

Darcy shrugged. 'Did even doctors buy that hippie rubbish? I was a son of the fifties, and I wanted everything my old man never had. I couldn't grow up quick enough.'

Darcy was preoccupied. He was only giving Michael Wickham's rambling talk a fraction of his attention. All evening he had only been able to forget his anxiety for a moment, as the party commanded his concentration, and then it would come skittering back to him like a black spider emerging from a web.

Michael glanced at him, noticing for the first time that Darcy was not as eager as usual to play the role of expansive host. He seemed tired, and his tanned face had a greyish tinge. He wondered if he might be ill.

'No, Darcy, you are an example to us all. Nobody could ever accuse you of left-over hippie idealism. And look what you have to show for growing up so eagerly – Wilton Manor, several cars, wives and children. A place at the very epicentre of Grafton society.'

Darcy would not rise to the bait. He turned away from the dancers. 'Let's get another drink. You've spilled most of that one.'

Jimmy Rose was less affected by the spectre of his middle age. He had no children to catch him up, and his wife knew better than to follow him around at parties. He felt entirely free to admire Lucy Clegg's exposed thighs and the twists of coloured cloth she had wound in her hair, and to melt into the noise in the conservatory in pursuit of her.

The Clegg twins drew him into the dance, one on either side of him. They smiled and waved their fingers and undulated their slim hips in time to the music. None of the hulking boys in the vicinity seemed inclined to lay a claim on either of them. Jimmy slid his arm around Lucy's waist, and danced for a moment with his cheek pressed against hers. She smelled very young and fresh, like a bluebell stalk.

When she wriggled out of his grasp he grinned at her in rueful acknowledgement, and lifted a full glass of champagne from a passing tray as a consolation. Jimmy had been drinking steadily, but the only effect that alcohol ever had on him was to increase his capacity for mischief.

A little later he looked across the dance floor and saw Marcelle. She was standing on her own, her head and arms seeming to hang awkwardly. He left the twins and their friends and skirted around the edge of the floor until he reached her.

'Dance with me?' he asked.

'Yes. I will.' She held out her hands, rather stiffly, and he guided her. He knew that they made an odd contrast, a pair of waltzers with the loose-limbed young around them. He drew her closer to him. She was wearing a full-skirted dress made of blue-green taffeta that rustled around his legs. Her head drooped, and then rested on his shoulder. Her perfume was heavy and musky, quite unlike Lucy's, and intensified to the point of sickliness by the dry heat of her skin.

'You don't want to dance.'

'Not really,' she admitted.

'Let's sit out, then.'

He took her hand and drew her behind him. Marcelle focused on his shoulders, and on the reddish prickle of hair at the back of his neck that reminded her of an animal's scruff.

Jimmy knew Darcy's house as well as he knew his own. He opened the door to a small room under the angle of the stairway. It was half cloakroom, half gunroom, furnished with hung-up coats and mackintoshes, dismantled fishing rods in green canvas cases, creaking wicker chairs and too-pristine sporting prints introduced by Hannah. It was empty, as Jimmy had known it would be.

Marcelle sank down into one of the chairs, letting her head fall back with a long sigh.

'Too much champagne,' she said, swallowing a laugh and a hiccup together.

Jimmy sat beside her. He turned her wrist in his fingers to expose her underarm, where the skin puckered in tiny folds towards her armpit. He put his mouth to the blue vein in the crook of her elbow. Marcelle looked down from what seemed like a great distance on to his bent head.

'Tell me all,' he commanded, rubbing his mouth in the hollow.

'Nothing to tell.'

He lifted his head and circled her with his arm. 'Yes, there is, I can see there is.'

Now he bent forward so that his mouth reached the top of her breast left exposed by the taffeta bodice.

Marcelle knew that there were minute crepey folds between her breasts, too. They reminded her of the vertical seams in a dowager's top lip. She was afraid that the dusting of powder she had applied there might have turned into grey wormy threads in the heat. She felt suddenly shy, inexperienced and full of anxiety about her body's imperfections, like an awkward adolescent. Michael had not found the time to tell her that she was looking pretty when she had hustled him out of the house earlier on.

'Jimmy, don't.'

'Ah, why ever not? Isn't it nice?'

It felt good to him. At this minute Jimmy loved Marcelle, and he loved Hannah and Janice as well. All the women with their different shapes and textures and scents appealed to him, like so many dishes on an endless table, and the fact that he couldn't consume all of them did nothing to diminish his appetite.

'Yes,' Marcelle said sadly. 'It is nice. Only not now.'

Jimmy grinned at her. 'When? When Mike's at the hospital?'

'You know I didn't mean that.'

This was how Jimmy was, each of the wives knew it. Marcelle always parried his advances, very gently and with a touch of regret. She didn't know what the others did, not exactly, not even Janice, although they joked together out of Star's earshot about there always being Jimmy to fall back on.

'What a shame. Well then, talk to me instead. Tell Jimmy your troubles.'

The combined effect of his attention and sympathy following

on from the champagne made Marcelle's eyes fill with unwelcome tears.

'Oh, it's nothing. Just domestic bickering.'

'Only that?'

He stroked her wrist with the tip of his finger, little soothing strokes. She watched the movement, hypnotized by it, wishing that she had not drunk so much. Drink always loosened her tongue. She hesitated, trying to think of something light to say, then she opened her mouth and the words came spilling out anyhow, although she wanted to keep them in, to preserve the marriage myth.

'No, not only that. It's much more. And less, in a way. Michael seems to have . . . gone away somewhere. I don't mean actually away, although God knows he's in the house with us less and less of the time, the hospital and patients and committees seem to consume him. It's as if he's retreated into himself, closed a door on me, and I find myself . . . at one minute angry with him for rejecting me, and bitter and resentful, and at the next what must seem, I don't know, cloyingly *there*, with my claims and expectations, wifely, needing to be loved. Like an obligation.'

Marcelle took a breath.

'I don't know when we stopped being partners, and became antagonists. The two of us, drawn up on either side of some battle line. Looking back, I don't know when it happened, only that it *has* happened. We quarrel and the arguments are never resolved, and then there are silences, and times when we preserve this terrible politeness, and then there are arguments all over again.'

She was crying properly. Tears spouted out of her eyes and she felt them making hot runnels down her face. There would be tracks in the foundation she had applied to give herself some colour.

Jimmy murmured, 'Poor thing, poor old Mar. Here you are.'

He produced a big, clean white handkerchief, right on cue. Marcelle sniffed into it and bit her lips to stop herself crying any more.

'This evening, for instance. We were late, it made me anxious, and then my anxiety made us both irritable so we quarrelled.'

'You hate being late, you hate apparent failures. Nobody notices them except you, but then you are a perfectionist.'

'Am I? I don't believe I am. Do you and Star make each other happy?'

As she looked at him then, through the sodden blur of tears and champagne, Marcelle thought she saw an evasive mask slip over Jimmy's cunning-fox features.

'Oh, Star and I have evolved our own systems. After so many years long-married couples do, don't they?'

Marcelle thought of Star's aloof dignity at the parties where Jimmy flirted and murmured and kissed. She had seen her tonight, with a diamante star clip holding her hair back behind one ear, dancing with Andrew Frost while Jimmy skimmed between the Clegg twins. The Roses would have to have a system.

'Michael and I loved each other, I thought that was our arrangement, but it seems not to be. I don't believe he loves me any longer.'

Jimmy was still stroking. 'I'm sure it's not as bad as that. Do you think he's got someone else?'

Marcelle shook her head. 'No. He seems too cold for that, too frosted up inside himself.'

'Have *you* got someone else?'

'Of course not.'

They were quiet for a minute. The music from the conservatory filtered through to them, a thumping bass beat. The party was reaching full momentum. Gathering her wits, Marcelle wished she had not cried, had not been seen to give way, even here, even only by Jimmy. She cast around for some way of diminishing in his eyes what had seemed only a moment ago to be such an important confession.

'It's probably our age, just restless *ennui* before we settle down to a comfortable twilight together.'

'Perhaps,' Jimmy said. He shrugged, a little comic contrivance

154

of bafflement. Then he rolled her hand into a fist for her, placing it back in her lap, ready to fight.

Partly to reinforce her claim, partly to shift the focus from herself, and a little because she wanted to reward him for this moment of intimacy that she knew was ending, Marcelle smiled faintly and said, 'It isn't just Michael and me who are having our problems.'

'Hmm?'

Jimmy's face sharpened, but his eyes held hers.

'Perhaps we are all going through it, in our different ways.' It was a comfort to identify herself with the group. She wanted to share what she knew. 'I saw Gordon, the other day, with Nina. They were in Nina's car together.'

As soon as it was out she regretted it, but it was said and she smiled at him again, a smile of complicity now.

'Together?'

'Oh, yes. I don't know exactly how I knew, but I did as soon as I saw them. It was unmistakable. I felt it, here.' Her fist, still clenched, gestured at the pit of her stomach. 'They were horrified to see me.'

Jimmy grinned. 'I imagine they would have been.'

He looked pleased, smiling his narrow-eyed smile, and intent, as if he was so busy digesting this new piece of information that he had forgotten her. The tip of his tongue appeared at the corner of his mouth. The look of him made Marcelle feel slightly disgusted, and this distaste surprised her.

'How interesting,' he mused, more to himself than her. 'How interesting it all is. Don't you think so?'

'I don't know. I suppose so, if you can detach yourself sufficiently not to feel concern.' It was as if Nina and Gordon and Vicky had dwindled away to tiny organisms that divided and recombined in some Petri dish under Jimmy Rose's observation. 'You won't say anything, Jimmy, will you?' she asked.

He touched her hand once again. 'You know me,' he assured her.

Marcelle reluctantly nodded. 'I suppose we should go back and join in, shouldn't we?'

He leaned forward and kissed her on the mouth, but only very lightly, dismissively.

'I think we must, but you should go and fix your face up first.'

Outside the gunroom they went their separate ways.

Jimmy strolled into the noisy thick of the party, his hands in his pockets, smiling and joking his way through the various groups. At the buffet in the dining room he helped himself to a plateful of the excellent food that Hannah's caterers had prepared. He made himself comfortable in the niche of a padded window seat half-hidden by a curtain, and watched the procession in front of him as he ate.

He saw Nina in her black dress, and noted the way her face fell into sad lines when she thought nobody was looking at her. He watched Gordon solicitously steering Vicky to a comfortable chair, and bringing her a plate of food and cutlery and a napkin, and then looking up over his wife's bent head towards Nina, standing with her back turned to him. Jimmy fluently read the brief contraction of his dark features as an expression of powerful longing.

Jimmy took a long, meditative swallow of his wine. It was very palatable, of course. Darcy never served plonk at his parties. Jimmy spent an enjoyable minute calculating how much this year's party must be costing the Cleggs.

From his vantage point he also saw Andrew, flushed with champagne, and Janice following him with Marcelle, her face now freshly powdered. Hannah was commanding them to come and eat, laughing a great deal and wobbling slightly on her pin-thin heels. Behind them came his own wife with her arm in Michael Wickham's. They were the same height. Jimmy tried to imagine what he would want if he were seeing Star for the first time. He thought her androgynous, mysterious air would still interest him.

There was no sign of Darcy, the person he really wanted to

see. Jimmy left his dirty plate on the window seat cushions and slipped away in search of him.

He found him in the drawing room, leaning with his arms outstretched on the mantelpiece, smoking and observing his guests.

'Howdy, pardner,' Jimmy drawled, flicking at the fringes on Darcy's Gaultier jacket.

Darcy said nothing. It was silently recognized between them that they needed one another as a focus for aggression, but tonight he could not summon up the energy to spar with Jimmy, who ranged himself beside him gazing outwards into the room. Darcy felt, as he sometimes did, that the disparity in their sizes made them both appear a little absurd.

'There are demons abroad tonight,' Jimmy announced.

'That was Hallowe'en, surely. The last time we all gathered together.'

'Ah yes, it was indeed. The first time we saw your Belle Veuve. And now you've lost her.'

Darcy turned his head. 'Lost her to whom?' His voice was soft.

The currents between them shifted like dry sand.

'To Gordon Ransome, I believe.'

The *tick-tick* of mutual reckoning was almost audible. At first Jimmy was pleased with the effect of his news; he liked to overturn Darcy's easy assumption of sexual pre-eminence.

'How do you know?'

Jimmy shrugged. He hazarded, 'Ask any of the women. The women always know these things.'

To Jimmy's surprise Darcy began to laugh. It was a big, genuine laugh that welled up out of his chest, betraying none of the disappointment or pique that he had expected.

'Gordon Ransome? Is that so? Good for Gordon, then. It was bound to be somebody, I suppose.'

'Not you?'

Darcy was still laughing. 'I'm not going to live out your fantasies for you, James, you should know that by now. Has Vicky heard about it, according to your information?'

'I wouldn't have thought so. Not yet. No doubt she will.'

Jimmy was irritated. It seemed that he had traded his information for no return.

Darcy patted him on the shoulder. 'Happy Christmas,' he said triumphantly.

Jimmy couldn't gauge quite why Darcy was so pleased with himself. He looked at his watch, trying to conceal his annoyance. 'Thanks. The same to you. And thanks for the party. I have to go.'

'So early?'

'I'm going to midnight mass.'

'Forgive me, I'd forgotten that. Pray for us sinners, Jim, won't you?'

Jimmy left him. He went out into the cold, clear night and found his small car in the lines of bigger, glossier models. Star would get a lift home with the Frosts.

Vicky sat feeding Helen in the armchair in the corner of the Cleggs' big bedroom. Mandy, Hannah's Australian au pair girl, had searched her out to tell her that the baby was crying in her basket upstairs. It gave her an unreal, dislocated but none the less pleasant feeling to be suddenly translated from the brightness of the party to the silence upstairs, and to the familiar small intimacies of ministering to Helen.

She had laid a towel on Hannah's quilted bedcover and changed the baby's nappy, gently swabbing the inward-turning folds of skin with her concentration pleasingly blurred by champagne. Then she undid her dress and sat down in the armchair. After a minute's hungry attack Helen's sucking gradually moderated into a sleepy rhythm. Vicky began to hum to her, long, low notes that did not connect into any recognizable tune, but were soothing to both of them.

Darcy found her sitting there. 'Do you mind if I come in?' he asked.

Vicky smiled, caught out in her humming, 'Of course not. It's your bedroom.'

158

Instead of edging around the room, as she would have expected, in search of a fresh shirt or a stud or a handkerchief, he came directly to her and stooped down, turning back the corner of Helen's white cellular blanket with one finger so he could see the baby's face.

'She is beautiful,' he said.

The floor of the bedroom vibrated under their feet with the bass notes of the music pounding below. There was the distant sound of shouting, and then the crack of breaking glass.

'Is that your conservatory?' Vicky whispered.

'I don't care about the conservatory.'

Darcy knelt down. He put out one hand to cup the baby's head and felt hard bone under silky skin. The currents of air in the room slowed and became still, and the noise from the party grew irrelevant and then inaudible.

As he stroked the small head Darcy felt a sudden calm. The shocks of anxious energy and fear that made his muscles jerk entirely subsided. He forgot about the party and Hannah and Jimmy, and about the business and all the coloured balls of his concerns that were about to fall out of their juggled sequence.

In their place there was an intense and luminous fascination with the small distance that separated him from Vicky and her baby. It was as if he could see the components of the air, the Brownian movements of the atoms, minuscule and at the same time vast in their significance and simplicity.

He found that he hardly dared to breathe in case he upset the physical balance of light and air and warmth that held the three of them suspended here. Very gently, flexing his heavy fingers, he stroked again, once and then twice. He heard the contented sound that the baby made, a soft half sigh as her jaws slackened and released her mother's nipple. Darcy withdrew his hand and Vicky laid her in the hollow of her lap.

'Half time,' Vicky explained. Her lightness, her matter-of-fact acceptance of his observation, filled him with amazement and pleasure.

While Darcy watched, mesmerized, Vicky drew the white

elasticated cup of her bra over the breast and clipped the silvery hooks into the corresponding eyelets. Then, with the deft opposite movement, she released the other side.

He saw the rounded, down-drawn heavy weight, and the net of blue distended veins around the nipple, and the brown shiny nipple itself. It seemed to Darcy, in his trance state, that she was offering it directly to him.

Darcy leaned forward over the bundle of the baby in her lap and put his lips over the nipple.

He heard Vicky gasp, the tiny but sharp indrawing of breath making the exact opposite of the baby's satisfied exhalation. At once his mouth filled with the thick, sweet, secret taste of milk.

The effect of it was extraordinary.

It took him back to the jealous possessiveness he had felt when he watched his mother feeding his next youngest brother, and way beyond that, back past the boundaries of memory, to his own connection to his mother and his infantile need for her. Even as with one part of his adult, analytical mind Darcy recognized this, the rest of him was overwhelmed by the physical shock of his longing for Vicky Ransome once his mouth had connected with her breast.

He became aware that her hand had come to rest at the back of his head, neither drawing him closer nor pushing him away, but simply holding him, as he had cupped the baby's head a moment before.

If it had not been for the baby between them he could not have done anything but push her backwards, covering her, pinning her underneath him on the wide space of the bed.

As it was he painfully withdrew his head and saw a whitish dribble of milk trickle down the lower curve of the exposed breast and threaten to drip on to her unfastened evening dress. He put out one finger to stop it, and then licked the fingertip. The taste in his mouth was an echo of his longing. He wanted to submerge himself in Vicky, to submerge himself and simultaneously to obliterate everything else as he had never wanted anything else before.

'Darcy? *Darcy?*'

He made himself look up into her face. There was no hostility in it, only the aftermath of surprise and – was this possible? – the faintest kindling of a response to him.

They held still for a moment, staring at each other.

Darcy had come straight from Jimmy Rose to look for Vicky. He had come in concern and sympathy, which was commendable enough, but he knew that there had also been a baser intention to measure and then, perhaps, to make use of her vulnerability. He had always found Vicky attractive, and in the last months of her pregnancy and since the birth he had found her even more interesting. The peaks of his interest in his two wives had also coincided with the production of his own children. There was a secretive, intent side to a woman absorbed in a baby that was intensely arousing.

Yet now, as Vicky lifted Helen once again and pinched the nipple – *his* nipple – expertly between fingers and thumb for the baby to latch on, Darcy recognized a counterpoint to his expendable desire.

Vicky was watching him, not her baby. She had round brown eyes, he saw, with bronze flecks at the outer rim of the iris. It came to him that he loved her as well as wanting to smother himself inside her.

'My God,' Darcy said aloud.

He would not let anything harm her. He would not let her gauche husband and his skinny widow breathe any hurt on her, nor anyone else in Grafton either. He would protect her and defend her.

Vicky put her fingers over his mouth.

'Shh.'

It was to make him contain his promises, even before any of them could be formulated.

He was still kneeling in front of her, between the end of the quilted bed and the padded and filled armchair Hannah liked to curl up in with her copies of *The World of Interiors*. The noise from downstairs swelled up to them again. Darcy had forgotten that there were more than a hundred people drinking and dancing in his house.

'Darcy?'

It was Hannah who called his name, not Vicky. Hannah had come in behind them.

Darcy turned around to look at her. She was flushed, a breadth of crimson skin showing above her gold dress and two red patches burning through the creamy makeup on her cheeks. Hannah walked forward into the room. Her hips swung in the tight swathe of satin.

'I've been looking everywhere for you. One of Barney's friends was fooling round with a chair, pretending to dance with it or something stupid, and managed to fall through the French windows and cut his hand open. Didn't you hear the noise?'

'Yes, I did. Is he hurt? Is Mike Wickham still here? Or David Poynter? How many other medics have we got on the bloody premises?'

'Bloody's about right. Mike's seeing to him. You'd better come down. What's the *matter* with everyone this evening?'

Hannah faced them, the red spots burning in her face. Darcy stood up, stiff from kneeling and suddenly conscious of his age in front of the younger women.

He remembered Jimmy's words. 'Demons are abroad,' he murmured.

'*What?*'

Hannah was angry. Her face reminded him of Laura's in the midst of one of her fits of temper. Darcy glanced down, and saw there was a white stain of milk on the satin lapel of his coat.

'Don't worry, I'll sort everything out downstairs,' he said, and left them.

Hannah looked coldly at Vicky. 'Have you got everything you need?'

Vicky blushed. She felt caught, by Darcy and by her own surprised and guilty pleasure in what had happened. She was further trapped by her semi-nakedness, by the weight of the baby, by the splendour of Hannah's bedroom.

'Yes, thanks. I'll finish her feed, and then I must take Gordon home.' And then she offered, because she felt that she must say something even if it was not the truth, 'Darcy was only keeping me company while I did this.'

Hannah shrugged. 'It's quite all right. I know what Darcy likes. He is my husband, after all.'

Nina had been dancing with Andrew when a boy with one of Hannah's curlicued-metal garden chairs in his arms had tripped and crashed forward through the glass doors. For a long moment he had lain quite still with the chair on top of him, under a ragged blanket of glass, while the music thumped on over his head.

Nina was the first to reach him. The glass crunched under her thin shoes as she lifted the chair away.

'Christ,' the boy said, blinking.

More people pushed beside Nina. There was a confused babble of orders and instructions. The boy raised his arm to look at it and a broad, bright fountain of blood sprayed from his wrist.

'*Christ*,' he repeated.

Nina knelt over him. She put her hand down to balance herself and felt a sharp stab.

'Keep still,' she said. 'Keep your arm up like that.'

Andrew fumbled beside her with a big white handkerchief in his hands. Nina snatched it and tied it around the boy's arm, knotting it over the shirtsleeve that was already soaked in blood. *Tight*, she told herself. *Is that an artery?* The boy's face had turned paper white. *How long before I must loosen the tourniquet?*

'Where's Michael?' Andrew was shouting. 'Get Mike, will you?'

Nina heard herself saying to the boy, 'It's all right, you're all right.'

There was more shoving in the crowd of people surrounding them and then Michael Wickham emerged. He had stripped off his jacket and rolled up the sleeves of his shirt. Hannah hovered in a nimbus of gold behind him.

'Let's see.'

Michael pressed his thumb over the cut and undid the hand-kerchief. Nina saw the blood ooze and felt her head swim. Michael glanced briefly at her.

'It's all right,' he echoed her own words. 'He'll live.'

Someone helped Nina to her feet.

'Well done. Give them some room. Oh, God, you're covered in blood too. Look at your dress.'

Nina recognized Darcy's big, blond son. Janice Frost had pointed him out to her earlier.

'It doesn't matter.' But she spread her hands out in front of her in helpless disgust. They were smeared scarlet like a murderer's.

The large young man took hold of one of them regardless. 'Come on. Let me take care of you. Tom will be okay with Mike.'

She let him lead her away. A path lined with sympathetic faces opened for them through the onlookers.

In the huge kitchen he made her sit down, and then filled a bowl with warm water and brought it to her. He sponged her hands and Nina saw the brown clouds of blood shadow the water when he rinsed the cloth.

'You've cut yourself, too.'

She looked at the clean slice in the fleshy base of her thumb. 'Only a scratch.'

He took a packet of Elastoplast out of a drawer, found a dressing of the right size then applied it for her. Nina noticed that his large hands were clean, but roughened and split at the fingertips as though he did heavy work with them.

'I'm Barney Clegg,' he said.

'I know. I'm Nina Cort.'

They shook hands, Nina's undamaged left held in his right.

'I don't know what we can do about your dress.'

There were dark, sticky patches on the bodice and the skirt. Barney dabbed at a fold of skirt with his cloth.

'Don't worry. Please, don't. You've done everything.' Now

that the drama had subsided Nina felt a bubble of laughter rising inside her. 'It's just that I can't stand the sight of blood.'

Barney began to laugh too. 'Neither can I. I never have been able to. A guy at college put a rake through his foot and I was the one who passed out.'

'We have both been heroically brave tonight, then.'

They continued to laugh. The party had taken over the kitchen once again; there were caterers clearing up at the sinks and guests passing through in search of one another and the music had boomingly restarted in the conservatory. Then Nina saw Gordon watching them across what seemed like an acre of quarry-tiled floor.

Her laughter faded. She wanted him to come to her and take Barney Clegg's place, but she knew that he wouldn't. He would look and then look away, and afterwards he would ignore her as he had done all evening in case anyone else saw them and made an incriminating connection between them.

Michael Wickham led the pale-faced Tom into the kitchen and made him sit down near Nina. His shirtsleeve had been cut away, and his arm was bandaged from wrist to elbow and supported in a makeshift sling made from someone's silk evening scarf.

'Are you all right, my son?' Barney enquired in mock Cockney.

'Yeah. Sorry, all.' To Nina he said, 'Sorry about the mess.'

Gordon had turned away, as she had known he would. Nina made herself smile at the boy. 'Don't worry. I'm glad it's not as serious as it looked.'

Michael said, 'Still, he needs someone to drive him to casualty to get that arm stitched. I'm damned if it's going to be me.'

Barney sighed. 'I guess that's my job. I'm just about fit to drive.' He patted Nina on the shoulder. 'See you again, I hope. Come on, Thomas. Let's go and join the festivities in the accident department.'

When they had gone Michael rolled down his sleeves and fished for his cufflinks in his trousers pocket. Without thinking,

Nina held out her hand for the gold links, and when he gave them to her she threaded them through the double cuffs for him as she had always done for Richard.

'Well done,' he commended her.

'Well done, doctor,' she returned.

Michael sighed. 'It's one of the hazards of the job, never quite to get away from it.'

She saw that when he was not frowning he had a good, plain, likable face.

'Join me for one last drink?' he asked her. 'Before we head home for Christmas? A proper drink, not bloody champagne.'

'I will. Thank you.' She already knew that Gordon was nowhere to be seen.

When Gordon crossed the hall Marcelle stepped out and put her hand on his arm. Gordon stopped at once. They saw Darcy hurrying down the stairs but he brushed by them, unseeing, heading for the kitchen.

'I feel like the Ancient Mariner.' Marcelle's mouth made a sad, acknowledging twist. 'Can we talk for a minute?'

He looked down at her fingers, the red-painted fingernails against his black sleeve. She had capable domestic hands and the red varnish seemed slightly incongruous. Gordon's head was full of Nina's pale, imploring face and the little swimming movements she had made with her smeared hands. He answered vaguely, but with a cold sense of impending catastrophe, 'Talk? Yes, of course.'

'In here.'

Marcelle opened the door of the gunroom. There were the two creaky wicker chairs that she and Jimmy had occupied, and Jimmy's empty glass on the floor where he had left it.

'Parties, these parties. Getting together and talking and drinking and being good fun. At all costs, good fun.' She put her hand up to her neck, where she could feel a vein pumping. She was very tired now.

'Marcelle? What do you want to say?'

She nodded, feeling that her skull was too heavy for her spine. Was it only this evening, how many hours ago, that Jimmy had kissed her in here and she had worried about the creases in the skin between her breasts?

'I know it isn't any of my business,' she began, and then faltered. 'Gordon, I'm sorry. That's what malicious gossips always say, isn't it?'

'I wouldn't know.' His mouth became a grim line. 'Do you listen to gossip?'

She felt rebuked, but also that the rebuke was justified. 'All right. I'll just tell you how it is. You know what I saw the other day, and you should also know that until this evening I hadn't mentioned it to anyone, not to Michael or anyone else.'

He said stiffly, 'Thank you. You were right, of course, at the beginning. It isn't any of your business.'

A retrospective, wasted prickle of anger went through Marcelle. 'Even though Vicky is my friend?'

'It would be an act of friendship, wouldn't it, not to pass on speculative whispers about a brief glimpse of two people? A glimpse that might easily have been mistaken or misinterpreted?'

'But I don't think I was mistaken, was I?'

When Gordon said nothing she rushed at her admission, wanting to get it over with so she could escape from the horrible room,

'This isn't coming out the way I meant it to, not that I know how I meant it. We know each other well enough, don't we? I wanted to say that I meant to keep my mouth shut, but I didn't, stupidly, and I'm very sorry. I told Jimmy Rose about it.'

Gordon repeated, 'You told *Jimmy*?'

His fuddled mind filled up with images of Jimmy's cunning fox-head bent close to a circle of heads, and then the heads turning to more circles of listening heads, and mouths whispering, all of them Jimmy's mouth, on and on in widening ripples into infinity.

'I'm very sorry. It was a thoughtless and damaging thing to do.'

'Yes.'

He could think of nothing else to say, other than to acknowledge the truth of it.

Marcelle's hand wavered towards him, as if to offer meaningless comfort, but he made no move and she let it fall to her side. Then she turned sharply and ran to the door.

Gordon watched the door close behind her. He stood and stared at it, his eyes retaining the blue-green swirl of her skirt. He felt a leaden pity for Vicky and Nina, for himself, even for Jimmy and Marcelle, which he knew would shortly flower into pain.

The party was coming to an end. Couples were filtering into the hallway to stand in their coats under the pine garlands and exchange the last words of the evening. The music had turned smoochy and it was punctuated by the slamming of car doors outside and by headlamp beams raking over the conservatory glass. The smashed door had been hastily patched up with a flattened cardboard box.

Darcy had stationed himself near the front door to say good night to his guests.

Gordon and Vicky came down the stairs together, Gordon carrying the baby basket. Darcy kissed Vicky on the cheek and she leaned against him for an instant, looking up at him, her fingers closing on his arm. Gordon was stiff and dark beside her.

'Good night. Merry Christmas.'

The Wickhams followed the Ransomes out into the cold darkness, with the Frosts and Star not far behind them. They called out, wishing each other a happy Christmas, separating into the old pairs for the drive home into Christmas Day.

Marcelle stared ahead, watching the way the car's headlights sliced at angles over the flat-topped hedges. She wanted to build a bridge to Michael now, before they reached home, where Michael's visiting parents might not yet be in bed.

'Was the boy all right?'

'Yes, more or less. He was quite lucky.' Michael glanced at her. 'Did you enjoy the party? I didn't see much of you.'

He was aware of all the evenings of their years together meshed behind them. He thought of the parties they had been to following the one at which they had first met, the clothes and places and friendships that had been discarded, temporary attractions to other people flaring and fading, leaving just the two of them. The weight of so much history pulled at his shoulders as if he was wearing a heavy train.

Marcelle thought of Jimmy with his head bent to kiss her lined skin, and Gordon's rebuke, and his cold face. She also remembered the furtive delight that she had glimpsed in the red Mercedes.

'Yes,' she lied. 'Yes, I did.'

Michael took one hand off the wheel to touch her arm. 'Let's try to have a happy Christmas, shall we?'

'Of course,' Marcelle answered.

Vicky rested her head against the cool glass of the passenger window. She was smiling. There had been a guilelessness in Darcy's advance, a childish directness that she found deeply appealing. She was also pleased that he had so plainly wanted her; after what seemed like years of feeling huge and milky and bovine it was good to be reminded that she was alive and interesting. She could feel the stirred-up blood now, singing inside her.

Vicky had no idea what would happen next, or if anything would happen, but she contemplated whatever it would be with sleepy equanimity.

Gordon negotiated the familiar twists of the country road with frozen concentration. He could see the lights of another car, probably the Frosts', winding ahead of him. He thought Vicky must have dropped into a doze and he tried to drive smoothly in order not to wake her or the baby. He needed this interval to think.

He was certain that he would have to tell Vicky the truth, before she heard someone else whispering the story.

He would have to tell her as gently and as honestly as he could manage, although he could not imagine what words he would use. Nor did he have any idea of what might happen once Vicky did know. But even in the midst of his dread he knew that he couldn't bear to give Nina up, even though that was what he must certainly do.

His whole head was alive with images of her this evening, in her black dress, with her head held up and her long hands painted with blood. It had been hard enough not to run to her then, to have to leave her to Barney Clegg.

How could he tell Vicky what he barely understood himself, only clung to with all the selfish and vivid need that had woken up in him?

And when could he tell her? He must warn Nina first, some-how, and that would be a second betrayal. A wild impulse to leave Vicky at home and then to turn round and drive straight to Dean's Row fuelled him for a second and then shrivelled away.

There was nothing to be done today.

There would be the enactment of a family Christmas with his children and their grandparents, and he would have to live through that with his knowledge of what was waiting for them. The next day, or the day after that, he would somehow find a way to tell the truth before Jimmy Rose did it for him.

Then, at the end of it, he would be left without Nina. As he considered this Gordon noticed, as dispassionately as if he were registering it in a third person, the first sharp twist of pain.

Darcy sat down on the edge of the bed and took off his shoes. Hannah was already in bed, lying curled up with her back to him.

'What's the matter?' he asked her. 'It was a good party. Good enough, anyway.' When she said nothing he undid his tie and shirt and then took off his trousers, dropping each item on to Vicky's chair. He could see the print of her body in the cushions.

'Is this to do with Vicky Ransome?' he asked. Hannah muttered something he could not hear. He told her irritably, 'Don't sulk, darling, it doesn't suit you.'

Darcy padded naked into the bathroom and looked at himself in the mirror as he stood at the lavatory. There was a thick roll of flesh around his midriff and the hair on his chest was grey, but the muscles of his belly remained satisfyingly taut. He was not, he told himself, in bad shape for his age.

When he slid into bed beside her, Hannah still had not moved. Darcy eased across and pressed himself against her bulky warmth. He loved the generosity of flesh; it was Jimmy Rose's mistake to imagine that he could have been drawn to Nina's dry bones.

'Hannah?'

He reached an arm over her shoulder and found her breasts. The looseness of them connected him to Vicky again and he felt himself harden.

'Stop it, Darcy. The kids will be awake in three hours' time.'

'Let Mandy see to them, or the twins.'

'It's *Christmas*.'

'All the more reason to spread a little cheer.'

Her only response was to push his hand away and hunch her shoulders in self-protection. Darcy was too sleepy to make more than a token protest; he knew this was Hannah's revenge for his interlude with Vicky, and he also knew that by tomorrow it would be forgotten.

When he reached to turn out the light Darcy was smiling. He had remembered his earlier absolute conviction that he loved Vicky Ransome. He wanted to fuck her, that was true; he still did. But there was no need for love to be a factor in the equation.

Jimmy came out of the church. He shook hands with the priest and nodded a greeting to some of the other worshippers, although he knew none of them well. This was a matter of choice; he preferred to slip out of the currents of the day and come to mass alone.

The Catholic church was a modern brick building in a quiet road. Jimmy walked a little way away from it, down the street, to get away from the people and their cars. It was a cold, clear night. The street lights spread a murky orange canopy overhead, but he could see through it to the sharp brilliance of the stars. When he was alone he stopped, and heard the tiny echo of his own footsteps.

He tilted his head back to look at the stars.

It was Christmas morning, and Jimmy felt entirely at peace.

Nine

The door of the house in Dean's Row was opened by a man Gordon had never seen before. His pale, indoor clothes looked incongruous in the metallic winter light and his feet were bare. It was the afternoon of Boxing Day.

'Is Nina here?'

Patrick said, 'Yes, she is.' He knew at once that this was the man. Reluctantly he held the door open wider. 'Come in. She's upstairs.'

Nina and Patrick had been watching a film, the Branagh *Henry V.* They had spent many afternoons like this together, immersed in a movie, barricaded by sofa cushions. There was a box of Belgian chocolates on the floor, and a comfortable litter of empty coffee cups and wine glasses. The King's dirty, weary army limped across the television screen in the corner.

'I much prefer the Olivier version,' Patrick had sighed, before the knock at the door. 'Such romantic Plantagenet splendour.'

'You would.' Nina laughed at him through a mouthful of chocolate. 'Don't you think mud and dead horses are more realistic?'

'And is realism a real benefit?'

Now Gordon stood in the doorway. Nina was startled, still warm with laughter, sitting in her corner of the sofa with her knees drawn up against the cushions. Gordon saw the evidence of an indulgent, adult afternoon of a kind that he had almost forgotten. His own house today was a dense, humid mass of children and grandparents and festive detritus. Nina's bare, elegant drawing room and even the unknown languid man formed a tableau that entirely excluded him.

'I'm sorry. I'm disturbing you.'

Nina jumped to her feet. She was wearing leggings and a loose cashmere tunic that he remembered seeing before. It had felt soft enough to melt under his hands.

'No, you're not. Of course you're not.'

He clearly saw the pleasure and anticipation in her face, and wished that he had come to tell her something different.

'Only I thought, today . . .'

She gestured with her long fingers that he wanted to take hold of. She meant that it was Boxing Day, a time of new dolls' houses and noisy parlour games and family attachments.

'I said I had a headache and needed some fresh air. The truth, as it happens.'

For a moment he had forgotten the pale-coloured man behind him, but Nina had not.

'Gordon, this is Patrick Forbes, an old friend of mine. Patrick, this is Gordon Ransome.'

Gordon said stiffly, 'How do you do?'

Patrick shrugged, smiling a little. 'Hi.'

They shook hands, conscious of immediate mutual dislike. Gordon saw, now that they faced each other, that Patrick must be queer. He was always uncomfortable with homosexuals, and Patrick's defensiveness of Nina made him prickly.

Gordon was also disconcerted to realize that he had never considered that Nina might not be alone, even on the day after Christmas. They hadn't discussed their separate holiday plans. Patrick's presence, among the cushions and pairs of wine glasses, conjured up another world of Nina's friends and diversions and allegiances in which he played no part. He felt a desolate, paradoxical jealousy.

He said, with his eyes fixed on her face, 'I hoped we might be able to talk for a few minutes.'

Patrick's eyebrows lifted. 'I'll go and make some tea, shall I?'

Nina smiled at him. 'Could you?'

Gordon felt as if he had blundered into a game in which the unwritten rules were too subtle for him to comprehend. But as soon as Patrick had gone Nina came to him, putting her hands on his arms and reaching up to kiss him. He held her, longingly and unwillingly.

'He knows about us, doesn't he?' Gordon asked.

'I had to talk to somebody. I couldn't keep so much so secret. Do you mind very much?'

She was bright-faced with happiness. He considered, briefly, whether he might not be able to conceal the real reason for his visit. Then they could sit down together in comfort amongst the discarded television pages and hollowed cushions. He hesitated, but her face was already changing, the happiness fading out of it.

'What is it?' she asked.

He noticed that in the time he had been in the room the light outside had faded from midwinter afternoon to premature dusk. In a moment the street lamps would come on at the margins of the green. When he didn't answer at once she repeated,

'What is it? Tell me.'

He sat down on the edge of the warm sofa. He remembered that he had lit the fire for her, on the first afternoon, and they had admired the view of the west front before it was obscured by scaffolding. Not many weeks ago. He could number them exactly, and the days, counted out in intervals by the number of times they had managed to see each other. In retrospect they seemed very few, for the weight of what he was having to do now.

'Marcelle told Jimmy Rose that she saw us together.'

Nina gazed at him. The firelight polished her cheeks and the golden shields of her earrings.

'Well. That is a pity.'

He waited, but she had nothing else to say. Her passivity irritated him until he remembered that she was an outsider and did not understand the shorthand of the Grafton couples.

'If Jimmy knows it means everyone knows. Jimmy has never been one for keeping a titbit of gossip to himself.'

'Vicky?'

'Vicky will know soon enough, obviously. Someone will tell her.'

Nina was silent again.

Gordon had not thought directly of Vicky since he came into the room, but now he saw her as she had been when he left home with his headache to drive to the cathedral. Her mother and father had been with her, and he had noticed the way their features foretold her progress into old age just as Vicky's predicted her own daughters' maturity.

He had been quick with his gabbled excuses, and his wife had sighed, not looking him in the face. Her silence had made him afraid that somehow she must know the truth already, and the fear had made him hurry away to do what had to be done.

Nina raised her eyes to meet Gordon's. In his head the features of the two women were briefly superimposed, as he had once envisaged their bodies at the start of the affair.

She said very quietly, 'I see. What does this mean?'

'It means that I must tell her the truth, before somebody else gives her a distorted version of it. And it also means that I can't go on seeing you. I'm sorry. I wish I didn't have to be so clumsy. I feel as if I have broken something that is irreplaceable.'

Nina sat still. Her eyes slid away from his, to the fire. When she spoke it was in the same quiet voice.

'Don't worry. Nothing's broken.'

Whatever it was that Gordon had been afraid of, tears or protests or blame, did not come. Her face was immobile, and her silence meant that he had to talk, continuing to offer her some other currency now that the old, thrilling one had become invalid.

'This is very painful, Nina. You made me so happy. Guilty, but happy as well. I went through our tapes, in the racks at home, and dug out the old rock numbers and fed them into the deck in the car. I used to drive along, going to work or some bloody site meeting, with the volume turned up, music blasting out. Singing along, grinning and drumming my fingers on the wheel. I felt like a boy.'

He spread his hands out, offering her this.

'A middle-aged engineer, burdened with debt and children and responsibilities. I couldn't believe that it was happening.'

Nina said nothing.

'I loved you. I love you now.'

She looked at him at last.

'And so what happens to it, this *love*?'

He considered it, knowing that he owed her as much.

To feel love had been seductive and intriguing and flattering, and it had lent him an animation that he had not felt for years. This woman, whom he had believed he understood and now suspected that he did not, had accepted and reciprocated his love, and all of this had been enclosed within a frame of secrecy that had been part of its delight. Gordon had enjoyed having a secret, after so many years when his interior life had been as clean and plain and colourless as the external world. The possession of it had added an extra erotic charge to everything that he and Nina did together.

But once the secrecy was gone, he did not see how the rest could remain. Whatever different gloss he wished to give it, it had been a private affair that was now public property.

'I love you still,' he said helplessly.

That was the truth. Greedy and possessive as he knew it was, he wanted to keep her. Even now it would have been easy, delightful, to reach out, to undo buttons and expose the white, tea-freckled skin.

Gordon touched the tip of his tongue to his lips.

'But I am married, and therefore responsible to people other than myself. I thought you understood that. Nina?'

'Understood that wives must be protected at all costs?'

Her eyes were as flat as the discs of her earrings.

'Wives, and children . . .' Gordon said.

As he spoke the words he gained another surprising perspective. This loss of love and Nina hurt him, and would continue to hurt him, but he also wanted to be saved. Salvation was in sight, and this glimpse of it filled him with relief.

'What about me?' Nina asked. Her voice was dry, toneless.

He shook his head slowly, from side to side, accepting the darts of pain inside his skull as his due. He was eager for the pain of losing her to begin, too, as the penance he must undergo.

'I don't want to hurt you. I want to wrap you up and make it better for you, but I can't. I can't bear the thought of hurting you.'

'But, clearly, you *can* bear it.'

It was fully dark outside. The street lamps made an ugly, amber haze in drifted snow-shapes of condensation at the corners of the window panes.

In the silence that followed Nina went to the nearest of the tall windows and unfolded the shutters from their panelled niches, carefully fitting the old iron catch with its curled tail into the slot to hold them securely closed. She did the same with the other two windows, moving carefully behind the Christmas tree to reach them. Nina's tree was hung with silver trinkets and illuminated with pure white light. Gordon made an automatic comparison with Vicky's, which was loaded with crayoned ornaments made by the girls and lit with multi-coloured lanterns.

Nina finished the task of closing out the darkness, and came back to her place.

'Thank you for coming to tell me first,' she said. 'Before Vicky.'

He had never seen this coldness, this composure, in her before. After the very beginning she had always been warm and eager, generous with herself in a way that had been enticingly at odds with her physical slightness. He wanted to defend Vicky, who had done nothing, but he restrained himself.

'I'm truly sorry,' was all he could think of to say.

'Yes. However, nothing is broken,' Nina repeated.

But she is *strong*, Gordon thought. Much stronger than I am.

Her strength unbalanced him, and revealed his own weakness.

Now that the business was done he felt a terrible, humble urge to throw himself at her, to hide his face and to cry and wail in her arms and have her comfort him, the way Vicky soothed Alice with inarticulate murmurings after a bad dream. The smell of her and the texture of her skin and hair returned sharply in his imagination. He propped his elbow on his knee, and rested his head in his hand. She did not reach out to soothe or console him, as he wanted her to do. Instead she looked at her watch, and the loose cuff of her tunic fell back to expose her thin wrist and the freckles on her arm.

She said in her cool, unemphatic voice, 'I wonder where Patrick is with the tea.'

Gordon lifted his head again.

'I don't want any tea.'

'Yours will be waiting for you at home, of course.'

The glimpse of her bitterness stirred him. She was not unaffected, after all, and he felt himself melting. He made a tiny move towards her, but she held up her hands, fending him off.

The conversation was over. He could not put any other interpretation on it. She would not look at him now.

There was nothing for him to do but stand up and take the coat that he had put aside when Patrick led him into the room.

He blurted foolishly, 'Will I . . . will we see each other again?'

Nina sat amongst the cushions, one side of her face gilded by the firelight.

'At the Frosts, or the Cleggs, I imagine.'

'Don't be hard.'

'Don't you be soft, then.'

'I'm sorry,' he attempted for the last time.

'Yes,' Nina said. He was dismissed.

Gordon nodded. Then he went down the stairs and let himself out into the Row. His Peugeot was parked beyond the archway that led on to the green. He drove out of the city in the opposite direction from home, and stopped in a field gateway off a lane that led in the direction of Wilton. In the distance he could see the lights of Darcy's house on its little hill.

He sat for a long time with the car heater making a small burr of warmth around him. The hedge trees loomed in the darkness, and no other car passed. Once he reached out to the tongue of the cassette tape protruding from the player, but he stopped before pushing it in to play. He thought about all the households between here and the city, imagining the rooms and the decorations that had been put up for the holiday and the complicated arrangements of families gathered for Christmas. He felt omniscient, elevated by his sadness, as if he could look into each of the houses and interpret its secrets.

Then he thought about his own fireside, with a sudden affection coloured by relief. It only remained for him to make his confession to Vicky, and then he would be safe.

At length, when he began to feel stiff and cold even with the heater running, he restarted the engine and turned the car back in the direction he had come.

In the empty room Nina leant forward and picked up a shred of gold wrapping paper from the rug. She folded it and buffed it with her fingernail to make it shine, and then twisted it around her ring finger to make a wedding band, as she had done as a child in games of getting married.

My husband will be handsome and rich, and we'll have eight children, four of each.

My husband will buy us a big house in London and another by the sea, and we'll have eight children as well.

The paper made a gaudy triplet with Richard's rings.

She asked him, *Why aren't you here? Why did you go and leave me, when I needed you? We had our houses and your money and our happiness.*

No children. I'm sorry for that, my love.

And then you had to go and die, and leave me here.

Nina stared at the blank wooden shutters that closed out the cathedral and the restoration works. A month ago, even a week ago, she would have cried and battered herself against the wall of her own grief. Nothing had changed, only herself, but this time she did not cry.

Now that he had stumbled away with his needs and his confusion, Nina knew that she had only tried to make herself a shadow husband out of Gordon Ransome. She had imagined his strength and protection, and her instincts had been hardly more developed than those of the little girl playing weddings.

It was harsh to be angry with Gordon because his strength had turned out to be an illusion, and because his protective instincts were all for himself and his wife and his children and not for her.

She took off the paper ring and screwed it into a ball before throwing it at the fire. The only strength that was valuable to her was her own, and for the protection of friendship there was always Patrick.

She found him sitting in the kitchen, the room she still disliked with its faux-rustic cupboards and tiles. The tea tray was immaculately laid and waiting on the table beside him. He was smoking a coloured Balkan Sobranie with gold filter, a Christmas indulgence.

'I heard him leaving,' Patrick said.

'The final exit.'

He raised his eyebrows at her, squinting through the smoke, making his Noel Coward face. Nina began to laugh.

'Funny?' Patrick enquired.

'Not really. No.'

'Tell me, then.' He lifted the teapot and poured for her, passed her the cup.

'It's just how you would have predicted. You warned me at the beginning, didn't you?'

He made a gesture modestly dismissive of his own prescience, and now they both laughed.

'One of the wives, one half of one of the couples, happened to see us together. She told someone else, one of the husbands, who will in his turn tell the others. And so Gordon's wife will get to hear of it. And so it has to end, so that he can confess to her and ask for forgiveness.'

Patrick demanded, 'How can you bear it? This provincial world of couples pecking away at each other, at each other's secrets?'

Nina drank some of her tea. 'It isn't quite like that. This isn't a metropolitan world, there isn't the same luxurious privacy that cities give. But there is a feeling of us all being here together. Of having committed ourselves to the same life. It was a mistake to have an affair. I suppose I had overlooked the fact that it would be more . . . significant here.'

She was thinking of the different faces of the Grafton couples and the ways that their friendships and allegiances seemed to knit them together, and remembering her reluctance to join Darcy Clegg in his mild mockery of them.

Patrick was watching her face. 'So it is over, your love affair?'

'Oh, yes.'

There was a moment's silence. 'He *was* wearing those shoes. The ones that look like pork pies that have been left out in the rain.'

'Don't laugh at him, Patrick. I liked him very much.'

'And now he's made you sad.'

'Yes.'

Patrick took hold of her hand and then he put his arms around her. She rested her forehead against his shoulder.

'Why don't you come back to London instead of staying out here in bandit country, with bandits in pork pie shoes?'

Nina shook her head. 'I like it here,' she said. She was thinking of the statues in their cathedral niches, and their faces re-emerging from the lime bandages, images of regeneration.

Patrick let her go. 'Well. I suppose that's that, then. Do you want to watch the end of the film?'

'Why not? We could have a glass of champagne at the same time. It *is* Christmas.'

'That's my girl.'

They finished their tea, and then drank champagne in front of the television. Later there was another knock at the door, and Nina went downstairs to answer it. A car was parked with two wheels on the pavement, and Barney Clegg and his friend with the bandaged arm stood on the step. Barney held up two bottles and Tom carried an ivory-flowered plant wrapped in green tissue paper in the crook of his good arm. They both beamed at her.

'You did live, then,' Nina said to Tom.

'I did. We've called to say thank you. And to give you this. Whatever it is.'

'It's a Christmas rose,' Barney Clegg protested. '*Helleborus niger*. For your garden. I suppose you've got a garden, back there?'

She took the offering. The fragile cup-shaped flowers were tinged with green, with a central boss of golden anthers. 'How beautiful. My garden isn't worthy of it. Would you like to come in and have a drink? Provided you don't bleed on anything.'

The boys trampled in, seeming huge in her hallway.

'Eleven stitches,' Tom said proudly, holding out his arm.

'After eleven hours sitting in casualty, or thereabouts,' Barney cheerfully complained.

They followed Nina up the stairs, filling the quiet house with noise.

'We've been round to Mike Wickham's, to thank him as well.'

'And how were they?'

The boys snorted with laughter. 'Pretty dire. Howling kids everywhere.'

'Like Barney's place, in fact.'

Nina opened the drawing room door for them.

'Well, there are no kids here, howling or otherwise. Only Patrick and me.'

Patrick uncoiled himself from the sofa.

'This is Barney and his friend Tom. They've come to thank me for doing not very much when Tom cut his arm on Christmas Eve.'

After the handshakes Barney offered his bottles of wine.

'I don't know what these are. Is it drinkable? I lifted them from Dad's cellar.'

Patrick examined the labels. 'Better than drinkable. A rather good Pomerol.'

'Shall we open them? Let them breathe, and the rest?'

More glasses were brought, logs were put on the fire and the humming television was switched off. The boys made themselves comfortable, arms and long legs folded somehow into Nina's cushions. Patrick and Nina refilled glasses and passed plates, and learned among other things that Barney was a student of landscape design and horticulture at agricultural college, and Tom was at the nearby poly. They had been friends since their not-very-distant schooldays. They had been vaguely planning to move on to Grafton's one disco later in the evening, but Barney complained that it was full of kids, 'Lucy and Cathy's crowd'. Soon it became clear that Barney and Tom were staying to dinner.

When Patrick and Nina found themselves alone for a moment in the kitchen, Patrick said, 'I thought you said you knew no one in Grafton except middle-aged married couples.'

'Surprise, surprise.'

It was a convivial supper. Patrick was never predatory or even openly camp, but the wine melted his reserve and made him funny and loquacious. It was clear that he liked the company of the two large boys. He seemed too often to be an observer nowadays. For herself, she was amused by Barney and Tom's good humour and their enthusiasm for everything from her food to Patrick's wry jokes.

When she remembered Gordon and experienced the twist of angry sadness that came with the thought of him, she made herself close him off and concentrated instead on the friendly faces around her kitchen table. It was odd to hear the laughter and clatter of plates in this room, when she had so deliberately determined that it would always be empty and silent.

The Christmas rose stood stripped of its paper on the draining board. There were crumbs of earth around the lip of the clay pot, and more mud rimming the bottom of it. Nina brushed some of it away with her fingertips. Barney came with a neat pile of dirty plates to stand beside her at the sink.

'I lifted it from the nursery bed especially for you,' he told her. He was a head taller than Nina, and she had to look up at him.

'Did you lift one for Mike Wickham too?'

'No, of course not.'

They both gazed at the ivory petals with their faint suffusion of green. Nina was disconcerted to find that she was blushing. Behind them she heard Tom explaining to Patrick the rules of some complicated word game that he had suddenly decided they must play.

'Shall I plant it for you?' Barney asked her. 'It's too hot for it to be happy in here.'

Nina turned on the outside light and led Barney to the doors that looked out on to her tiny courtyard garden. It was a dismal prospect of bare earth drifted over with dead leaves and windblown litter.

'I did say that my garden wasn't worthy of it.'

Barney unlocked the door and carried the plant outside. Nina watched him as he found a sheltered corner and tenderly heaped up dead leaves around the pot to protect it from the frost. He rubbed his large hands on his jeans and ducked back into the kitchen.

'I'll come in the daylight to plant it properly for you. I could tidy up the rest and plant some other stuff as well, if you like.'

He waited.

Nina said gently, 'That's very kind of you. But I don't think you should spend your time doing my neglected garden for me.'

Richard had always been the gardener. He had loved his garden in Norfolk, the garden where he had died. Carefully Nina picked up the last specks of earth from the stainless steel ribs of the sink drainer.

Barney shrugged. 'That's okay. It's my job; or it will be if I ever get qualified.'

Tom called to them, 'Are we going to play this game, then?'

They had had a good deal to drink, Nina realized. But she took another bottle of wine from the rack and opened it, and sat down at the table again.

The game was a rambling, open-ended affair of inventing words and then supplying meanings for them. Patrick was the best at devising words and definitions; he had always been good at crosswords and riddles and charades, but Barney came in a surprisingly sharp second. Nina was hopeless, her wits were too scattered, but it was a pleasure to see Patrick enjoying himself so much.

At length, long after midnight, the boys decided that they must after all make a late raid on the disco. They tried to persuade Nina and Patrick to accompany them, without success, and finally, with promises to come back another day, they left in search of new diversions.

Patrick leaned against the duck-egg blue cupboards and drank the last of a glass of wine.

'Do you think I'm a silly old queen?' he asked, 'Enjoying a pair of nice, straight boys like those?'

'No more than I'm a silly old woman,' Nina answered. She was smiling, but Patrick was not deceived.

'Are you thinking about pork-piefoot?'

'Yes.' And about Richard, too, only she would not burden him with that.

'Then don't,' Patrick ordered her.

Vicky's parents went home on the day after Boxing Day. Gordon carried their tartan suitcases out to the front of the house and stowed them side by side in the boot of Alec's Vauxhall. The old people moved slowly in his wake, arranging their car rug and Marjorie's handbag on the back seat, arguing protractedly with each other about the need for petrol and the best route to take home. Mary and Alice ran out after their grandmother and hung on to her arms, while Vicky stood in the doorway holding Helen wrapped in a white shawl.

Patiently Gordon helped his parents-in-law to settle themselves ready for the short journey, answering Alec's queries about the nearest filling station likely to be open and reassuring Marjorie that of course he would make sure Vicky got enough rest.

At the same time, he was trying to imagine how he and Vicky would be together when they had reached the same age as her father and mother. He thought that the small irritations with one another and the tetchiness generated by minor interruptions to routine would be solidified in just the same way, set in the rock of another twenty-five years. They would go visiting at Christmas time and Mary's husband would humour him, exactly as he was humouring Alec now. The idea was profoundly depressing.

At last the old people were ready to go.

Vicky came out and stood beside him in the driveway, and Alice and Mary waved, and Alec revved the engine too fiercely before letting in the clutch, as he always did. The Vauxhall bucked forward, narrowly missing the rose bushes bordering the front lawn, and then achieved the correct momentum to pass between the gateposts and swing left into the roadway.

The children shouted gamely, 'Goodbye, Granny, goodbye, Grandad,' and Gordon and Vicky raised their arms in salute, frozen for an instant in a happy-family tableau.

When the Vauxhall had finally passed out of sight they turned back into the house. Vicky lifted the baby to her shoulder and massaged her back through the thickness of the shawl.

Gordon looked carefully around him, as if he was seeing the interior of his home for the first time. There was a hard, yellowish light that revealed the chipped paint of the skirting boards and the sticky handprints on the walls, and now that he and Vicky were alone together again the rooms seemed to contain a sullen, implacable silence.

They went into the untidy kitchen, and while Vicky put the baby into her basket Gordon covertly watched her face. The skin seemed puffy and unhealthily smooth, as if water had seeped underneath it. It came to him that she was suffering too.

He had decided that he would talk to her this evening, when the children were asleep. It was the anticipation of what he must do that gave the house and surroundings their queasily unfamiliar aspect, and for the hundredth time he played with the idea of saying nothing, of trusting to luck and the hope that Vicky would never hear what had happened. But ever since Christmas Eve he had been imagining the invisible snake of gossip twisting between the Grafton couples, and he knew he would have to make his confession because he couldn't hope that the secret would be kept.

Vicky was listlessly piling toys into the wicker hamper where they were supposed to live. Someone had spilled sugar on the kitchen floor, and her slippers made a gritty protest as she moved.

Gordon said, 'I thought I might take them all out for a walk, down as far as the river. I could put Helen in the buggy. You could go to sleep for an hour, if you like.'

She straightened up, and he saw her brief flicker of surprise replaced by disbelief.

'You look tired,' he offered. 'Go on, have an hour's rest.'

Vicky dropped another toy into the basket, looking away from him again. 'Thanks. I might, if you don't mind.'

After he had searched for and found the necessary pairs of mittens and wellingtons, and helped Mary and Alice into their coats and wound scarves around their necks, and once Helen was zipped into her padded bag and strapped into the nest of her buggy, Gordon's patience was almost exhausted. Vicky had gone upstairs without a backward glance.

'Off we go,' he encouraged his daughters.

They set off down the road. Gordon felt conspicuous wheeling the high-framed white buggy, but the world seemed deserted. The neighbours' front doors were tightly closed and their windows were screened by the scrawny arms of winter trees. Alice wanted to stop at every corner, but he made her hurry on with the objective of the park beside the river in his mind.

'Mummy always lets me say hello to the spotted dog,' she complained.

'Don't you want to get to the swings?' he coerced.

When they reached the park after their slow journey they stood in a line and peered through the railings at the river. It was swollen and brown, carrying crests of dirty foam on its back. The wind was very cold. Helen's tiny nose had turned red, although the rest of her was almost invisible in her swaddling covers.

'Sometimes we throw sticks,' Mary told him.

'Shall we swing, today?' Gordon asked, recognizing that this numbing outing must be a regular part of Vicky's routine. He left the baby parked against the railings.

Mary ran to a swing and hoisted herself on to the seat.

'Push me,' she called.

Alice ran to one side, to a yellow plastic cockerel mounted on a heavy spring.

'How high can you go?' Gordon asked Mary, giving the small duffel-coated back a tentative push.

'Much higher. Push harder,' Mary shouted, sticking her legs straight out in front of her. 'That's better. Like *that*.'

To Gordon she seemed terribly fragile, a small cargo of precious humanity rushing backwards and forwards through the hostile air. Her hair streamed out under her knitted hat and she shouted with excitement, defying his adult anxiety.

A second later he saw the red blur of Alice's coat out of the corner of his eye. She had abandoned her cockerel and was rushing towards them.

He shouted, 'Look out!', but he was frozen in mid-push with his hands stretched vertically in front of him. Alice zigzagged in front of the swing and the sole of Mary's wellington boot caught her on the temple before the seat soared on upwards over her head.

Alice collapsed on the tarmac and the arc of her sister's swing returned above her. Gordon caught at the chains and held them, arresting Mary at the high point and almost wrenching his arms out of their sockets. He stilled the swing and scooped Mary out of it before sprinting to where Alice lay in a heap.

'She ran in front,' he heard Mary babbling.

He bent over Alice and saw her face contract and her lips draw back from her teeth. There were three full seconds of silence before the first howl found its way out of her. He was almost crying with relief himself as he snatched her up and held her. Her screams grew louder, and she went rigid.

There was a blue and white graze on her temple, and as he looked at it tiny scarlet beads sprang out between the shreds of skin. The caterpillar print of Mary's sole was clearly visible.

'Mummy puts cold water,' Mary said, pointing to the drinking fountain. Gordon carried the screaming child over to the metal cup and soaked his handkerchief in icy water. The side of Alice's head was already turning red and beginning to swell. Gordon pressed the cold compress to it and soothed her, feeling the panicky jumps of his heart.

'It isn't too bad, darling. It will hurt for a bit and then it will go away. It's just a bump. Just an old bump. Something that happens at the swings.'

After a while the child's screaming diminished and then stopped, fading away into hiccuping sobs.

'Good girl,' he whispered to her, rocking her in his arms. 'Brave girl.'

'She's stupid,' Mary said at his elbow, needing to state her own case now that the panic was subsiding. 'She ran in front. It wasn't my fault.'

'It wasn't anyone's fault, it just happened.'

Gordon extended his other arm to hold Mary too. He hugged his daughters close to his chest, daunted by their vulnerability and by the scale of the work involved in keeping them safe, helping them to grow. He felt weighed down by the responsibility of parenthood, but at the same time a different, narrow perspective opened up, of reluctant admiration for Vicky and satisfaction in their partnership. They had achieved these three tiny individuals, at least. After this evening, he thought, he would make sure that everything was set right again.

The lump on the side of Alice's head had grown to the size of a small, shiny egg, but the graze had stopped bleeding and he could see that there was no serious damage done. Gordon stood up, setting the two girls side by side on the tarmac.

'We had better go home,' he told them. 'Helen will be waking up soon and needing her feed.'

In the evening, after the children had been put to bed, Vicky made dinner, a random assemblage of leftovers that seemed even more half-hearted than her recent efforts in the kitchen.

'I'll do a big shop tomorrow,' she defended herself, before Gordon could complain. Her brief nap in the afternoon seemed only to have increased her tiredness. She moved heavily between the table and the fridge with the congealed dishes.

'It doesn't matter,' Gordon said. He felt clumsy and guilty. He opened a bottle of wine, and made himself a cold turkey sandwich. When they were both sitting down he began, 'Can we talk about something?'

'I'm very tired,' Vicky answered.

'It's important.'

She waited in silence, holding her wine glass between her hands. The puffiness of the skin around her eyes had narrowed the sockets, giving her a Chinese look.

Gordon put down his sandwich. Staring at the plate in front of him he said, 'There isn't any gentle way to tell you this, I wish there were. I have been having an affair with Nina. It's over now.'

Behind him the refrigerator gave its familiar shudder as the motor started into life.

Vicky looked as if he had hit her. Gordon made a move to touch her, but she pushed him away with a stiff, panicky gesture.

'Nina?' she repeated.

'I'm so sorry about it. I wanted to tell you.'

After a moment Vicky sank down, her shoulders sagging against the back of the kitchen chair.

'I knew there was something. Oh, God, I knew there was something.' She shaded her eyes with her hand. 'How long have you been having this affair?'

'It started when you were in hospital.'

'When I was in hospital? When I was in *hospital*, having our baby?' She shook her head from side to side, as if she couldn't quite make sense of the words.

Gordon thought, This is terrible. He had tried to imagine how it would be, over and over, but he had never envisaged this sick, shocked look of Vicky's.

'When did it end?' she asked.

'I went to tell her yesterday afternoon.'

'Why yesterday afternoon?'

He paused, and then said, 'Marcelle Wickham saw the two of us together a few days ago. She told Jimmy about it on Christmas Eve.'

'But why did you end it?'

'Because I wanted to,' he lied. 'And because I wanted you to hear about it from me, not from Janice or Star or somebody else.'

Vicky nodded her head, his words seeming to come clear to her at last.

'Christmas Eve? You ended it because you had to.'

'No, that's not true.'

She let her hand drop away from her eyes. They stared at each other as if in the last minutes they had become different people. Gordon felt himself beginning to shake.

'So, what was she like in bed, your Nina? Was the sex wonderful?'

'No,' he lied again.

Vicky was still staring. Then, with terrible suddenness, her face began to melt. Her mouth split wide open, showing her teeth and her tongue, and her eyes narrowed to slits. She started to cry, the tears running down her face. Her shocked composure followed by this collapse reminded Gordon of Alice's stunned silence and then her screams of pain and outrage in the park. He reached out now and did manage to take Vicky's hand.

'I'm very sorry,' he said humbly. 'It was a terrible thing to have done.'

Vicky was sobbing aloud, thick uncontrolled sobs that went *ahahah* in her throat.

'What can I say?' Gordon muttered wretchedly.

Vicky tore her hand away from his. She made a grand sweep with her arm and knocked her glass to the floor, and the red wine splashed up the cupboards and over a drawing of Mary's that was pinned to one of them. Broken glass glinted on the tiles and Vicky got to her feet, staggering as if she was drunk, and ploughed through it to the sink. With another sweep of her arm she cleared the draining board of cups and plates, sending a wave of china crashing around her.

'Don't say anything,' she shouted at him. 'Don't! I don't want to hear it, whatever you say.'

She stretched out, her fingers clawing for something else to throw and smash. Gordon jumped to his feet and ran through the sea of broken crockery to catch her wrists.

'Stop it,' he ordered her.

Vicky jerked one hand free. She swung it back and delivered an open-handed blow to the side of his face. His jaw snapped upwards, catching his tongue between his teeth and making his eyes water with humiliating pain. He stepped away from her, angry now, his shoes crunching in the shards of china.

With a last wild swing Vicky knocked the bottle sterilizer off the worktop. As it hit the floor the top came off, sending a plume of sterilant and dancing bottles that descended over Gordon's feet. He thought she was laughing as she whirled away from him, out of the kitchen, slamming the door so that the unbroken plates on the shelves perilously rattled.

Gordon stood still, breathing hard and tasting the blood on his tongue. Feeding bottles rolled and settled amongst the mess of broken plates, and sterilant ran in uneven tongues towards the bulwarks of the cupboards.

He put his fingers to his stinging cheek, and then wiped the blood from his tongue on the back of his hand. The refrigerator motor cut out, and the machine shrugged itself comfortably into silence again.

Gordon stooped down and picked up the first pieces of broken plate.

He set to work slowly and methodically, mopping up the wet, then sweeping up the debris and wrapping it in newspaper before putting it in the outside dustbin. He came in and locked the back door carefully behind him, then filled a bucket with soapy water and washed the wine stains and splashes of sterilant off the walls and cupboard doors. His cleaning went beyond the immediate damage; he swept up a mixture of crumbs and spilt sugar from under the table, and flicked the accumulation of household dust from the corners of the room.

After half an hour his anger and guilt had subsided.

He went out of the kitchen, intending to look for Vicky, and saw that the front door was open. Cold air funnelled down the hallway. There was a bulky pile of what looked like jumble heaped in the driveway beyond the front step.

As he stood there, slow-witted, Vicky came down the stairs. In one arm she carried a tangle of his belongings. He saw the jacket of his Tory suit, and his squash racket. The other hand dragged the largest of their suitcases. It bumped down the stairs in her wake.

Vicky threw his things on to the pile outside, and pushed the suitcase after them. She was panting with exertion, wiping her mouth with her hand.

'Go on!' she shouted at him. 'Go on, we don't want you. Get out of here. Go to her, if that's what you want.'

Her face was burning. He had never seen such anger in her.

Still only half comprehending what was happening, Gordon ran outside to see what she had done with his things.

The front door slammed behind him.

He turned round and heard her sliding the bolts, and the rattle of the chain as she secured that. Then there was the faint, bland *beep* that signalled the switching on of the burglar alarm.

It was a bitterly cold night, and he was in his shirtsleeves.

Over his head, in the room that looked out over the driveway, one of the girls had woken up. He heard her, Mary or Alice, whichever it was, beginning to cry.

Ten

The chalet rented by three of the Grafton families for their February skiing holiday was in the upper, quieter part of Méribel, near the Rond Point and the ski school. It was a modern building, but the exterior was pleasantly faced with wood and it had a first-floor balcony in rustic Alpine style. Inside, most of the walls and ceilings were lined with tongue-and-groove pine boarding.

Darcy lay on the bed in the best bedroom in the chalet, the only one with its own adjoining bathroom. His hands were folded behind his head and he was staring up at the wooden ceiling. The window opposite him was partly masked with snow and snow was still falling in thick, aimless flakes.

'This is like living inside some damned great sauna. It even smells the same. I keep wondering why I'm not sweating,' Darcy remarked.

Hannah was unpacking, taking her silk shirts out of wreaths of tissue paper and hanging them in the tiny wardrobe.

'Don't start complaining already,' she said sharply, without turning.

Darcy did not answer. Hannah was not usually tart, but recently she had become increasingly so. He continued to stare at the ceiling, counting the knotholes in the wood, irritated at the margin of his consciousness by being unable to arrange them into a satisfactory pattern.

He was thinking about money, about the shifting and massaging and redeployment of figures, and making flurried computations in his head. Darcy's business was money. In all the years he had worked in the City, looking after money for other people and earning it for himself, he had dealt in it with confidence, certain of his own expertise. Then, when he had semi-retired to Wilton with Hannah, he had retained responsibility for half a dozen of his previous clients. He managed their assets from his office in the manor house, making the journey to London as often as it was necessary.

But in the last few months it had begun to seem to Darcy that money was not the abstract, docile commodity he had once imagined. It had started to assume characteristics that he did not understand, slyness and capriciousness, like an irresistible but unreliable woman that he was obliged to court and propitiate.

As he lay on his bed in the chalet Darcy's heart began to thump uncomfortably. The knotholes in the pine boards jumped and then blurred as he gazed at them too intently.

He closed his eyes, forcing himself to breathe evenly to suppress the anxiety that heaved inside him. There was a telephone here in the chalet, but no fax machine. He was glad of that; he needed the respite and the altered perspective of this week in the snow. He was away, legitimately away, on holiday. There was nothing to be done now.

When he looked again, Hannah was finishing unpacking clothes. She placed the last folded pile in a drawer and then zipped up the empty suitcase with a vicious rasp. The door opened and Freddie appeared, already dressed in his brand new ski suit. Laura had been left at home with the au pair because Hannah had judged that she was too young to learn to ski, but this was Freddie's initiation and he was boiling with excitement.

'Can we go out in the snow? Jon and William are having a *snowball* fight, and I want to as well. Mummy, can we?'

Hannah turned to Darcy. 'Why don't you take him out?'

It had been a long drive from the airport up to Méribel. Outside it was almost dark. The snowflakes spun out of the darkness to bat themselves briefly against the wet glass.

'For Christ's sake, not now,' Darcy said. 'There's plenty of time for that tomorrow. I'm going downstairs for a drink.'

He rolled sideways off the bed, feeling weighty and sluggish, as if his body was too heavy for him to carry.

'Thanks,' Hannah called after him.

The chalet telephone was in the first-floor living room, sitting on an orange linen table mat on top of a pine cabinet. In Darcy's mind the personification of money as a tantalizing woman had become entangled with thoughts of Vicky. As he came into the room he glanced at the phone, but he knew he couldn't call her. Perhaps there would be a chance later in the week, when everyone was out on the slopes.

Michael Wickham was the only person in the room. He was drinking whisky and reading a Sunday newspaper that he had brought out on the plane from England. Darcy had not bought any liquor on the journey, because he could not be bothered to stand in a line in a duty-free shop in order to get a few pounds off a bottle of Scotch, but he was pleased to see Michael with his large bottle of Johnny Walker uncapped at his elbow.

Michael glanced up, then pointed out an empty glass to Darcy. Darcy poured himself a measure, drank it at a gulp, and then refilled the glass.

'Thanks.' He stood at the window, gazing through a patch of condensation at the falling snow. 'Should be a good week, when it stops.'

Michael folded his newspaper. 'Yeah. For those of you who can ski.'

Darcy had momentarily forgotten that Michael had not yet progressed beyond shaky blue runs.

'Hannah will keep you company.'

Hannah was the same standard as Michael; it was one of the reasons why the Cleggs had agreed to accompany the Frosts and Wickhams this year. Darcy himself was an excellent skier.

Michael smiled only rarely, but when he did his face was entirely lit up by it. The illumination came now, surprising Darcy.

'There is that to look forward to,' Michael agreed. 'What's your room like?'

'Like the sauna in a council-run sports centre.'

'Lucky. Ours is like a locker outside the sauna in a council-run sports centre.'

The two men laughed.

In the next room the chalet girl was banging the cutlery as she laid the table for the children's supper. The Grafton couples had already annoyed her by asking for the children's meal to be served early, before their own. The back door of the chalet blew open to admit a blast of cold air and a swirl of snow, together with the Frost boys and Jonathan Wickham who had been pushing snowballs down each other's backs. The boys fell into the room, a tangle of arms and legs and crimson faces.

'Close the bloody door!' Michael shouted at them.

Hannah came downstairs, dressed in black velvet jeans and suede ankle boots, with Freddie trailing sulkily behind her.

'Why couldn't I play in the snow like the others?' he was demanding.

'Any chance of a drink?' Hannah sighed, not looking at Darcy. Michael stood up and poured her one.

'Happy holiday,' she said, firmly clinking her glass against his.

Later in the evening, after the children had dispersed to their bunk beds and the dinner had been eaten, the parents gathered in the pine living room with their drinks. It was still snowing, and the unmarked depth of it beyond the windows seemed to enclose the six of them, silently cutting them off from the ordinary world and heightening the intimacy between them. They felt cosy and at the same time adventurous, as if there were some unacknowledged risk in finding themselves isolated together.

No one said as much, but they knew that what had happened to Vicky and Gordon and Nina had unexpectedly shaken up the pieces of some tidy, established pattern. It had caused them to look differently at one another, speculatively, as if after so long they knew each other much less well than they had always imagined.

After Christmas Gordon had bleakly camped out in his office, and then he moved into the modern hotel on the fringe of the business park. Then, some time later, the others heard that he was at home once more. Evidently Vicky had taken her husband back.

In the weeks since Christmas no one had seen very much of the Ransomes, either together or separately. Andrew told Janice that Gordon was working very hard. 'And a good thing too,' he had muttered in conclusion. Janice told the other women what she had also heard from Andrew, that Nina had gone back to London for a while, but none of them had anything else to report.

Each of the women, in turn, had taken care to let Vicky know that she was there for her, if there was any need. Vicky had thanked them, but in the end she hadn't talked much to any of them. It seemed that she was busy with her children.

But some of this new awareness of a break in the old pattern had accompanied the Frosts and the Wickhams and the Cleggs to Méribel.

Hannah stretched out in front of the fire. She had left her hair loose and a thick, shiny cascade of it half-covered her face and hid the hand propping up her head. Her jeans accentuated the hollow of her waist and the rounded swell of her hips. Andrew and Michael were both looking at her, and Hannah knew that they were looking. There was a triumphant curve to her lips that went with all the other curves of her, still just confined on the right side of the dividing line between voluptuous and fat.

Darcy was the only one who seemed unaware of the effect Hannah was having. He had been drinking steadily since before dinner, and his attention was fixed on the window where the snowflakes were visible in the last instant before they melted against the glass.

'Well,' Janice said softly, breaking a little silence, 'Are we all glad to be here?'

She glanced round at them, waiting for an answer.

Janice was wearing a loose, silky kaftan because she was at the upper limit of her weight range, the phase she described as Fat Jan. Soon a savage bout of dieting would reduce her to Plump Jan once more, and then the cycle would begin again.

'Of course we're glad,' Michael murmured. Away from the hospital and his bleeper and the considerations of tomorrow's list he was cheerful, almost light-hearted. The wine at dinner and the whisky seemed to have unpinned him. His legs splayed out in front of him and his long arms and surgeon's fingers dangled over the arms of his chair.

Andrew sleepily laced his hands over the small mound that his stomach made under his sweater.

'I need a holiday,' he said.

It had been a difficult couple of months. The recession was affecting business, and until recently Gordon hadn't been pulling his weight. Andrew told himself with satisfied conviction that he deserved a break, if anyone did.

Marcelle said nothing. She was wearing jeans and a sweat-shirt, an ordinary, workaday translation of Hannah's velvet and cashmere, and she knew that she looked old and faded. It had seemed a bigger struggle than usual, this year, to find everyone's ski belongings and to wash them and pack them, and to close up the house and to arrange a week's cover at work, and she had not found time to buy anything new for herself. She was worried that there were no other girls in the party to keep Daisy company. She was irritated that the dinner cooked by the sulky chalet girl had been less good than anything any one of her students could have produced, with the possible exception of Cathy Clegg. She felt tired, and anxious, and sad, and she would have liked to tell Michael so, and have him comfort and reassure her. But she knew that she could not tell him, indeed that she would have to pretend to be cheerful and to enjoy herself, so as not to increase either his irritation with her or her own sense of disappointment in him. They had existed since their last big argument in a state of careful politeness.

'Mar?' Janice was looking at her, her smooth forehead puckered with concern.

'Oh, yes.' Marcelle summoned a smile, only just able to remember what the question had been. 'So long as the ski-ing's good.' She had been a keen skier from childhood, and was probably the strongest in the group, better even than Darcy. Until this year, perhaps even this month, the promise of a week in the snow would have raised her spirits from any depths. That it failed to do so now only increased her fear and sadness.

'So, what shall we do with the rest of this evening?' Hannah asked. 'It's late, but it's too early for bed.'

She shook her hair back from her face, revealing her white throat. Behind her head a log fell in the hearth, sending up a tiny shower of sparks.

There was another small silence.

In the quiet room, hemmed in together by the snow while their children slept, they were reminded of Nina and Gordon. Even Marcelle, through the isolation of her sadness, sensed the possibility of something new and dangerous happening; even unimaginative Andrew sensed it.

'Play a game?' he suggested, not meaning quite that, but wanting to deflect this moment and steer the evening back to normality. There had been a period when the Grafton couples had been enthusiastic about after-dinner games, in the time when they had felt they knew everything there was to know about each other and needed new diversions.

'For Christ's sake, *no*. Not some fucking game.'

Darcy looked away from the window at last. The strength of his objection made the others realize that he was drunker than they were. But the tradition of deference to Darcy meant that no one tried to argue in favour of starting up a game.

Hannah looked at him, her smile disappearing for a second. Then she stood up, lazily reaching out her arms and flexing her fingers. She had taken off her suede boots, and her toe-nails were painted with the same bronze varnish as her long fingernails.

'I know.'

She went across to the cassette player provided as part of the chalet's equipment. There was a neat stack of cassettes beside it and she flipped through them until she found one that suited her. Michael and Andrew watched her as she bent down to fit the tape into the player. Janice lay back in her place with her head resting on one arm, waiting to see what would happen.

'I think we should dance,' Hannah said.

The tape she had chosen was Tina Turner's *Private Dancer*, no longer particularly new, more or less familiar to each of them. She began to hum, low down in her throat, while she searched for the place she wanted in the tape. Then, when she had found it, she stretched her arms wide, threw back her head and began to dance.

They had seen Hannah dance before, all of them, dozens of times, but not quite like this. Her eyes were half-closed but she was still smiling, moving her hips rhythmically to the music, slow gyrations that seemed to ripple up the length of her spine and down her arms to her fingertips. She was absorbed in herself but sang as she danced, 'I'm your private dancer, a dancer for money, I'll do what you want me to do . . .'

Nobody else moved.

As a performance it was overdone, veering close to parody, and there was a second when someone might have laughed and then the laughter would have spread and Hannah's solo would have lost its power to transfix any of them. But there wasn't a sound except for the music and Hannah's singing, and there was a crackle of tension in the room.

Janice lifted her head from her arm and watched, her mouth slightly open. Andrew was fully awake, and Michael put a finger up to rub a bead of moisture away from his top lip. Each of them thought, in their different ways, of the change that Gordon and Nina had begun. The imminent unravelling of the old pattern and the possibility that a new one might catch them up was threatening but now, also, it was made fascinating by Hannah's erotic dance.

Only Darcy had turned his attention back to the window and the snow drifting beyond the glass.

Hannah held out her hands to Andrew, not inviting but

insisting that he dance with her. He groped his way to his feet as if he was hypnotized and at once Hannah's arms snaked around him. Her head rested on his shoulder and her eyes closed.

'Dance, all of you,' she said.

Michael's limbs had connected themselves again, and he leaned across to Janice.

'Will you?'

He had wanted to dance with Hannah; he was amazed to discover how much he had wanted to dance with her when she had chosen Andrew.

Janice's silky robe swished as she uncrossed her legs and stood up.

She half stumbled, because she had drunk plenty of the wine at dinner, but Michael caught her hand. Her loose sleeves fell back, baring her pretty, rounded arms to the elbows as she made a mock-subservient offer of herself to him.

Michael took hold of her and as they began to dance she came closer, and he let his hands slide down over the soft stuff masking her back. She felt much bigger than Marcelle and there were pads of flesh on her shoulders and over her hips; confusingly the ampleness of her became identified with the image of Hannah dancing that he carried behind his eyelids. The perfume of Janice's hair and skin caught in his throat and nose, making him think that he would sneeze.

Past the swaying bodies of the other couples Darcy saw Marcelle sitting awkwardly in her place. Her head was up, but something in the stiffness of her posture betrayed her unhappiness. He left his place and edged past the dancers, feeling as he had done earlier that his own body had grown too bulky to manoeuvre properly.

'Marcelle?'

'You don't have to be kind, Darcy.'

The expression in her eyes made him suddenly angry with Hannah for doing this. It was her way of demonstrating her displeasure with him, of course, and she would not bother to consider beyond that.

'It isn't a kindness,' he said roughly.

When he took them between his, Marcelle's surprisingly small, cold hands reminded him of a little boy's, of Barney's years ago when he had come in from playing in a wintry garden. She felt brittle, too, as they moved together, unfamiliarly light and dry, quite unlike Hannah or Vicky, and tall, so that her eyes were almost level with his.

They danced clumsily together, and to smooth over this and to turn the moment to advantage against Hannah, Darcy pressed his cheek against Marcelle's, and then found the corner of her mouth with his own. He heard the small catch of breath in her throat, and opened his mouth to kiss her. As he did so he noticed that with Hannah's limbs wound around him Andrew had begun to look like a rabbit caught in the headlights of a car, and that Janice and Michael danced with their eyes shut, heads close together, seemingly unaware of anyone else.

He brought his attention back to the business in hand, that of kissing Marcelle. She was the opposite physical type to the one that attracted him, but there was an interesting novelty in exploring the contours of her lips and face. He moved his face, rubbing himself against her, but Marcelle neither responded to him nor removed herself. He had the impression that her eyes were open and she was looking away somewhere beyond him.

Another track began, slower than the last, and the three couples swayed and circled. The fire had burnt down to a red glow, and the room had grown dimmer.

Darcy wondered if they were going to continue with this, if the clinches would get closer and if they would slip away, each pair in turn, to bedrooms that did not contain their own clothes that had been folded and packed at home in Grafton. The scenes played themselves in his head, while he went on slowly circling with Marcelle Wickham and nuzzling her motionless face. He tried to work out what he would do, who would make the first move. The bizarreness of these imaginings, together with the possibility that they might become reality, made him speculate whether the ordinary old procedures of marriage and friendship were about to change, and to move in new and uncontrollable directions as his business life was doing. His heart began its uncomfortable thumping again, and he felt a small, needling pain in his chest.

Somewhere else in the chalet, from somewhere over their heads, someone began to scream.

Darcy thought for an instant that the sound might be to do with the sensations within him, but the three couples froze and then broke apart. They were blinking, momentarily bewildered and embarrassed. The screaming stopped, broken off short with a different cry, and then there was a long second's silence followed by a loud thump. The parents heard the sound of a child's bare feet running overhead.

'Who is it?' Marcelle cried.

Janice was already on her way to the door, with Michael behind her. The others heard panicky feet thudding down the stairs. A moment later William Frost appeared in the doorway with Janice swooping to catch him. His face was flushed and wet with tears and his round eyes stared only half-seeing at the semicircle of adults.

'A dream,' he sobbed. 'Terrible dream.'

Janice put her arms around him and smoothed his pudding-basin of blond hair.

'It's all right,' she murmured, 'I'm here. Only a dream, nasty old dream.'

They made way for her to lead him to the sofa, stumbling a little in adjusting to this different focus, no longer quite catching each other's eyes. Janice sat down and hugged William and Andrew leant over him.

'It'll go away, Will. You're awake now. He's been having these dreams,' he explained to the others.

Hannah pushed her hair back from her face, gathering it up with one hand into a bunch at the nape of her neck. Michael looked at the crescent of white skin that was momentarily exposed, and then made himself bend down to see William Frost instead.

'Poor old chap,' he said pleasantly. He felt the child's forehead and then ran his fingers lightly under his jaw. 'Nothing to worry about, I'm sure. Some hot milk, perhaps?'

'I'll do it,' Hannah said. With her hair pulled back, in the changed atmosphere, she appeared almost matronly. Marcelle sat down in her old place, and Darcy went to the table where the whisky bottle was waiting. Someone turned off the music and the room became bright and ordinary, as it had been at the evening's beginning.

Janice sat on the edge of the bed to take off her slippers, and then slid sideways into the warmth under the covers. She reached to turn off the light, then curled herself beside Andrew.

'Are you asleep?' she asked. She had waited up to make sure that William had settled down properly again.

'Not quite. Is Will all right?'

'I think so.'

Out of habit Janice listened for the ticking of their bedside clock, as she always did in the intervals of their night-time conversations, then remembered that they were not in their own bedroom. The evening had left her with a knot of anxiety that she knew would keep her awake.

'What were you doing with Hannah?'

Andrew sighed. 'What was Hannah doing with me, don't you mean?'

'Is there a difference?'

'Of course there is. She was trying to make some point for Darcy's benefit, I suppose. Whatever it was, do we have to analyse it now?'

'You didn't look as if you minded.'

'I didn't. That was then, and now is now and here we are in bed, my love, and it's time to go to sleep.'

He settled the hard French pillow under his head, offering more of himself to her as he did so, but it was as a comforting gesture, without any suggestion of sex.

Janice mumbled to him, with her face pressed against the

warmth of his shoulder, 'Do you mind that I don't look like Hannah?'

'What? Certainly not. What do you think I want? Anyway, in a couple of years Hannah will look like you.'

She waited in the absence of the clock's ticking for Andrew to realize what he had said, and when he did not she was nearly angry.

Then she understood that he was sliding into sleep, and she knew that it was easier not to have an argument than to wake him up and insist on one. She found suddenly that she was smiling, out of affection for his clumsiness and relief that the evening had harmlessly ended.

Marcelle lay on her back and stared up into the darkness. She was thinking about the separate wooden cubes of the chalet rooms stacked above and below her, and of the walls that separated the couples from each other, two by two.

Michael was breathing evenly beside her. She was not certain that he was asleep, but when she had put out her hand to touch his side he had made no response. That was the pattern now. If one of them was awake the other was asleep, or seemed to be.

She turned away from him, on to her side, and began to think about the evening. It was Hannah who had set it off, but Marcelle knew that she had only been the trigger. Since the day she had seen Gordon and Nina together at the level crossing she had known that the possibility of collapse, of the destruction of their tidy lives, lay quietly just beneath the surface of these featureless days. Dissatisfaction and the desire for change, for the sharpness of some new feeling, whether pleasure or pain, was like a virus that had reached Grafton with Nina Cort. The virus must spread, Marcelle thought, whichever direction it took.

She put her hand to where Darcy's mouth and cheek had rubbed against hers. She could still taste the whisky from his tongue.

She closed her eyes, willing sleep to come.

If it had been Jimmy, Marcelle thought. If it had been Jimmy, tonight, what would I have done then?

She was not certain, but she thought that she might have clung to him, and begged him to rescue her.

Hannah put on the oyster-grey silk robe that matched her pink and grey lace and silk nightgown, and loosened her hair from the bunch she had tied at the nape of her neck. Standing in front of the small square of mirror fixed to one wall, she examined her reflection. She gave it her full attention, knowing that by doing so she was avoiding the necessity of thinking about less pleasant things. She spread her hair over her shoulders, admiring the way it rippled over the sheen of the silk.

Not bad, Hannah thought. Not bad for thirty-four, after having had two children. Better than Vicky Ransome, anyway.

She had seen the way Andrew and Michael had looked at her. It had given her a wonderful surge of power, to switch on the magnetism and see that it worked. The pleasure of their admiration stayed with her, energizing her. She lifted her chin, and met her own eyes in the mirror. There had been a time, when she and Darcy had met and fallen in love, when Darcy had looked at her like that every time she came near him.

But it was not all bad. Whatever Darcy thought, whatever he thought he wanted, the truth was still partly palatable. She was still objectively desirable.

She watched the reflection of her mouth, and saw how the corners of it had begun to take on a downward curl. She made herself smile, reversing the expression.

Darcy came out of the box of a bathroom and walked across to the bed without glancing in her direction. He took off his robe and lay down in his pyjamas, easing himself into the unfamiliar bed. Watching him, as he turned on to his side and his body slackened under the sheets, Hannah realized that he looked heavy and old. She felt a quick and surprising beat of sympathy, as she might have done for her father, or for Freddie if he was unhappy or ill.

She turned out the lights and got into bed beside her husband. Carefully, she fitted herself against the loose curve of his back. Then she edged her arms over and under him. She waited, acknowledging to herself and waiting for Darcy's acknowledgement that the evening had excited her. Darcy did not pull away, but he did not respond either.

Hannah whispered against the meaty slab of his shoulder, 'Come on, come to Mummy.'

Darcy turned over then.

He did not say anything, but he put his hands under her nightdress and spread them over her breasts.

Hannah pulled him closer, needing to exact another tribute from the evening. Without saying anything more to each other they went through the customary agenda of their love-making.

Afterwards, when they lay side by side again, Darcy said to the empty space over his head, 'I didn't very much like what you did this evening.'

Hannah made a small sound in her throat, not quite a laugh. 'Were you jealous?'

'No, not at all. The opposite. I didn't like the way what you did affected Marcelle, and Janice.'

'I'm sure they understood. Women do understand these things, don't they? They have to.'

'What is that supposed to mean?'

Hannah felt the sudden tension in him. It made his arm and leg quiver, tiny shivers that were transmitted to her own warm limbs. She felt the charge of power again, this time the power that her knowledge gave her. She chose her words with pleasurable care.

'It means what I said. Women have to understand what their husbands do. Their little lapses, their small betrayals and the lies that don't quite cover them up. They have to look on, don't they, and pretend not to see, or not to mind? It's kind of you to feel for Janice and Marcelle. But why doesn't your ready sympathy extend to me? Or is it used up on poor, poor Vicky?'

'On Vicky?'

'Yes, on Vicky. Alone in that house with her lovely, innocent baby girls, without her wicked, unfaithful husband.'

'Hannah –'

'Don't *Hannah*, with all your pretend bewilderment. I know you're fucking Vicky. What else would you be doing on the mornings your car is trying to hide itself in her driveway? Advising her on her investments? Why did you think *you* could get away with it, in a place the size of Grafton, when Gordon and his widow woman couldn't?

'Linda Todd who lives opposite the Ransomes is a customer of mine. She couldn't wait to tell me how many times she's seen you there. I drove past myself, just to check. Including the day you said you were going to Bristol.'

Darcy said calmly, 'There's no reason why I shouldn't call on Vicky. She does need advice, as it happens. That doesn't mean I'm sleeping with her.'

Hannah drew away from him so she could no longer feel the quivers under his skin. She said softly and finally, 'But you are, Darcy, aren't you?'

'What can I say to convince you otherwise, as you seem to have made up your mind?'

'Nothing, darling. We were talking about what women are obliged to understand. I'm not going to worry about Janice and Marcelle because their husbands can't take their eyes off my backside.'

Hannah turned over. She was surprised to find that she was sleepy, that her body felt pleasantly warm and heavy. She had told Darcy what she knew and there was nothing else she wanted to say. He didn't speak again, and after a few minutes Hannah drifted into sleep.

Darcy lay awake for much longer. He was thinking about Vicky.

Apart from a handful of trivial lapses that were easy enough to discount, Darcy had been faithful to Hannah ever since their marriage – until a month ago.

*

After Vicky had locked Gordon out of their house she had stayed alone with the children for a night and half a day. And then, emerging from a daze of distress and needing to talk about what was happening to her, she had telephoned Hannah at Wilton. Only on that day Hannah had gone to her shop to make everything ready for her post-Christmas sale, and it was Darcy who answered the telephone.

'I'll come over,' he said at once.

In the Ransomes' house he found a litter of toys and children's detritus underfoot, a half-eaten meal on the kitchen table, a broken-down central heating boiler and Vicky in her dressing gown with Helen in her arms.

Darcy had tidied up some of the mess and called out his own central heating repair man. He had made tea and toast for Vicky, fed the older children and found the whisky bottle. The business of creating order for her had filled him with happy energy and he whistled softly as he worked.

Vicky watched Darcy moving around her house.

'It seems that I can't manage on my own,' she said sadly.

'Yes, you can,' Darcy told her.

Neither of them mentioned Christmas Eve in Hannah's bedroom. But when it was time to feed the baby he saw the tender and businesslike way that Vicky settled herself to the task, and it tightened some string inside him that pulled at his heart. He reached out and with the tips of his fingers he brushed her cheek. The colour came into her face, but she kept her eyes fixed on the baby in her arms.

Darcy left her with the name and telephone number of his London solicitor, and promised to come back the next day.

It was not very long before all the couples in the Grafton circle knew Vicky had turned Gordon out.

The wives visited or telephoned her, offering their different versions of support and advice, but it was Darcy she looked forward to seeing. She knew that he came unknown to Hannah, and his secret presence in the house seemed to change the quality of it for her – the light in the rooms became sharper and brighter, and the weight of her anxiety dropped away to leave her feeling calm and decisive. When she told him this Darcy laughed and said that Hannah would say the opposite about him at Wilton, but Vicky could see that he was pleased.

Gordon telephoned constantly, from his office and then from the hotel, but Vicky told him that she did not want to see him until she had had more time to think. As the days passed her first hot anger with him curdled into weary disappointment, but she held firm, telling him that she did not want him to come back yet. She surprised herself with the strength of her own resolution.

One morning, after Gordon had been away for two weeks, Darcy came to visit Vicky, leaving his Range Rover parked to one side of the house where it was hidden from the road by a screen of evergreens. It was a clear day, and as she went to let him in Vicky saw in the changed angles of the shadows the first intimation of spring.

Darcy sat at her kitchen table while she made coffee for him. The older girls were at school, Helen was asleep in her cot and there was a thick, expectant silence in the house. Vicky turned to the table with his cup in her hand, and when she had put it down she hesitated beside him.

'I'm very grateful,' she told him. She meant for the solace of his company, as well as for the practical advice he had given her.

Darcy reached out and took her hand and she looked down gravely at him. He remembered in that instant that he had imagined himself in love with her, as well as wanting to take her to bed. He stood up, and she did not move when he held her by the shoulders and kissed her. She smelt of baby scents, innocent soap and milk.

'Come upstairs with me,' Darcy said.

The double bed was unmade, with lacy pillows tumbled on the floor and the quilt still rucked in the contours of her solitary sleep. Standing beside the bed Darcy unbuttoned her loose shirt, and rediscovered her distended breasts and the curves of her belly marked with pregnancy. She made a move to cover herself with her hands but he pushed them aside and knelt so that he could follow the silvery lines with his eyes and the tips of his fingers.

'Vicky.' He said her name to himself, confirming their arrival together, here and now.

Her hands rested on his head, and she stroked his hair absently, almost maternally.

'Take your clothes off too,' she said. 'Then I won't feel so exposed. I'm ashamed of the way I look these days. I wish I was thin and tight-skinned, like Nina. I wish I had long legs like knitting needles, and no tits. That must be what Gordon wants.'

'It isn't what *I* want. I want you. Look at you.' He weighed her breasts in his hands, and saw that a colourless bead of liquid appeared at the brown nipples.

'Take your clothes off, then,' Vicky said again. 'Before Helen wakes up.'

He loved this brisk practicality in her. Hannah liked the transactions of sex to be swathed in the ribbons and tulle of romance, even after seven years of marriage.

Vicky helped him to undress, putting his clothes tidily to one side as he discarded them. She thought that for a handsome man he had a surprisingly ugly body. His chest and shoulders were covered in thick grey hair and the muscles of his stomach must recently have given way because when he was not holding it in his belly coyly protruded as if it were not quite part of him. His small, thick penis looked like some hairless burrowing rodent. When he took her in his arms the grey pelt crinkled minutely against her skin.

They lay down together in her bed, and while one part of her mind was occupied with the attentions that Darcy required, the rest of it seemed free to wonder if this act was revenge against Gordon, or if it was something she had wanted for the sake of itself.

It was startling to discover that Darcy was not such an adept lover as her own husband.

He came quite quickly, very noisily, and the detached part of her remained untouched and unaroused, dreamily watching this scene as if it were nothing to do with her. She wondered what it could be that Hannah liked, and it came to her in a moment of pure perception that Hannah liked herself – it was her own vanity that gave her her habitual glow, and Darcy functioned as a suitably impressive mirror to reflect her back at herself. The certainty of this insight lessened Vicky's guilt.

'You didn't do that out of gratitude, did you?' Darcy asked afterwards. They had been lying with their arms around each other, separately contemplating the room and his presence in it.

'No. I did it because I wanted to.'

That was the truth. For the two weeks that Darcy had been visiting her she had known it would happen, and she had been waiting for it, neither putting it off nor willing it to come.

'Will you let it happen again?'

'Yes,' Vicky said, because she knew that she would.

And so Darcy had called on her the next morning, and the one after that. On the third morning, after they had made love, she found herself examining his blunt, handsome face on the pillow in Gordon's place. There were creases and pouches in it that she could not remember noticing before.

'You look tired.'

'I don't sleep well, at the moment.'

'Are you worried about something? About business?'

He was startled by her percipience. Hannah never asked him about his work.

'There are some investments I have made on behalf of other people that haven't performed as I hoped they would.'

Her clear eyes gazed into his. 'Is it serious?'

'No,' Darcy said.

'Do you want to talk to me about it? Would it help?'

'It wouldn't be very interesting for you.' With the tip of his forefinger he touched the hollow of her throat. 'And it isn't very important, because it is easily put right.'

'That's good.' Vicky smiled, and it touched him to see her relief. He kissed her, and burrowed deeper into the warmth and safety of the bed.

*

It was another two weeks before Vicky answered one of Gordon's telephone calls and heard him say,

'Won't you let me come home? I miss the girls. I miss you.'

It was the middle of the morning, the safe, domestic time that she had always liked and which had lately come to belong to Darcy's visits, or to the possibility of a visit. She looked at her kitchen, seeing the cups and plates in glass-fronted cupboards and hearing the industrious thrum of the washing machine and the dishwasher.

This is the life Gordon and I made, she thought, seeing it as a once-clear picture now confusingly cross-hatched with images of Nina and Darcy.

The few hours that she had spent with Darcy had been stolen, and retaliatory, but they had also woken her out of some stale, isolated maternal trance. She felt grateful to Darcy, and under his spell like some narcissistic girl newly and shallowly in love, but she also felt strong. She was suddenly sure that she was much, much stronger than Gordon.

Vicky looked down at her hand, with her engagement and wedding rings, and extended her fingers for her own pleased contemplation as if she had just had a manicure.

'Yes,' she said. 'All right. I'd like you to come home.'

She had told Darcy the same day, 'I said he could come back.'

'Is that what you want?'

After a moment she had answered, 'Yes. I was angry with him, but I'm not any longer.' She touched his hand gently. 'Doing what you and I have done has made me less . . . less censorious of Gordon. Do you mind that?'

'How could I? What about you and me? May I still see you?'

'Like Gordon seeing Nina, do you mean?'

'Yes, I suppose I do mean like that.'

He had heard the smile in her voice before he met her eyes and saw it. 'I don't know. I'm not sure. But you know where I am, and I know where you are. Is that enough, for the time being?'

'I suppose it will have to be,' he had answered. Darcy had felt slow, and out-manoeuvred, and he had also felt hurt. He remembered again that at Christmas he had momentarily imagined himself to be in love before dismissing the idea with a coarser intention.

He had been right the first time, Darcy thought. His mistakes seemed now to multiply in thickets around him.

Later, in Méribel, Darcy carried the telephone to the window as he dialled her number, and stood staring across the balcony to the sunny slopes while he listened to the ringing tone.

'Hello?'

'Hello.'

He did not need to identify himself, that was an acknowledgement of their intimacy, but there was an infinitesimal pause before Vicky said,

'Darcy? Is that you? Is something wrong?'

'Why do you think there's something wrong because I've called you?'

'You're on holiday with Hannah and Freddie . . . I didn't expect to hear from you.'

He looked out at the skiers, coloured matchstick people zigzagging in the sunshine. Everyone was out in the snow, except for him.

'I wanted to talk.'

'Oh. Well, do you know what's happened? I'm going back to work part-time. I had a call yesterday from the director of therapy at the centre, and they need someone to take on a limited caseload, just two or three days a week, and I talked it over with Gordon last night and we agreed that I should do it. I've got to find someone to come in and take care of Helen . . .'

Darcy listened to her plans, leaning against the window glass with the telephone crooked under his chin. There was snow on the balcony floor, and a white rim in the rustic cut-outs and on the curved rail of the wooden balustrade. The light danced and sparkled, hurting his eyes.

'That's good, I'm glad,' he heard himself say. He felt dirty and creased in the sunshine, full of a weariness that seemed to spread all through him, and weak as a child in comparison with Vicky's procreative strength.

'Why *did* you call?' she asked him at last.

It was too much of an effort to dissemble.

'I talked to Hannah last night. Or, rather, she talked to me. Someone called Linda Todd, who lives opposite you, has been monitoring my movements. Does that sound likely?'

'Yes. Shit. Yes, it does. What exactly did Hannah say?'

'Not much. It was more what she did. A bit of a dance, not quite a striptease, for the benefit of Michael and Andrew, and a warning shot for me at the same time. It stirred up the passions a bit.'

'I can imagine.'

Vicky knew how it would have been. Hannah dancing, lit up with pleasure at herself. She had been friends with Hannah for a long time, and she wondered if she liked her at all. She said quietly, so quietly that he had to think for a moment before he was sure that he had heard her correctly,

'I think you and I have come to the end of the road, Darcy.'

'This particular road, perhaps. For now,' he said, wishing that he could contradict her.

A moment later they had said goodbye, and he replaced the receiver in its cradle.

Darcy slid open the glass door and stepped out on to the balcony. The cold air caught in his throat. He leaned on the balcony rail, and looked across at the nearest slope. Suddenly he saw Hannah in her silvery ski suit with its fur-trimmed hood, and Michael Wickham in navy-blue that appeared black at this distance. Their ski teacher made a series of fluent turns, and Hannah and Michael obediently followed him.

Hannah had improved, Darcy noticed.

She lifted her arms in triumph and waved her poles as she completed the last turn. Michael punched the air in front of him in laughing acknowledgement of their achievement.

Eleven

All through this time, the work on the west front of the cathedral went on behind the contractors' screens of scaffolding and tarpaulins.

One afternoon in February Nina stood at a corner of the green, where a gap in the coverings offered a narrow view of one column of saints and archangels. The stone figures in their niches were enveloped in dust or swathed in dingy protective coverings, and workmen passed in front of them with plaster-coated tools and buckets. Watching them, Nina could not imagine how the details of folded hands and serene stone faces could ever be recovered from this desecration.

The wind was cold. At length, wrapping her arms around herself, Nina turned away from the cathedral front and began slowly to cross the green. She would have liked to go on in through the west door, to look at the columns and arches of the interior, but she did not. Ever since Christmas she had avoided the cathedral, because it was associated with Gordon. She had been afraid to begin with that she might meet him there, and so be thought guilty of pursuing him. Lately she had simply preferred to keep away from the places that were most closely connected with him in her mind, because she missed him and it was easier to spare herself this much.

When she reached the opposite, sheltered side of the green she saw a woman sitting on one of the benches that bordered it. The woman was wearing a flamboyant long mackintosh made of some light, banana-coloured material. She was watching Nina coming towards her, and eating a sandwich. Nina recognized Star Rose.

'Hello,' Star said, in her cool voice. 'I heard on the bush telegraph that you'd left and gone back to London.'

Nina hesitated. Of the Grafton couples, she had seen only Janice and Hannah since Christmas and those meetings had been accidental. The women had not been unfriendly, but just as it had been easier for Nina to avoid the places that were connected in her mind with Gordon, so it had also been her choice not to meet his friends, and Vicky's.

'I did go back for a time. But I'm here again now. This is where I live.'

She had spent almost three weeks staying in the Spitalfields house with Patrick, but it had become increasingly hard to ignore the truth that she had left London for Grafton to escape the memories of one man, and had then fled back to London for the same reason and a different man. Patrick had not tried to hide his concern.

'You can't flit to and fro for ever, you know, running away from yourself and imagining you can leave your losses behind you like last year's overcoat.'

'I know that,' Nina said humbly. 'I'll go back to Grafton to confront myself, shall I, and wear the coat until the better weather comes?'

He took her hand, and she rested her head against his shoulder for a minute.

'You know you can stay here as long as you like,' Patrick said.

But in the end Nina had come home. In any case she had work to do, and needed her studio.

Star screwed up her sandwich paper. 'I'd offer to share my lunch with you, but that was it. We could go and have a cup of coffee in the cloister, if you like. I am as free as air, it being half term.'

Surprised, and pleased by the suggestion, Nina said, 'Yes. All right. Let's do that.'

Star stood up, brushing the sandwich crumbs from her

raincoat. A pair of pigeons swooped down on them. The two women began to walk towards the cathedral.

'Where do you teach?' Nina asked. She had met Star a number of times, but it had always been at dinners or at parties or with permutations of the Grafton couples.

'Williamford. Modern languages.'

Williamford was the big mixed comprehensive that had been created after Nina's time by an amalgamation of her girls' grammar with the boys' school where Andrew Frost had gone.

'I went to the Dean's School.'

'Did you? Oh yes, Andrew said something about it. We still use the same buildings, you know. Very inconvenient they are, too.'

There had been red-brick classrooms with tall Victorian windows that let in thin coils of fog in the winters, and concentrated the sun's heat in the short summers. Nina remembered the old-fashioned desks and blackboards and the sharp fins of the green-painted radiators.

'I should think it's very different now.'

'Should you? You'd probably find it's much the same. Who used to teach you French?'

'Mr Jenkins. Gawaine Jenkins, that was his name.'

Filaments of memory unwound in her head. Mr Jenkins had been an awkward, unpopular teacher with a half-guessed at, unhappy private life.

'He retired last year. I took over from him as head of the department.'

It was as if Star had tied a tiny, invisible knot, fixing Nina within Grafton again in a mesh of people and the rubbed, familiar places of her childhood. She had not thought of Mr Jenkins for more than fifteen years, but now she heard his thin, correct voice reading from Molière and saw the reddened wings of his nose and the ancient corduroy jacket he wore every day to face the ordeals of his classroom.

'Just hearing his name makes me feel seventeen again.'

Star hunched her angular shoulders inside the yellow raincoat.

'I feel seventeen most of the time. If some gang of kids runs in the corridor at school I start running too, then I have to rein myself in and make myself shout at them.'

Nina laughed. 'You don't sound like Mr Jenkins. The children must like you.'

'Most of them do,' Star answered in her dry fashion.

They had crossed to the side of the cathedral and went through an archway into the cloister. One side of it had been glassed in to make a combined bookshop and tearoom for visitors. Nina and Star passed by the stands of books on cathedral history and architecture, and the displays of teatowels and leather bookmarks with their pictures of the west front, and came to a long, glass-fronted counter displaying dishes of salads and quiche and flapjacks and wholemeal scones, and a row of refectory tables with bench seats. Most of the places were occupied by pairs and trios of women, eating salad and talking

Star surveyed them. 'We could have gone to the Eagle and had a drink amongst the menfolk of Grafton.'

'This is fine,' Nina said quickly.

She bought two cups of coffee in thick pottery mugs and carried them over to an empty table. Star sat down, swinging her coat out behind her. She lit a cigarette and stared out at the yew tree in the middle of the cloister garth. Nina covertly examined her face. Star had high cheekbones and a wide mouth, and she wore her hair pushed back behind her ears and no make-up, which emphasized her bones and revealed the clarity of her skin. She was not in any way beautiful, but her height and her faintly inimical manner made her interesting.

After a moment Star looked back at Nina. She picked up her coffee mug and tilted it towards her in acknowledgement.

'Welcome home,' she said. 'I'm glad you haven't abandoned us.'

Nina was surprised and pleased again. Unguardedly she asked, 'What has everyone been saying?'

Star's eyebrows lifted. 'Everyone? I've no idea what *everyone* has been saying. I haven't read any reports about your love affair in the national press, or even in the *Grafton Advertiser*. If that's what you are asking about, of course.'

Nina felt her cheeks redden. She was irritated by the quick bite of sarcasm, but she also had to admit that she had probably deserved it. Solitude was making her focus too closely on her own concerns.

'Not everyone in that sense. I meant the coterie of Grafton couples into which I've made such a disastrous intrusion.'

Star smiled at that. 'Yes. I thought that was probably what you did mean. *Was* it disastrous?'

'In the sense that it caused pain, yes, it was.'

'Ah.' Star spooned brown sugar crystals into her coffee and then meditatively stirred. There was a silence, and then she said quietly, 'I've always thought that if I were going to have an affair with anyone else's husband, it would have been with Gordon.'

Nina thought that this conversation was moving too rapidly for her, or that she had somehow missed some crucial intervening pieces of it.

She said uncertainly, 'I didn't know that. I . . . have this impression of history, shared history, stretching back behind you all. Do you remember when you changed that toast at Janice's dinner party? You said, not just to friendship but to *loving* friendship. I was impressed, by that and by all of you so handsome and happy, and by the way that you seemed to affirm each other.'

Star shrugged, using what appeared to be a characteristic gesture.

'I'm such a romantic with a few glasses of wine inside me. There isn't any history stretching behind Gordon and me. Unfortunately.'

Nina remembered then, on that same evening while she had been talking to Darcy Clegg, that she had also covertly been watching Star and Gordon murmuring quietly together in a corner. She had thought at the time that perhaps Star was crying.

Star put out her cigarette and immediately lit another. It was after two o'clock and the pairs and groups of women were beginning to filter away, back to their offices and shops. A girl in a green overall was loading cups and plates on to a tray.

'What was he like?' Star asked.

Nina looked up, and their eyes met. It would have been easy to be affronted or disconcerted by the question, but this directness in Star and the simplicity of her manner appealed to Nina. It was as if she very much wanted to know the answer to her question, and trusted that Nina would understand why, and how.

Nina found that she did not even hesitate, but answered with the same simplicity.

'I suppose the word to describe him would be wholehearted. He gave himself with great enthusiasm, and I found that very touching as well as erotic. He was also very straightforward. Not unimaginative, but not particularly poetic either. He used words like fuck and dick, and in turn that made me say things, and do things, that I've never done before. I felt . . . unleashed.' After a moment she added, very softly, 'I suppose it was the best sex I have ever had.'

It was an unexpected solace to talk about him, after two months of trying to suppress even her passing thoughts. She realized that she could easily go on, might suddenly spill out across the refectory table every remembered detail.

Star nodded her head. She said sadly, 'Yes. I thought that was how he might be.'

They looked at each other again.

And then, unmistakably, Nina felt a thin, piercing shiver of some different awareness that was nothing to do with Gordon, but was directly between Star and herself.

For as long as it lasted she became acutely conscious of the contours of her hand resting against the wood grain of the table, the curl of smoke in the air over Star's head, the insistent rattle of cutlery and crockery behind them.

Star put out her hand and touched the tips of her fingers to Nina's hand.

'I'm sorry for you that it was painful.'

'It was. It is, but I deserved it. I should have known better,' Nina said.

'One never does know better.' Star lifted her hand again. 'It's like really being seventeen for ever.'

The tearoom, the table and cups and everything else slowly resumed their normal density. Nina said, 'I regret it more for Vicky's sake.'

'Do you? Do you think Vicky is blameless?'

Star did not wait for Nina's answer. She gazed round at the almost deserted tearoom and impatiently pulled the folds of her mackintosh closer as if to insulate herself from it.

'Shall we have a walk somewhere?'

Nina had planned to spend the afternoon working, but even as she began her refusal she changed her mind. Since coming back to Grafton she had resumed her solitary country walks, but now she discovered that she minded her solitude more. Sometimes she felt almost disabled by it as she followed the paths and lanes that wound around Grafton. But this afternoon Star had unexpectedly arrived in the middle of the empty landscape.

Nina wanted their talk to continue, because she wanted to see where it would lead. An intimacy had sprung up between them so quickly that it made her aware of how much she needed a woman friend in Grafton. She suspected Star needed a friend also.

They went out on to the green and walked away in the opposite direction from Dean's Row. Star walked briskly, with her head up and her hands in her pockets.

Their route took them along Southgate, the best street in Grafton. It was lined with the bow-fronted façades of eighteenth-century shops, Hannah Clegg's La Couture amongst them. There were no cars in Southgate. Shiny, black-painted bollards closed off either end of the street, and the city council in its civic pride had placed dark green and gold litter bins along the pavements and hung flower baskets from the arms of the Victorian lamp posts. The baskets had been planted for the winter with universal pansies and variegated ivies, and the trailing leaves were browned by the wind and lack of water.

Nina and Star walked down the middle of the cobbled street. Pedestrians with plastic shopping bags crossed between the bollards and fanned out towards the shops, and Nina scanned the people as they passed her. Every one of them looked respectable, even the youngest ones. They were dressed in muted colours and serviceable shapes as if they had been outfitted by the same civic department that was responsible for the tasteful liveries of the Southgate shopfronts. Not one of them looked as if a deviation from the routine path would be welcomed.

There was a prosperous, provincial solidity in Grafton that sometimes reassured her, and at other times did not.

Star was laughing.

'What's funny?' Nina asked.

'The tidiness of it. Tidy lives. That's what you were thinking, wasn't it?'

They came out into Bridge Street, where traffic flattened the polystyrene litter blown outside McDonald's.

'Something like that.'

'Grafton is tidy. Socially and emotionally tidy. Pain and passion are mostly kept well out of sight, especially by people like us. It's easy to sneer at it, but I rather like it. It's dignified.'

Darcy had tried to recruit her into a conspiracy of urban superiority against Grafton, Nina remembered.

'Why should you think that I would sneer at it? I came back to live here, so I must like it too.'

She was thinking about the handsome couples, who had at first seemed so smilingly enviable and secure in their comfortable houses, and the contradictions that wove around them now. Into her head at the same time came an image of the stone figures of the west front, blackened and pitted by the centuries, but still enduring.

'Not you, I didn't mean you,' Star said.

They were walking towards the river. Ahead of them, as they rounded a curve in the street, they could see the old bridge and

225

a pewter-coloured expanse of water. On the far bank were the playing fields and dim red-brick blocks of the Dean's School, now part of Williamford.

'What did you mean when you asked me if I thought Vicky was blameless?'

Star flicked a glance at her, a look that was speculative and amused and faintly malicious.

'Just that.'

'Oh. So, do I think that Vicky is to blame because I blithely started a hot affair with her husband while she was in hospital delivering their third baby by an emergency Caesarean?'

Nina saw the tiny contraction of the muscles around Star's mouth that gave away her hurt, and wondered for how long she had loved Gordon. No wonder Star liked Grafton for its bloodless dignity. She possessed exactly the same quality herself. Star would be good at suppressing her own pain and passion.

Nina said more sharply than she had intended, 'No, I don't think Vicky is to blame.'

'That's not what I asked you.'

Nina followed the thread of Star's insinuation.

'I see,' she said at last, unwillingly. And afterwards, 'Who is he, then?'

Star nodded, as if Nina were a slow pupil who had at last grasped something.

'Darcy.'

They had reached the point where the road turned parallel with the river. Iron railings separated the road from a path that ran beside the water under the naked branches of willow trees. The river was swollen and little crusts of yellowish foam eddied in the current and were caught in the twiggy debris beside the bank.

'How do you know?' Nina asked automatically.

'I know because I've heard. Small towns don't keep secrets for long. As you discovered.'

'Yes. I did, didn't I?'

They had crossed the bridge, and as if they were acknowledging that they had left Grafton behind they stopped to stand shoulder to shoulder, looking back at it. The cathedral's twin towers rose over the steps of rooftops, sombre against the graphite sky.

'Does Hannah know?'

'Oh, I should think so. I'm sure she's reeling in his line. Hannah may never have read a book in her life and she may also think Wittgenstein's a ski resort, but she's not a fool. She has Darcy placed exactly where she wants him, whatever the old poseur may imagine to the contrary.'

'And Gordon?'

'I don't think Gordon knows.'

To assimilate this information Nina leaned against the limestone pillar that marked the end of the bridge.

As her cold fingers rubbed the gritty stone she remembered that it was exactly here that she had been kissed for the first time. There was a triple-globed ornamental lamp mounted on the pillar, one of four put up by the people of Grafton to commemorate the Coronation, and when the boy had put his arms around her and begun to rub his mouth against hers she had been afraid that they were too clearly visible in the pallid circle of light. She had also been afraid that he would rub away the coat of white lipstick she had applied in the school cloakroom and expose the babyish rosebud of her real mouth. They had been on the way home from the third-year Christmas party in the Williamford hall, but Nina couldn't recall anything about the boy except his name, and the amalgamated taste and smell of Clearasil.

The realization that more than twenty years had elapsed since that night, the conviction that nothing in Grafton had changed, and the news that Star had just given her, combined as a tremor in the back of Nina's throat that forced its way forward and emerged between her teeth as a spurt of laughter.

She saw Star's expression, the mixture of amusement and malice and cleverness in it, and then Star began to laugh too.

'It's funny,' Nina explained.

'You're right. It's so funny that it hurts.'

They leant against the limestone pillar, oblivious to the passing traffic, until they stopped laughing. And then they turned their backs to Grafton and walked on, newly comfortable with one another.

'I don't know why I've marched us out here,' Star remarked. 'Force of habit, I suppose.'

They had come to the school gates. They were locked, but there was an old man in an overall beyond them, dispiritedly brushing long-dead leaves from the tarmac drive.

'Hello, Ted,' Star called to him.

'Afternoon, Mrs Rose. Can't you keep away from the bloody place, then?'

Nina stood with her fists locked on the railings, like a convict, gazing into the grounds. The line of trees that had marked the far boundary were gone; she supposed that they must have been elms. There was a new housing estate on the slope beyond where there had once been farmland. Threads and snippets of unimportant memories swam and merged in her head.

'Mrs Cort's an old girl of the school, Ted. Can we slip inside so she can have a look around?'

This was so much what Nina wanted without even having expressed it to herself that she stared at Star in surprise.

'Can't let you in the building, Mrs Rose, it'd be more than my job's worth. But I'll open these gates for you, if your friend wants a stroll round.'

Star and Nina walked up the driveway to the Victorian red-brick slabs of the building. At the nearest window Nina leaned on the sill, shading her eyes to look in at the rows of desks. As soon as she saw the shape of the room she immediately became the fomenting schoolgirl she had once been, full of dreams and illusions, unwillingly hunched over her work. The exercise books they used had had stiff grey covers and Nina had drawn all over them, obsessively creating derivative op-art designs and then filling in the divisions and subdivisions with her black pen, as if she could reduce the confusions of adolescence to mosaic patterns.

'It's all different, furniture, colours, everything, but it's still exactly the same. This was the geography room.'

It had smelt of hot dust from the radiators, and chalk, like the other classrooms, but also of the sticky, oiled canvas of the big old-fashioned maps that hung on the walls. The room had had a soporific hum that made it difficult to stay awake in there on warm afternoons.

These shreds of recollection knitted together. Their coalescence was painful because the life that had contained them was gone, but the revival of so many tiny memories made Nina feel suddenly that she had her place here in Grafton more securely than anywhere else she had ever lived, even with Richard. She knew that her instinct to return had been the right one, even to this mutating city of car parks and micro-industries and modern couples.

'My theory is that the essence of a place never changes,' Star said. 'Because it is to do with the layers of time and experience variously contained within it, not the colour of the walls or the style of the furnishings.'

'I don't know if your theory would stand much analysis. But I know exactly what you mean. It's rather comforting, isn't it?'

They began to walk around the outside of the building, stopping to look in through the tall windows.

Now Nina could recall the shiny tiles of the corridors and the submerged green of the cloakrooms and the beams and arches and echoes of voices as vividly as if she had left them behind only yesterday. She felt that she was linked to Star by their separate paths through the same high classrooms, and as they reached their starting point again she put her arm through Star's so that they walked in step.

'Enough?' Star asked.

'Yes. I liked seeing the place again. Thanks.'

'It wasn't difficult to arrange.'

Ted let them out into the road again, and morosely locked the gates behind them. Nina and Star turned back towards the bridge. The sky was already darkening, leaving a faint outline of phosphorescent green around the roofs and chimneys and the cathedral towers.

Nina gazed ahead of her, measuring the familiarity of what she saw, the unfamiliar comfort of Star's arm linked through hers, and noticing how the thin, cold wind made her eyes smart. It came to her in that moment that she was content, not happy but content, as she had not been since the day of Richard's death.

As if their thoughts were common to each other, perhaps because as they came back into Grafton they remembered the couples, Star abruptly asked,

'Were you and your husband happy?'

'Yes, we were very happy.'

'Tell me what it was like.'

Just as she had asked about Gordon. Nina suddenly felt such a plaintive, bewildered need in Star Rose that she wanted to stop and hold her, to comfort her. She held her arm closer, as if that would do.

'What can I tell you? It was a marriage. A friendship, a contract, good and bad, like any other.'

They were on the bridge now, midway between the two pairs of commemorative lamps.

Star nodded, staring away over the parapet at the water.

'None of us can look into other people's marriages, can we? There is only our own, and the continual mystery of the rest.'

'Yes,' Nina said, knowing that was the truth. They walked on quietly together.

When they reached the Dean's Row house Nina asked Star if she would like to come in, but Star shook her head.

'I have to go. But can I see you again?'

The form of the question did not strike Nina as odd.

'Of course.'

'I'll call you, then.'

Star stepped forward, and they put their arms around each other and hugged. Then Star turned away and recrossed the green, walking briskly so that her long yellow coat flared out behind her.

In Méribel, as soon as it stopped snowing, the families zipped up their padded suits and clumped out into the white world to ski.

The children went to ski school, while the Frosts with Darcy and Marcelle set out every morning to conquer new and more distant peaks and steeper gullies. They came back each evening with pale circles printed by their sunglasses across their reddened faces, to sit around the dinner table and talk about how high and how far they had been, and how much farther and higher they planned to venture the next day.

On previous holidays the families had taken in their various permutations, there had never been such determined concentration on skiing. There had been longer lunches, and more hours spent sitting in the blade-bright sun. But this year, after the first evening, they were wary of each other although Andrew and Janice cheerfully acted as if nothing was different. Marcelle was quiet except when she was with her children, and Darcy was irritable. To gloss over the feeling of discord the four of them skied longer hours, and talked about it all evening.

By unspoken agreement the children were allowed to stay up later, and the extra exercise meant earlier nights for everyone. The threatening intimacy of the snowy chalet was dispelled.

Michael and Hannah were left out of this determined nucleus of the party because they could not ski so well. They took lessons every day with a private teacher, a lean-hipped French boy called Thierry who smoked Marlboro cigarettes on the chair lifts and wore his mirror-lensed sunglasses even inside the mountain restaurants.

Michael found that he looked forward to the moment every morning when Hannah appeared in her silvery suit, and they waited outside together for Thierry to ski down to them in a flurry of exhibitionist turns. Hannah was good-humoured and courageous throughout their lessons, and while Thierry flirted routinely with her it was Michael she turned to to share their small triumphs and the comedy of their failures. He was flattered, and pleased, and felt himself thawing out in her warmth. Even his joints seemed to loosen. His stiff knees flexed and to his surprise his turns became fluid and confident.

The two of them met up with the group of children for lunch, and Michael liked the easy way Hannah dealt with them. She let them order French fries and Cokes, found their missing belongings for them and marshalled them efficiently for the afternoon without making a difficulty of it, as Marcelle would have done.

'Do you know, I've even enjoyed having lunch every day with the bloody kids?' Michael said to her when they set off on the Friday afternoon. They were standing in a queue for a chair lift, with Thierry a little behind them because he had lingered to talk to a likely-looking girl. Hannah's face was framed in the silvery fur of her hood. She smiled, pausing in the act of rubbing some kind of cream into her lips. He could smell the fragrance of it.

'Why not? They're fun, aren't they? And think of the brownie points we've earned.'

She tipped her forefinger with a tiny extra peak of cream and then reached out and dabbed it on Michael's mouth. He was encumbered with his ski poles whereas Hannah had looped hers neatly over her forearm. She rubbed the cream in for him, following the lines of his mouth. Her face within the rim of fur was serious, concentrating. He had seen her perform the same service for Freddie.

Michael wanted to kiss her, but he transferred one ski pole to the other hand instead and in an awkward gesture put his arm around her. The skiers shuffled forward as the chairs scooped them away from the front of the queue. Hannah put her suncream away and zipped the pocket securely. She slid forward, holding her poles ready for the lift and he reluctantly lifted his arm to let her move freely.

Michael had not admitted as much, but he did not enjoy these lift rides. The empty space seemed to yawn nauseatingly under his encumbered feet and he was always relieved at the point at the opposite end when the chair sailed over the safety net and the bar lifted to allow him to slither forward and stand upright.

This was a three-seater chair but as the columns formed in the throat of the installation Michael saw that there were two trios ahead of them and no one on Hannah's other side. He was thinking, Good, we'll be on our own, as they stood at the barrier and then the little gates opened to admit them. They slid forward shoulder to shoulder, readying themselves and looking back at the chair as it rotated towards them.

Then there was some laughter and scuffling behind, and someone crashed through the third gate just as it was closing. A skier slithered hastily forward to the third position, almost falling as the chair swept behind them and caught all three of them off balance.

'Careful,' Hannah warned, her voice sounding sharp. There was more laughter following them and some jeering in French.

The three of them collapsed awkwardly into the chair and as it swept fast upwards Michael had to struggle to reach and pull down the safety bar. He managed to sit upright and place his skis on the footrests and saw that Hannah had worked herself into the right position too.

The chair sailed upwards over the snow-covered tops of some conifers and then a rocky gully. There was a pylon on the other side of the gully and the chair juddered as the cable passed over the rollers. They were swinging uncomfortably and Michael suddenly realized as he craned forward to see past Hannah that the third skier was rocking the chair because she was trying to rotate her legs from the side to the front. She had fallen into the seat sideways with her upper body twisted and her legs hanging out sideways. He caught a glimpse of a scared face, very young. She was a girl of perhaps fourteen, in a red and black ski suit.

'Sit still,' Hannah cried as the thin dark legs flailed wildly.

The girl's skis looked very long and heavy as they swung over the treetops.

'For God's sake,' Michael heard himself call out.

'She's slipping!' Hannah screamed. The chair lurched wildly.

It seemed that the girl was being dragged under the safety bar by some cruel invisible hand. Her mittened fists caught at the armrest and at Hannah's leg.

'*Je vais tomber*,' she cried. Her legs flailed again; Michael saw how the skis made arcs against the white slope.

They were over open ground now, a white piste a long way beneath them spiked with marker poles. It was steep, a black run.

Hannah threw herself sideways to try to catch at the girl. Her ski poles fell away as the chair bounced on the cable and confused voices shouted in French. There was a scream as the girl lost her precarious hold and Hannah clumsily fought to catch her wrist.

Then there was a terrible instant when the girl was sliding downwards, a blur of red and black and skis like scything blades, and after that a jolt that set their chair violently oscillating. Michael's head jerked backwards and his teeth snapped on his tongue; for an instant he was blinded by the pain.

When he could see and hear again there was more screaming and he saw that the girl had indeed fallen, but as she fell the hood of her suit had caught on the end of the opposite footrest.

Now she hung suspended by the neck over the empty windy space. Her head lolled forward and her slack body rotated a little, to the side and then back again. The lift had stopped.

Hannah had edged along the seat and was leaning down to her, her own body almost beneath the safety bar. Michael was swept by a suffocating wave of vertigo. His mouth was full of blood from his bitten tongue. His hand shot out involuntarily and clamped on Hannah's arm. The ground forty feet beneath them seemed to swing dizzily up into his face.

'Don't,' he choked. 'You'll fall. *Sit up.*'

'I've got to help her.'

Hannah knocked his hand away. Through the confusion of his fear Michael felt a kind of wondering admiration for her bravery. He looked upwards in order not to have to see the drop beneath them. In each of the chairs suspended ahead there were three white faces gazing back down at them. In the chair immediately behind there were three boys, the girl's companions. They were motionless, transfixed with fear. A long way down, still over the gully, Michael could see Thierry's red *moniteur*'s suit.

Hannah lowered her head as close as she could to the girl's.

'They'll come quickly,' Michael heard her say. 'Can you hear me? They'll come soon, I know they will.'

The red and black bundle stirred. The skis swung lazily, first one and then the other, up and down.

'Don't look down,' Hannah ordered. 'Look at me.'

Michael was amazed that the girl was alive. He had been imagining the cervical vertebrae, the functional purity of the bluish-white bone laid bare of skin and muscle tissue as he might have exposed it on the operating table; he was sure that her neck would have been broken. But she had slid rather than fallen, he recalled.

A group of skiers had collected on the piste below. Their upturned faces were like discoloured blotches on the snow. Two *pisteurs* in orange jackets arrived in the centre of the huddle. One of them held a short-wave radio to his mouth. Hannah looked back over her shoulder to Michael.

'How will they reach her?' she whispered.

'I don't know.'

Vertigo made him afraid that he would vomit or faint.

'What can we do?'

'Keep still. Nothing else.'

It was very quiet. A moment ago the air had been full of shouting.

Hannah turned away from him again. She was talking to the girl in a low, steady voice. He couldn't catch all the words.

'. . . can't speak French . . . all right . . . get your skis off . . .'

Amazingly, the girl responded. Her head lifted. They could see her face, grey-white, and black eyes sunken in their sockets. Her lips moved, but they couldn't hear what she said. Her eyes darted to one side, and they knew she was looking in her terror to see what was holding her suspended.

Hannah went on talking in her low, soothing voice. She told the girl that she couldn't fall, that she was securely held, that all she needed to do was wait until the rescuers came. The girl's eyes fixed on Hannah's face, and never moved.

A long time passed. Michael knew that it was a long time because he began to feel cold, and then the cold seeped into his bones. The group on the piste below swelled into a crowd. There was a flurry of coming and going but none of it seemed to relate to the three of them suspended in terrible isolation high above the snow. Michael tried to work out how long it would take for a helicopter to reach them, but he had no idea where rescue helicopters came from. He couldn't think why they didn't winch the chair slowly along to the next pylon, about fifteen yards ahead. Then he saw a man in a *pisteur*'s jacket climbing like a monkey up the ladder at the side of the pylon.

The girl began to swing her legs. The chair picked up the movement at once and began to swing too. Michael realized that she was trying to kick off her skis and nausea gripped at him again.

'*Non, non, attend,*' he heard Hannah's urgent murmur.

The climbing *pisteur* had reached the cable. He was wearing a webbing harness, and they saw him attach the harness to the cable and launch himself forward. He was winching himself slowly down towards them, swinging awkwardly past the two intervening chairs.

'He's coming, you'll be all right now,' Hannah's incantation continued. The girl was too numb and terrified even to turn her head.

With a sliding rattle down the length of the cable the man reached them. He had a brown face seamed like a walnut. At the sound of his French voice the girl detached her eyes from Hannah's at last and stiffly turned her head.

Michael could not work out how the girl could be freed and lifted to safety. There was a bag of tools suspended from the man's waist, but no second harness, and his own could not have accommodated two people. Then he saw something that made the ground begin to spin again.

236

The group of rescue workers below had been cutting free the big orange plastic-coated mattresses that padded the base of every pylon along the piste. They were heaping them into a pile directly below the chair.

Hannah saw it at the same time, and her head swivelled so that her eyes met Michael's. He snatched at her hand and imprisoned it under his arm as if it were Hannah the mattresses were waiting for.

The rescuer was calling out in rapid French to the people below. A stretcher on ski runners had materialized at the side of the piste. Then the man reached forward and down to the girl. He caught one of her legs and with a deft twist he freed the boot from the binding. One ski and then the other looped downwards to the snow.

Michael closed his eyes against his dizziness and in that instant the man had cut the girl free.

He heard Hannah gasp, and looked, and saw a blur of red and black falling and then not falling; the girl hit the heap of mattresses and they saw her roll, and her arms came up to cradle her head before she lay still again. Immediately she was surrounded by the rescuers.

Michael pulled at Hannah's arm. He knew that the force of his grip must be hurting her, but he could not release it. Very slowly she sat upright, and he held her as best he could.

The rescuer hauled himself up the cable in his harness and dropped into the empty place in the chair. He muttered in French and when he saw they didn't understand him he shrugged and looked away.

They didn't speak. They sat in the frozen silence of shock, watching the activity below them. At last the stretcher was brought across and made ready.

Then Michael said, 'She must be okay. If it was bad they'd be waiting for a helicopter to take her off.'

Hannah was visibly shuddering now. 'It was such a fall. She's only a young girl.'

'The mattresses broke the fall for her. Did you see her roll and cover her head? That's a good sign. She was conscious and probably her legs and back are all right.'

He heard himself offering this wisdom and good sense after the event, whilst in the crisis he had been hopeless and Hannah had bravely done everything she could. He was swamped with admiration for her.

'I think she is good.' The Frenchman stabbed his finger downwards.

The loaded stretcher was finally sped away. Michael and Hannah were both shaking with cold and reaction before the chair lift jolted again and their seat began to rise upwards on its mechanical progression.

At the top they stood to one side and watched the three boys who had been with the girl ski shakily away towards the point where she had fallen. Hannah's poles had gone, and they could do nothing themselves but wait for Thierry to reach them. Michael put his hands on Hannah's shoulders so he could look into her face.

'You were wonderful. Amazing.'

Hannah smiled, denying her white face and blue lips. 'I couldn't remember a single word of French. Nothing. I thought she was going to be killed.'

Michael drew her closer to him, rubbing her arms in an effort to warm her.

'All I could think of was that we were going to be killed along with her. And I'm supposed to be the doctor.'

'I know you don't like heights.'

He was amazed again. He didn't think he had given any sign, but somehow she had seen it, and understood it, and excused him. He felt safe and protected, like Freddie, and filled with love for her.

Thierry skied away from the chair and stopped beside them without any flashy display of his skills. He had even removed his sunglasses.

'That was bad, I think. I never have seen it happen before.

How is my 'Annah? And Michael? Perhaps we have a drink in the bar and then go home for today?'

'I think a drink would be a good idea,' Hannah said.

In the chalet they were the heroes of the evening. The news of the accident had already travelled around the bars and ski rooms, and the children and adults alike were entranced to come home and discover that Michael and Hannah had been so closely involved.

'Tell us all the details,' the Frost boys demanded. 'Was there any blood?'

'For God's sake,' Michael protested, but Hannah only laughed. She had bathed and changed, and either the colour had properly come back into her face or else she had skilfully applied some.

'None. I couldn't have handled that. Remember Barney's friend on Christmas Eve?'

Michael telephoned the Securité des Pistes, and managed to establish that the girl was in hospital in Moutiers, not badly hurt. He made a plan with Hannah to visit her the next day.

This good news was taken as reason for a celebration. Andrew went out and bought bottles of champagne, and even the chalet girl found herself able to smile as she served the dinner. Michael drank two glasses of whisky and two more of champagne and, as he had intended, became rapidly and pleasantly drunk. He embroidered Hannah's role and his own as a comic pantomime of bravery contrasted with abject terror. Everyone laughed, egging him on as he sprawled at the foot of the table. It pleased him to be the failure of the story, and to make Hannah even more the heroine. He looked at her, shaking her head at the opposite end of the table, and knew that nothing could be more pleasurable or desirable than to undress her, and hold her, and have her for himself.

He saw that Darcy was proud of Hannah, and that his own wife, his Marcelle, was looking at him for once without disapproval or anxiety. Michael sat up straighter and focused his eyes on the golden nimbus of the candle flames, and on Hannah's bright hair beyond them.

It was a good evening. The tensions of the first night seemed to have been forgotten, and Andrew and Janice laughed and nodded their relief and approval. The couples sat up later than usual, basking in the unexpected glow of shared happiness.

There was only a moment, when everyone was on the way to bed, when Michael wandered into the kitchen and found Hannah searching for mineral water in the fridge.

He went to her and put his arms around her waist as she stood with her back to him, feeling the breadth of her hips and the roundness of her backside against him.

'I'm a bit drunk,' he told her, with his mouth against her neck.

'I know.' She eased herself away, but smiling, indulgent with him.

He lifted her hand and turned it so that he kissed the pulse point inside her wrist.

'There,' he said tenderly. 'That's all.'

He stumbled to the door, and up the stairs to his bedroom and Marcelle's.

Marcelle was in bed, but with the bedside light on.

Watching him undress she said, 'You were nice tonight.'

'I am nice.'

'I know that.'

He groped his way across to her, and half fell on to the bed. Then he switched off the light before turning to her. He tried, but the buttons of her nightdress defeated him.

'Take that thing off.'

He heard the whisper of the sheets and flowered cotton and his wife's skin before she pressed herself into his arms.

He made love to her, feeling the familiar hollows and ridges of her. And all the time, as he did it, he was aware as if he was contemplating some magical photographic negative, guiltily and delightedly, of Hannah's silvery curves above and beneath and all around him.

Twelve

Barney Clegg stood back to admire his work, brushing the earth off his large hands on to the legs of his jeans.

'There. What do you think?'

Nina stood in the doorway to survey her tiny square of back yard. The early March sunshine felt warm on the top of her head, and Barney's opulent clumps of daffodils and grape hyacinths added to the brightness.

'I think it's the best instant garden I have ever seen.'

He had arrived in a van loaded with sacks of compost and pots and tubs of plants, and in the course of the morning had dug over and fed her patch of starved earth and filled it with splashy green shrubs and spring bulbs in full flower.

'I feel fraudulent, though.'

Barney raised his eyebrows at her. 'Why's that?'

'I haven't sprinkled the seed or hoed or watered.'

'Well, neither have I, exactly.'

'Where did the plants come from?'

He grinned. 'Don't ask. But it looks good, doesn't it?'

'It does. I shall come and sit out here and admire it, all summer long.'

'And think of me.'

Nina laughed. 'Of course. I'm very grateful, Barney. I'm not quite sure why you've gone to so much trouble.'

She was not sure, but she was glad to have her garden so deftly transformed. Nor would she have denied to herself that it had been a pleasure to sit on a kitchen stool pretending to be busy, and covertly watching him humming and digging out in the sunshine. Barney was comfortable in the open air.

'I promised I'd do it for you.'

'I didn't really expect you to keep such a rash promise.'

'I always keep my promises, actually.'

They were standing by the French doors into the kitchen. Barney was leaning on a spade, with his shirt sleeves rolled up. There was a rim of fresh earth around his wrists.

'Now I've offended you.'

'Not seriously. You could make amends with a cup of tea.'

She had offered one earlier, but Barney had told her he wanted to get the job finished first.

'Do you really want tea? Wouldn't you rather have a drink?' It was the middle of the afternoon, an indeterminate and featureless hour. The idea of a drink seemed appealingly decadent.

'Yes, I would rather, since you mention it.'

Barney followed her into the kitchen. He stood at the sink washing his hands while Nina foraged in cupboards. She put bread and cheese and fruit on the table, and poured two glasses of wine. The lush greenery outside kept catching her eye. The afternoon had mysteriously become an impromptu celebration.

'You'll have to teach me what these plants are, you realize. I only know the Christmas rose.'

The hellebore he had brought her on Boxing Day had been joined by two more. Their new leaves stood up from the earth like eagerly raised hands.

'Easy. There's *Choisya ternata, Fatsia japonica, Hedera* Goldheart and Ravensholst –'

'Stop. I'm lost already. My husband was the gardener.'

He hesitated. 'I'm sorry.'

'Don't be. It's all right.'

It was, she thought. A year, almost, since Richard's death. Now she was drinking wine in the middle of the afternoon in her house in Dean's Row with an amiable blond giant of a boy, and she had been pierced by a sudden arrow of happiness.

Barney was thinking that when Nina smiled, when she was caught unawares, she reminded him of a picture. Cathy had had a print of it pinned on her bedroom wall. Botticelli, was it?

'Go on,' Nina told him. 'Have something to eat.'

He began with a fist-sized chunk of bread and cheese.

'You'll have to water out there a lot to start with. Even if the weather's wet. The beds won't catch much rain, being overhung by the walls.'

'What do I use? A watering can?'

'If you've got all day. Or I could come back and rig up a hose and a sprinkler for you.'

'I can't ask you to do anything more.'

'I'd like to do it. And we Cleggs always do what we like.'

Barney had reached across and refilled Nina's glass for her. She could see his father in him, only Barney was so likeable.

'Do you? All right, then,' she agreed, knowing that it had not taken much to persuade her and resolving that she would not worry about it. 'If you can. Come back and fix up some water for me.'

'I'll come on Wednesday, then.'

He finished his chunk of bread and began on another.

'Wednesday?'

'There's a lot of college that's worth bunking on Wednesday.'

'Am I supposed to agree to you missing college in order to come and fiddle with hosepipes for me?'

He put his head on one side and examined her face. In the strong spring light Nina knew that the fine lines around her eyes and the furrows at the corners of her mouth would be clearly visible, and at the same time she could see the boy's ruddy open-air skin and the unclouded whites of his eyes. Untroubled healthiness and good humour beamed out of him.

'You needn't agree to anything, Nina. Only I know that practical experience, actually doing the job, beats any amount of classroom theory. I've never been any good on paper.'

Belatedly Nina understood that there was a whole subtext to this talk of hosepipes and practical experience, that the boy was

243

flirting with her, and that she was not displeased by the discovery. She began to laugh, and Barney laughed with her, and their amusement sealed the impromptu celebration between them.

At last Nina took a deep breath. 'Yes. Well. You're old enough to know your own mind. But if you've finished your wine and had enough to eat, Barney, I should think about doing some work now.'

'I'll see you on Wednesday,' he said, as she opened the front door for him. 'I'll bring along everything to finish the job.'

'I'm sure you will,' Nina said crisply.

She glanced across the green to the tarpaulins masking the west front. In the spring sunshine, the world looked newly bright and clean. The statues would surely re-emerge from their lime poultices as crisp as unfurling leaves.

'Where are you going?' Cathy asked her sister.

Lucy was examining her face in the magnifying mirror that extended on a bracket from the wall of their shared bathroom. She had been plucking her eyebrows and now she turned her head from side to side with a sharply critical expression.

'Just out, okay?'

'I'm sorry. I only asked.'

'You're in my light, actually.'

'You're always going *just out*. Who is it?'

'Shut up, Cathy, will you? And move, so I can see what I'm doing.'

'You look divine, darling. But that's my shirt.'

Lucy snapped the cap on to her lipstick. She gave her reflection a last narrow-eyed appraisal, then she turned her back on the glass and faced her sister. The mirrored walls doubled and redoubled their twin likenesses, but the effect was too familiar for them to notice it.

'You don't mind, Cath, do you? And can I take the car?'

Cathy sighed. 'I hope it isn't who I think it is.'

Lucy crammed her Chanel purse into her handbag. 'Don't say anything. Just don't. I've got to go now.'

Cathy followed her, frowning with concern. They met Barney coming up the stairs. He was whistling, but he stopped and took his hands out of his pockets when he saw Lucy.

'Hey. You look real.'

'Don't try to be hip, Barn. You're too old.'

Lucy framed a kiss in the air. On her way out she looked into the kitchen. Hannah was standing in front of the Aga in her dressing gown, heating up bedtime milk for Freddie with a fretful Laura balanced on one hip. Hannah had a cold, and so did the two children. Her eyes were puffy and her nose was red.

'See you,' Lucy called to her.

'Your father telephoned.'

Hannah yanked the milk pan off the heat.

'Is he okay?'

'Mmm. I think. He won't be back for a few days, he said. He's still got some things to sort out.'

Darcy had gone to London and then, saying he had some business to do, had told Hannah he had to go to Germany. He had never been away from Wilton for so long before.

At least Vicky Ransome was at home, where she should be. Hannah had seen her, from a distance, in town. Hannah tilted the pan, staring at the flat moon of milk without seeing it, but Lucy was too busy to interpret her anxiety.

'Bye, Hannah. Don't worry if I'm late.'

Lucy ran out to the car she shared with Cathy. It was dark, but there was a faint luminosity in the sky that promised lighter evenings. She backed the car hastily and made a turn that sent an arc of gravel pattering over the grass beyond the driveway. Hannah, carrying Laura and the hot milk, saw her tail lights through the glass of the front door as a pair of red eyes in the darkness.

Jimmy Rose waited in his car.

They had arranged to meet at a place they had used before, in a quiet lane between Grafton and Wilton. It was the same field gateway where Gordon had sat on Boxing Day after making his last visit to Nina, and Jimmy also could see the distant lights of Darcy's house on its hill. After a few moments he was able to distinguish the lights of a car coming towards him. The glow brightened and switched direction with the sharp bends in the lane, and he knew that she was driving much too fast.

The dazzle of lights approached him, separated abruptly into twin beams as Lucy braked her Renault, and raked over his face as she swung into the gateway beside him. In the darkness that followed the door of her car opened and slammed shut, and he saw the pale blur of her face and hands as she ran to the passenger door of his car. A second later she was inside in the warmth beside him.

They kissed without speaking, her fingers splayed on the back of his neck as she pulled him closer to her.

'You were driving too fast,' he said at last, when he lifted his head.

Lucy's smile showed her white teeth and the glint of her tongue in the dim light.

'I always drive too fast.'

'You're a silly girl. I don't want you to smash yourself up.'

She answered him by winding her arm around his neck again, searching for his mouth with her tongue, an eager girl. Jimmy's hand found her knee, then her long thigh in some thick, dark stocking material and the stretchy hem of her tiny skirt.

'Ah, God, Lucy, I've missed you. A week's too long.'

'It isn't my fault that we haven't seen each other for a week.' Her voice was soft, teasing him, but Jimmy had sharp enough ears to hear the scratch of complaint in it.

'Of course it isn't. If I could do anything more I would, you know that. Only the truth is that you shouldn't be wasting your time with an old married man like me.'

He felt the muscles of her smooth cheek move against his. Her hand touched his leg and then insinuated itself between his inner thigh and his groin. Jimmy winced pleasurably at the effect of it and shifted his position a little.

'It isn't a waste of time,' Lucy whispered.

Jimmy knew that. It wasn't difficult to respond to Lucy Clegg, but she took her own pleasure in him in turn as eagerly and directly as anyone he had ever known. He shifted his hand under her jacket to the front of her blouse, sliding his fingers inside it to find warm silky skin as his mouth searched for hers again.

But Lucy sat up abruptly and flicked her hair back from her face.

'Where are we going tonight?' she asked.

'Ah, to heaven and back, I hope.'

'Where are we going first? I want to go somewhere, Jimmy, not just to sit in the car. I've got all dressed up for you.'

There was a distinctly plaintive note now. Jimmy sighed inaudibly.

'I can see. You look, and smell, fantastic.'

In fact he did not much mind what Lucy wore, so long as it came off easily. But she rewarded him for the compliment by sliding closer again, warming his face with her breath.

'I want to go somewhere with you, for once, the two of us as if you were really mine.'

For once? Jimmy thought. He had only been seeing Lucy Clegg for two months, but perhaps that brief interval felt like a much longer time to a nineteen-year-old.

'I *am* yours,' he soothed. 'Look, here I am. It's these precious hours that count, not the ordinary ones in between.' He was thinking rapidly as he spoke. 'Come on, I'll take you for a drink.'

There was a pub about ten miles the other side of Wilton that should be safe enough, and there would still be time afterwards. Star would be back from the Williamford parent-teacher evening, but that couldn't be helped. He would think of something. It was Darcy finding out that he really wanted to avoid; it was comfortable knowing he was away.

Jimmy switched on the ignition, and Lucy's triumphant smile was illuminated for him in the glow from the dashboard. She put her hand back on his thigh, her fingers grazing against him so that his dwindling erection immediately recharged itself.

*

247

Star came home and found the house in darkness, although Jimmy had not mentioned that he was going out. She went into the kitchen and made herself a cheese sandwich and a cup of tea, listening to the mixer tap dripping into the sink without bothering to turn it off or to switch on the radio to drown it out. She carried her supper into the dining room and sat down at the table with a pile of exercise books that were waiting to be marked.

Star picked up her red pen, but the silence of the house pressed into her. She could feel it like a weight on her head and on her hands.

When she looked at the walls she saw that the striped wallpaper was beginning to peel at the joins, and there was a film of dust on the shallow skirting. The vertical blinds at the windows were of a design she no longer liked; everywhere her eyes turned there seemed to be evidence of neglect. Jimmy and she lived in this house, but it was a long time since they had done anything to improve or cherish it. Star tried to offer herself the excuse that they lacked the money; it was true that they had her income, but Jimmy's conference-organizing business had recently almost collapsed. He had never been as successful as the other Grafton men, but until quite lately they had been able to make wry jokes about that to one another. Now there were no jokes, but she knew quite well that there was enough money to look after the house, if either of them had cared sufficiently about it.

The truth was, Star thought, that it was good enough as it stood to enclose what existed within it.

She twisted the top off her pen and drew the pile of books closer to hand. Even in here she could hear the drumbeat of the dripping tap.

It was five minutes to midnight, and she was on the second-to-last book, when she heard Jimmy's car pull into the space in front of the house.

'Hello there,' he called out as the front door rattled shut behind him. 'Shall I lock up?'

Star waited until his sandy face appeared round the door, his pointy eyebrows raised.

'Unless you're planning to go out again,' she said.

'Would I be, at this time of night?'

'How would I know that?'

'Oh, dear God, what's the matter now? How was the school evening?'

Star gazed down at the work in front of her. Gary Burdett's translation, covered to a point halfway down the page with little red hieroglyphics.

She wondered if somewhere in some defiant corner of herself she loved Jimmy still, or if she hated him, or if she was simply tired and ashamed of them both, and finally indifferent. She wondered who he had been with, and if she knew her, or whether she was some mysterious and therefore incalculably alluring stranger.

'It was exactly the same as usual. Where have you been?'

'I went over to the golf club for a quick drink. Do you want a nightcap?'

He had opened the sideboard and found a bottle of Johnny Walker about one third full.

'No, thank you. Who was there?'

'Where? Oh, nobody much.'

'Have you eaten?'

'Yes, I had something at the bar.'

Looking at her, at her angular face, Jimmy thought, She knows, but the realization did not dismay him particularly. She only knew in the way that wives always knew, with a mixture of suspicion and intuition that shied away from wanting to find out the real truth. He wondered how he would feel if she was unfaithful to him, and decided as he always did that he would not care for it at all.

He leaned down to her, intending to kiss the top of her head, to make an offering of affection.

'You look tired.'

Star jerked away from him, out of his reach, letting her anger show.

'It's late,' she said coldly.

249

Her arm struck against his as she stood up, making him spill some of his drink. Jimmy felt an answering kick of anger within himself, fuelled by whisky.

He wondered if Lucy's scent clung to him. He felt immersed in her. After their drinks, in the confined space of the car, she had wound her long legs around him in the gymnastic enthusiasm of their lovemaking. Now he was home and the bloom of guilt he had felt when he arrived was burned off by a jet of resentment. He did not want to come in and see Star with her face made stiff with accusation; there was a way a man's home should be and Star did not make it so. He hated her when she did this. She could have made things easy and pleasant for both of them, for herself as well as for him, but there was some rigid determination in her that would not adopt the comfortable way.

His free hand grasped her shoulder, his finger and thumb pinching her flesh.

'What's the matter with you? I've only been out for a couple of drinks.'

Star looked at his face.

His eyes were reddened and there was a flush across his cheekbones that made the fair hairs above the shaving line stand out, but he was a long way from being drunk. A sequence of images passed, dreamlike, through her head. They were violent images, in which she struck out and Jimmy hit back at her, blow for blow. Star shrank. She was bigger, but he was stronger. The scenes in her mind were not all imaginary. Some of them were simply recollected.

Carefully, almost gently, she removed his hand from her shoulder. She walked past him, without saying anything.

Upstairs in their bedroom Star took off her clothes very carefully, and hung them in the old painted wardrobe that they had never quite got around to replacing with fitted alcove models like those in the bedrooms of the other Grafton couples. In bed she turned on her side and waited.

Jimmy followed her up after a few minutes. She heard him in the bathroom, and then he came in and undressed. There was the clink of loose change as he emptied his pockets on to the dressing table. As she lay there Star remembered other evenings that had followed this pattern. She thought, if he tries to touch me, wanting to show what he can do, then he hasn't been with anyone else. If he doesn't try, then I'll know he has.

There was a draught of cold air on her skin as he lifted the covers. Jimmy lay down, turning his back as he composed himself for sleep.

The next day Star telephoned Nina. She felt like some laboratory animal that had explored all the avenues leading out of a cage and found them blind, except for one that she could not remember encountering before. As she listened to the ringing she imagined Nina in her studio, although she had never seen it. It would be tidy and full of white light.

'Nina, this is Star. Can we meet? I'd like to talk. I thought I'd forgotten how to, and then I half remembered on our walk. I enjoyed our walk.'

There was a brief silence and then Nina's warm response. 'So did I. I'm glad you called. Come round and see me. When? Are you busy this evening? I could make us some supper.'

'Thank you. I'd like that.'

Star was surprised by the house. Nina showed her over it, right up to the studio at the top. There were pale walls, a very few pieces of furniture, most of them antiques that looked impressive even with Star's limited knowledge of such things. She liked the feeling of space and air, the sense that fine things had been confidently acquired and then placed exactly where they belonged, without the necessity for compromise. There was nothing makeshift or mass-produced; it was a spare, metropolitan look that made the tastes and styles of Grafton, even Wilton Manor, seem effortful and hopelessly provincial.

They went back to the drawing room on the first floor. Nina poured wine and gave Star hers in a thin glass with a knobbed stem.

'Are you rich?' Star asked her. 'You must be, to have a house like this, with these things in it. That's an impertinent question, isn't it? You see, I have forgotten how to talk.'

'My husband was rich. I didn't really know, until he died.'

Star felt something that it took her a moment to recognize as envy.

Nina was free, she possessed the luxury of wealth and independence. It would be easy for Nina to go where she wanted, to make herself whatever she wished. It was no wonder, she thought, that Gordon had been attracted to her. Gordon was as defined by the limits of Grafton as she was herself.

'I know what you're thinking,' Nina said.

'I rather hope you don't. I'm not proud of it.'

'I found it harder, rather than easier, to have so much, and still to be alone. To have it because I didn't have him. In the beginning, just after he died, I wished that my external circumstances matched the way that I felt inside. I sold the houses in London and the country, the cars, put his art collection in storage. I wanted to dispense with what he had left me, as brutally as I could, because he had left *me* so brutally.

'I came here because he had never been here. It was my past, not our joint history. And I was so jealous of you, when I first arrived. All you couples.'

'Ah. Us couples. But you are right, that's what I was thinking without thinking about it carefully enough. Are you still very sad?'

Nina rested her head against the high back of her chair. It was her instinct to deflect the question, but Star herself made her want to answer it.

'Sometimes. At other times not. And sometimes when the grief does fade I feel guilty, as if I ought to keep it fresh. Then occasionally I feel sharply happy, as if I've never really noticed what it was like to be happy before. Gordon made me feel like that. And so did you, when we had our walk the other day. And Barney Clegg, who came to do my garden for me.'

'Barney *Clegg*?'

'Why not?' Nina protested, but they were both laughing. It

seemed that they had passed over some interim stage of acquaintanceship and had become allies.

'And you?' Nina asked.

Star gave her shrug.

'You said you wanted to talk,' Nina prompted. 'You haven't forgotten how to. It happens like this, like we are doing now. Was it about Gordon?'

'No, not about Gordon.'

'About Jimmy, then?'

Star examined the rim of her glass, and then tapped it very lightly with her fingernail. It gave a tiny, clear ring.

'Are you still envious of us? Now that you have seen us more closely?'

Nina said, 'Now that I know about Vicky and Darcy, do you mean, as well as what happened between me and Gordon?'

She did not try to speculate beyond that, not out loud, but she had the sense that the couples were held in some precarious suspension, as if another breath of passion might overbalance the prosperous order and send them toppling.

She added, very softly, 'It was you who said that none of us can look in on other people's marriages. I don't know what Vicky and Gordon are like, or Darcy and Hannah, or you and Jimmy. I can only see the surface. It seemed smooth and shining when I first came here.'

Star lifted her hands and chopped a box shape in the air.

'Did you ever feel that there was nowhere to go?'

'Yes, I did. But there always is. There is somewhere to go, if you look hard enough for it.'

Star drank her wine, admiring the glass again, and the carved wooden arms of her chair, and the pretty room that contained them.

'Could we be friends, do you think?' she asked at length.

Nina nodded her head. 'Yes. I think perhaps we could.'

On Wednesday, Barney came as he had promised with two lengths of different piping, an armful of garden hose and a

253

toolbag. He whistled as he carried the load through the kitchen into the garden.

'Have this fixed for you in a trice, lady,' he called. 'Nice place you got here.'

Nina watched him roll up the sleeves of his overalls and set to work. She had not realized that he planned to install an outside tap for her.

'I'll have to turn the water off at the mains for half an hour, is that OK? I like plumbing,' Barney said confidently. 'I can always be a plumber, if all else fails, can't I?'

'I don't think all else will fail, somehow.'

She had begun to believe that Barney possessed the necessary talents to make a success of whatever he chose.

He quickly became engrossed in the job. Nina put her red jacket on, and went to where he was laying plastic piping under the sill of the door.

'I'm going out for half an hour, Barney, to buy us some food for lunch.'

He sat back on his heels, rubbing a grease mark on his cheek.

'I was hoping you might let me take you out for lunch. Only to the pub, or somewhere, if you wouldn't mind that?'

She looked down at him. 'I would like to. But I still need to do some shopping. I'll be back soon.'

Nina pulled the front door to behind her, but she lingered for a moment on the top step. It was a pleasure to feel the spring sun on her face, and the warmth trapped in the black paint of the iron handrail under her fingers. The green was dotted with people, the first of the new season's tourists, and the benches on the opposite side where she had met Star eating her lunch were occupied.

Gordon saw her before she saw him. His first thought was that she had changed, and then he realized that she seemed different because the lines in her face had somehow altered.

'You look beautiful,' he said, when he reached her. 'You look happy.'

'Do I?' She was startled by his sudden materializing in front of her, when she had almost stopped wishing for him.

'I wanted to see you.'

'Did you? Why, after all these weeks?'

'You had every right to be angry,' he said humbly. 'You still have. Nothing has changed. I can't offer you anything, any more than I could at Christmas. I wanted to see you, to see —'

'To see how I am surviving without you? Well enough, thank you. Did you think I wouldn't be?'

Even as she spoke she was disappointed with herself, for making a pointless charade of anger that she no longer felt.

'Please, Nina, couldn't we go inside and talk?'

'No. Barney Clegg is here, doing some work in the garden for me.'

'Barney *Clegg*?'

He said it in exactly the same tone of disbelief as Star had done.

Nina smiled, and he noticed the difference in her face again. Nina said, 'Let's walk, instead.'

She took his arm, folding her own comfortably within it, and they crossed the cathedral green between the knots of tourists to the west door.

Inside there were scaffolding towers around the pillars on the left side of the nave. They were screened with polythene sheeting but the screens did not cut off the clamour of high-speed drilling and workmen calling to each other. There was a group of Japanese listening intently to a guide in the middle of the central aisle.

Gordon and Nina passed on the opposite side. They walked over stone tablets with their worn inscriptions and the brass memorials to armoured knights and mitred bishops.

'Do you remember when we first came? When I showed you around?'

'I remember.'

They came behind the quire stalls and the high altar, to the Lady Chapel in the apse. The glass in the windows here had been destroyed and then pieced together after the Reformation in a fractured pattern of crimson and cobalt. They stood side by side, looking up at the brilliance of the mosaic.

Nina felt the fragility and the importance of the threads that briefly held them here, tenuously woven together in their joint and separate places, the Grafton couples and their families, and herself in her own place, and the filaments that stretched beyond them into infinity.

She was convinced for a moment that they were in a pattern with its own brightness and darkness, a pattern that was not always legible or comprehensible but was nevertheless there, and the notion comforted her. She thought of Vicky and Darcy, and whatever it happened to be that they needed from each other, and how Gordon did not or would not know about it, and of Star and Jimmy, and the other precarious links of marriages and the desires and disappointments surrounding them.

The frailty of the connections saddened her, and she felt the loss of Richard as a blank within her, but at the same time she felt her own single strength, and she knew that she would survive.

Gordon turned away from the dislocated beauty of the stained glass.

'Are you ready to go on?' he asked.

'Yes, I'm ready.'

They moved on, down the opposite side of the nave, so that they made a complete circuit of the cathedral under the great vaults of the roof.

Outside the light seemed even brighter. Gordon walked her back across the green to the steps of the Dean's Row house.

'Is the restoration work going well?'

'Slowly, always slower than anyone expects, but yes. Behind those screens there is a logical, expensive miracle happening. It's a perfectly explicable miracle but it's still wonderful to watch it.'

He was suddenly animated, full of pleasure in the work. She loved him for his enthusiasm.

'Are you all right?' he asked her.

'Yes, I am.' Nina released his arm. 'I hope you will be too.'

They didn't touch each other again. Gordon smiled at her, and nodded his head, and then turned to walk away.

*

In the enclosed green space of the garden, Barney had almost finished work. The coil of hose was lying beside the new tap.

'Can I help you carry the shopping in?'

'I didn't get it in the end. Never mind.'

'Watch this.'

He turned on the tap and water splashed over the paving stones. Nina clapped her hands and Barney bowed to her in his overalls. For an encore he coupled the length of hose and from a spray nozzle at the other end a jet of water arced upwards, catching the light to make a brief rainbow. Droplets pattered on the leaves and released the scent of wet earth from the ground beneath.

'Barney, thank you.'

'My pleasure entirely. Shall we go across to the Eagle to celebrate?'

'I should be buying lunch for you.'

He came closer to her, so that his shadow fell over her face. He was very large, and young. But he leaned down, serious-faced, and kissed her on the mouth and Nina thought, whatever next?

'Barney . . .'

'You didn't mind that, did you?'

'No. No, it was nice. Surprising, but nice.'

'There can be other lunches, then, can't there? If you want there to be?'

Why not, Nina thought. Why not, after all?

Thirteen

Vicky was giving Mary and Alice their breakfasts. She was dressed for work, in a cream blouse and a pleated skirt, so she moved carefully to avoid splashes of milk. The little girls sat at the kitchen table eating Rice Krispies out of blue bowls with their names spelt out in white lettering around the rims. Helen was strapped in her bouncing chair with a string of coloured plastic balls suspended in front of her. Gordon came downstairs in his shirtsleeves, collecting the morning's post from where it lay scattered on the hall floor.

Vicky put his breakfast in front of him as he slit open envelopes and frowned and placed the bills in a pile beside his plate. The radio was tuned to the *Today* programme, because that was what Gordon preferred. The two girls chattered through the election news; Alice had turned five now and joined her sister at proper school. The kettle boiled, and Vicky caught it before the whistling properly started. She spooned tea into the pot from a blue tin caddy.

Gordon glanced up at her as she put the teapot on the table. She saw anxiety contract to a dark pinpoint in his eyes, but Vicky only smiled and turned tranquilly back to spread honey on Alice's toast.

It gave her a twist of satisfaction, after the months of confusion that had followed Helen's birth, to look at the domestic order that contained them. Gordon was back in his place at the table and Nina's name was no longer mentioned between them. Even Mary had stopped asking, in fearful moments, if Daddy would have to go away again. Vicky had heard him reassuring her once, 'No, darling, I'm not going away anywhere any more.'

She had not tried to meet his eyes because she had felt no need of it, any more than she did now.

Vicky was not sure how she had done it, when she had imagined that she was weak and defenceless, but by some instinct she had won a victory in the campaign between them.

As soon as she had shut Gordon out of the house, and the fearful days immediately afterwards had passed, she felt strength coming back to her. She had cooked for the children, and put them to sleep and wakened them again with a kind of robotic determination that was centred in herself and not in her dependence on anyone else.

It had made her feel stronger to take Darcy in, and then to discover that it was her motherliness he craved, the very part of herself that had seemed so undesirable in comparison with Nina Cort.

Darcy had sat where Gordon was sitting now, and she had made tea for him too, and listened to his talk and then calmly taken him into herself. She did not trouble herself with feeling guilty about her affair, as she would once have done. What had happened was past, as she believed that Gordon's love affair was also past. Instead she looked back with interest, even curiosity, as if it had happened to someone else.

Vicky understood that she had taken pleasure in going to bed with Darcy because it had been a retaliation, and an unexpected tribute, and a comfort in her solitude. She had felt greedy, and the greediness itself had reassured her that she was still alive, better than alive, a functioning woman as well as a mother and a wife. But it had also left a part of her untouched.

The truth was that Darcy's attentions had sharpened her appreciation of Gordon. She had no wish to be Darcy Clegg's mother. In fact the exposure of his secret infantile interior within the familiar, assertive shell had been surprising, and faintly repulsive.

The end of their affair had come as a relief.

Vicky knew all through the weeks that Gordon was away from them that she would eventually let him come back. She counted off his begging telephone calls like beads on a rosary, and finally, almost languidly, she judged that he had paid enough.

When he was home, and had fallen with wary gratitude into the old pattern of their life, Vicky made another discovery. Although the acknowledged transactions between them indicated that Gordon looked after her, the underlying reality was the opposite. It was she who did the caring, mothering again.

Perhaps, she thought, Gordon had discovered this too. Now he knew that he could not survive without her and his children, whereas they could survive without him, and had done. Vicky thought that it must be this awareness that made the pinpricks of anxiety show in her husband's eyes.

But she was not complacent, not any more. She did not know for sure, and it was equally possible that Nina had rejected him; or that he had decided it was simply more comfortable to live with the wife he knew rather than the lover he did not. It was here that Vicky's reasoning began to blur, and she allowed herself to shrug off the speculation. He was home, and she did not think he would wander again.

All she did know for certain was that the balance of power had subtly shifted between them. She felt calm and strong. If Gordon heard about Darcy, from Linda across the road, or Hannah, or Jimmy Rose or anyone else, she would deal with it. Vicky knew she would survive. She felt secure, and content with what she had.

Vicky looked at the oven clock. It was half-past eight. Marcelle would be here in five minutes. It was Marcelle's day for the school run and she was never, ever late. Gordon looked at the clock too, and put his breakfast aside to wipe the toast and honey from the girls' round faces and find their belongings.

Marcelle's shadow appeared at the front door.

Mary ran down the hall, chanting, 'It's time, it's time!'

The women briefly smiled at each other on the doorstep.

Marcelle would drop five children off today before driving on to the Pond School. The map of her day was already laid out in her head like some endurance course that she must negotiate before she could subside into sleep again.

Vicky stood on the step and waved until the car was out of sight, as she always did, then turned back into the house.

In the kitchen, Gordon had lifted Helen out of her seat and was holding her up to the window to see the cats in the garden. Her small fists waved in the air to show her pleasure.

'Marcelle seems tired,' Vicky said.

'Marcelle will never rest while there is some arrangement within her reach that falls short of perfection. She must be exhausting to live with.'

'Not like me, then.'

He looked at her over the baby's head, with the dark points in his eyes again, to see if this was contentious. Vicky only smiled, and scooped the breakfast detritus, crusts and eggshells and teabags, into the sink where they settled around the cups and plates that she had already stacked there.

'No, not like you,' he agreed.

'Have we got time for another cup of tea?'

Gordon checked his watch. The middle-aged woman who came in to look after Helen on Vicky's working mornings had not yet arrived; when she came they would leave together.

'I should think so.'

Vicky poured tea into two cups. The tea was stewed, but the cups were clean. Gordon supposed that Helen's carer would put the breakfast things in the dishwasher while the baby was asleep, or that Vicky would do it when she came in, or that he himself would do it at the end of the day. He told himself it didn't particularly matter which it was. They stood at the sunny end of the kitchen and drank their tepid tea, aware of the silent re-establishment of normality between them, like a long-awaited truce.

Later he drove her to her therapy centre, and watched her walk briskly away from him with her leather bag full of case notes

261

swinging at her side. She was still wearing her hair in the short bob that she had had cut just after Helen's birth. He remembered that he had come home one evening from Nina and found her looking quite different, and he had stared helplessly at her as if she were the stranger, and not Nina. But as Vicky left him now he saw that a younger man on the pavement glanced after her, following her with his eyes. Gordon was touched with admiration for his wife, for her grace and strength and good humour.

He turned the Peugeot around and headed through the town towards the office. The windows of many of the buildings were plastered with election posters. Most of them were blue, because Grafton was at the centre of a safe constituency, but the Conservative candidate was a new man, an unknown, and both Labour and the Liberal Democrats were fielding strong candidates. Gordon had voted Conservative all his life, but he was beginning to be afraid that some tide had finally turned against them, and that the new government would be a Labour one.

At lunch only the day before, Andrew had complained, 'If they get in this time there will be no end to this recession. I can't see how the building trade can ever hope to recover.'

Andrew was on the committee that had selected the new Conservative candidate, a barrister from London. Inevitably, the Frosts were holding an election night party.

'Let's damn well pray there's something to celebrate,' he had said to Gordon when he delivered the invitation.

Gordon's mind was elsewhere as he negotiated the traffic in the town centre. He was thinking that the time he had spent away from home, sleeping in his office and then the hotel, pleading with Vicky and all the time longing for Nina, had faded until it had taken on almost the remembered quality of a vivid dream. He had felt as if he was in a dream when he met Nina yesterday outside her house.

He had longed to touch her when they stood side by side staring up at the stained glass. It made no difference that he could not, and that they both knew he would not; the longing was no less intense. The reality that had replaced the dream was home, and Vicky, and his daughters, but he still loved Nina.

He knew that he was probably an object of pity amongst their friends: Poor Gordon, whose wife had thrown him out and who had eventually been allowed to creep back home once he had come to his senses. He did not even mind that. He had failed some test of bravery or initiative and turned back instead of running forwards, to Nina and whatever would come after, so pity was no less than he deserved.

The loss of her, his recognition that he was the man who would stand still with his eyes open instead of leaping into space, that was the worst he would have to live with.

Gordon reached the bypass, driving the route he took every day without seeing a metre of it. But as he turned towards the business park he recognized a car coming the other way. It was driven by Michael Wickham, who raised one hand to him in a negligent wave.

Michael drove on, towards Pendlebury, in the opposite direction from the hospital. He and a group of other surgeons were to spend the day attending a fund management conference, but the first session that was relevant to his own speciality did not start until midday. He had started out too early, knowing that one of the routes he could choose would take him close to Wilton. He had hardly seen Hannah since Méribel, and when he rounded a corner and caught a glimpse of the house on its hill he knew that he had intended all along to call on her this morning.

His car rolled slowly up the gravel drive under the trees that were fuzzed with the first green of spring. Michael eyed the house when he reached it. There seemed to be far too many windows, each with the glass polished and the white paint fresh and clean, and with the internal layers of blinds and thick curtains and ruched pelmets hinting at the further opulence within. There was no expense spared at Wilton.

But Darcy could afford it, Michael thought. Why should

Hannah not enjoy the benefits, if that was what pleased her?

The Range Rover and Hannah's BMW were parked to one side of the house, but Darcy's Maserati was missing. Michael had been perfectly prepared to encounter Darcy. He would have drunk a cup of coffee with him and declined the offer of an early drink, and they would have talked desultorily about the election prospects and health service funding before he drove on to his conference. But he was pleased to discover that there would be no necessity for that. Nor was there any sign of the cars belonging to Darcy's grown-up children, or the au pair girl's Fiat.

He left his own car and walked swiftly around the side of the house. There were banks of daffodils in the narrow beds along the wall, and a bird singing somewhere in the trees on the other side of the path. Michael skirted the conservatory, where the pane of glass smashed by the boy on Christmas Eve had long ago been replaced, and crossed a paved yard at the back of the house. The garages in the stables were empty too. Michael tapped on the glass of the back door, and then when there was no response he opened the door.

'Hannah?' he called out.

There was no answer, but he thought he could hear a radio playing somewhere in the depths of the house. He called her name again. A black-and-white marble tiled corridor in front of him led through the conservatory to the kitchen.

A second later Hannah appeared at the opposite end with a bread knife in her fist, blade upwards and outwards. She confronted him in the humming silence of the house.

'Hannah, it's only me,' he said.

'Michael? Oh God, you frightened me.'

'I'm sorry. I did knock and call.'

'I thought you were an intruder.'

He went to her and took the knife away. Her hand was trembling slightly.

'And you were going to go for him with this?'

'Yes, I suppose so. Protecting the nest. I don't know. What should I have done?'

He put his arm round her, sorry for having frightened her and admiring of her absurd courage again.

'Called the police or pressed the burglar alarm.'

She shrugged. 'Well I didn't, did I? Lucky, seeing it was only you. What are you doing here, anyway?'

He released her, so he could look at her properly.

'I was just passing.'

'No, you weren't. Nobody just passes this place.'

'I wanted to see you, then. Not at a party or at dinner in someone's house or in town, but simply to see you.'

'I wish you'd called first. I've got a filthy cold and I look a mess.'

The thought that she might want to look her best for him delighted Michael. He saw that her eyes were puffy and reddened, and her nose and lips were flaky and swollen. Her face was bare of make-up and her hair was loose, in need of washing. Two or three darkened strands clung to her neck, inside the collar of her housecoat. There were marks down the front of the silky fabric, and she held it closed with fingers that revealed chipped nail varnish. She was barefoot, and her toenails were similarly neglected. Michael found this spectacle of her sluttishness entirely beguiling.

Hannah suddenly smiled at him, forgetting her fright.

'You'd better come in properly, now that you're here and I haven't stabbed you.'

He followed her into the kitchen. The room was messy but Hannah appeared not to notice it. Marcelle would have launched into embarrassed apologies. Hannah simply went to the coffee pot that was keeping warm on the Aga, poured out and handed him a cup. Michael put the bread knife down amidst the clutter on the table.

'It's funny to see you dressed like that,' she said.

He was wearing a business suit. It surprised him to realize that Hannah only saw him on holiday, or in the evening and at weekends.

'I'm on my way to a conference.'

She made a small face, pulling down the corners of her lips, mocking his importance.

'Where's Darcy?'

She had removed her hand from the front of her housecoat and it gaped a little where there was a button missing. Michael imagined the texture and taste of the warm, unwashed skin underneath. This private, unkempt revelation was far more enticing than any of the public versions of Hannah in her shiny golden party frocks or her silvery furred ski suit. Hannah shook her head, pushing her hair back from her face in irritation. He tried to concentrate on what she was saying.

'London again, or so he said. Working, anyway. Dealing or fixing or whatever it is.'

'Don't you know?'

'Who knows anything, with Darcy? He isn't exactly easy to predict, because he always does what he wants and he never wants the same thing for two days at a time. He makes me angry.'

'All husbands make their wives angry. It's axiomatic.'

He had said it flippantly but then he saw bleakness behind the chapped planes of her face. Without any preconsideration he reached across the corner of the table, resting his forehead against hers for an instant, and then kissed her. After a moment she tilted her chin and kissed him back. Automatically, awkwardly because of the table separating them, he lifted his hand and slipped it inside her housecoat, where the missing button left a place to admit him.

'Well, Doctor Wickham.' Hannah's voice was amused now. She caught his fingers and held them away from her.

'Mister, actually.'

'Oh. Sorry.'

The legs of his chair scraped on the tiled floor as he stood up. He went to her and lifted her to her feet so he could reach her better. She smelt of Vick, and tasted of coffee and very faintly of toothpaste. After a moment Hannah raised her arms and locked them around his neck but she was neither actively encouraging nor positively discouraging.

266

'I've wanted to do this ever since Méribel,' Michael whispered. He thought of her dancing on the first night of the holiday, and back beyond that, seeing a long line of colourful, sinuous Hannahs weaving through the plain fabric of Grafton. 'No, that's not true. Since long before.' At the corner of his mouth he felt the sly curve of Hannah's smile. 'What are you wearing underneath this thing?'

'Nothing.'

'I want to take it off you.'

Her hand held it closed against him. She laughed properly this time, a deep sound in her throat.

'You can't just walk in here like a burglar and expect me to let you do that.'

'Why not? Wouldn't it be nice?'

'What about Marcelle?'

Michael tilted his head. He could see her bare neck, and her hair pushed back behind her ear, and the criss-cross stitching of the quilted fabric covering her shoulder.

'What can I tell you about Marcelle?'

As he spoke he saw his wife, first of all her face with its neat brown bird-like features, and then Marcelle in her kitchen at home with cooking utensils professionally laid out in front of her, her quick hands moving and her head turned aside in concentration on what she was doing. He tried to shuffle the images to find a more pleasing one, but he could only conjure up Marcelle hurrying children into the car, or jabbing the iron over the empty limbs of a shirt, or holding Daisy on her lap and looking accusingly at him over the child's head. He knew that there were happy recollections buried under these sharper images, but he couldn't reanimate them. Always he could see her face with her mouth compressed in its thin line of disapproval of him, and he couldn't recollect exactly when this later mask had disguised the girl he had married.

'She is my friend,' Hannah said piously.

'Yes. I don't know whether she's mine, any more.'

Michael looked down at her, and she unwound her arms from his neck.

'Is that what you want?'

'I think it's what everyone wants, isn't it, once the beginning is past? Companionship and continuity. A shared history and the understanding that comes with that.'

Hannah hitched her robe more closely around her. She sat down again in her place and wrapped her hands with the flawed nails around her cup of coffee. He immediately regretted the change of mood and wished that they could go back to where she had put her arms around him. He felt awkward, hovering over her in his dark suit, and so he reluctantly moved back and sat down facing her in his own chair.

'It isn't what I want,' Hannah declared. 'Anyway Darcy and I don't have that much shared history. His stretches right back through Barney and Lucy and Cathy to the first wife and the first business, and the businesses after that, and includes all the old friends and the old places that I know nothing and care less about, not to mention the women who came before, during and after the first wife and then after her and before me.'

'But you have Laura and Freddie and this place together.'

'*I* have them. It's not really a joint enterprise. They're my children and I run the house and Darcy pays the bills.'

Michael was amused by the casual dismissiveness of a rich man's wife. 'And so what do you want?'

Hannah regarded him. 'I want to be loved, of course. Loved madly, passionately, addictively, to the exclusion of all others.'

She said this grandly, with a red-tipped flourish of her hand, but Michael understood that she also meant it.

'And doesn't Darcy love you?'

'Oh, *Michael*. What do you think?'

'I think he does.'

'Wrong. Darcy loves himself, getting the best of a deal, making money, drink, food and cigars, in that order.' She counted off on her fingers. 'The children, me, our life here, are

268

just home comforts to him. I'm not sure where Vicky Ransome fits in. A non-home comfort, perhaps?'

Michael stared at her. 'Vicky?'

'Didn't you know?'

'No. I had no idea.' Vicky Ransome had always seemed a quiet, faintly bovine presence in the Grafton circle. He was amazed, and embarrassed by his innocence, and troubled by the beginning of a sense that as well as Gordon and Nina and now Vicky and Darcy there were a hundred other secrets and nuances that he had never even dreamed of as he plodded to the hospital and home again.

'On Christmas Eve I found him with her up in my bedroom, after that boy sliced his arm open. Then after she pitched Gordon out he was there the whole time. He's got a real thing about women with babies, it's what turns him on. Mothers. Breasts, mothers' milk. It's what he wants himself, inside, in the secret place under the skin. He wants to be mothered. He'd like me to be his mother, only I get tired of it.'

Hannah gave the faintest shrug, tolerant and dismissive at the same time, and she seemed to Michael wonderfully female and knowing as if she had seen and accepted all the quirks and weaknesses of men.

'I don't want you to be my mother,' he told her.

'Good,' Hannah said, looking straight into his eyes.

The kitchen seemed to expand around Michael until it became an infinite space filled with light, a much warmer and more liquid light than the brittle spring sun shining into the conservatory. He felt an unfamiliar awareness of limitless possibilities, energy in his limbs, the luxury of the day, of this minute, and realized it was happiness.

He reached out for Hannah's hand.

'I'm sorry that I came in and made a clumsy pass at you.'

Her other hand held the strands of hair back from her cheek. He had never seen her look plain before, and he had never wanted so much to go on looking at her, holding her face in front of him.

Her hand linked in his. She was tolerant of him as well as of Darcy. 'Isn't that what men do?'

Michael hesitated. He thought it must be what men did to women who looked and acted as Hannah did, and so that must be all she knew.

'Not necessarily.'

Then, miraculously, she leant closer to him and touched her hand to his mouth. 'I didn't mind. I'm glad you did.'

The light intensified around him. 'I still want to take this thing off you.'

'Not now. I can't let you now. Mandy will be back soon with Laura.'

'Then when?'

'I don't know. Does that matter?'

He smiled at her. 'No. So long as it is when, not if.'

'When,' Hannah said, softly and seriously.

On election day the windows of the Frosts' house were papered with blue posters, and there was a blue rosette fastened with blue and white streamers to the front door knocker. Andrew and Janice had invited their Grafton friends to a late supper and to watch the election results, and an hour before the polls closed the couples began to arrive. They parked their estate cars in the quiet road and greeted one another with questions and predictions about the night's outcome as they crowded into the house. They congregated in the den where a big blank television screen faced the room. There was an air of uneasy but pleasurable expectancy.

'A hung Parliament, I think,' Michael said in answer to someone's question. 'And another election within a year.'

Andrew overheard him. He was jovially busy, pouring wine with a bottle in each hand while his face radiated confidence and satisfaction.

'Don't you believe it. Share prices are up, the word is that exit polls are promising. I wouldn't have bet on it a week ago but the last couple of days have been crucial. My money's on a small majority for us.'

Gordon was standing in the same group. He had searched quickly through the rooms for Nina, with a beat of illogical hope, even though he knew she had not been invited. Andrew had explained to him discreetly that he need not worry. Janice and he had nothing particular against Nina Cort, he said, because it took two people to create such involvements and in any case it was none of his business, but it was much easier for everyone not to ask her to the same evenings as Vicky and Gordon. Gordon had even thanked him. He glanced around the crowded room and remembered how she had looked in her chiffon dress on the night he met her, and how the revolving lights had made different colours in her hair. They had only talked about politics once, lying in the bath together in a motel room. He looked back on that as if on some remote, precious time of unrecoverable happiness.

To Andrew and the other familiar irrelevant faces gathered around him he said something like, 'I wish I felt as confident. I think we may well have a Labour government tomorrow morning.'

Gordon had gone with Vicky to vote before he dropped her at the clinic. They had walked past the playground railings and into the primary school that was their polling station. There had been the usual officials, local people all known to him but wearing expressions of absorbed self-importance for the day, and the representatives of the parties sitting behind their rosettes at rickety card tables, and voters with too little else to do lingering to gossip. Inside the big classroom he had taken his ballot paper into the usual flimsy half-screened cubicle and held the string-tied stub of pencil poised over the list of names.

He had been overcome by a feeling of *ennui*, by a suffocating recognition of his own predictability and the predictability of Grafton.

He read the candidates' names and their parties, and he wondered if there would be a flash of lightning and a clap of thunder if he voted Labour, or Green, or Dog-Lovers Rights or Monster Raving Loony. There seemed little enough to choose between the neatly printed inscrutable English names even though he knew that the Labour man was considered sound, that the Conservative had an irritatingly patronizing manner and the Green woman was an energetic housewife married to a man in the county planning department. He thought of everyone else, of the seventy or so per cent of franchised adults in the country who would take the trouble to go to the polling stations that day, and wondered how many of them felt clogged as he did with repetition and banality and the unheard voice of mediocrity.

The voters in the cubicles on either side of him had come and gone. Gordon felt the scrutiny of one of them directed at his back as he passed. If only by making a different mark he could change the condition of England or even himself in the smallest detail, he thought.

Gordon's pencil wavered.

Then he marked a firm cross in the space beside the Conservative's name, folded his paper and dropped it through the slot in the black tin box before walking to the door where Vicky was waiting for him. She looked serene, with an air of pleasure in having done the right thing.

'Trouble making up your mind?' she joked as they left.

'A brief meditation on the responsibility of the voter.' He smiled at her.

At Andrew's party Jimmy Rose answered him. 'The night will tell, but I hope to God you're wrong. Still, they can't make me pay tax on what I'm not making, can they?'

Star had left his side as soon as they arrived. She was wearing a black-and-white striped jacket with a red rosebud in the buttonhole. It was a joke among the couples that Star was the only Labour voter who was allowed to cross Andrew Frost's threshold, and Star had been known to retort that Andrew was as guilty of tokenism as the BBC.

The noise level was rising. There was a deliberate gaiety as they absorbed enough wine to fortify themselves for the results. Andrew plied his bottles and Janice ordered everyone to come and eat while there was nothing else going on. There was an elaborate cold buffet laid out in the dining room.

The Cleggs arrived late, complete with Barney and the twins. Barney was carrying a case of Bollinger which Darcy presented to Andrew.

'Put the whole lot in the fridge. We'll crack it as soon as we know we've won, and I'm not going home until it's all drunk.'

There was a mottled flush across Darcy's cheeks and a new looseness about his throat that made him look unkempt, although his hair was sleekly brushed and he was wearing one of his emphatic chalk-striped suits. He declined wine, and filled himself a tumbler of whisky.

The three younger Cleggs and Hannah melted into the thick of the party. Hannah was wearing a bright green dress made of some shimmery material.

'I'm announcing what I voted,' she proclaimed.

'Save the Hedgerows, Hannah?' someone teased her. 'Andrew, did you know we've got a traitor to the cause here?'

'It's not quite obligatory to vote Conservative,' Marcelle protested. 'I voted Lib Dem, as it happens.'

'The Pantsdown party? Adulterers unite?'

There was a small, shivery silence in the heart of the party before someone else's boisterous laughter crashed over it and the waves of talk washed it away.

'*Please* come and eat,' Janice begged.

They crowded into the dining room and spooned her good food on to their plates, settling to eat and drink and talk before the television coverage began. Only Lucy Clegg ignored the food, but she filled and refilled her glass of wine. Marcelle found a corner of a sofa and picked at a salad until Jimmy came and sat beside her.

'Sad face,' he said gently. 'Why's that?'

Marcelle gazed at the animation round them. She could hear the ebb and flow of three different conversations but couldn't think of anything to contribute to any of them. Tiredness dragged at her.

'Do I look sad? I don't mean to.'

Darcy was in the nearest group, talking loudly and stabbing with his fork to emphasize his words. Marcelle thought wearily that she must have been to a hundred Grafton evenings with the same or similar permutations of people.

'Talk to Uncle Jimmy,' he cajoled her. He did not look much like an uncle, with his bright eyes and demonic smile.

'I talk too much as it is.' Gordon and Vicky were across the room, in a group that included Barney Clegg and the Kellys. Jimmy followed the direction of her glance.

'These things pass,' he said smoothly. 'See?'

At eleven o'clock the big television was turned on. Jon Snow's face filled the screen.

'Is that a positively impartial tie or has he just spilled something?' Hannah called.

There were other cries for quiet. The experts' view at the close of polling was that the result was too close to call. There were ironic cheers and whistles.

Andrew had photocopied the newspapers' lists of marginal and key seats and he distributed them amongst the watchers. The political enthusiasts prepared themselves for the first results while the rest of the party congregated in noisy groups in the kitchen and elsewhere. Cathy Clegg indicated to Lucy that they might slip away soon, but Lucy mutely shook her head. She hovered at the margin of the gathering, holding firmly to her glass and keeping her face turned away from Jimmy. She was paler and less pretty than usual.

Star sat on a tall stool by one of the kitchen counters with a half-full bottle of wine beside her. She looked elegant in her striped jacket. The rosebud in her buttonhole was beginning to unfurl in the warmth. Gordon slid into the place next to her and filled his glass from her bottle.

'How long until Darcy's champagne, I wonder?' he murmured.

'For ever, I hope,' Star said crisply.

He smiled at her. 'I'm sorry, I forgot. And you're wearing your party badge, as well.'

There was a shout from the television room as the first result was declared.

'Don't you want to go and watch?' she asked.

'No. It won't make much difference, whoever gets in.'

'Yes, it will.' Her contradiction was vehement, and Gordon envied her the conviction that altered and animated her face. But he did not want to embark on a political argument with Star tonight.

'How are you?' he asked instead.

'Nothing has changed. You know how I am.'

It was an acknowledgement of some unfinished business between them that now never would be completed. Star drank her wine and Gordon noticed as he had done before that she wore her sadness like armour.

Vicky was watching the television in the other room and no one else in the kitchen was in earshot.

Star looked up and said, 'I have been seeing Nina. I like her. We made a kind of agreement that we might be friends.'

It gave him pleasure to hear her name spoken with plain affection.

'I'm glad. I know she needs a friend, and she couldn't find a better one than you.' He was aware that he had been less than stalwart for both Nina and Star, and there was the flat taste of disappointment in his mouth.

There was a chorus of groans and some booing from the television room.

'Sounds like we won one,' Star said.

Darcy looked at his watch. It was not yet one o'clock, and although the signs were promising there was no clear victory yet. He glanced around for Hannah, but could not see her. He did not particularly want champagne. His head felt fuzzy as if his skull no longer properly defined it and there was a weight beneath his diaphragm that threatened to expand into pain. But

275

the moment of victory and the uncorking of champagne to mark it gave him something close at hand on which to focus his attention. He heard himself shouting some imprecation at the red and blue figures on the television screen. They suddenly began to dance in front of his eyes, and the burst of laughter that followed seemed to come from a long way off. He reached out for his glass which had been empty and found that it had been refilled for him. He drank down some more of the whisky.

Barney sat on the stairs talking to the two Frost boys. They had been allowed to stay up for the first results, and Janice had not yet noticed that they were still out of bed.

'We had a mock election in our class,' Toby told him. He was much more confident and articulate than his younger brother. 'I was the Labour candidate and I got seven votes.'

'Seven? That's not much,' William jeered. In William's face the rounded contours of babyhood were plainly visible, whereas his brother's were just firming into the beginnings of maturity. Barney did not usually take much notice of children, even Laura and Freddie, but he was struck by this difference in the boys.

'Wait a minute,' Barney said. 'How many in the class? Eighteen? So Toby polled about forty per cent. That's not bad, William. I think even Mr Kinnock would be fairly pleased with that.'

Lucy had been sitting in Janice's bathroom. It had been a welcome refuge for a few minutes, but Jimmy had not noticed that she was missing and come in search of her. It made her angry that he was so easily able to ignore her in the midst of this braying, opinionated party of her parents' friends. She took a comb out of her bag and tried to rearrange her hair. As she stared at herself, the wine she had drunk made an acid knot in her stomach and she leaned experimentally over the basin to see if she would be sick. When nothing happened she straightened up and decided that if Jimmy would not come and find her she would search him out instead.

*

Hannah had grown tired of listening to Darcy and Jimmy shouting out their politics in front of the television. She wandered through the chintz-patterned drawing room where quieter groups were sitting and talking, and past the stairs where Barney was good-naturedly entertaining Janice's boys. Hannah patted his shoulder and wandered into the deserted dining room. She hesitated beside the wreckage of the supper table, and then realized that Michael was standing with his back to her, staring out through the French windows into the dark garden. She felt a distinct lift of happiness at the sight of him.

When she went across and put her hand on his arm he moved a little to one side, as if he had been waiting for her.

'Don't you care about the results?' she asked.

He shook his head. Then he quietly opened the door.

'Come out here with me,' he said.

They stepped out into the darkness. The mild air tasted damp and clean. It was exhilarating to walk away from the over-lit house into the less familiar territory of the garden. There was a pergola along the side of the house and an expanse of paving and lawn, monochrome flat in front of them. Michael took her hand and they stumbled away from the lights of the party. Beyond an arch in a black hedge they came to the swimming pool, closed up under its winter cover. Michael guided her around the perimeter until they came to the cedarwood pool house. He tried the door and it creaked open. Inside they could just distinguish the black outlines of summer garden furniture. There was a dried-out scent of grass clippings and canvas and mower oil.

Hannah shivered and Michael took off his jacket and covered her shoulders. They felt their way forward through the thicket of wood and metal until they came up against a paler glimmer. There was a crackle of polythene sheeting as Michael pulled the cover off the Frosts' canopied swing seat.

'Sit here with me,' he whispered.

The swing rocked and creaked under their weight. Hannah found that she could remember the fabric exactly. It was a pattern of green leaves and blowsy coral flowers against a white background.

'It'll soon be summer,' she murmured.

'And then autumn again, and Hallowe'en, and Christmas,' Michael said with his mouth against her hair.

From the refuge of the seat they could see through the half-open door down the length of the pool towards the house and the curtained windows of Andrew's television room. They were both recalling summer afternoons when children dived and splashed with their wet, dark heads like seals and the couples basked in deck-chairs with drinks in their hands, and there was the scent of charcoal smoke and grilled meat and sun-cream.

Hannah asked, 'Does everything break up in the end?'

It seemed that there were long cracks underlying these remembered images, although the surface of them remained unbroken like the glassy pool water before the swimmers shattered it.

Michael reassured her, without any certainty of his own, 'No, not everything.'

He kissed her because he didn't want to think of anything beyond here and now. They lay back against the flowered cushions and his hands found her bare shoulders under his jacket and the tight band of the top of her green dress.

'Is it when now?' he asked her and she laughed softly into his ear.

'The beginning of when.'

The seat rocked and gave out its mild summer creaking as he undid the zip of the dress. His tongue moved slowly over her skin and he tasted the faint spiritous burn of her evaporated perfume.

Lucy stalked through the party, feeling that no one could have paid her less attention if she were invisible.

She found her father in the middle of an augmented crowd in front of the television, but to her relief Jimmy was no longer ensconced beside him. She saw Star Rose leaning in the doorway, looking at the television watchers with her habitually superior expression. Lucy slid past her, eel-like, with her face turned away. Barney was nowhere to be seen. She thought he must already have gone off in his own car in search of livelier company. Even Cathy seemed to have deserted her.

The dining room smelled unpleasantly of congealed food and cigarette smoke, even though Janice and Marcelle Wickham were pecking about in it with trays and cloths. She breathed shallowly against her nausea and then in a group at the far end containing the Kellys and a quartet of dull, golfing people Lucy caught sight of Jimmy.

She darted to his side, and as the faceless people made room for her she turned her shoulder on them to isolate Jimmy from the group.

'I want to talk to you,' she said. Her voice had risen in pitch.

'Lucy, my lovely girl. Talk away,' he said warmly. His brogue seemed to have thickened and she thought he half winked over her shoulder at the eavesdroppers.

'Somewhere else. Please.'

Jimmy's benevolent expression didn't change but when he took her arm he gripped it a little too tightly. Jovially he excused them both from the group and steered Lucy away. Out in the empty hallway she saw that his mouth made a tight line and his eyes had gone flat. She had made him angry, and the thought that all she had wanted to do was to have him to herself for a moment in public as well as in thick, fumy secret, caused her eyes to sting with tears.

Jimmy glanced around them and then opened the front door and propelled her outside. He hustled her through the cold until they reached the safety of his car. Once they were inside it in the dark Lucy felt they were in their own territory where he had acknowledged her as the queen.

'I needed to see you,' she said with a touch of hauteur.

'Don't be an idiot. In front of your father, and everyone else in there?'

Lucy understood that he was still angry even though they were alone. Her imperiousness dissolved at once into helpless tears.

'I love you. I can't bear to see you and not to be with you.'

'I know that, but you must. How do you think it is for me?'

He was softer-voiced now. Lucy flung herself against him and sobbed. 'I want you, I need you now.'

'How much have you had to drink?'

'Quite a lot. I feel sick.'

He sat upright against her. 'Are you going to be sick?'

'It isn't that.' She pushed her hair back from her smudged eyes and turned to look full at him. She made her face solemn with the importance of what she had to say. 'I think I feel sick because I'm pregnant.'

As she looked at him in the dim light reflected from the house his features seemed to contract, sharpening and hardening as the reactions ticked through him.

'I thought you took the pill?'

'I do. Only I don't always remember it . . .' Lucy bit her lip and her voice trailed away.

'How many days late are you?'

'Eight.'

Jimmy relaxed a bit. 'Ah, that's not so much. It might not be what you think. A week's no time.'

Lucy found her own determination in this softening of his. 'And what if it is that?'

'We'll fix it, don't worry.'

She put her fingers on his arm. They felt claw-like as she dug into the layers of his clothes.

'I don't want it fixed. If it's your baby, our baby, I want to have it. I've thought of nothing else for a week, Jimmy —'

He shook off her hand and then grabbed her by the shoulders. Her head wobbled and she sobbed a little because his face in the half-light combined all the familiar features that she loved with a different and frightening expression that made her want to get out of the car and run.

'You can't have any baby. I'm not your husband, I'm married already, and you're nineteen years old. See sense.'

'Sense? Is *that* sense? Don't you want a child, your own baby?

You haven't got any children. I can give you this one. You *must* want to be a father!'

Her teeth rattled in her head with the shake he gave her.

'No, I don't. Not like this. Neither do you.'

Lucy breathed in a gulp of air against the wails of loss and fear rising up through her chest and into her throat. Her thoughts and intentions blurred and skittered in her head and then began to slip ahead of her, out of her reach, dragging her in their wake.

'If you won't hear me I'll tell your wife. I'll tell Star and she will know you want to murder your own baby.'

Jimmy grabbed at her but Lucy had already flung open the car door. She staggered for two steps and then tensed as she heard him springing after her. Fear made her run faster as she fled up the Frosts' driveway and plunged in through their front door.

A burst of noise seemed to strike her in the face. There were people in the hallway cheering and jostling, chanting, 'Five more years.'

Lucy slipped past them, searching for Star in her black and white stripes, needing to find her before Jimmy caught up with her. She sensed rather than saw that he had been enveloped in the hubbub inside the door, and she stumbled on with the crowd around her into the kitchen.

Lucy saw her father in the middle of the room with a dozen people laughing around him. Darcy himself was not laughing. His face was solemn as he lifted a bottle of champagne in the air in front of him like a trophy. Lucy could see his thumbs whitening as he pressed upwards on the cork.

The room was full of noise but there was an eye of silence in the centre of it, containing him. The effort of forcing the cork showed in his face. His mouth drew back from his teeth and his eyes began to close.

Everything seemed to happen very slowly, there in the silent eye.

As Lucy watched him her father's face darkened and distorted into a mask of pain. There was a sheen of sweat on him that glinted in the light. The champagne bottle fell out of his hands and rolled away, unopened.

Then Darcy's body buckled underneath him and he slipped sideways, toppling into the thicket of people.

There was a gasp that shivered into the silent bubble, but even as she heard it there was a jubilant voice beside Lucy.

'A majority of at least twenty. Break out the bubbly,' it cried out.

'*Darcy!*' Someone else was calling out his name. A note of shock and disbelief.

A press of people surged around him, and he disappeared from her sight.

Andrew and Vicky were closest to him. Andrew tried to fend off the willing hands and looming faces.

'Keep back. Give him some air.'

Vicky knelt beside the tumbled body. She put her hands to Darcy's grey face and found that it was clammy. Then she lowered her face to his in the parody of a kiss and felt the faint stirring of his exhaled breath. With fingers thickened with fear she struggled to loosen his tie and dragged open the neck of his shirt. There was a violent movement in the silent circle above her head and Lucy fell beside her.

'Daddy? *Daddy?*'

Andrew put his arm around her and tried to lift her away but she was clinging to her father's hand. Vicky looked down into Darcy's face. She had no idea what she should do. She heard her own voice begging,

'Find Michael. Somebody get Michael.'

She bent over Darcy again. Her fingers pinched his nose and she dipped her head once more so that her mouth covered his. She blew air into his lungs and when she listened she heard the sigh of his exhalation. His lips moved, forming a word that she could not distinguish. The realization that he was alive fanned her desperation.

'For God's sake, where's Michael?'

The question rippled outwards. No one in the kitchen had

seen him. Lucy and Vicky knelt on either side of Darcy with Andrew at his head. His face was grey but he was breathing. They could hear the painful indrawn gulp and the rasp in his throat as the air escaped again. His mouth was open and a thread of saliva looped from it. Vicky wiped it away.

'Call for an ambulance,' Andrew ordered.

Lucy heard Jimmy using the kitchen extension a yard from her head. She looked up and saw him with Star at his side.

There were voices beyond the kitchen, calling for Michael. Marcelle and Janice came in from the dining room, their faces white with shock.

'He's here somewhere,' Marcelle was saying. 'Isn't he watching the television?'

Barney and Cathy appeared together, from the upstairs room where they had been playing games on William Frost's computer. The kitchen doorway was jammed with murmuring people.

'Keep everyone else out, Jan,' Andrew said.

'Where's Hannah?' Barney asked from his father's side.

The flesh of Hannah's inner thigh was as soft as butter. Michael rolled the tight nylon skin down to her plump knee and then knelt to slide his tongue upwards. Hannah lay back against the cushions, a serene odalisque in the darkness. When he lifted his head he could just see the lazy glint of her smile.

He heard a voice, and then several voices calling out, but he did not listen. No one would come to the pool house, and his senses were occupied with the taste and the scent and the softness of Hannah.

Then he heard his name. It was his name that was being called. The seat creaked and Hannah sat up, and then they did listen, frozen into stillness.

'Michael. Where's Michael?'

'Someone is hurt,' he whispered. 'Shit.'

He scrambled to his feet, brushing at his clothes and raking his hair with his fingers, a pantomime adulterer. Hannah held out his jacket and he took it from her, pushing his arms into the sleeves.

'Wait here for a few minutes,' he told her.

He left the pool house and ran, slipping on the damp grass. The French windows were open and light spilled through the pergola and over the flower beds. There were knots of anxious people peering into the garden. He stopped running when he saw them, and tried to stroll with his hands in his pockets.

'He's out here, in the garden,' someone called.

'What's going on?' Michael asked, as he stepped into the house.

Darcy was lying on the kitchen floor with his children and Vicky and Andrew kneeling around him like saints in some religious tableau. His eyes were open.

'Don't crowd him,' Michael snapped. 'Has someone rung for an ambulance?' They moved back, silently and obediently, to let him through with his package of doctorly skills.

As he bent over Darcy, he could hear the murmuring voices, 'Where's Hannah? Somebody must tell Hannah.'

'We'll have to get you to the hospital, Darcy,' Michael said. 'Can you hear me?'

Darcy looked up at him, his eyes unnaturally dark in his ghastly face. Then, just perceptibly, he nodded.

'You have had some kind of cardiac seizure. I can't tell much more until you've been examined. Lie still until the ambulance comes.'

There was a flurry amongst the watchers and then Hannah appeared in the midst of them. She stared down wide-eyed at Darcy. Barney stood up and put his arm protectively around her. Hannah's bare arms and shoulders were goose-pimpled with cold, and there was a bracelet of earth and grass around the two black satiny spikes of her stiletto shoes. She could only have been outside. Another small shock-wave travelled outwards from the centre of the circle. Across Darcy, and over the heads of his twins, Michael saw Marcelle look at Hannah, and then turn her brown eyes on him.

'He's all right,' Michael said to Hannah. 'We'll get him to hospital as soon as we can.'

She put the back of her hand up to cover her mouth, from where he had kissed away her lipstick.

The ambulance came, and the men with their stretcher to carry Darcy out to it. Michael and Hannah followed them, and Marcelle stood to one side of the kitchen door to let them through.

'I'll get home when I've made sure how he is,' Michael murmured to her as they passed, but Marcelle did not look at him.

In the speeding ambulance, Michael and the crew man watched attentively over Darcy while Hannah sat huddled in the opposite corner. They did not speak to each other. Barney and the twins followed behind the flashing blue light in Barney's Golf.

The party was abruptly over, and almost everyone had gone quietly home. Marcelle sat at Janice's kitchen table with her hands folded around a mug of tea, as she had done a thousand times before. This normality, the reminder of familiar domestic life, made what she had seen appear all the more ugly. Michael had been out in the garden making love to Hannah. She kept seeing their faces when they stumbled in, over and over, and having to understand that there was no explanation other than the obvious, humiliating one.

Marcelle unwrapped her hands and ducked her head to the comfort of her mug of tea, seeing Michael again with cobwebs on his clothes and Hannah, shivering with cold in her grassy shoes.

Janice came to sit beside her and put her arm around her shoulders.

'You okay?'

'Yes, I'm fine.'

She would not let even Janice know that she was not, because that would be too much to give away. Small currents of anger, and bitterness, fear and disbelief passed through her like electric shocks.

'Andrew'll take you home,' Janice said. 'Or we could call a taxi.'

'No, I'm fine to drive. I'll finish my tea and then I'll go.' She kept her voice cheerful, denying the possibility of Janice's sympathy, as if neither of them had seen anything.

Janice sighed. 'These parties,' she said. 'All of us, giving and going to parties. What is it we want, I wonder?'

It was seven o'clock in the morning, fully light, but the day was dim and cold, promising no warmth.

Nina had been awake for more than an hour. She was lying on her back, staring up at the ceiling from her boat bed, when she heard someone knocking at her front door. It was a gentle, interrogative knock and not a summons, but she got up at once and wrapped herself in her dressing gown.

Barney stood on the doorstep. He was unshaven and seemed utterly exhausted.

'What has happened?' Nina asked, with fear in her throat. Her first irrational thought was of Gordon.

'Can I come in?'

'Yes. Yes, of course you can.' She held the door open wide for him.

In the kitchen, where it was warm, he told her what had happened to Darcy.

'It's all right. Michael was very good, and then the cardiologist or whoever he was came and told us he'd had a heart attack, but it was a minor one. He's in intensive care now, under observation. There was nothing else for us to do there. I took Hannah and the girls home, but I didn't want to go to bed.'

He lifted his shoulders, and then dropped them again helplessly. He looked very young.

Nina went to him and put her arms around him.

'Don't worry,' she soothed.

'I went back to Wilton and I saw Hannah and the twins to

bed. But I knew I wouldn't sleep. I wanted to talk to you.' He moved a little, circling her with his arms in return so that they held each other. 'Do you mind?' he asked.

Nina shook her head. 'No. Do you want to try to go to sleep here?'

Barney's hand found hers, and he held it between them. They looked at each other for a long, quiet moment.

'I'd like to lie down if you will come with me.'

She knew she should have laughed, as if she were being teased, and gently extricated herself. But she also knew how comfortable and natural it would be to lie down against the warmth of him. The subtraction sum, the difference in their ages, slipped out of her head.

'I'll come and hold you until you fall asleep.'

Upstairs in her bed the rumpled quilt still held the warmth of her sleep.

Fourteen

Michael was driven home from the hospital in a taxi. He had a busy list for the next day, and he had already reassured himself that Darcy was out of danger for the moment. It was four o'clock in the morning, and the darkness seemed to enclose the cab like some cube of solid matter that travelled with him and closed off all the avenues of escape.

He was thinking about Marcelle and his children; he could clearly see Marcelle's face as it had been when he had stepped in from the garden, but he was thinking mostly about Jonathan and Daisy.

Michael knew that he had never been a wholehearted, enthusiastic father to them in the way that he had blithely imagined he would be before Jonathan was born. He loved his children, but quite often they seemed to be unpredictable obstacles that needed to be negotiated in the pursuit of a civilized life. They consumed Marcelle's time, and his own, and although he was proud of them he knew that they did not entirely repay this investment of energy. They did not always act in the way he wanted them to. Sometimes they turned on him and gazed with mute, accusing faces and he felt his heart twist inside him with the knowledge of his own guilty inadequacy.

Now, on the over-familiar road with the silent, tired cab-driver hunched beside him, there was a different perspective. Michael knew that with Hannah he was trying to meet a need that Marcelle no longer answered, but he also knew that in doing it he was risking Marcelle and his children. And when he imagined the state of being without children he suddenly saw them much more clearly. He saw Jonathan's stubborn, interrogative stare and Daisy's convex upper lip buckling with the onset of her too-frequent tears, and they seemed both complicated and separate from himself and Marcelle. He felt the demands of his responsibility for them sharpening, and he was fearful for their safety, and yet he was filled with a kind of awe because they were themselves, and unique.

He remembered how Darcy had looked in the hospital A and E room, lying grey-faced at the mercy of the cardiac crash team. Michael had known most of the nurses and doctors at least by sight, some of them much better than that, and it had been shocking to see Darcy solitary in the midst of them, robbed of his personal stature, reduced to a body on a trolley. With the thought of him, and with the fear for his children, Michael found his eyes so blurred with tears that he could barely see.

When he went into the house, carefully relocking the doors behind him, the silence and the darkness were even blanker and thicker than outside. There was a faint smell of stale food, a fainter trace of the clear varnish that Jonathan used to finish his model aeroplanes. Michael trod softly, his steps weighted by familiarity.

Marcelle was awake. She had not slept, although she had come home a long time ago from the Frosts'. She lay in bed, having heard the crunch of car tyres on the gravel outside and then the small, blindfold movements of Michael within the house.

The bedroom door opened and then closed again. The floor creaked as he passed the end of the bed and Marcelle was gripped by the fear that it was not Michael, but an intruder.

'I am awake,' she said in a clear voice edged with alarm.

'Are you? It's very late.'

It was him, of course, but she did not feel any sense of relief. She clicked on her bedside light.

'How is he?'

Michael was standing with his shoes in one hand and his jacket in the other, the picture of stealth.

'Oh. Probably all right, in the short term.'

Marcelle listened as he told her about Darcy and the hospital. He undressed as he talked, putting his cufflinks in the carved wooden dish that stood on the chest of drawers, dropping his shirt and underclothes into the wicker laundry basket. Marcelle thought of the thousands of other nights that had slipped by and now stretched behind them, their joint history.

'And Hannah?'

Michael lay down on his side of the bed.

'Worried, naturally. But coping with it well enough.'

Marcelle wanted him to put his arms round her, making some gesture of reassurance, but she knew that he would not.

'So what was going on tonight?' she asked.

There was a small silence, and then he said, 'I'm sorry, I know how it must have looked. We'd both had a few drinks, we'd agreed that we were sick of the election. So we went outside, that's all. There was a bit of fooling around. You know what Hannah's like.'

'Not really, evidently,' Marcelle said.

Within her head gnawed the conviction that Michael was lying to her. She turned his words over and over, trying to prise the truth out of them, but they stayed defiantly flat, refusing to admit her.

'What does "fooling around" mean?' she persisted. The expression was not quite right. She had never heard him use it before. Was that the false note?

'I kissed her. A friendly, flirtatious kiss. These things happen between people.'

'Do they?'

Michael moved his arm awkwardly, and then found her hand. He squeezed it.

'Yes, they do. I'm sorry if you were hurt.'

She knew that she would get no more out of him, and in a way she was relieved. There was nothing for her to do but accept what he told her, and it was easier to do so than otherwise because it allowed her to step aside from her anxieties. These things did happen, she told herself. Between people of their age, with their histories behind them. She knew as much, from Jimmy.

Michael withdrew his hand, settling himself for sleep.

'I'm tired,' he said. 'And I've got a busy day tomorrow. How about you?'

'The same.'

Marcelle closed her eyes experimentally, and they lay next to each other with their separate thoughts.

Nina lay on her side and looked at Barney's naked back. His spine was a strong groove like a thumb-line pressed in soft clay.

Barney was sitting on the edge of her bed, talking on the telephone to the hospital. She closed her eyes, and then opened them again. There was still the narrow space of crumpled sheet and then the startling, solid shape of him. She stared at the lines of his neck, and imagined the hard outline of his skull under the scrolls of hair. His face was hidden from her but his questioning voice sounded like an anxious boy's, contradicting what she saw.

Barney replaced the receiver and turned back to Nina.

'He's stable, and his heart is being monitored. He's asleep at the moment.'

'Good. That's good news.'

'May I call Hannah now?'

'Of course. Don't tell her where you are, will you?'

'Not if you don't want me to.'

He dialled again, and almost at once began talking to Hannah. Nina knew that she must have been sitting at Wilton waiting beside the telephone. She turned over on to her back and thought about the morning in order to disconnect herself from Barney's conversation with his stepmother.

They had come upstairs together, and in the shuttered silence of her bedroom Barney had seemed neither a tired boy nor a predatory man, but simply himself. He kissed her and undid her dressing gown, and she stood quietly while he looked at her. Then he touched her arm.

'Don't get cold,' he said.

He lifted the quilt and she slid into the warmth underneath it. He took off the clothes that he had put on for the Frosts' party, ages of time ago, and gratefully lay down beside her. She held out her arms to him.

'May I?' he had asked, and he had sounded so much like a polite boy at a birthday party that it made Nina laugh.

'Well, yes, since we've come this far.'

Barney laughed too, with relief, leaning over her and kissing the corner of her mouth.

'Thank you. It would be quite difficult to go to sleep right now.'

Nina had not wanted to compare him with Gordon, but she could not help it. Barney would not make her forget herself, and the time and the place and everything else except what he did, as Gordon had been able to do, nor did she want that from him. She could feel his eagerness, and his clumsiness, and she wanted to reassure him.

'It's all right. I want you to be here. I'm glad you are.'

Barney closed his eyes and sighed, and then murmured, 'I wanted to be. I have for ages. I thought you knew.'

'I did.'

They both laughed again, acknowledging that the gap between them was temporarily diminished.

It was easier, after that. She had given him confidence, and he was as warm and natural as she had imagined he would be.

Afterwards Barney said with his mouth against her cheek, 'Thank you. Did I tell you that you are beautiful?'

'I think you did, more or less.'

'Less isn't enough. You *are*.'

Nina smiled. 'Thank you,' she said in her turn.

She was pleased that they had safely negotiated their way to this comfortable moment. She dismissed the hovering spectres of common sense and responsibility, and concentrated instead on the joint pattern her breathing made with Barney's. After a moment she realized that he had drifted into sleep and saw from the looseness of his mouth and the circles under his eyes that he was exhausted.

Barney slept for an hour, while she lay quietly beside him. Then he opened his eyes again, at once wide awake and seeming completely rested. It made her realize again how young and healthy he was.

'I should telephone,' he said.

After he had spoken to the hospital and to Hannah his anxiety visibly lifted.

'I told her she should go to bed and try to sleep,' he said to Nina, adding, 'She thinks I'm at Tom's.'

He lay down beside her again. They contemplated each other openly for a moment, squinting a little because of the closeness of their faces, each of them evaluating this new stage of their intimacy and trying to work out what should happen next. Nina put her fingers up to his mouth, approving of the shape of it, and the other remembered details of the early morning. It came to her that she liked him being where he was, and then she felt afraid and unwilling to be the predatory widow who had lured him to her bed.

'This is just between you and me, Barney. It was very nice, very surprising, but I don't want the rest of the world to know about it.'

'I want to tell everyone. To climb up on the roof and shout about it. How could I not?'

His wide smile disclosed his white teeth as he propped himself on one elbow to look down at her. His uncertainty had evaporated now. He was pleased with himself and his conquest. Cocksure was exactly the word, Nina thought with a touch of weariness, feeling herself to be dry and disparaging and ancient by comparison. She would have been relieved to dislike him, but recognized that the truth was the exact opposite. The spectres gathered around the bed again.

'Even so, I don't want anyone to know.'

'Of course not, if that's what you prefer. Are you ashamed of me, is that what it is?'

'Not at all. Perhaps ashamed of myself.'

He was surprised. 'Why is that? Didn't you like what we did?'

'Yes, Barney, I did like it. But there's the matter of . . . suitability.'

'Because we aren't quite exactly the same age? If you and I feel that this is suitable then who else matters?'

His very reasonableness was appealing. Seeing that he had gained a point Barney persisted.

'If no one knows about us, whatever it is we are, can I come and see you again? I'll steal in secretly, in the dead of night, if you insist.'

She saw that he was laughing, and his lightness lifted her too. She had been thinking of Gordon, and preparing herself instinctively for pain to be connected with the acceptance of pleasure. Barney's view of the world was so simple that she wanted to respond to it.

She reminded herself that they were both adults, of free will and corresponding inclination, however temporary that inclination might turn out to be.

'You'll have to visit under cover of darkness, and wearing a false beard and a long raincoat.'

'Whatever turns you on,' Barney said philosophically. 'Can I, then?' Nina nodded, and the flash of pleasure in his face was her reward.

Cathy and Lucy went to the hospital to see Darcy. Two days after his heart attack he was sitting up in bed in a general ward. His face was still an unhealthy colour, but he seemed to have recovered some of his impatient energy.

'Diet and exercise,' he complained to them. 'These damned doctors come and stand around the bed with their long faces, telling me what I can't eat and can't drink and how I must walk and swim and guard against stress. What kind of a life does that sound like?'

'You must do what they say,' Cathy told him. She turned to her twin. 'Mustn't he?'

Lucy sat with her chair at an angle, winding new knots in the teased and plaited tails of her hair.

'Yeah. Give up cigars and eat grapefruit.'

Darcy flapped the covers around him. 'I'll promise them whatever they want, so long as they'll let me out of here. And if I don't get some answers soon I'm just going to get up and walk out.'

Cathy shook her head. 'What's the hurry? Why not have a proper rest?'

'I don't need a rest. There are things that I want to do. Need to do.' She was startled by the vehemence that broke through his predictable complaining. Darcy wiped his mouth and Cathy glanced uneasily at her sister, but Lucy appeared to be intent on the knots of hair that hung in front of her eyes.

'Listen to what they tell you, Dad. We love you, you know.' She put her hand over his, and her father's eyes settled on her face although she could feel the currents of impatience jerking within him.

'Do you? All of you? Even you two and Barney?'

'You know we do,' she reassured him.

Lucy peered through the curtain of her hair. She had gnawed the skin of her lower lip until it was sore.

'Barney said he'd be in to see you tonight,' she contributed.

'Did he? Where is he? At college, I hope.'

'I dunno.' She pushed back her hair and shrugged. Lucy felt how difficult it was to hide her exhaustion, especially confronted with this unpleasant sight of her vigorous father beached and helpless in a hospital bed. She was relieved when Cathy looked at her huge black watch and said,

'We should go, Dad. Marcelle'll kill me if I miss any more of her demos.'

'Off you go, then.'

They kissed him, one on each cheek as they used to do when they were tiny. Darcy straightened up for them, but he allowed himself to sag against his pillows as soon as they turned away down the ward together. He could feel the muscles in his face and neck pulling in different directions, and his heart seemed too big, and dull, and heavy for his chest.

Cathy was driving the Renault.

'Can you stop in town? I want to get something,' Lucy asked her as they skidded out of the hospital car park.

'Where?'

'Boots.'

'Okay.'

She was away from the car for only five minutes. When she came out of the chemist's she was stuffing the plastic bag containing her purchases into the neck of her black rucksack.

The following morning Lucy did the pregnancy test that she had bought, carefully following the instructions on the leaflet enclosed in the box with the chemicals and the test tube. She left the glass tube in the holder provided and went downstairs.

Cathy had already left for her day at the Pond School but Hannah was in the kitchen with Freddie and Laura and their au pair. The children were eating boiled eggs while Mandy cut buttered toast into fingers for them. Lucy went to lean against the warmth of the Aga and tried not to look at the mess of food.

'Coffee's fresh,' Hannah offered.

'No, thanks,' Lucy said through dry lips.

Hannah regarded her. Lucy was supposed to be studying to retake the A levels she had failed and searching for a part-time job, but there was no sign of either activity. She looked pale and heavy-eyed this morning, and sulky as well. Irritation with the girl broke through Hannah's preoccupation.

'What's the *matter*?' she snapped at her. 'Were you in late last night?'

'No, I wasn't. Nothing's the matter, why should there be? Everything's utterly wonderful.'

Lucy whirled and ran out of the kitchen, leaving Mandy and the children making round-eyed mock-gloomy faces at each other.

tights. Jimmy knelt in front of her, his eyes on the white skin of her thighs and the lick of fair hair exposed by the ridden-up elastic hem of her skirt.

He undid himself, thick-fingered with haste, and Lucy leaned forward, greedily taking him in her mouth.

He let her for a moment, and then he forced her backwards on to the crumpled bed of their clothes. He ran his fingers over the veins that were faintly visible under the white skin, and then he slid his fingers inside her and watched her face as her eyes closed and her mouth opened, inviting him.

'*Jimmy*,' she whispered.

He withdrew his fingers so that a recollection of a scowl formed between her eyebrows, and then he extricated himself from his own clothes, hurrying, and pushed himself inside her.

'*Jimmy*.' He felt the breath in his ear, rather than hearing her voice. Her legs tightened around his waist and her fingers knotted in his hair as he thrust at her. They rolled over, locked together and blind to everything, and brambles tore at Lucy's hair and her bare legs. Jimmy's anger with her melted into his greed and became one and the same thing, and he bit at her mouth and her throat as they twisted over and under each other. He knew he was hurting her but her fingers still dug into the muscles of his shoulders, and her legs wound more tightly around him to hold him where he was, buried in her.

When she cried out there was a whirring of wings in the trees overhead as the wood-pigeons took fright. Jimmy didn't hear her or the birds; his eyes were closed and his lips were drawn back from his teeth as if he were snarling. At last, after he came, he collapsed on top of her, his ginger fox's head resting at an exhausted angle on her shoulder. Lucy lay back, staring up at the sky laced with twigs and fresh, optimistic leaves. Her face was burning and her throat felt dry and sore.

After a while Jimmy lifted himself so he could look at her. There were leaves in her hair, and long bramble scratches, beaded in places with droplets of blood, on her calves and thighs. He sat up, pulled his clothes together, then found a handkerchief in the pocket of his trousers and gently dabbed at the blood. When he looked at her face he saw that she was silently crying. He touched the handkerchief to her cheek but she rolled on to her side, drawing her knees up to her chest.

'Don't cry,' he said.

'I'm crying because I'm angry. It isn't fair. Why is it like this? We could be happy, couldn't we, if you weren't married. If you were mine –'

He interrupted her. 'I don't want you saying anything to Star. Do you hear me? I don't want anything like the other evening. You are not to run after her and tell her any of this.'

Something in his voice or the set of his mouth reminded Lucy of the different, frightening Jimmy she had tried to run away from that night. It came to her that the other Jimmy had always been there, only she had not looked at him hard enough. Her voice when she answered him came out somewhere between a sob and a whine.

'I wish I was her. I wish I was your wife.'

To her relief, his hard face softened. 'No, you don't,' he said. 'You don't really wish that.' He stroked her hair, and picked the leaves out of it.

'What's going to happen?' Lucy whispered.

'What will happen is what you know must happen.'

While he waited for her to assimilate this, Jimmy listened as patiently as he could to the repetitive calls of the wood-pigeons.

Lucy shivered, and then plucked at the blades of grass a few inches from her eyes.

'You don't want our baby. You don't want me.' Her expression changed from disbelief to desolation.

Jimmy summoned up his patience again.

'Lucy, darling, the truth is that I can't have you. I am married already.'

He helped her to sit up, and then shook out her sweater and pulled it over her head. When she was dressed he took her face between his hands and gazed into it for a moment, and then he kissed her on the lips.

'There,' he said. 'That tells you what I feel for you, and what you mean to me. But I thought you understood how things have to be between us. Hmm?'

He tilted her chin up with the tip of his finger. Even now her distraught look was half irritating, half enticing. He murmured, 'Don't worry. We'll see each other through this. I promise you. And in time you'll look back on it, and on me, and wonder why you ever thought you wanted me.'

Lucy rubbed her face with the cuff of her sweater.

'I do love you,' she mumbled. 'Only I'm so confused.'

'I know you are. Of course you are. Now, do want me to find out what you should do? Where you should go?'

'No,' Lucy said. Her chin had lost its wobble. 'I will do that, if I have to. If that's what I must do.'

'If you need money . . .'

'Okay.'

She picked up her black tights from the tangle of his jacket, and held the jacket out to him. He watched her roll the black Lycra up over the scratched white skin of her legs. She put on her shoes and then stood up, towering over him until he scrambled to his feet. He tried to lean close and kiss her, but she turned away from him. They began to walk back along the path, the way they had come.

Jimmy was not angry any more; he was relieved and also sad, for the end of their affair but much more for the extinguishing of the baby. Only it was not a baby, not yet; he had assured Lucy of that, whatever might be taught to the contrary. This much he told himself too, but he knew he would have to make his own amends for the severance of its thread of life. Only he would not let Lucy know this, any more than he had let her know one of his true thoughts. Nor would Lucy ever come close to guessing it.

They reached the car park.

Lucy was pale, remote, entirely occupied with her perception of herself at the centre of some broad, tragic canvas. Jimmy walked with her in silence to Darcy's Range Rover, and with the ritual glance around them to make sure that no one was watching they let their lips just touch. Then Lucy stepped into the driver's seat, and checked her reflection in the driver's mirror before putting on her Ray-Bans. Jimmy stood back, lifting one arm in a salute as she drove away. Once she was out of sight he crossed to his own car and drove gratefully back to work.

When Lucy reached Wilton Cathy was parking the Renault in its place at the side of the house.

'Where on earth have you been in Dad's car?' she gasped.

'I had to go somewhere. To see someone.'

Lucy took off her dark glasses. At once her face crumpled and she began to cry properly, without regard for how she looked or sounded.

Cathy ran to her and put her arms around her.

'You have to tell me what's been happening. Please, Lucy?'

'Oh, Cath. I need to tell you. I really do need to.'

With their arms around each other, both of them in tears now, they went into the house and up the stairs to Lucy's bedroom.

After they had held hands sitting on Lucy's bed, and Lucy had poured out everything between sobs and half-smoked cigarettes, the twins sat back to look at one another. They felt their childhood closeness, somewhat lapsed of late, renewing itself.

'Why didn't you tell me about him, about this, before now?' Cathy demanded.

'I don't know. I suppose I felt partly ashamed of myself, but I did love him. I *do* love him.' Lucy blew her nose, ran her fingers through her knotted fringe and reached for another French cigarette.

'I think I'd guessed, without knowing I'd guessed, you know?'

'I should have told you. Only I was afraid of what you would think of me.'

'How could you have been afraid of that? You must have known what I would think. That if he made you happy that was fine, and if he hurt you or made you sad then I would want to *kill* him.'

'He did make me happy.'

'So I won't kill him. What do you want to happen?'

Lucy stared down at her hands, at her fingertips with bitten nails and raw skin. She was thinking. Then at last she said,

'I suppose I wanted to have the baby, for him to leave Star and marry me, for us to be together. A family.'

Cathy waited, but her expression betrayed her scepticism.

'And I suppose what I realized, in the wood today, is that it won't happen. He won't leave her for me. He never even thought about it. He won't stand by me. Isn't that what they say?' Then Lucy laughed, sniffing back her tears at the same time. 'Dumb of me to think he would, really.'

They heard a car coming too fast up the drive and a peppering of thrown gravel as it braked in front of the house.

'Barney's back,' Cathy remarked.

Lucy looked up. There were more tears in her eyes. 'I'm so lucky I've got you, and Barney. Now Dad's ill, and Jimmy's not here where I thought he was. We can stick together, the three of us, can't we?'

'You know we can.'

They sat on the bed, with cigarette smoke curling around their heads, knowing they were allies.

'Luce, what do you want us to do about this?'

With the thought of Cathy and Barney to support her, Lucy's will reasserted itself. She said with new determination, 'I don't want Dad or Hannah to know anything about it. I don't want Star to, either.'

'That will suit Jimmy,' Cathy said.

There was even defiance now. 'It suits me, too. And I don't want his help. If it has to be done, we'll do it on our own.'

And then, as the tide of her momentary courage ebbed again, Lucy curled on her bed as she had done beside Jimmy in the clearing, and gave herself up to tears once more. Cathy sat beside her, patting her shoulder and rubbing the curve of her spine, waiting for the storm to blow itself out.

They heard running feet on the stairs, and Cathy leaned to look out of the window. A moment later she saw Barney jump into his Golf and drive away again.

'I wonder where Barney's going in such a hurry, all smartly dressed?' she mused.

At last Lucy sat up, swollen-eyed. Cathy lit yet another cigarette and gave it to her. 'Thanks.' Lucy blew out a long, meditative plume of smoke. The first glimmer of considerations beyond her own broke through to her. 'Why are you home? I thought you had to be at the Pond today or get thrown off the course.'

'Yeah, I did. But Marcelle was ill, so her class was cancelled. She came in, but she had to go home with a migraine. She looked pretty awful. Not like her, really. I've never known Marcelle call in sick before.'

Lucy was sitting smoking with her chin resting on her drawn-up knees. She had no views on Marcelle to contribute.

Michael walked down Southgate, the best shopping street in Grafton. He had left his car in the multistorey park, in a remote corner of the top level, although in these last few minutes of the shopping day there were plenty of spaces lower down. Most of the shops along the street were already closing. The jeweller's steel shutters had been drawn down, and also those of the expensive wine merchant two doors further along.

He had already seen that La Couture was still open; the curly gold lettering on the navy-blue shop front was lit by two brass spotlights. There was a single dress in the bow window, a black velvet sheath with a nimbus of gold-coloured gauze around the bodice. He could imagine Hannah wearing it, with her creamy shoulders set off to perfection by the golden halo.

Michael paused at the door of the shop. There was a sign hanging against the glass that announced 'Open' in the same curly script as the shop front. Then he looked beyond the sign into the honey-coloured interior. He saw Hannah sitting at a spindly desk towards the back of the shop. She was reading, with a pair of tortoiseshell-rimmed glasses slipping down her nose. A bell tinkled somewhere over Michael's head as he pushed the door open.

Hannah looked up. Her hair was piled up on top of her head and she was dressed in a navy-blue suit with big gold buttons down the front. The clothes and her spectacles gave her a businesslike appearance that was new to Michael, and completely enticing.

'I'm afraid I haven't come to buy a cocktail dress,' he said.

Hannah took off her glasses and chewed meditatively on one of the arms.

'No? You don't want a little number for the golf club dance? The parents' party? I'm sure I could find something to suit you.'

'Ah, I don't think so. But do you mind my calling by like this?'

Hannah folded her glasses and placed them on the desk in front of her. She put her stocklist aside and stood up. He thought she was coming to him and he clumsily lifted his arms, but she slipped past in the confined space and went to the door instead.

'Do I mind? No, I don't mind. I looked up and there you were at the door like the beginning of a fantasy. I was about to lock up. It's gone six, isn't it?'

She flipped over the sign, turned a key, and locked them inside the shop. Then she went to a row of switches, and the lights illuminating the window and the shop front blinked out. They were left cocooned in the glowing interior.

Michael gazed around him. He had never been inside La Couture before. It was like stepping into a box of elaborate, expensive fondant sweets. Everything was pale and soft and scented, and every surface was padded and buttoned and puffed. There were thick carpets and curtains and drapes in cream and honey beige and dull gold, and in the middle of the floor was a plump satin-covered chaise longue heaped with glossy magazines. The clothes hung around the walls, spotlit at intervals like pieces of modern art. They were all velvets and silks and clouds of net; there was nothing here that acknowledged the world of work, of lives lived before six o'clock in the evening.

Michael felt the exotic scent and softness of the place rising around him like a tide. The remoteness from reality seemed female and mysterious and drowningly erotic, and he saw

Hannah in the midst of it, pale-skinned and luscious, the very embodiment of these sensations. He remembered the pool house, the creaking of the swing seat and the contrasting musty scents of canvas and creosote and dried grass.

'Are we safe here?' he whispered to her.

Hannah nodded, smiling, her mouth incurving and offering him dimples and tiny cushiony recesses.

'Yes. No one will come in now.'

'But they can see in, from out there.' He gestured to the wet cobbled reality of Southgate, Grafton, beyond the curved glass of the window.

'Not through here, they can't.'

Hannah took his hand to guide him. He followed her at right angles beneath an arch. There were more curtains here, striped cream and honey, and thick gold tassels to fasten them. Michael saw a wall of mirrors, and the fabric over their heads gathered like an Ottoman tent. Hannah turned off more lights, and then let a curtain fall behind them so they were enclosed in the secret space with only their own reflections to observe them.

'Fitting rooms,' she whispered. 'Women need privacy to be pinned and tucked and stitched into their own fantasies.'

Michael stood behind her as they faced the mirrors. For a long moment they just looked at one another.

Then he put his hands up to cover her breasts. There was a deep V at the front of her dark vendeuse's jacket. Watching himself as he did it, and with Hannah's reflected wide eyes on his face, Michael undid the gold buttons one by one. Underneath there was black lace, and her white powdered skin, and the cleft between her breasts. Little rims of flesh were pushed up above the waistband of her tight skirt, which had been hidden from him by the peplum of her jacket. He loved the ampleness of her, the promise of softer folds and curves to be released from the constriction of her clothes. He found the zip at her waist, and Hannah dreamily arched her back against him.

'Have you done this in here before?' he said into the curve of her neck. 'In front of these mirrors?'

'No. But I have imagined how it would be.'

'Like this?'

'No,' Hannah confessed. 'Not nearly as good as this.'

She turned to face him, and over her bare shoulder he watched his hands slipping over her hips and her bottom, then greedily drawing her against him. He ducked his head to kiss her, closing out the mirror images, so there were only the two of them left in the world.

Hannah undid his buttons.

'Striped shirt, gold cufflinks,' she murmured. 'The very picture of a professional man.'

'Half-dressed? In the changing room of a ladies' frock shop?'

They were laughing as they stripped off the last obstacles of each other's clothes. Michael let the shreds of her black lace drop on the floor behind him. And then, as suddenly as it had begun, the laughter stopped.

He put his hands on her waist and Hannah raised herself on tiptoe to bring her mouth level with his. He looked down at the roundness of her belly and the heavy swell of her hips, and at her small hand closed around him and the red marks in her flesh left by her constricting clothes, and he was filled with tenderness and longing for her.

'Lie down,' he told her.

Obediently she knelt and then lay back, and he knelt beside her and lifted her arms and then her legs so that she made a star for him against the pale carpet. He leaned over her and let his mouth travel slowly, exploring the map of her skin, until her head fell back and she lifted her hips and he found the soft centre of her.

'Yes,' he heard her whisper. 'Yes, oh *please*, yes.'

Their striped and mirrored tent became a miraculous kingdom.

As he entered her, Hannah's legs wound around his waist and they looked sideways to see their reflections, light and dark, locked together. Their faces appeared suffused, abstracted, unlike themselves and yet like each other, conspirators in

309

pleasure. It was a long time since Michael had known pleasure like it. He felt that he was drowning in it, a death he reached out for, welcoming as it came.

Afterwards, when they lay wrapped in each other, Michael whispered to her, 'I don't want this moment ever to end. I don't ever want to have to leave you.'

Her fingers touched his spine. He felt the caress of her fingers with their painted nails so intensely that he could see them, and he lost the distinction between felt and seen, mirrored and plain.

Hannah's face had all the taut lines rubbed out of it. She lay gazing at Michael, half smiling, blurred by her own hair.

'You make me happy,' she said. 'I didn't expect you to.'

'I can't ever remember feeling so happy. I love you.'

She touched his mouth, warning him. 'Be careful.'

'I can't be careful. It's too late to be careful. I love you, Hannah.'

Warmth spread through her, under her skin, unpinning her. *It's too late to be careful.*

'I know,' Hannah said simply, with her mouth against his.

Fifteen

'I could have done this,' Janice said in her comfortable, insistent way. 'I should have done. It's our tennis court that's being christened, after all.'

She stood with her hands on her hips, head on one side, contemplating the two garden tables and the company of unmatched chairs arranged on the Ransomes' terrace. Janice wore candy-striped Bermuda shorts, familiar from other summers, although this May Sunday evening was their first appearance this year. Their re-emergence seemed to mark the official opening of the summer season. The cuffs of the shorts came just above Janice's plump, pretty knees.

Vicky shook out a William Morris print tablecloth and smoothed it over the sun-warmed wooden slats of one of the tables.

'No, I wanted to do it. It's time I did. We haven't had anyone over for ages.'

She couldn't even remember the last time she and Gordon had properly entertained the Grafton couples. It must have been before Helen was born. Long ago.

'Will this be all right, do you think?' she asked. 'If we sit at this one, and put the children over there?'

'Of course it will,' Janice said. She was laying knives and forks on the flowered cloth, polishing each one with a tea towel before placing it. 'There. Two, four, six, eight, and two more if the Cleggs make it. And six children, eight if the Cleggs ditto. Perfect.'

Janice wished she could bring everything else to order as easily as she marshalled the cutlery. She was troubled by the suspicion that too many familiar features of their lives were changing, and by a more obscure and generalized fear that she could not place, and found all the more alarming for that. She kept her anxiety under control by her attention to the glasses and plates.

Star had been wandering in the garden. It had been a hot day for early May, and the first cool of the early evening was welcome. The Ransomes' garden was not as big as the Frosts' but she had always liked it better. There were damp, wild corners here under the shade of tall trees, and even the flower beds nearer to the house were tangled with an unkempt mass of foliage that was the opposite of Andrew's manicured borders.

She came back across the grass towards the house, with her hands full of lilies of the valley and scilla. She was thinking as she skirted the children's noisy game of rounders that the three women on the terrace made a pleasing picture. Marcelle was sitting in a deck-chair, with one arm crooked behind her head. Janice and Vicky in their pale summery clothes moved calmly between the tables, and the sun slanted on the glasses they were laying out, making them look as if they had been poured full of light. The scents of grass and leaf mould mingled with barbecue charcoal, smoke and warmed earth.

Star held out her flowers to show Vicky. 'I picked these for the table, is that all right?'

'They're lovely. Here, put them in these.' Vicky held out two of the glasses and Star arranged the flowers in them, admiring the freshness of the tiny white and azure bells.

'I was saying that I should have done dinner for everyone,' Janice explained. 'But really this is much better, thanks to Vicky. Otherwise it would have been tennis all evening as well as afternoon.'

'It's nice here,' Star reassured them, as she was meant to do.

It had been a tradition amongst the five Grafton families to come together for a barbecue party in the first spell of fine weather of every summer. It was one of the cycle of parties and gatherings that made the landmarks in their year.

This year there was a new development. Andrew had recently installed an all-weather tennis court in his garden, and he had invited the men to play an inaugural afternoon match. And so the women had gathered in the Ransomes' garden with the children to make companionable preparations for the evening, as they had done often enough before.

Only this evening everything was not quite the same.

The absence of the Cleggs was part of the difference. Darcy was out of hospital and installed at Wilton again, but the couples had not seen much of him. They agreed amongst themselves that he did not look fully recovered, although Hannah was determinedly cheerful. He needed rest, she insisted, that was all. She had promised that they would try to come to the barbecue, if Darcy was not too tired, but there was no question of his playing tennis. The others felt the chill of that. A month ago Darcy would have pitched himself into any match, energized by the competition and his own determination to win.

And yet, it was not only Darcy's illness that had altered the pattern. Marcelle sat in her deck-chair with her head turned slightly to one side, seemingly a part of the little group but also separate from it.

Janice leaned over her once and asked, 'Are you okay?'

'Yes,' Marcelle said immediately. 'It's just so nice, sitting here watching the children. But there must be something I can do to help. Vicky, what is there?'

'Nothing. Sit right where you are.'

Marcelle did not know whether they exchanged concerned glances behind her head. She remembered how the women had murmured their anxiety for Vicky, and the concern that Janice and the others sometimes privately voiced for Star when Jimmy behaved badly, but she felt too withdrawn even to speculate about what they might think of her. Marcelle let these reflections slip away out of her head almost as soon as they had entered it.

It was enough to do to hold herself quietly, only half listening and half watching.

Vicky was smiling, busy with her arrangements for the evening, and Star was intent on arranging her flowers, her dark face momentarily lightened by her pleasure in them. Janice strolled across the lawn to the children, her hands in the pockets of her shorts.

The women had drawn closer. No one had mentioned the change in the air, but each of them was aware of it. There was the thin vibration of watchfulness and anxiety between them, but also the low, steady note of friendship.

Marcelle's eyes fixed on her children again.

Jonathan was almost the same age as William Frost, but he was physically much smaller. There seemed to be an anxiety about him, a tentativeness that made him poke nervously at the rounders ball instead of hitting out when it was pitched to him. When her turn came, Daisy was bolder. She swung out with the bat and the ball soared in a triumphant arc and dropped into the green waves of ivy and honeysuckle at the far end of the garden.

'*Daisy, Daisy's lost the ball, we'll never find it in there* . . .'

'*It's not fair* . . .'

The children's voices rose in complaint and then faded again as Janice found another ball and threw it to them.

'They should be here soon,' Vicky said, meaning the husbands.

But it was another half-hour before they did arrive, in their tennis shoes, wet-haired from their swim in the Frosts' pool. They came out into the garden with beer cans in their hands, full of the reports of their game, breaking the net that the women had woven between them.

Jimmy and Gordon had beaten Andrew and Michael, but the match had been close enough for them to feel satisfied. Gordon put his hand on Vicky's shoulder.

'Are we very late? I'm sorry. They took us to five sets, by some fluke, and it was eight six in the last one. Do you want me to start barbecuing?'

'Well done, Daddy,' Mary Ransome said. She wound her arm around his leg and he rested his other hand on the top of her head, feeling the fine hair warmed by the sun. The three of them stood for a moment, connected by his hands, until Vicky moved easily away.

'Do the children's sausages first,' she ordered him.

'And what about me?' Jimmy demanded of Mary. 'Don't I get a well done?'

He swung her up by her arms so that she shrieked with delighted fear, and then he settled her on his shoulders and cantered across the grass.

'You're a horse, well done, horse,' Mary shouted.

Marcelle sat in her deck-chair. She had watched Michael as he came out of the French doors, the last of the group, and saw how he glanced at her, lifted one hand in a wave and then went to where Star and Andrew and Janice were standing, laughing at something one of them said as he wiped the froth of beer from his top lip. Marcelle did not even know what she had been hoping for from him, but the denial of it cut her so she had to blink and the hard edges of the terrace in front of her grew threateningly blurred.

Jimmy lifted Mary over his head and set her on the ground again. His shoulders and arms ached pleasurably from the hours of tennis, and the glow of the win was still with him. He stood in front of Marcelle's deck-chair, his shadow falling across her. He noticed that she was wearing big earrings that looked too large for her face.

'Hey, Mar, you haven't got a drink.'

'I haven't, have I? I'll have a glass of wine, whatever there is.'

He brought her one, and one for himself, and then sat down on the flagstones at her feet, resting his back against her legs.

There were wood-pigeons in the tall trees. The thought of Lucy came into Jimmy's head, followed by a surge of relief that Darcy was not here. It was more than a week since he had heard from Lucy, and he was beginning to be afraid that she might tell her father. Jimmy had resolved on each successive morning that he would telephone her and determine when the abortion would take place, but each day he had found some reason for not making the call.

Marcelle felt the warmth of Jimmy's shoulder. It seemed to spread through her, and she realized that she was cold. She touched the collar of his shirt with the tips of her fingers, intrigued in spite of her detachment by the solidity of him, the prickle of rufous hairs at the nape of his neck and the scent of beer and swimming pool that emanated from him. By contrast Michael had become insubstantial, slipping away from her, so that on the rare occasions when they did touch it surprised them both and they drew back, unsure of themselves. Neither of them spoke of this new degree of separation between them.

Marcelle found that she wanted to press her face against Jimmy's neck. She wanted to cry and have him stroke her hair and murmur comfort to her. She was appalled by her own weakness.

'Your fingers are cold, Mar,' Jimmy said, turning to face her. She withdrew her hand at once but he seized it and began to rub it between his own.

'Talk to me,' Marcelle said, to cover her distress.

'What shall I tell you?'

She saw that Jimmy was pleased with himself and the evening. *Tell me you can see me, that I'm not invisible, that I still exist,* Marcelle cried silently. Aloud she said, 'Oh, whatever you like. Some gossip.'

He pretended to think. He did not like the idea of gossip now; it had become uncomfortable to him. The throaty calls of the wood-pigeons seemed to grow louder.

'Hmm. Gossip. Do you know, I don't think there is any? Dull bunch, aren't we?'

Michael sat astride one of the garden chairs, watching Gordon flipping sausages on the barbecue. As soon as he'd arrived in the Ransomes' street Michael had been hoping for the sight of one of the Cleggs' cars, and he had carried his disappointment inside with him in the vain hope that Hannah might somehow have arrived with one of the other couples, or even have sent some innocent-sounding message via Janice for him to hear. But there was no sign of her, and no word either, and now the evening stretched pointlessly ahead of him. He fiddled with the tongs, getting in Gordon's way and not knowing what else to do.

At length the children were called to the table. The parents had another drink while Gordon turned their steaks on to the heat. The sun moved behind the trees and the dimensions of the garden seemed to change, expanding beyond the indistinct margins of green and grey.

The four couples were already sitting down to eat when the doorbell rang. Gordon went to answer it while Vicky hastily relaid the two places she had removed.

A moment later Darcy and Hannah emerged into the garden with Gordon at Darcy's elbow on the other side from Hannah. The talk around the table stopped expectantly.

At first Michael could take in nothing but Hannah. She was wearing a vivid yellow linen shirt, and white trousers that stopped short of her bare ankles. The evening light seemed to brighten again and settle around her head. With this focusing came sharpened recollections, how taut and silky her skin had felt, the entire scent and taste of her, the wonderful secrecy of the curtained ottoman tent within her exotic shop and the infinity of mirrored reflections. He realized that he had half risen from his place, and made himself sit down again, awkwardly bumping the table as he did so. Darcy was no more than a dark shape beside Hannah.

There was a confused babble of greetings, but the only voices were the women's. Jimmy sat unnaturally silent in his place, and Andrew was staring at Darcy.

Darcy detached himself from Hannah and Gordon and seemed to launch himself at the table. He loomed suddenly at the end of it, fists on the back of Gordon's chair, surveying them. There was an instant's quiet, even the children at their table falling silent, and then Darcy demanded,

'What is this? Don't I get a drink?'

'Darcy –' Hannah began.

He didn't turn his head. 'I can have a fucking glass of *wine*, can't I?'

Hannah lifted one buttercup-yellow shoulder. She sat down between Andrew and Jimmy without looking at Darcy again. It was Vicky who stood up, walked to the other end of the table and poured the drink for him. Everyone stared at the glass, as if the Californian Cabernet had taken on some significance of its own. Darcy sat in Gordon's place, pushing away Gordon's plate with his forearm. He drank half of the wine and then set his glass down with exaggerated care. It was obvious that it wasn't his first drink of the day.

'So who won the big match?' he asked. 'Jim?'

Jimmy was rigid with the anticipation of a different question. The certainty that Lucy must have talked to her father began to break up, permitting different, more hopeful interpretations of Darcy's mood. He grinned at Darcy.

'Ah, Gordon and me. Piece of cake.'

Jimmy heard the little musical jingle of Marcelle's improbable earrings as he dropped one arm around her shoulders, and he absent-mindedly squeezed her as if she were the trophy.

Andrew protested that it had been no piece of cake. Conversation resumed in relieved eddies. Darcy had been drinking, that was all.

Michael's eyes guardedly met Hannah's across the table. He saw now that she was carefully made up but the artifice did not quite hide some shadow in her face. She seemed less pretty than usual. He found this juxtaposition of public Hannah with the other Hannah he had discovered both touching and disconcerting. He made himself look away, to Darcy.

Darcy was loudly talking, tilting his glass, complaining that he had not been able to play tennis. Michael was belatedly shocked by what he saw.

There was a flush over Darcy's cheeks and nose, but the skin seemed loosened on the bone. There was a bluish tinge to his lips that bled out into the lined flesh around his mouth. He was still handsome, even imposing, but it was as if the good looks had all along been only pasted on to some crumbling substructure.

Michael's professional mind began to tick. He recalled the name of the Cleggs' GP, and resolved that he must have a quiet word with his colleague, Darcy's cardiac specialist.

Then, fully-formed, the thought delivered itself to him. What happens if he dies? What happens to Hannah? *Hannah* . . .

Once it had come to him, it seemed absurd that he had not asked himself the question before. But Darcy had always been a solid, massive presence amongst the couples and in Grafton itself. How much more invincible must he seem to Hannah? Yet he had suffered one heart attack in front of them, and he was plainly ill.

A new set of reckonings took root and multiplied as Michael looked across the table again, to Hannah. He shivered, torn between apprehension and desire for her. Hannah was talking, making Andrew laugh at something she said, and her hands moved fluently between them.

The children dispersed indoors. Gordon brought candles in holders to the table and the flames steadied within their glass chimneys. At once the darkness concentrated beyond the margin of the circle. Tiny moths were drawn to the light, and spiralled upwards in the treacherous heat.

The talk within the fragile dome of light fragmented, growing thin, as if they were each aware of other, unspoken and more significant conversations.

Darcy barely touched his food, but he drank steadily. He could not let the smallest talk begin at the other end of the table without leaning forward, his bulk weighty against the table, scowling and demanding, 'What? What the hell are you talking about?'

It was as if he wanted to demonstrate his supremacy here, at least, in the company of friends. The couples were kindly to him, making space for him as his interruptions and pronouncements grew louder, more insistent and less rational, until conversation almost foundered. Darcy's words began to slur and he frowned, as if affronted to find his tongue beyond his control.

'What do you know?' he pursued some argument in Andrew's direction. 'What the . . . what the *fuck* do you know?' His face contorted with anger and frustration, but the reason for the disagreement had already escaped him. His helplessness was apparent to all of them.

Hannah would not look at him.

Gordon left everyone's glasses empty. But then, with a small cunning smile, Darcy bent down and reached out for an uncorked bottle that was left half-hidden in the shadow beside the barbecue. It clearly cost him a physical effort to bend and twist and there was an instant, with the bottle in his grasp, when it seemed that he would not be able to heave himself upright again. But Darcy did sit up, and he placed the full bottle beside his glass with a hiss of triumph.

'Anyone join me?' he called.

His fist tightened around the neck of the bottle. He lifted it, brandished it over his glass, and then tilted. Misjudging the distances, he clipped the rim of the glass with the bottle. The wine gushed but the glass was already falling. Darcy tried to catch at it, but his confused hands fumbled and the bottle fell too, a dark plume of wine making a twisted arc in the candlelight. A crimson jet sprayed across the cloth and the wine glass rolled over the edge of the table to smash on the paving.

There was a confusion of movement. The bottle was caught, hands reached to mop up the rivulets of wine.

Michael said, 'Darcy? Are you all right?'

Darcy did not answer. His head was bowed, so that he seemed to be staring down at the shattered glass. Very slowly, painfully, he lifted one arm and then the other until his elbows rested on the table. Then he covered his face with his hands.

Very quietly he said, 'Oh God.'

In the candlelight the faces except Hannah's were like pale moons, reflecting their separate concerns and their diffidence and embarrassment.

Michael had begun to stand, but Vicky was quicker. She reached Darcy's side before he lifted his head from his hands.

'Yes, I'm all right,' Darcy said.

He seemed suddenly completely sober, surprised to see them staring at him.

Vicky touched his shoulder. 'Come inside. I'll make you a cup of coffee. It's getting cold out here.'

'Yes. Yes, it is.' Darcy went with her, heavy-footed but as obedient as a child.

Gordon watched them go. He was impressed by the calm directness of Vicky's intervention, and he felt a quiver of renewed love for her as she led Darcy out of sight into the house. And at the same time, as if some subconscious recognition swam towards the surface of his mind, a question formed in his head.

Janice began to collect the plates and Gordon bent to pick up the broken pieces of glass. The others pushed back their chairs, feeling the release of tension. A buzz of concern centred on Hannah.

'I'm sorry,' she said to Gordon. 'We shouldn't have come. Only he wanted to, and he isn't stoppable when he wants something.' She spread her hands helplessly.

'How is he?' Michael asked. The others were quiet, deferring to his superior medical insights.

Hannah hesitated. 'Well . . . perhaps if I could talk to you about it, some time . . .'

Their eyes met again, mutely signalling to each other, *I must see you, I need you.*

Gordon was prompt. 'If you want to have a quick chat, if you think Mike can help, why don't you go in there, in my study?'

There were French windows, open on the garden, on the other side of the house from the kitchen. Hannah nodded.

'I'd be grateful. That's if you don't mind, Michael? I'm sorry the evening's ruined.'

Marcelle held herself still, listening to the rushing sound her blood made in her ears.

321

With the yellow linen shirt brushing against his sleeve, Michael walked with Hannah into the house.

Inside, Gordon's study was dim. He closed one half of the doors behind them, leaving the other ajar, wondering how closely Marcelle was watching. Hannah faced him, stepping backwards a little in the thick blue dusk. He saw the cushiony oval of her half-opcn mouth. Without saying anything Michael took hold of her. There were seams in her tight clothes that constricted the flesh beneath and made him think of the swollen hemispheres of summer fruit. He breathed in the scent of her hair and her skin as he kissed her, his fingers at the neck of her yellow shirt. Michael's head revolved with dizzy calculations about the desk and the open windows, and the compound scents of the Frosts' pool house came back to confuse him.

'Not now,' Hannah whispered. 'We can't now.'

Michael felt the tiny twist of her smile as she kissed him in return. Hannah liked her own power, and it gave him a pleasurable, abject sense of his own helplessness to be made her victim.

'Yes, we can. No one will come in.'

She was already half lying on Gordon's desk. Michael could just make out a neat pile of household bills, a dish of paper clips.

'No. Marcelle's outside. Darcy's somewhere, you saw how he was.'

Irritation blurred Michael's desire. He knew that Hannah would not give way, and he wondered why he was trying to coerce her.

'When, then?'

'Come to the shop on Tuesday evening. At closing time.'

She had planned it already, and his desire for her renewed itself. There was no question that he would not go; he could not even remember what he was supposed to be doing on Tuesday evening.

'Yes. I'll come. You know that I will, I suppose?'

Hannah slipped away from underneath him. Outside a light clicked on, illuminating the garden. They could see each other clearly, and the arrangement of Gordon's paperwork on his desk, and they both heard the clink of plates and the scrape of chairs as the tables were cleared. Michael walked slowly around the desk and sat down in the chair. He swivelled it through an arc, and pressed his fingers together at the point of his chin.

'What about Darcy?' he asked reluctantly.

Hannah sat down in another chair. They were both aware of this parody in their positions of the doctor and his patient. Michael thought that anyone looking in from the garden would see them sitting in exactly the blameless way that they ought.

'You can see how he is tonight. I don't know if he feels afraid, or weakened, and can't bear to show it even to me. There are all these' – Hannah's hands chopped at the air – 'side issues of the booze, and his aggression, and the determination to go on doing business as if nothing has happened, and he makes them so dense that I can't see through them to the reality. But I *think* he is afraid. I can feel it seeping out of him when he's asleep. He sleeps badly, and his muscles quiver like a dog's.'

'Do you think there is anything else he is worrying about? Beyond the fact that he suffered a heart attack a month ago?'

After a moment Hannah said, 'No. What could there be?'

'I imagine that it is difficult for a powerful individual like Darcy to admit the truth of his own physical vulnerability. His reaction might take a dozen different forms. There might well be other manifestations yet, before he comes properly to terms with it. And Darcy is a complicated man.'

Michael offered her the reassurance, although he thought that Darcy's brand of bullish confidence was in fact rather straightforward.

Hannah nodded. She said, as if it was important to make the point, 'I still love him. And I think I hate him as well.'

'I don't think that is particularly uncommon,' Michael said softly. 'Do you? Sitting where we are now?'

He felt as if his ears were tuned to previously inaudible frequencies. He could hear the high-pitched humming of sexual conspiracy minutely disturbing the air between the couples and radiating beyond them, through his own and Hannah's and other people's marriages outwards into infinity.

Darcy might die, he thought again. All the possibilities of confusion, of responsibilities that he might have to bear nudged at him. I still love him, Hannah had said. She had her own weakness, he understood, in spite of her apparent power. He looked at her now, as if she were really a patient in the chair beside his desk, and felt himself caught between pity and desire.

'No,' Hannah agreed at length. 'I suppose it is quite ordinary.' Then she smiled at him, her face warming and lightening. 'I'm glad you are here. I'm glad of this, between us.'

'That's good,' Michael said, feeling his own fraudulence.

Star and the Frosts had gone inside with Vicky and Gordon, and Marcelle and Jimmy were left alone in the garden. Jimmy had secured the half-spilled wine bottle, and he refilled their glasses. Marcelle drank in the vague hope that alcohol might anaesthetize her. She wished that she was not here, but could not think of anywhere else to be. The lights on the house wall shone too brightly overhead; she closed her eyes for a second and a painful red glare burned behind her eyelids. There was no light showing at the window of Gordon's study.

'Let's walk down the garden,' Jimmy proposed, breaking the silence. He offered her his arm in an old-fashioned gesture.

The garden was dark and soothing beyond the glare of the terrace lights. The rank scent of earth and crushed grass grew stronger, released by their silent feet. It made Jimmy think of the last time he had seen Lucy, and the brambled clearing in the wood. He swallowed his anxiety slightly more easily. If Darcy knew anything, it would have come out tonight.

Jimmy and Marcelle sat down together on a wooden seat at the end of the garden, hidden from the house by the rounded bulwark of a silver-frosted ilex. Marcelle wrapped her arms around herself. She felt as if she were slipping out of sight, down some treacherous slope into a mire of isolation. She wondered, as she identified the sensation, if this were no more than weakness and whether some act of self-discipline might set her upright again in the landscape of ordinary life. Jimmy stuck up in the middle of the slope like a healthy tree that might break her sliding descent.

'Do you think I'm a fool?' she asked abruptly.

He answered at once, 'No. Not any kind of fool. What makes you ask?'

Marcelle's head fell back. Jimmy's arm rested along the seat behind her; it was a luxury to lie against him. She had felt the same earlier, when she had touched his collar and noticed the prickle of reddish hair at the nape of his neck. The confirmation of touch, she thought absently. The comfort of it. There had been nothing with Michael, neither touch nor comfort, for a long time. Her loneliness focused sharply, burning like the pinpoint of sun through a magnifying glass. And then, with a sudden flare of anger she thought, Why should I be denied it, why only me? When everyone else takes what they want . . .

Without any warning, she was overtaken by a jolt of longing, a need for love that was stronger and seemed more affirmative than anything she had felt for a long time.

She had almost blurted out her fears about Michael and Hannah, but now her queasy anxiety contracted, diminished by the urgency of the new feeling. She remembered clearly what had happened on Christmas Eve, the secret she had shared with Jimmy and then wished she could take back into her own custody. Jimmy was not the right recipient for her confidences, if there were anything to confide. But Jimmy felt like her friend. More than a friend, as he had offered to be on dozens of occasions in the past. Jimmy was what she needed.

'What makes you ask?' Jimmy repeated softly. She could tell he was smiling.

Marcelle was thinking that they were like dominoes standing in a tidy row. Then Nina had been set down carelessly at the end of the line and she had toppled over, and the couples had begun falling on top of each other in obedient sequence all along the line, and now the momentum had reached her and it was her turn to fall too. The thought made her want to laugh, and then to her surprise she realized that she was laughing, out loud, resting her head against Jimmy's arm and looking up at the stars in the dark sky.

'Nothing. Nothing,' she managed to say.

'I'm glad it's funny, whatever it is,' Jimmy said.

Marcelle stretched her arms and legs, cat-like, recognizing the cords of tension that had kept her hunched into herself for weeks.

The need for love and attention had not evaporated with her laughter. It had become a quite specific itch.

Slowly she turned her head to him. There was the outline of his small-nosed, tidy profile. Like a pleased dog, she thought. Or some nocturnal animal, tilt-eared and poised. When she lifted her hand to the nape of his neck the hairs felt very soft under her fingers. She stroked, tiny encouraging movements in the reddish fur. There was a thick, viscid heat between her thighs.

Jimmy's top lip lifted, showing his teeth. He looked full at her. Marcelle was singingly glad of the darkness. She felt beautiful and queenly in it.

Then Jimmy leaned forward an inch and kissed her. It was a light, brotherly little kiss that fell at the corner of her dry mouth. Marcelle waited, imagining that she could trace the course of her blood through the cells and ventricles of her body. Then, in the flush of warmth, she tilted her head so that their lips touched again, and opened her mouth and kissed Jimmy in return. She had kissed him before, in the hazy glow of evenings when the couples drank and laughed and danced in each other's houses, but there had never been an invitation in it until now. Tonight she made the invitation explicit with her tongue and her fingers knotting in his hair, drawing him towards her.

Jimmy's arm was awkwardly trapped behind Marcelle's shoulders. He noticed that her skin was hot; there was a faint, scorched scent coming off it as if she had a fever.

Jimmy liked Marcelle, because she was part of the spread of other men's wives that was there for him to admire, but also because she was herself. He had imagined, quite pleasurably and not infrequently, what kind of lover she might be. Nor had he ever dismissed, in their amiable skirmishes, the interesting possibility that one day one of them might lead to his discovering whether or not his predictions were accurate. But now, with Marcelle's tongue in his mouth and the pulse in her cheek ticking wildly against his, his only feeling was of dismay. He shifted on the bench, resisting the need to clear his throat.

Marcelle's other hand came to rest, palm up, on his thigh. He grabbed hold of it and used the business of kissing her knuckles as an excuse to detach his mouth from hers.

He could only think of Lucy, Lucy white-limbed in the clearing in the wood and all the other times they had been together, but without any flicker of retrospective passion that might have come to his rescue now. He could only think of her as pregnant, a confusing double identification of her as both his innocent victim and the malevolent repository of a brood of accusations that might swarm out of her at any time, to home in on himself. He was smitten simultaneously with longing for her, and with the desire to escape from Grafton as quickly as possible before Darcy came for him. The relief he had felt at dinner was eaten up by certainty that it was only a matter of time before he was found out. Darcy had acted freakishly enough tonight to make Jimmy afraid of what there might be to come.

And now there was the painful irrelevance of Marcelle.

Jimmy wondered, with a tangential flicker of curiosity, if had it not been for Lucy he might have taken up Marcelle's offer. A brief image entered his head of the two of them on this bench, with Marcelle straddled barelegged across him, her face tipped back in a spasm of pleasure. He dismissed the thought, with the possibility that he might return to it later, as he kissed the knuckle of Marcelle's little finger again.

'You don't really want this, do you?' he chuckled.

Marcelle hesitated. He felt the shiver of confusion in her.

'This? Oh yes, I do.'

Who was he to tell her what she might or might not want? There had been perhaps a minute for Marcelle when everything had seemed sweet and intense and also perfectly simple. She was desirable and desired and Jimmy would love her out here in the rustling garden and later, without knowing exactly how, she was sure she would close up this secret and carry it safely back into the couples' evening and all the other evenings like an amulet.

Only now, she understood too late, she had opened herself up, like some saleswoman opening a case, and Jimmy had declined her.

'Mar' – his voice was cajoling, cracked with their mutual embarrassment – 'you know I love you, but –'

Marcelle coldly interrupted him. 'But you don't want to fuck me. Have I got that right?'

Anger foamed up inside her. She would not try to laugh, to make it easy for him, so they could dismiss this as another episode in the saga of Jimmy's flirtations. He had asked her often enough. What did he say, with his foxy little grin?

When? When Mike's at the hospital?

He had allowed her – no, *made* her – think of him as her resort, for when she needed him. But it had been only to flatter himself, and nothing to do with her or her feelings and least of all to do with the unsavoury package of her needs and desires.

Marcelle had never felt such anger.

Mercifully the anger burned up her humiliation. She drew away her hand and wondered whether she should slap him with it. Her fingers itched, and she could already hear the way the sharp, satisfying crack would be taken up and amplified by the black air.

'Of course I do,' he mumbled. 'Only here, in the garden, with Star and Mike in the house . . .'

'Don't lie about it,' Marcelle said. 'Don't you know how disgusting it makes you seem?'

The desire to hit out left her. She stood up instead, and then ran back over the grass to the house.

'Marcelle, wait a minute,' Jimmy called after her.

Marcelle could see Michael. He was standing in the kitchen,

his back to the window, talking to Gordon and Andrew. She put her fingertips up to her face and pushed the folds of burning skin back, taut, to open her eyes and drag her mouth into a smile. She stepped on to the terrace, into the glare of the lights. She was afraid of the feelings that would come later, but for the moment she had the armour of her clean, bright anger. She opened the door and walked into the kitchen, where all of them could see her.

Jimmy sat on the bench. He took out a cigarette and lit it, but he smoked only half before he threw it away from him with a quick gesture of distaste. Then he stood up and followed Marcelle to the house, stepping in his turn into the lights.

Vicky's bedroom was the same, but Darcy's memories of it seemed to belong to a much more distant past than the reality of a few months. He sat tentatively on the end of the bed in a ruck of cushions and what looked like a crocheted shawl with long, tangled fringes.

He was thinking back to the other times when he had come here, of Vicky standing in the thin, chilly sunshine of wintry mornings to unbutton the loose layers of her maternal clothes. He had entirely submerged himself, forgetting everything, in the blue-veined folds of her exposed body. He could recall the precise choreography of their passion as clearly as he could see the lace-bordered cushions, the intimate terrain of the white bedcover, but it was like studying a series of photographs of their encounters. He was cut off from that sweet series of mornings by the intervention of chaotic time as effectively as if by a steel door. He was possessed by the knowledge that he could not go back, or obliterate what had intervened, or even hope to make a partial repair. An overwhelming sense of loss weighed him down, and a nostalgia for his life as it had been then. His heart contracted and expanded in his chest, forcing a muddy and sluggish current around his body.

It was only when he was drunk that a proper perspective opened to him. Sober, Darcy knew, it was possible to feign a kind of busy blindness, to deceive himself as well as he deceived the others. But the day's drinking had cleared his sight and he wondered if he should make some move before it was too late.

Still he went on sitting at the end of Vicky's bed. He was tired, and he had no idea where to run to.

Vicky put a slopped cup of black coffee into his hand. 'There. Drink it.'

He bent his head. As the warmth fogged his face some other recollection stirred, the pale eye of a cup held for him, the elusive warmth of his mother.

Vicky sat down beside him. 'How do you feel?'

Darcy considered the possible responses. 'Drunk,' he offered. 'Sorry about the evening.'

'The evening doesn't matter in the least. But you shouldn't drink so much.'

Simple, he thought. Good, wholesome advice. Too late.

'Hannah . . .'

'No.' Very gently. 'It's Vicky.'

'I know that. I'm not so far gone. Vicky, Vicky. I remember. I was going to say, Hannah tells me the same thing. And the doctors. Ha. Bad for the heart. Only I keep thinking it might have been easier to go the first time. Saved a . . . saved what? I don't know.' Darcy shrugged. 'Saved a lot of formalities.'

Vicky took the empty cup away from him. He felt the mattress absorbing the shift of her weight and he was reminded again, with the same detachment, of the far-off mornings they had spent on this bed. Vicky put her arms around him. She was murmuring to him, cajoling.

'You mustn't say that. You mustn't even think it. You've been ill, but you're getting better. You have to let yourself get better, wait for it to happen naturally, not think it's something you can fix like you're able to fix everything else.'

Her broad hands rubbed his shoulders, her fingers cupped his jaw, holding the weight of his head for him. The associations stirred in him again.

'*Was* able to.'

Slowly Darcy let his head drop forward until it rested against her and Vicky held him, her words becoming indecipherable croonings as she cradled him in her arms.

'I'm tired,' Darcy said. It was true. He could feel sleep thickening at the back of his eyes.

'I know.'

Then he told her, 'I'm afraid, as well.'

To Vicky he sounded like a child acknowledging his fears at the end of the day.

'I know,' she said again. 'It's all right.'

'No. It isn't. It can't be.'

'Darcy, don't go to sleep now. Hannah will want to take you home.'

Later, after the couples had gone, Gordon went upstairs. Vicky was already in bed, sitting up in her nightdress. He perched on the edge beside her so she had to put down what she was reading.

'What did you make of Darcy?' he asked.

'Beyond the obvious, you mean? He told me that he was afraid.'

'Of what?'

'I don't know. The same things that we are all afraid of, I suppose.'

His wife's smooth face and clear eyes seemed to Gordon to deflect his questions. He could have asked her if she had had an affair with Darcy, but he did not think Vicky would divulge her secrets. He understood that perhaps he should not try to make her, and that more probably he did not want to know the truth.

He stood, and she calmly picked up the magazine she had laid aside. He was thinking of Nina as he undressed, in her cool house in the close. He wondered if it would be his fate to think of her with longing every night from now until he was an old man.

The next morning Darcy was downstairs early, before anyone else in the house was awake. He had not been able to sleep and so went to the kitchen and made tea. He sat at the table with his cup, staring out at the garden and the view beyond it.

A car came up the driveway from the lane. It was quiet enough in the house for Darcy to hear the driver leave the car and cross the expanse of gravel to the front door. A moment later the bell rang. Darcy pulled his bathrobe tighter around him and went to answer it.

There was a man standing under the umbrella of wisteria that shielded the front door. Darcy knew him quite well. He was an accountant called Geoffrey Lawson. The last time they had met was when both men had played in a charity golf tournament.

'Geoffrey? You're very early. We're not scheduled to meet today, are we?'

'No. But may I come in?'

The man followed Darcy through the quiet house to the kitchen. He stood in the doorway holding his briefcase, stiff in his dark suit.

'What can I offer you? Coffee? Or breakfast, perhaps?' Darcy asked. He glanced pointedly at the kitchen clock. It was not yet eight a.m.

'Nothing, thank you. Darcy, I'll come straight to the point. I had a call from Vincent Templeman yesterday evening.'

Darcy stood without moving. He could only wait for what would come next.

The man said, 'Could we go through into your office?'

'Of course,' Darcy said.

In his briefcase, Geoffrey Lawson had the books of his client Vincent Templeman's private company. Templeman was a property magnate, now retired to Jersey. Darcy had managed his private funds and assets for almost five years. Lawson laid the books on Darcy's desk.

'When Vincent called me last night, he told me that there are one or two aspects of these figures' – he tapped the folders under his hand – 'that are troubling him. I promised him that I would drive down here first thing to see you.'

There was a moment's silence. From upstairs, Darcy heard

one of the children, Laura or Freddie, running the length of the landing. The au pair girl was calling them to get dressed. Soon Hannah would be downstairs.

'May I see the company cheque books?' Geoffrey Lawson asked.

Darcy went to the safe, took them out and handed them to the accountant.

'And may I sit here?' Lawson indicated Darcy's desk chair.

'Of course,' Darcy said again. Now that this was happening, after the weeks of convincing himself that it could not, he felt only a merciful detachment. He watched the man set out his papers, his neat silver pen and his calculator in a leather folder.

'I will go and put some clothes on,' Darcy said. He left the man, head bent over the accounts at his own desk, like some threatening doppelgänger.

Hannah was out of bed. When he went into their bedroom Darcy heard her singing 'Eleanor Rigby' in the shower. He went into his own bathroom and shaved, and then dressed himself in a dark suit, better cut than the accountant's, and a silk tie, as if it were one of his days for going to London. Then he went slowly back down the stairs. He could hear Mandy talking to Laura and Freddie over their breakfast in the kitchen. The man in his office looked up at Darcy when he came in, then returned to his work.

A little while later he replaced the cap on his silver pen. His fingers rested on the calculator keypad while he spoke. His voice was perfectly level.

'Darcy, it appears that five unaccounted cheques have been drawn on the Templeman company account. Three are in your own name, the others are to Kleinwort Benson. The sum in question amounts to something over nine hundred thousand pounds. Is there any explanation you would like me to relay to my client?'

'Not immediately,' Darcy said. The explanations would come. He would have to begin the counterplay, even though he was so tired that he wondered if he could even lift the telephone.

'I shall have to call Templeman. You do understand that, don't you?'

Darcy inclined his head. He watched as Lawson gathered up his papers and the cheque books and locked them in his briefcase. He escorted the man to the front door and watched him as he climbed into his car and drove away.

Hannah came down the stairs. 'Who was that?'

'Geoff Lawson. Came to pick up some papers.'

Hannah clicked her tongue as she kissed his cheek. He could smell her scent. It was one he liked, but he couldn't remember the name of it.

'How do you feel? I didn't know you were going to town today.'

'I'm not,' Darcy said vaguely, turning away from the door. 'I forgot, when I got dressed.'

He went back into his office, and sat down at the desk.

Hannah put her head round the door to say goodbye before she left for the shop. He heard Mandy leaving to drive the two children to nursery and school, and then Cathy scrambling downstairs and running out to the Renault. It was another sunny morning, he noticed, as the light warmed and brightened the silent room.

Darcy sat at his desk, and waited. Somewhere in the house either Lucy or Hannah's cleaner was playing loud music. The cheerful sound intensified his sense of isolation. He gazed at the black file drawers ranged against the opposite wall, but he did not move to look into them.

The fingers of sunlight crept across the wall. Darcy drank the cup of coffee that the au pair brought him at lunchtime, but he ate nothing. Once his hand reached out to the telephone, but he did not pick up the handset. He thought of how Vicky had held him the night before, and her assurance that everything was all right. He would have liked to speak to her, but he remembered that she was at her clinic. His business line rang only two or three times and he sat motionless in his chair, letting the answering machine click and hum in response.

In the afternoon the house came to life again. Laura and Freddie were at home; he saw Laura run past his window and across the striped breadth of lawn. The sun had moved round the house; his desk was in shadow. Hannah came back too, although she did not look in to see him.

Then, at gone six o'clock, when he was stiff and chilled from sitting for so long in the same position, he heard another car coming up from the lane. The front doorbell rang again. Darcy waited, his senses strained to anticipate what would come next.

He heard the sound of voices, and the swift click of Hannah's high heels. And then she knocked at his door.

'Darcy? There are some people here to see you.'

There were three of them. They wore dark blazers, unemphatic striped ties and cheap watches. When the door had closed on Hannah one of the men introduced himself and his colleagues. They were from the Fraud Squad.

The senior policeman explained that they came with a search warrant, under the special procedure provisions of section 9, Police and Criminal Evidence Act. Still Darcy sat at his desk, where he had been waiting all day for this. He turned his head and saw Laura running back over the mown grass to Mandy.

And then, because there was nothing else he could do, he gave the three policemen access to his safe and file cabinets. They stayed in his office for three-quarters of an hour. When they left, they took with them most of the books and ledgers and files relating to Darcy's business.

When they had gone, with their evidence, in the grey Ford Scorpio that had brought them, Darcy walked into the sunlit drawing room. There were bowls of fat blood-red peonies on the tables on either side of the chimneypiece. Hannah and the twins were standing in the middle of the room, watching.

'Who were they?' Hannah said. She came to him and put her hands on his arms, but the twins stood together, defending each other. 'Darcy, what's happening?'

'They were policemen,' Darcy said.

He saw the identical stiffening of shock and fear in his

daughters' beautiful faces and the way that the colour changed in his wife's, leaving two dull blotches of crimson high on her cheekbones.

Darcy said, 'Don't worry, it's all right. There's nothing to worry about.' His voice sounded brittle, with the bass resonance gone. He turned away from the eyes of the three of them.

'I have to go and ring my solicitor,' he said, in his different voice.

Sixteen

'Mrs Clegg for you,' the medical secretary's nasal voice announced to Michael in his poky office at the hospital on Tuesday morning.

'Put her through,' Michael said. The long day ahead with its cargo of patients was like some sentence that must be served before the evening, and Hannah, could be delivered to him.

'Michael?'

He smiled into the receiver. 'You only just caught me. I'm about to do rounds.'

'Something's happened. To Darcy.'

'His heart?'

The complex of possibilities that he had already imagined delivered themselves to him again. Even as he envisaged them, Michael realized that his own heart leapt with a momentary wild hope.

'No. He's all right. Nothing like that.'

'Then what?'

'Michael, it's very weird. The police came yesterday evening. They had a special warrant. They took away Darcy's files and books, everything to do with the business.'

'What does Darcy say? Is he there?'

'Yes. He says it's a mistake. He was on to his solicitor for an hour last night after the police left, and the man has just arrived. They're shut in Darcy's office. It means I can't see you tonight, although I want to so much. I have to be here if Darcy needs me, don't I?'

337

'Of course you do. Don't worry. It must be some kind of mistake, if Darcy says it is.'

But even as he reassured her Michael was already sifting the grains of likelihood in his mind, weighing the possibility that Darcy might in truth be guilty of something. There had often seemed to be too much money at Wilton, an over-heated largesse spilling out of Darcy in a way that Michael suddenly and perfectly clearly recognized to be ominous.

'I hope you are right,' Hannah whispered.

A vibration of doubt and anxiety in her voice was plainly to be heard, the rich confidence faltering. Michael understood that she was not convinced by Darcy's protests either.

'Listen,' he said. He had to grasp at a thread of hope because the promise of their evening had been snatched away.

'Next week I had planned to go to a medical conference. Two nights away, Wednesday and Thursday. Marcelle knows I'm going. I'm supposed to be presenting a paper, but David Keene, who is one of my colleagues and the co-author, came to ask me this morning if he could read it instead. There isn't the funding for us both to go. If you could manage to be away too, we could go somewhere together instead. Could we?'

Since Darcy had further hemmed them in with uncertainties it seemed vital to have this much to hold on to.

'I don't know.' Hannah was distracted. He couldn't blame her, but it was imperative that she should agree to what a minute ago had only been the vaguest possibility.

'Please,' Michael said.

'I . . . I could do it, if I said I was going on a buying trip for the shop. If this is resolved by then . . .'

'It will be. That's what we'll do.' Michael could see a posse of white coats in the corridor outside. He was already late for rounds. 'I have to go. Hannah, I love you.'

He had said it before, in the cushiony sanctuary of her shop. He wasn't even certain that he meant it, but in the shabby and pressured reality of the hospital morning it seemed better, even nobler, to feel this threatening and disorientating love rather than to feel nothing.

'Do you?' Hannah doubted him too, but he could not stay to tell her any more.

'I'll call you tomorrow,' Michael promised.

On the evening of the same day, Cathy and Lucy Clegg sat in the upstairs room at Wilton that Hannah had designated as the older children's sitting room. The room had a pretty view of the garden and the fields that dipped towards Grafton, but it was underdecorated compared with the rest of the house. The curtains were no more than striped ticking hung on plain wooden poles, and the walls were bare except for a series of tired Guns n' Roses posters that were beginning to peel away from their Blu-Tak anchorages. There were two sofas, on either side of the empty fireplace, both of them heaped with magazines and cracked paperbacks, and a folding snooker table belonging to Barney rested against one wall. In the past, the room had been a place of refuge for the twins and Barney from Hannah and the upholstered extravagance of the rest of the house.

Lucy was sitting on one of the sofas with her hands folded behind her head. Cathy flicked at the pages of a book. They had been sitting in silence for what seemed a very long time.

Then Lucy said, 'I hate this waiting. It's horrible being suspended, not knowing how to go forwards or back. I don't know what to do, and now there's this with Daddy too. What's going to happen?'

Cathy watched her as she stood up and went to the window. They were waiting for Barney to arrive, because Darcy had said that he wanted to speak to the three of them together. The house was full of a queasy silence within which the confusion of the day was barely contained.

'I don't know,' Cathy answered. 'I don't understand what's going on. But I do know one thing. *You* can't wait much longer. You have to decide what to do.'

Lucy did not turn from the window.

339

'He's not going to do anything, is he?' she whispered. 'I thought he might. I thought he might come after all, when he had had time to realize what it meant. Me, and his baby. And then how would it have been, if I had already had an abortion?'

'Jimmy isn't going to come for you,' Cathy said. 'How could he? Think of the damage it would cause.'

They had trodden this circuit before.

'He hasn't even called me.'

'I know that. Lucy, do you want to go ahead and have the baby by yourself?'

Lucy crossed her hands over her chest and massaged her arms. Even up until today, although she understood the reality perfectly well, she had let herself hope that Jimmy might contradict everything she had learned about him and come to her rescue. That he had not was not surprising, but it was the tiny hope itself that had become precious. She longed to hold on to it.

But now there were other reckonings to be made.

Darcy had always been the secure and generous rock in his children's lives. Yet here he was, not only ill, betraying a frailty that she had never imagined before, but there were also other more disturbing intimations of his fallibility. Lucy could only dimly conceive what the visits from policemen and lawyers and the urgent telephonings, and Hannah's half-concealed tears might really mean, but she felt that some entire structure of security and insulation, never so much as questioned before, was being knocked out from underneath her. Lucy began to be afraid that not only might her father not be able to look after her for ever, however shockingly the world might assault her, but that he might without warning have ceased to be her protector and be instead in need of her protection.

The thought made her feel exposed and precarious, but also suddenly and surprisingly older. She pressed her fist into her stomach, as if she wanted to reach inside herself.

'No,' Lucy said. 'I don't want to go ahead and have the baby by myself.'

'Then there's only one possibility, isn't there?' Cathy lifted her blonde head. 'Listen. I think Barney's here.'

They heard Barney's voice, and the rumble of their father's. Then the door opened and Barney appeared with Darcy behind him. Darcy was wearing a shapeless sweater. His shoulders hunched forward.

He's old, Lucy realized with a surge of panic stronger than anything she had felt when she witnessed his heart attack. He's an old man.

Darcy waited while his children sat down. Barney glanced at his sisters, his face telling them that he didn't understand this mysterious summons or the air of foreboding in the room any more than they did.

Darcy wouldn't sit himself. He began to walk, traversing the floor and back again, his big head half turned away from them. As he walked, he told them that they had better hear what would soon be public knowledge.

'I am accused of theft,' he said. 'My client Vincent Templeman and his accountant claim that I have by means of forgery and false accounting misappropriated certain funds belonging to Templeman's private company for my own use.'

Darcy turned, completing one negotiation of the room and beginning another. It seemed that he was intent on fitting his words to the number of paces. His children sat waiting, with their eyes fixed on him. Lucy had opened her mouth in protest but Barney took her hand and held it, silencing her.

'The police were informed, which is why they came here last night. They have taken away various sets of books, without which I can't continue to do business. My solicitor advises me that there will be some charges to answer. I don't know yet exactly what will happen. But I think there will be . . . publicity, difficulties before everything is set right again. Because the business is based in this house it won't only be difficult for me, but for you and Hannah too. I wanted to tell you.'

Darcy reached the window yet again. This time he stopped and stood as Lucy had done, with his back to them.

'I wanted to tell you myself, and to say I am sorry.'

There was a silence as his words began to make threatening sense out of random impressions.

Lucy sat upright. 'They can't accuse you!' she shouted. 'They can't just say you've done something you haven't. This is a free country not . . . not some police state.'

Barney still held her hand. She realized that he was hurting her by trying to hold her down, and she snatched it away.

'Dad?'

Darcy turned again, and each of them could see from the sluggishness of the movement the weight he was carrying.

'I know you didn't do it,' Barney said, 'but what's the basis of the accusation?'

Darcy smiled, the upward lift of the muscles not quite aligning and his upper teeth showing so he looked momentarily, grotesquely, as if he had suffered a stroke.

He's being brave, Lucy thought. He's being brave because he has to be.

'I haven't done anything dishonest. But you know who I am. I'm not always conventional. I have been a maverick. I wouldn't be where I am now, would I, if I had never broken a rule?'

He shrugged his shoulders with a gesture of dismissal. Out of bravado he was trying to be the father they had always known, and the threadbare attempt made the difference in him all the more disturbing. For a few seconds none of them could think of anything to say, so that the fragile construction of Darcy's assurances might not be dislodged. The three children sat, looking nowhere, trying to assimilate what he had told them and to piece together their own interpretation out of the windy spaces between his words.

'Then that's all right,' Cathy said at last. She stood up and went to Darcy, and he put his arms gratefully around her, stroking her hair as she leaned her head against him.

'That's my girl,' he said.

Lucy and Barney followed her lead. They wrapped their arms

around their father, and their combined strength made his discovered frailty more apparent to each of them.

'Don't worry,' Lucy told him.

'I'm not worried. Only for what it might mean for the three of you, and Hannah, and Laura and Freddie. If I hadn't been ill, I could have put everything back in order. No trouble. A matter of days, that was all it was.'

They did not want to ask him any more. Their conjectures were enough.

'There we are then,' Darcy said, with his terrible, hollow, confident bluster. 'Now you know everything there is to know. Thanks for being such good kids. I'd better go back downstairs to your mother.'

This vagueness was telling. 'To Hannah, that is,' Darcy corrected himself.

Hannah was in the drawing room. The space filled with warm, diffused light and the planes and angles of polished surfaces and billows of soft fabrics seemed newly precious to him, and also troubling because of his fear.

'Did you tell them? Did they understand?' Hannah asked.

'Yes, of course they did. Why not?' Darcy responded in the cheerful, positive manner that it seemed important for him to adopt. He went to the silver tray and picked up a bottle from the shining rank of them. Alcohol would blunt the sharp edge of his anxiety, he knew that, although it would not dispel the dark mass itself. 'Let's have a drink, shall we? Celebrate getting to the end of today?'

Upstairs Lucy had begun to cry. She cried in thick sobs that bubbled out of her slackened mouth. Barney looked at her, his good-humoured face creased in concern.

'He'll put it right. It doesn't sound too healthy now, but I'm sure he will.'

'It isn't only that.' She took a ragged breath, staring at him with streaming eyes. Lucy was ugly when she cried. She shouted at him, 'I'm pregnant. I don't know what to do. I want to tell Dad about it.'

Barney turned to Cathy, who nodded sombrely.

'Who?' Barney asked.

Lucy told him brutally, 'Jimmy Rose.'

While his sisters watched him, Barney assimilated this.

'Then you can't tell him.' Barney was rarely angry, but they saw his anger kindling now. 'You can't bloody well dump that on him as well. You can see how he is, can't you?'

Lucy's cheeks wobbled with her sobbing. Her outrage at this turn that her life was taking emerged in her cry, 'What about *me?*'

'I'm sorry about you.'

'You sound it.'

'Barney,' Cathy warned him. 'Look at her.'

Barney sighed. His big hands floundered in the air around his sisters' shoulders.

'I am sorry, Luce. I am. Only you can't run down to Dad, at this minute of all times, and tell him his best friend's got you pregnant. What were you doing with Jimmy Rose anyway? He's old enough to be your father himself. How can you have let it happen?'

'The pill. I forget it sometimes. And I thought I loved him.'

'*Jimmy Rose?*' Barney let out a long, derisive breath. And then he nodded, understanding her even though it was unwillingly. 'Yeah. Okay. I can imagine how. Poor Lucy, but you can't tell Dad about it. What you have done is tell me instead. And what I ought to do right now is go round to see Jimmy Rose and kick his arse up his windpipe.'

'Put his balls in the Magimix?' Cathy murmured.

'Yeah. And his dick on a skewer. The little rat.'

There was a small sound from Lucy that wasn't a sob or a sniff. She had let out an unexpected squirt of laughter.

'That's better,' Barney said. He sat down next to her, holding her and cradling her head against him. He murmured with his mouth close to her ear, persuading her that there was a chink in her misery, 'So we can sort this out ourselves?'

Lucy slowly nodded her head. 'I want to have an abortion. And get away from Grafton.'

'Sure thing.' Barney promised her.

Nina opened her front door and saw Barney standing on the step.

'Are you working?' he asked her.

'Yes.'

'Can I come in anyway?'

She held open the door. Nina was not surprised to see him; Barney had taken to calling on her without telephoning first, as if he felt that it might be too easy for her to turn him down on the telephone. What was surprising to her was that she was not displeased by his arrival in the middle of her working day.

Barney followed her down to the kitchen. He gestured for her permission, then went to the refrigerator and took out a can of the beer she had begun to keep there for him. Nina also liked this familiarity and freedom he took with her tidy arrangements. It made her empty house seem populated. Barney pulled at the metal ring and over the hiss of gas before he drank asked her his invariable question.

'How's it going?'

Instead of irritating her this made her feel much younger, as if she were part of some conspiracy in which work and responsibility were inconveniences to be negotiated before the real business of pleasure could continue.

Nina laughed as she told him, 'Well, thank you. I've done lots of work. Been to London about a new commission. And you?'

Barney drank some more of his beer. 'Not so good.'

Nina recomposed her face, ready for a recital of catastrophes that might have befallen Barney's car or his studies.

'Tell me.'

He stood up from the corner of the table where he had been leaning and came across the kitchen to her. He was awkward with surplus energy and also graceful, and she knew before he

345

reached her that she wanted to touch him. When he took hold of her she let herself fit neatly against him.

'Come upstairs?' he asked, when he had kissed her.

'We can't always go up to bed.'

'Why not?'

'Um. I can't think of any specific reason, now you ask me. Just that one shouldn't always give way to one's urges. As a matter of principle. Self-discipline.'

'Crap,' Barney said.

In the end, she led him upstairs to her room.

In bed he was awkward and graceful in the same way as when he sloped across her kitchen or worked in her square of garden. He acknowledged his over-eagerness and occasional clumsiness and when he smiled at himself, with their faces close together, his eyes seemed to flatten and slide apart so she imagined that she was looking into the mask of some friendly, healthy, silent animal. Then if she tried to guide him with a small movement of her thighs or wrists, his face would sharpen with the intensity of his concentration, like an animal again, and she would be quick to reassure him with another movement in order that he should not misunderstand her intention and be hurt.

The second or third time he came into her bed Nina asked him, 'How many girls have you made love to?'

'Half a dozen. Six,' he corrected himself in case this should sound dismissive. 'Including you.'

'The same as me. Lovers, that is,' Nina said.

This limited history of hers diminished the distance between them. But unlike Gordon, Barney did not ask her to talk about Richard or any of the other features of her invisible and therefore irrelevant past. Barney's appetites were for the present. After Gordon, and the rawness from him that was left under her skin, Barney's puppyish immediacy seemed natural, and inevitable, and welcome to her.

With the palms of her hands Nina traced the solid muscles of his back while Barney made love to her. She began by dreamily staring up at the ceiling, beyond him, but his insistence drew her in and made her an equal participant as it had done each of the times before. This, as well as other things about him, surprised and pleased her.

'You said before that something was the matter,' Nina said afterwards. 'Was that why you came to see me?'

'Nope.' He moved his finger along the prominent ridge of her collar bone and grinned at her, flat-eyed, like the satisfied animal. 'But there is something. Can I tell you?'

'Of course you can.'

He told her first about Lucy and Jimmy Rose. Nina listened, and although Barney's account of Lucy's difficulty was brief and bloodless it propelled her back fifteen years into her own late teens.

In her first year away from home Nina had fallen in love for the first time, with a painter of difficult and uncommercial abstracts who also taught at her art school. Within three months she was pregnant, and within as many weeks the painter had faded out of her orbit and resubmerged himself in his life with a wife and two small children.

After she had listened to what Barney had to tell her, Nina offered her own story in response.

'His name was Dennis O'Malley,' she confessed. 'He was not that unlike Jimmy. I haven't thought about him for years.'

'What did you do?'

'Had an abortion.'

The thought of Lucy Clegg sharpened the memories of it for her. Nina found that she could recall exactly the metal-framed furniture in the office where an unsympathetic doctor had interviewed her, the street in a London suburb where she had walked up and down under the plane trees for an hour before deciding finally to enter the clinic, and the nauseous complex of feelings, fear and loneliness and anger, with the alarming longing for the baby itself that was all the more disturbing because it must be pinched down and denied. When it was over she had felt empty and stricken.

Those brief weeks carrying the flutter of fear had been the

only pregnancy Nina had achieved. When Gordon Ransome had admired her flat and unmarked belly, she had not told him quite the whole truth. Nor had she kept the promise to herself, made when she re-emerged into the suburban street, that she would never again entangle herself with a married man.

She thought of Star, and the cool and dignified way she moved through the Grafton parties with her face turned away from Jimmy's antics, and the offer of friendship she had extended to Nina. Nina wondered how many other Lucys there were, and whether Star knew about them, and, with a kind of internal shrinking as if to deflect a blow, she also thought of Vicky Ransome. Nina shifted, turning away from Barney on to her back, so she could look up again at the impassive ceiling.

'Lucy is going to have an abortion too,' Barney said.

'As long as that is what she wants. And Jimmy?'

'Jimmy nothing.'

'Yes, I see.'

Barney moved closer to her. She could feel the tiny currents of displaced air between them in the places where their naked skin did not quite touch.

Barney said, 'There is an added complication. To do with Darcy. Maybe I shouldn't tell you this, but I can't ask for your help without letting you know why. Can I?'

Nina sighed. 'I don't know. I think you imagine I'm much wiser than I really am. The truth is that I'm full of confusion and misgiving.'

'Please. I need to tell you.'

'Then do.'

She listened again, this time to Barney's much longer account of the police arriving at Wilton, and the suppressed concern in the house, and Darcy's blustering, clay-footed explanation of the events to his children. Nina was filled with sympathy for Hannah, and for Darcy, because she liked him, although she did not believe that he would be entirely incapable of a criminal act.

And then an image came into Nina's head, as pin-sharp as if it were projected on to the blank plaster above her. She saw the

Grafton couples dancing, two by two, as she had first seen them at the Frosts' Hallowe'en, only the smiles they wore were the Hallowe'en masks, and behind the masks there were the hollowed faces made unfamiliar by the shadows of secrets and fallibility. She saw herself amongst them, first with Gordon and then, in response to some unseen dance-master, changing her partner for Barney. Around her the couples changed their partners too, and danced on in their broken gavotte with their faces hidden behind the grinning masks.

'Are you asleep?' Barney whispered.

She had kept very still, but she had heard every word he said. He had not asked her what she thought, nor even suggested that his father was anything but innocent. Nina liked him the more for it. She thought that Darcy would be generously supported by his family.

Nina turned her head. 'No, I'm not asleep. Poor Darcy. I'm sorry.'

She kissed the corners of the boy's mouth, and held him. Now she did feel the span of the years separating them.

'Do you see what it means?' Barney was intent on his explanation. 'Lucy wants to tell Darcy what's happened to her, so he can make it better. That's what he does, always has done for her. Only she mustn't, now. He shouldn't have to worry about anything else.'

'I think your instinct is right,' Nina said.

'It's just that Lucy isn't particularly . . . stable, or reliable. She needs someone who knows what to do, to help her get through it. So I'm asking you. Is that trespassing too much, on this?'

The small movement he made took in their proximity, and the tiny world they made together between the curled ends of Nina's bed.

'No. It isn't trespassing. I could give Lucy the number of my gynaecologist. He's in Harley Street, although there are plenty of other places and different agencies that Lucy could go to. But I know that Mr Walsh will understand what she needs and how it

349

should be handled. I should think that with his help Lucy could be in and out of a clinic within a couple of days.'

'How much will it cost?'

The memories of that distant, suburban clinic and the doctors behind their metal desks and her own long-ago desolation gathered around Nina again. She was not sure whether to interfere in Lucy Clegg's life would be damaging, but since she had come this far she resolved that she might as well go on.

She said very carefully, 'You can tell Lucy that I can easily afford to help with that too. Perhaps she can pay me back one day.'

Barney touched her cheek, and then her mouth, with the tips of his fingers. She could see the relief in his eyes. Nina was pleased to be able to offer him what he and Lucy needed, but she knew she was also doing it for Star's sake. If Star could be shielded from at least this much, then it would be something.

'And if Lucy would like somewhere in London to stay, before or afterwards, just for a day or so, we could always ask Patrick.'

'Thank you,' Barney said humbly.

'Not at all,' Nina murmured. He answered by kissing her, and she felt the neat contraction of her own pleasure in response to him.

It was raining. Thick ropes of rain twisted out of the grey layers of sky overhead, bouncing up and breaking into steely threads as they hit the streaming pavements. Hannah and Michael ran, hand in hand, with the wetness plastering their hair to their skulls and cheeks and soaking in black patches across their shoulders to glue their clothes to their skin. They ran and dodged the rain-stalled London traffic until Hannah was gasping for breath and stumbling in her ruined shoes.

'I can't run any more.'

'It's not far,' Michael called to her.

There were lines of taxis in the streets but not one of them offered the comfort of a yellow light. He pulled her on behind him, across the murky rivers swirling in the gutters, until they turned a corner and saw the windows of their hotel. A minute later, with the doorman offering them the pointless protection of his umbrella, they reached the revolving door and were delivered by its rotation into the mirrored warmth of the hotel lobby.

'Safe,' Michael proclaimed. He was exhilarated by the dash through the rain. He took Hannah's soaking arm and steered her into the lift, and they were swept upwards in the company of their own dripping but flatteringly tinted reflections. Down the corridor to the door of their room they left a trail of watery steps.

'Let me dry you,' Michael said. He came out of the bathroom with an armful of towels, and he unbuttoned Hannah's clothes, bundled them away from her and knelt down to unstrap her shoes from her feet. He swathed the towels around her and patted her face dry, seeing how the black stuff with which she made up her eyes had touchingly blotted over the soft, pouchy skin beneath the lashes. The rain clattered against the windows, isolating them in the hotel bedroom with its glazed chintzes and empty cupboards. Michael thought the moment was both sexy and melancholy, but when he turned his mind to try to pin down either his excitement or sadness they both slid away from him, leaving him standing awkwardly in his wet clothes, with Hannah in her towels held against him.

'I'm cold,' she said.

'Have a bath and get into bed. I'll order us some tea.'

It was five in the afternoon. They had already spent one night together, under the grey eye of the television perched at the foot of the bed. Michael had tried to submerge himself in Hannah, until his insistence had made her ask him, only half-jokingly, 'What are you trying to prove, Mister Wickham? This isn't a competition.'

'I just want you,' he had answered. 'I can't help it. Do you want it to be different?'

Only he had not been able quite to submerge himself, however intimately he connected himself to the folds and fissures of Hannah's body, and so he was troubled by a sense of

351

separation from her. She was still herself, and desirable to him, but they were not quite easy with each other. Michael found that he was thinking about Marcelle and his children, that their faces and voices inserted themselves between Hannah and himself when he had wanted to dismiss them for these few hours.

Today Michael had followed Hannah to some designers' showrooms. He had sat apart, uncomfortable in a visitor's chair, while house models paraded clothes in front of Hannah. He had liked to see this other, businesslike side of her, but she shrugged at his questions.

'It's just a matter of picking what I like, what I think I can sell. I don't even need to go to the showrooms, really. I made the appointments to give myself an alibi for being here with you.'

He had been flattered by that, but the sense of distance between them had not been dispelled. They ate an indifferent lunch in a restaurant he had chosen from *The Good Food Guide*, and afterwards, without admitting that they felt at a loss, they went into the National Gallery. They had wandered through the Sainsbury Wing with the tourists, exiled from their proper setting along with the Japanese groups and elderly American couples, and had emerged into the downpour.

Michael felt energized by the plunge through the streets, and the stinging rain, as if the woolly insulation between Hannah and himself had been washed away. When she emerged from her hot bath, pink and glowing, his desire for her recharged itself without any tinge of guilty melancholy. The tray of tea with silver teapot and thin china was brought by a white-coated waiter, but when he had withdrawn they left it to go cold on the side table. Michael knelt over Hannah's rosy body so she could close her warm mouth around him.

He felt as he had done the first time, within the curtains of her shop, and afterwards clean, hollowed out, reconciled. He lay for a while, drifting in the trivial backwaters of his own imagination.

Then, when he looked at Hannah's face on the pillow beside him, he was amazed to see that she was crying.

'What is it? Hannah, what have I done?'

At first she wouldn't say anything. She shook her head, and more tears squeezed out from beneath her eyelids.

'You must tell me. I can't put it right, unless you tell me.' A flicker of irritation came with a sense of his own powerlessness.

'It's all right,' she muttered, contradicting everything he could see. 'It's nothing to do with you. Or not really. I felt lonely, suddenly.'

'Lonely, when we are this close?' He smiled, with his mouth against her cheek, to comfort her. But his awareness of the distance between them returned, intensified by Hannah's recognition of it too. Looking at the close tangle of her hair, robbed by the rain of its springy lift from her skull, he saw that the roots were darker than the honey-coloured strands. Her vulnerability oppressed him.

Hannah cried for a minute, snuffling damply against his shoulder. Then she lifted her head and stretched her round arm to the brocade-boxed bedside tissues.

'Sorry.'

'Don't be silly. But I don't like to see you cry.' That was true. It was the courageous, chair-lift Hannah he valued, the foil to his own cowardice, and her erotic mutation into the woman he had discovered within the Ottoman tent of her shop. He did not care so much for this weepy, sniffing version of his love.

'I'm worried about Darcy. I'm afraid of what will happen next, and he won't tell me anything except that it's going to be all right.'

'Of course you are worried.' Michael stroked her hair.

'I'm worried mostly that I won't be able to cope with whatever it is that's coming. Arrest, trial, I don't know. I want to be able to withstand whatever he has to face up to, and I'm afraid of letting him down.'

The tears had started to gather again at the corners of her eyes. She dabbed at them with her wodge of tissues.

'I am completely certain that you will be able to cope,' Michael assured her. 'I know you well enough for that.'

'Do you think?'

'I know.'

Hannah blew her nose. 'I think I just needed a good cry.' Then she laughed, with the corners of her mouth wobbling as if she were a film actress who had been told to go for a close-up. 'That's better. Stupid, isn't it? If this isn't letting him down, I wonder what is.'

'Do you wish we hadn't come?'

'No,' Hannah said, after she had thought. 'I don't wish that.' She snuggled closer to him and he put his arm around her, settling his chin against her ruined hair.

'What would you like to do this evening?' Michael asked.

'Nothing. Stay here like this and watch television. Have room service later, with those silver domes on a heated trolley disguised as a table.'

He picked up the television remote control and clicked it.

They lay back amidst the tangle of sheets and pillows and watched the end of *Channel 4 News*. Michael felt that the fragile shell of their intimacy had been tossed like a tiny boat through some storm and had pitched through it, waterlogged but still afloat, into a calmer sea.

It was this pleasure at the survival of some delicate organism that Michael took back with him to Grafton. Hannah had caught an early train, and Michael drove home alone. He realized that their brief, awkward time together had left him with a residue of happiness, and the happiness coloured the dull route and softened his apprehension at returning. He turned on the radio, and whistled as he drove. He felt a generalized affection and tolerance for all the world, and a new tenderness for his wife and children.

When he reached his house he first saw the front garden, the neat oval of raked gravel under the cherry tree and the peony bush heavy with red, taut buds, and then Marcelle's car parked in front of the garage doors. He had expected that Marcelle would be at the school at this time of day, but there was still the ghost of a whistle in his head as he lifted his briefcase out of the car. He put his key in the front door and let himself in. The house was quiet but there was a comforting note that it took him a second to identify as the smell of cooking.

Michael walked through to the kitchen. Marcelle was there. She was standing at one of the worktops in a muddle of bowls and utensils. When she looked at him he saw that her face was like a cold blade.

'How was the conference?'

He hesitated, apprehension prickling him. 'Fine. Like the others. Interesting in parts. Why aren't you at the school?'

'Was your paper well received?'

'Yes. Very well. Rather gratifying.'

Michael picked up the handful of letters waiting for him and flipped through them, seeing nothing. The tension in the air was like a smell, poisonous, the opposite of the wholesome scent of food.

'What are you cooking?' he asked.

When Marcelle didn't answer he looked across at her. Her hands were jerking in a mound of flour. A little puff of it rose and drifted like incense.

'I don't know,' Marcelle whispered. 'Isn't that funny? I've no idea what I'm doing.'

Her head fell forward, and the cords in her neck tightened as her mouth gaped and she began to cry. Appalled, Michael stared at her.

'You haven't been to the conference,' Marcelle said.

Michael thought of the volleys of accusations and lies that would follow if he attempted a denial.

'No,' he agreed.

'Where have you been?'

'In London.'

'Why did you lie to me?' The knifelike accusation had gone from her face. It was contorted with pain instead. Michael hunched his shoulders to protect himself against it.

'Because I didn't want you to be hurt.'

'Who were you with?'

'Marcelle, do you have to know that? Does it make any difference?' He took two steps across the immensity of space that separated them and tried to touch her arm.

Marcelle put her head on one side, as if giving the question due consideration.

'I suppose not. Not to the fact that everything has ended.' She lifted her hands and the flour puffed up again, as if it could whiten the blackness. 'This is how marriages end, isn't it? Ever since I met Caroline Keene on Wednesday and she told me how generous she and David thought you were to let him go in your place and present the paper, I've been thinking, so *this* is how it happens. Even to us. It just finishes.'

Michael tried to think back to a time when he and Marcelle had been happy in this house. He knew that there had been such a time, but he could not locate it now by a date, a particular year. Had it been when the children were smaller? Before they were born? It seemed that his feelings of tenderness as he drove down from London had been no more than post-coital sentimentality.

'If you say so,' he answered tonelessly.

'I telephoned Wilton,' Marcelle went on. 'Cathy told me that Hannah was in London for a couple of days.'

Caroline Keene, Michael reflected. It must be a year since she and Marcelle had last met. Why should they encounter each other on this particular, critical day? Then he was surprised by his own resentment. It was, wasn't it, inevitable that they should have done?

'This isn't anything to do with Hannah. It's to do with you and me, first, Marcelle, do you understand that? Hannah is only what happened next.'

Marcelle was crying again. These were not pretty, photogenic tears that asked to be brushed away, like Hannah's.

'What do you want to do?' Michael asked.

'I want you to leave. You can't come back here, strolling in with your bag and your fully-fucked smile expecting to be fed and fuelled and serviced ready for the next adventure. What happens is that you lose me and your children and your home. But you're half-gone already. Why not the whole way?

'You can find out how it is without us. See if you like it better out there. Perhaps Hannah will be able to do everything for you. If she can stir herself. If it doesn't mean she might break a red bloody fingernail.'

'You're angry. Don't be angry with Hannah. She has enough difficulties of her own, whatever you think of her at this minute.'

'Yes. I'm *angry*.'

There were white flecks at the corners of Marcelle's mouth and she ran her powdered fingers through her wild hair. He was afraid of her.

'I'm so angry that I want to kill you. I want to hurt you. I want it so that . . .' The words evaded her, and she licked her smirched lips and then clenched her fists, staring at the knuckles as if they belonged to someone else.

'. . . I want it so you know what it feels like.'

Then she turned her back on him. She stumbled away to the window and stood there, her face hidden and her whole body stricken with her crying.

'I'm sorry it's such a shock. I'm sorry for what I did,' Michael said helplessly.

Marcelle turned once more. 'I want you to *go*,' she screamed at him. 'Get out of here.'

'What have you told the children? What do you think it's going to mean to them, if their father suddenly isn't here any longer?'

'Why didn't *you* think about that?' She ran at him, with her arms swinging, and struck at his face and head with her floury hands. He had to struggle to hold her, to keep her at bay.

'Stop it. Marcelle, *fuck you!*'

They were both shouting. The front doorbell rang.

'It's the children. Janice brings them home on Fridays.'

Marcelle stepped back from him, panting. She wiped her mouth with the back of her hand and pulled at the whitish horn of hair that sprang from her forehead.

Michael walked down the hall to the front door. Through the frosted glass panels he could see the dark heads of his children and the comfortable bulk of Janice behind them.

'Hello,' she called. 'All well?'

Jonathan and Daisy sidled past him, pale-faced.

'Yes, thanks, Janice. Have a nice weekend.'

He closed the door against the bright outside.

'Hi, kids. Had a good day?' His voice sounded as false as a clown's red nose.

'Where's Mum?' Jonathan asked.

In the kitchen the two of them stood on either side of Marcelle. Trembling, she put her arms around their shoulders.

'What is this?' Michael asked, seeing how they ranged them-selves against him. He was rebuffed by the stares of his children.

'Daddy wants to tell you something,' Marcelle said.

'Marcelle,' he warned her. 'Don't do this in front of them.'

'Why not? Why not this? Are you ashamed now? And don't you think they have a right to know what their father does?'

The rounded eyes glanced from one parent to the other.

'It's okay,' Jonathan said. His mouth was tight with his efforts not to cry.

'Why do you always have to be like this?' Daisy burst out. Jonathan kept his anxiety within a shell of control but his sister was accusatory.

Michael wondered, are we always like this? He didn't even know how much of the discord between himself and Marcelle had seeped into the children's lives. He felt vanquished, defeated by the impossibility of trying to reassure them.

'Come here.'

He opened his arms to encourage them, but they stayed at Marcelle's side. Michael hated her for forcing this division on them, but then he thought that she would claim he had created the divide himself, long ago. Yet it seemed that Jonathan and Daisy had always belonged first to Marcelle, and to him only secondarily. That was the way Marcelle had ordained it.

Michael let his arms fall to his side. He said quickly, to get it over, 'Your mother is very angry with me, and she's right to be. I told her a lie about where I have been for the last two days. But that isn't the only trouble between us. We haven't been making each other very happy. I'm sure you know that, in a way.'

'So what's going to happen?' Jonathan asked, out of his tight mouth.

'I think I am going to have to leave. To live somewhere else, for now.'

Jonathan nodded very quickly two or three times, as if he were merely satisfied to get the facts.

'Daddy, I love you,' Daisy shouted. She ran to him and threw her arms round his waist, noisily crying. Over her head Michael looked at Marcelle. This was indeed how it ended, he thought. With a strip of the kitchen floor between them like a crevasse.

'See? Do you see what you have done?' he said.

She spat at him. 'I didn't do it. You did.'

Michael knelt down so he could look at Daisy. 'I love you too. I always will, and we'll always be your parents, whatever happens.'

Daisy began to wail. 'No. Nooo. I can't bear it.'

He stood up again. As firmly as he could, he steered her back to her mother. Then he left the kitchen and went upstairs, noting the scratches in the wallpaper and the chips like little eyes gouged out of the paint, the honourable scars of family life. He packed another suitcase and came down the stairs again. The house had fallen silent once more. He could not think how he would say goodbye, and so he did not try. He closed the front door softly behind him.

Seventeen

The front door bell began to ring. Once it had started it seemed that it would never stop; whoever was doing it must be holding his thumb pressed to the bell push.

Darcy was already awake, lying in bed beside Hannah in the room flooded with yellow early morning light, but the sound pierced his skull like a dart. He had not heard any car.

Hannah stirred and mumbled, 'What is it?'

Darcy left the bed, put on his dressing gown over his pyjamas. 'I'll see to it,' he said.

He met Hannah's au pair girl at the top of the stairs, also in her dressing gown.

'I'm going,' Darcy said to her. The bell stopped shrilling and there came a barrage of knocking. The stairway dipped in front of him, and the wide mouth of the hallway, and the slivers and lozenges of reflected sunlight lay like broken glass on the floor. He could hear the sounds of his children waking up, disturbed by the thunderous noise.

Darcy descended the stairs, flat-footed in his slippers.

He opened the door, but he already knew who would confront him.

There were five of them this time, not the same men but enough like the ones who had come before. They wore shirts and ties and short casual jackets, aggressive clothes, and in his nightwear Darcy felt disabled and exposed.

'Why are there so many of you?' he asked. It was half-past six in the morning, nearly the end of May.

'Darcy Clegg?' one of the policemen said.

'You know who I am. Yes. I'm Darcy Clegg.'

'My name is Detective Inspector Hely, Serious Fraud Office.'

The other four men had come into the house, and they stood in a phalanx around Darcy as if they feared that in defiance of them and his faltering heart muscle he might break out and try to run away across his own lawns and into the dewy countryside.

'I have a warrant for your arrest.'

The policeman recited the charges, and cautioned him. To Darcy the scene had a cardboard quality, like the cheapest of cheap police dramas. In his cold and rational moments he had understood that they would come in just this way, and had feared and dreaded it, yet now that it was happening it seemed insignificant, almost comical. He might even have laughed, until he turned and looked behind him and saw the ring of faces at the head of the stairs.

Freddie and Laura stood fenced behind the banisters, gripping the oak spindles with their hands, staring down in bewilderment. Cathy hovered beside them, her suntanned legs bare underneath her short robe. Lucy had gone to London for some reason, Darcy recalled. He knew that the policemen were staring up at his daughter too. Her beauty struck him anew, and he felt a spasm of despair that he should have exposed her to this scrutiny. He saw Barney with her, rubbing his face in disbelief, and then Hannah pushing past them and running down the stairs.

Hannah's robe was silk, like her nightdress, and the sheeny double skin seemed to slide over the loose curves underneath it as she ran. The policemen looked at her too, and Darcy knew that they would talk about this afterwards, and laugh about it. He clenched his fists and in a welter of hot images wondered if he tried to hit them whether they would pinion his arms behind him and warn him to come quietly. The urge to inappropriate laughter renewed itself and his heart squeezed, a needle of pain in his chest before inflating again, to remind him that he was old, and guilty.

Hannah grabbed his arm. 'What do they want?'

She held her hair back with one hand, and down the calyx of her sleeve Darcy saw the way the soft flesh of her underarm sagged away from the bone. This evidence of her ageing reminded him that he loved her, and the life here that he had seemingly destroyed by trying to preserve it. That was all he had tried to do, wasn't it? The mechanism of self-exculpation quivered wearily within him again and the detachment of a spectator at a bad drama faded and left him.

'We shall have to ask you to come with us,' Hely said.

Darcy wanted to lay his head on his wife's shoulder. He was tired enough to close his eyes.

'They have come to arrest me,' he said.

At the top of the stairs Mandy was trying to lead Laura and Freddie away. Laura began to howl.

Hannah spun round to the policeman. She looked ready to fight him herself, shouting at him, 'You can't come to an innocent man's house and drag him away in front of his children.'

'Don't, Hannah,' Darcy said. 'It's all right. There's nothing to worry about.' It was the litany he had repeated to her a hundred times already, but the crack of disbelief that he saw widening in her face made it seem a pointless reiteration. 'I may get dressed first, I suppose?' he asked the policemen.

Barney and Cathy were beside him.

'Can they do this?' Barney said to Darcy.

'Oh yes, we can,' one of the younger men said with relish. 'Even to your Dad.'

Two of the policemen accompanied Darcy upstairs. They let him dress in a dark suit, but they did not give him time to shave. When they came down again Darcy seemed shrunken inside the dark envelope of his clothes.

'When will you let him out?' Hannah demanded.

'I couldn't say,' the senior policeman replied. 'The charges are serious, and bail depends on a number of factors.'

'It shouldn't take long, perhaps only a few hours,' Darcy said.

'Call McIntyre and tell him what's happened. Tell him to come as soon as he can.'

The men took Darcy outside, the two of them who walked on either side of him holding his upper arms. They ducked into one of the waiting cars with him. Hannah, Barney and Cathy went out after them but Darcy did not look round as he was driven away.

Barney muttered, 'Oh, Christ, I can't believe it. Why didn't he say it meant *this*? What has he done?'

Hannah rounded on him, hard-eyed, as angry as when she had faced up to the policemen.

'He's done nothing.' Her forefinger with its red nail jabbed at Barney, as if she would gouge it into him. 'Nothing at all. Remember that, when they ask you.'

Then she turned away from them and ran into the house.

The news travelled quickly enough. By the evening of the same day the Grafton couples and apparently most of the rest of the world had heard about Darcy's arrest. Hannah grimly answered the telephone every time it rang. To the newspapers and the reporters with their insinuating or openly insulting questions she responded with a terse refusal to comment. To the friends who telephoned in shock or sympathy she said something like,

'It's to do with an alleged misappropriation of funds, but he's not guilty of anything. His solicitor is with him, he's very confident that he'll be out in a matter of hours. I'll tell him you rang. Yes, yes of course I'm okay. It's only Darcy I'm worried about.'

Almost as soon as she had replaced the receiver after one of these calls, the ringing would start again.

Barney and Cathy telephoned Lucy at Patrick's Spitalfields house.

'Shall I come home?' Lucy asked them.

'I don't think you need to if you don't want to,' Cathy advised her. 'How do you feel?'

'Worried about Dad.'

'Yeah. I meant you.'

After a moment Lucy answered, 'Strange. Sad, and small. But I'm relieved to be myself again. Just me, no one else to be afraid for. As if I can deal with anything, if it's just to do with me.'

'Good. That's good, isn't it? Stay where you are for now. It's probably better. I'll let you know as soon as anything else happens here. There are reporters hanging about outside, trying to see in.'

Lucy put the phone down and sat in her leggings and holey grey jumper, cross-legged amongst the needlework cushions on Patrick's Knole sofa. She pushed her thicket of beaded plaits and miniature pigtails away from her white face.

'My dad's been arrested, on a fraud charge. The police came this morning.'

Patrick had heard about Darcy Clegg from Nina.

'Poor Lucy.'

'Poor him, more. Don't sympathize too much with me, or I'll start crying.'

He patted her shoulder. 'Fine. Not another sympathetic syllable.'

Lucy looked up at him. 'Why're you and Nina being so nice to me? You don't even know me.'

Patrick shrugged. 'Nina has her own reasons, I can't answer for her. As for me, you can see I've got plenty of space.'

Lucy loved the spare grandeur of Patrick's house. Even though she was a stranger, even though she felt weak and dismayed, she had been comfortable in it as soon as Patrick had brought her here from the clinic, yesterday morning. The rooms were half-empty and wholly soothing compared with those at Wilton. The covers and cushions here, all made of dark heavy stuff that seemed to have been mended and made from something else, looked even better after they had been sat on and lived with, unlike Hannah's.

Lucy had slept surprisingly well, without need of the pills she had been given at the clinic, between darned linen sheets in a huge oak bed with an embroidered canopy.

'It's not really to do with having a spare bedroom, is it?'

'It is very spare.'

'Are you lonely?'

Patrick frowned at her. He liked this girl with her alternately disaffected and inquisitive manner, and he guessed that she was probably quite brave. There had been no sign of tears, despite her warning, but that did not make him think that the ordeal she had undergone had left her unscathed.

'Yes. But no more so than plenty of other people.'

Lucy reached for his hand and wound her fingers between his.

'I was lonely in that clinic. They were quite kind. I wouldn't want Nina to think it wasn't anything but fine in that way, only it was just me who was doing that thing. No one else could help me, and it was right that I should have to do it on my own. I felt very solitary. No baby, no nothing. Perhaps it was good for me. I've never had to be singular before, with being a twin. But I didn't even want Cathy to come.'

Very softly, almost to herself, Lucy added, 'It was right to do it that way. My responsibility. No one else to blame or judge. Anyway, you don't have to be lonely now, with me here, do you?'

'Thank you.'

Patrick settled beside her on the sofa, not trying to disengage his hand although the connection seemed strange. He did not hold hands much.

Understanding that she did not want to talk any more about her abortion he said, 'Tell me about your father.'

She tilted her head downwards so that the teased hair hid her face.

'All our life he has seemed so huge. When we were tiny he seemed to fill the sky and my sister and I thought he could do anything. Like fly, or stop the rain. He wasn't around that much, but when he was everything seemed to flow out of him, fun and excitement and money and reassurance and confidence. He never said no to things like our mother did.'

Seeing Patrick's expression Lucy grinned through her fringes. 'Yeah. Spoilt kids, eh? He was always telling us that himself.'

365

The grin vanished. 'Oh, God! Why am I talking about him in the past? When he got ill, it was – it was like the first time I'd understood that he really isn't everlasting. Now there's this, whatever's happening. I feel like *I* should be looking after *him*.'

After a moment, she said, 'I really love him. I don't care what he has or hasn't done.'

Patrick felt suddenly envious of Darcy Clegg, in prison or not. 'I'm sure he would like to hear you say that.'

She nodded. 'Yeah. I'll have to try and tell him, when we both get home again.'

Jimmy Rose rang Wilton as soon as he heard the news. Hannah had gone upstairs with Laura, and it was Cathy who answered the telephone.

'Lucy? Is that you?'

'Who is calling?' Cathy said coolly.

'Ah, don't be that way. I've been thinking and worrying about you. Have you decided what you want to do?'

'Lucy isn't here. She's gone to London.'

In the silence that followed, in spite of everything else, Cathy allowed herself a little smile.

Anger edged the brogue out of Jimmy's voice. 'Why did you not tell me it was you?'

'You didn't give me a chance.'

'All right. How is she?'

'Why do you want to know?'

'Jesus! Why would I not? Do you think I don't care for her?'

Cathy sighed. 'She's okay. She's staying with a friend.'

'Did she . . . ?'

'Yes. Yes, she did. By herself, because that was what she wanted. Are you happy now?'

'Of course not.' Jimmy twisted in the armchair to peer over his shoulder. He realized that Star had come in with her bag of exercise books earlier than usual. She put her burden down without looking at him and left the room again. Jimmy changed his tone.

'I called to talk to Hannah. Will you tell her if there's anything I can do she's only got to ask?'

'I'm sure she'll be grateful.'

Sarky little bitch, Jimmy thought. Both of them.

'But I don't think there's anything now. Daddy's solicitor just telephoned. He's been released on bail, and they're on their way home.'

'That's grand news. Who stood bail for him?'

'My uncle and Andrew Frost.'

Jimmy was shocked by this. He protested, 'He could have asked me. Why didn't he ask me?'

'I don't know. Because he asked Andrew, I suppose.'

'Yes. Well, if there's anything else, tell him.'

He hung up. Staring out of the window into the garden he saw the unpruned branches of shrubs whipped by an unseasonal cold wind, and the first threads of rain scribbling the glass. He was angry with Cathy Clegg and snubbed by Darcy. The sour view of his living room and the wedge of garden and the hedges and back windows and ornamental conifers of the dead-end of Grafton fed the anger with the fuel of his failure and disappointment. Jimmy sat with his fists clenched between his knees until Star came in again. She sat down in a chair, removed from him, and opened a book.

Watching her, Jimmy thought that her supercilious detachment was calculated to enrage him. A quarrelsome dialogue rehearsed itself in his head until, as if the preamble had already been uttered, he murmured,

'Why are you such a bitch?'

Star lifted her head. Her face was cold, her top lip lifting slightly as if she was aware of a nasty smell.

'If I am it's because you make me one.'

Her cool voice recalled Cathy Clegg. Darcy's failure to ask for his help took on the status of a deliberate insult. Had the destructive Lucy said something to him? Even as he thought of

367

her a wave of longing for her and the baby, and what might have been, weakly washed over him. His resentment fastened on Star, crackling, ready to ignite.

'It's nothing to do with me. Except that I have to live with you. Why is it me who has to be married to a frigid dyke?'

Star closed her book and it slid to the floor. She stood up and stepped deliberately towards him. Then she swung her hand and slapped him in the face. His head jerked backwards and a thread of spittle whipped from the corner of his mouth.

'Don't call me a dyke,' she whispered.

Jimmy licked his lips, then smeared them with the ball of his thumb, looking down at it for blood.

'I'll call you whatever I bloody like.'

She was already backing away from him but too late. His hand shot out and grabbed her wrist and he dragged her back within his reach.

'*No . . .*'

He hit her, a quick double blow, his knuckles smashing against her cheekbone and then the palm of his hand cracking against the other cheek, mirroring the slap she had dealt him.

'Fuck you,' he said.

Then he let go his hold of her, the taste of disgust thick in his mouth. There was an instant's white print on Star's cheek that filled with a quick tide of colour.

Star slowly turned, moving cautiously as if she was afraid that her legs would give way. She stooped, holding her back straight, to pick up her book and place it tidily on the coffee table. Then she went out, leaving the house and walking away down the suburban avenue without any particular destination in mind.

Jimmy poured himself a whisky. When he had drunk it he pulled the telephone towards him again.

'Andrew? Jimmy. Yes, I heard.' He listened to the snap and rumble of Andrew's voice.

'How much did you have to put up?' His mouth puckered in a soundless whistle. 'It'll be in the papers anyway. Two hundred and fifty grand *each*? Bit of a nuisance if he skips the country.'

Andrew spoke again and Jimmy nodded, looking at the empty room while he listened.

'Do you feel like a drink, later on? I thought I'd go down to the golf club. No? All right. Saturday, then.'

After Andrew had rung off Jimmy poured himself a second measure, and drank it down straight.

Star found herself walking along the path beside the river. The start of the summer had brought out the first tourists, and even in the intermittent rain there were pairs of them strolling under the snaky fronds of the willow trees. They were mostly elderly couples, filling in the interval between exploration of the cathedral and the hotel dinner. She passed them in her solitude with her head averted, eyes on the water, conscious of the bruises beginning to discolour her face. The wind was licking the surface of the river into glittering silver menisci.

The vista of old stone and water meadow opposite and the low hills in the distance had always pleased her, and numerous other corners and recesses of the city that had been rubbed and rounded by the passage of time, like stones on a beach, pleased her in the same way. It gave Star satisfaction and a sense of peace to have her small daily itinerary defined and contained by these medieval boundaries. She was thinking as she walked that it was such simple things that had kept her in Grafton, and her preference for order and routine over the risk of the unknown that had prevented her from leaving it.

But now she resolved as she threaded her way between the tourists and the flags of the willow branches that there would have to be a time to leave. She did not love her husband any more, if she had ever loved him. It was not even the acceptance of that truth that convinced her, but the recognition that this evening had provided a finishing point, a definitive break in the slow decline of her marriage. There could be no reversal or cosmetic redefinition.

Star began to make her plans. She walked for a long way, following the wide sweep of the river, until Grafton dropped out of sight behind her.

In the evening, twelve hours after his arrest, Darcy was driven home by his solicitor. Hannah, Cathy and Barney had been waiting in a tense huddle in the drawing room, but when they heard the car they stood in unison and hurried into the hallway, not knowing what they should expect. When the car drew up on the gravel sweep in front of the house, two of the pressmen who had watched the day's traffic to and from the front door jumped from the garden seat where they had been smoking and talking and ran towards it. Darcy emerged from the passenger seat.

Hannah and his children heard him from within the safety of the house.

'I have no comment to make. This is private property, and you will remove yourselves from it immediately. Either that or I will have you removed.'

Tim McIntyre, the solicitor, hurried in his wake. 'Mr Clegg told you. He has no comment to make.'

Darcy swept him into the house, slamming the door behind them.

'Have those rodents been out there all day?'

He was shouting, and he seemed to have swelled again to fill the confines of his dark suit. It was as if leaking air had been pumped back into him, smoothing out the creases in his flesh and puffing away the dark patches in his face. Hannah and the two children glanced at each other, startled and hopeful.

'Are you all right?' Hannah began.

'Of course I am,' Darcy insisted. 'Were you afraid I wouldn't be?'

His solicitor nodded in confirmation as Darcy shepherded them into the drawing room. 'Bail was granted without too much difficulty. It took a little time to arrange the formalities, as it often does in these cases.'

Darcy stood with his arm around Cathy's shoulders, surveying the room, once more the host and master.

'Hannah, we need a drink. Two or three drinks, after the day we've had in that place. Tim's done a good job. Everything is going to be fine.'

In the furnished flat that he was renting from the hospital, Michael waited for Hannah.

The flat was in an annexe to the main building that also housed the nurses' residence, and it was usually occupied by medical families new to the area while they searched for a permanent home. When he had heard that it was temporarily available it had seemed the answer to his problems, but now that he had moved into it Michael was less sure. The flat occupied an uncomfortable middle ground, neither part of the hospital nor completely separate from it. The kitchen windows looked out on the car park and a set of blue and white signs pointing the way to the X-ray and obstetric departments. The bedroom and living room windows faced the other way, on to a grassy area where groups of student nurses sat in the June evenings with their coffee mugs and ring-binders of revision notes.

After turning away from these reminders of the hospital into the silence within the flat itself, Michael would wander uncertainly through the small rooms. They were furnished with an accumulation of unrelated pieces, tables with brown Formica veneer and white chipboard shelves whose emptiness betrayed their lopsidedness, armchairs and a sofa upholstered in nubbly orange tweed, and a standard lamp with a burn on the shade that showed with the light behind it like a tumour revealed on an X-ray plate. All this reminded Michael of rooms he had occupied as a medical student, places he had passed through with the easy certainty that they were only temporary, only worthy of his attention in the question of whether they were convenient, or cheap enough, or not so uncomfortable as to be irritating.

It was as if in middle age he had acquired a forlorn clarity of vision. He saw the irregular stains of spilled wine or thrown coffee on the carpets as the ghostly imprints of previous occupants' uneasy lives, of their riotous parties or seismic quarrels, and the longer he lived in the flat the more shadowy

371

and insubstantial he felt himself to be. It was as if his removal from his proper home had reduced him to living an existence no more corporeal than that of these other vanished occupants of his rickety rooms.

Michael found it odd that he was waiting for Hannah, so emphatically flesh and blood herself, in this whispery no-man's land.

He was waiting for her, he realized. He had no idea whether she would come in the end, exchanging Darcy and the splendours of Wilton for whatever it was that he would prove able to offer her in exchange. Nor did he know whether he even wanted her to come, or whether what he really longed for was to be free of any obligation, either to Hannah or to Marcelle or his children.

He was simply waiting out the days, between the familiar routine of the hospital and the vacuum of the rented rooms, passively suspended in his solitude.

Then Michael looked out of his kitchen window and saw Hannah crossing the car park, away from her BMW. She walked quickly, in high-heeled sandals, with a little handbag swinging from a shoulder strap. It was more than a week since they had last met.

He picked up a smeared glass and some dirty plates from the table and hastily put them in the sink. He ran the cold tap on them and the water sprayed up over his shirt front, making him jump backwards.

Hannah knocked at the door. He crossed the box of hallway and opened it, taking in the sight and scent of her and the realization that he was happy she had come. He smiled, and tried to reach for her.

'I can't stay very long,' Hannah said. 'I told Darcy I was picking some things up for the shop.'

'Come in, anyway.'

He followed her through into the living room and poured her a glass of wine from the bottle he had bought for this visit. Hannah drank, then sighed as she let her head fall back against the sofa cushions. Michael looked at the white line of her throat and the rounded outline of her chin.

'I'm sorry I'm late,' she said.

'Tough week?'

'You could say.'

'What's happening?'

'Oh, more or less what I expected. Darcy is going full throttle into preparing his defence. He seems energized by it in a manic way. Endless meetings and telephone calls. His solicitor has briefed George Carman. Nothing but the best, of course. I hardly dare think what it will cost. I'm told that it could be a year or more before the case even comes to court.'

'What happens in the meantime?'

'I don't know. I don't know what we live on.'

'Darcy must have assets,' Michael said.

'I suppose so.' Hannah lit a cigarette and drew on it. 'I haven't a clue about any of that. If I needed money in the past it was there. Real bimbo behaviour, eh?'

'I don't think so. Wasn't it how Darcy encouraged you to live?'

Hannah looked sharply at him, wondering about the logic of defending her husband to her lover.

'What does it mean for you and me?' Michael persisted. It was not the first time he had asked the question.

After a pause Hannah said, 'I don't know that either.'

He put his hands on her shoulders, and their faces slowly drew together. When their foreheads touched they held still, not kissing.

'Poor Hannah.'

Hannah was thinking that she did not want his sympathy. She was too busy with her anxiety for Darcy and her own fears of the future. She was afraid of having to sell Wilton, of being cut adrift in a sea of insecurity when she had grown used to luxury and certainty. She did not have much doubt that they would survive being poor if they had to, but the threat of it repelled her.

When all had been well, and then even after Darcy's heart

attack, a love affair with Michael had offered itself as a pleasurable indulgence. Now it was incongruous; even unwelcome. She did not want Michael to feel sorry for her, nor did she want to have to feel guilty for what he had lost and sorry for him in return. It was not what had been intended in the beginning. It was not an escape, but a further responsibility.

She could not tell Michael how much she hated to see him in this sordid flat. It reduced his status in her eyes, and it was like a warning of what might be in store for herself and Darcy. Perhaps they would be reduced to living with Freddie and Laura in rented rooms like these, with burn marks in the nylon rugs and the outlines of other people's pictures on the bare walls.

'What about you?' she asked.

Michael gestured indifference, a new habit of his. He poured her more wine, slopping some over the rim of the glass. Hannah knew that it would make a sticky ring on the Formica-topped coffee table that he would not trouble to wipe away.

'Just what you see.'

'And Marcelle?'

'I can't fathom Marcelle. I took Jon and Daisy out for the day on Sunday. She seemed rather pleased to see the back of us.'

'Poor Michael, then.'

He laughed, but without much humour, and then took her hand.

'We shall have to take care of each other,' he said.

They sat side by side on the orange sofa, watching the light filtering through the leaves of the chestnut trees outside.

'I'm glad you're here,' Michael said finally, leaning across to kiss her. His hand travelled to the buttons of her silk shirt.

As she submitted to this Hannah wondered if it would be better to get up and drive straight back to Wilton. Michael's hand slid inside her shirt. She closed her eyes, and knew that she had no serious intention of doing so. It was pleasurable to be the focus of this much attention. It was satisfying to be about to take what she wanted from someone else, just for an hour. The strain of giving endless cheerful credence to Darcy was beginning to tell on her.

The sofa was cramped, and the tweed was tacky against her shoulders.

'Let's go to bed,' Hannah whispered.

The bedroom was small, with a pink-and-burgundy striped roller blind drawn against the sun and a beige sculpted carpet. The G-plan dressing table stood corner-wise, the mirror reflecting their midriffs. The top of the dressing table was bare except for the limited, mundane contents of Michael's pockets, keys and loose change and his wallet. The depositing of this handful of belongings had scratched a rough hieroglyph in a faint film of dust.

Hannah felt a sudden contraction of sympathy for him. She let him kiss her, concentrating on the warmth and the glow of light behind her eyelids, until the disabling sympathy receded.

They undressed each other and lay down on the bed. Michael had straightened it in readiness.

Hannah liked what he did, and his good, muscular body. Michael's love-making was pleasurable, even if he sometimes did it too vehemently, as if he had forgotten that there could be subtler rhythms. Her back arched as her hips reached upwards for him. It was good to forget her outside self in favour of the internal landscape that Michael slavishly created between them.

Afterwards, when they drew apart, Hannah lay on her side with her face turned to him, but Michael rolled on to his back. She drew a playful finger down his chest and over his belly to his flaccid penis.

'That was good.' She smiled, ready to be affectionate now.

Instead of responding Michael asked stiffly, 'Are you going to say anything to Darcy?'

Hannah sighed. She had not planned to talk about this. She would have liked another glass of wine, and then a bath before driving safely home. 'Do you want me to?'

His shoulders twitched. 'I don't know what this means, otherwise.'

'What should it mean?'

He rounded on her then. She had made him angry.

'It means that I've moved out of my home. Left my wife and children and come here, because of you. I need to know what, if anything, you are planning to tell your husband about it. I love you, is what I want it to mean. Does Darcy know anything?'

'No,' Hannah said carefully. 'Or only that you and Marcelle have separated for the time being. He's sorry, of course. We haven't talked a lot about it because he is preoccupied with other things.' There was no point in trying to explain to Michael the disconcerting, obsessive energy that had reflated Darcy.

'Would you rather he heard about this from someone else?'

'Will Marcelle tell him?'

'No, I don't think so.' Michael thought that he knew her as well as he knew himself; he didn't believe Marcelle would want even Janice to know the real reason for their split. She was too proud, too much of a perfectionist to betray it.

Hannah said softly, 'So, let me get this straight. You are warning me that if I don't speak to Darcy, you will?'

'That isn't what I said, or what I want.'

Michael felt that he had been manoeuvred into a confrontation that threatened to become a quarrel. They would not look at each other now, and a lengthening silence and six inches of cooling sheet separated them. Michael made an effort and said as reasonably as he could, 'Both of us know Grafton. How long is it likely to be before someone sees us and gossips?'

'Both of us know this place, yes.'

'Hannah, that's all I meant.'

Hannah bit her lip. The skin was bruised. Her instincts were to protect Darcy; the urgency of her intention surprised her. We do deserve each other, she thought. And then: I'm tired of my husband but I can't let go of him. Like a mother with a toddler.

She tried to focus her wits on what to say to Michael.

'I can't talk to Darcy at the moment. How could I? "You've lost your livelihood, and are likely to go to prison. And are accused in the filthy tabloids of being the biggest thief and fraudster since Maxwell. And, yes, I'm leaving you too." I don't

376

know what you expect from me, Michael. I didn't ask you to love me, and that's the truth.'

The light in the room was fading. The rays that struck through the paler stripes of the blind seemed heavy, as if they might drift downwards under their own weight through the still air. There was the sound of girls' voices outside, and the distant trill of an ice cream van. Sadness crept through their bones, like radiation.

'I know,' Michael said.

Their hands moved, and found each other again. They lay, a little apart, listening to the outside sounds.

At last Hannah lifted her other wrist to peer at her gold watch.

'I have to go,' she murmured.

Michael released her at once. She slipped from under the covers and then knelt upright, shielding her breasts with her forearm.

'I'll call you,' she promised. Her expression was sweet and serious in the dim light.

'I'm here,' he said.

He lay and watched her as she put her clothes on, thinking that they saved each other's dignity with these promises. He was glad they had not quarrelled.

After she had kissed him and closed the door quietly behind her, he wrapped a towel around himself and went through to the kitchen. He saw her crossing the car park to her car, walking briskly on her high heels. He stood at the window until she had driven away. Then, without bothering to dress himself, he began to wander through the empty rooms again, stepping between the marks of other people's lives as if they reared up like so many obstacles.

Sunday came once more. Michael drove home, as he had agreed with Marcelle, to pick up his children for the day. Jonathan was kicking a ball in the front garden when Michael's car turned in at the gate.

'Hi, Daddy.'

'Hi, Jon.' He hugged the boy and rubbed his hair. 'How was the week?'

'Okay. Daisy's waiting inside.'

Marcelle opened the door. Michael noticed that she was wearing a new shirt, made of some soft material in a cinnamon colour that suited her. She stood back to let him in.

'Daisy's just in the bathroom.'

They were like strangers to each other.

'How have they been?' Michael asked.

Marcelle shrugged. 'How would you expect?'

Daisy ran down the stairs. Michael shepherded the two children into the back of the car and drove them away from the house, noticing that the front door closed immediately.

As they turned towards the bypass, Daisy asked from the back seat, 'What are the plans for today?'

'I haven't made any,' he answered. 'What would you like to do?'

'Oh, Daddy!'

It was Daisy's protest, but neither child said anything else. In the silence that followed, looking in the rear-view mirror, Michael saw their white faces turned in opposite directions, and their eyes fixed on a view that could not have interested them. He did not know what to say or what to do with them, knowing that they would rather have spent the day at home with Marcelle.

Marcelle went upstairs with the Sunday papers. She found Jonathan's cassette player in his room, and then took a tape of Beethoven late quartets from the rack Michael had left in his study. With a feeling of unfamiliarity she slotted the tape into the player and carried it through into the bathroom with her. She turned the music up, so she could hear it over the bathwater. Then she undressed and faced herself in the mirror. Marcelle gave her body a long, shrewd appraisal. She even turned her back and looked at herself over her shoulder. She could see her ribs, and the knobs of her spine. She nodded her head. Her buttocks did not sag, nor were her thighs pocked with cellulite.

'Not bad,' she said aloud. 'Considering.'

Then she stepped into the hot water and lay down, shivering with pleasure as the warmth engulfed her. The music and the steam cleared her head. She closed her eyes, and let herself drift.

Marcelle could not remember the last time she had done exactly what she wanted to, such as she was doing now. Sunday mornings had always meant a family breakfast, after which Michael liked to go off and play golf. After that he had liked to come home to a proper Sunday lunch. Today Marcelle would not have to cook anything for anybody. Nor would she have to drive either of the children anywhere, or arbitrate between them, or go swimming or play tennis or attend to a late homework crisis. She did not have to do anything.

With the realization she felt her shoulders tighten under the skin of water, waiting for the fear to descend.

But then, as she waited, she knew that she did not feel afraid.

This would be the second Sunday that she had spent entirely alone, and the solitude was welcome, even blessed. Last Sunday, while the children were with Michael, she had filled up the hours with ironing and housework. She had crawled into bed tired, and then had lain there and asked herself if she had worked all day because she wanted to prove that she was a good mother, or because she could not think of anything else to do with the time.

The answer had come to her eventually. She had not allowed herself a day of freedom because she did not think she deserved it.

Why not? Marcelle asked herself, lying rigid under the freshly changed sheets.

Because your husband is having an affair with one of your friends? Because you are merely a wife and mother and teacher, and that means you are invisible and unworthy of consideration?

Why not you, if everyone else deserves a day off?

She had been angry with herself for her lack of care, and the hot anger had cauterized some wound that had been weeping for a long time. And without the disability of a wound to carry around, she had felt her strength returning.

Throughout the week Marcelle had noticed it, and hoarded it for herself. She did not miss Michael, although she felt the cold space that his going had left. She did not worry too much for her children. They were anxious, she saw, and needful of her, but their needs and their demands might easily grow and grow until they overpowered her. Coldly she resolved that the best thing for her to do was not to be overpowered. The best thing for her would also be better in the long run for the children. Marcelle liked thinking in this new, clear way.

All week, she had thought about herself. She did it awkwardly at first, with many false starts and mistaken directions, because she had grown rusty at it. But then, as her concentration improved, she began to feel small darts of gladness, even exhilaration. Once, after the children had gone to bed, she made herself a meal. Ordinarily she would have finished their leftovers or gone without. But on this evening she spent an hour chopping and sauteeing and arranging a salad, for herself alone. She laid a proper place setting at the table, opened some wine and sat down to investigate her own company. It had felt odd. There had been a quiver of sadness that so many years of marriage should have brought her to this, but there had also been a surprising, strong beat of assurance. She had eaten her own food with critical attention, relished the wine and afterwards – made pleasurably careless by the amount she had drunk – she had abandoned the washing up and gone straight to bed.

She lay with her limbs spreadeagled in the luxurious space left by Michael's absence and let herself sink, thoughtless, into sleep.

Janice and Vicky telephoned, and called on her so regularly and with such tidy alternation that Marcelle knew they conferred about her plight. She was grateful for their concern, and sometimes glad of their company, but it was satisfying to discover that she did not depend on it.

Vicky, in particular, was eager to talk. She would sit in Marcelle's kitchen with a cup of coffee or a glass of wine while

Helen rocked in her baby seat, and recall how she had felt when Gordon confessed to his love affair. She described her ways of dealing with the weeks when they had lived apart, and Marcelle listened and nodded.

'I found out things about myself that I never knew before,' Vicky confided. 'About my level of dependence on Gordon. About the way I used the children as a defence against the rest of the world. About my own sexuality, as well.'

Marcelle noted the flicker in her eyes when she mentioned this, but she didn't press her for more details.

'In the end it was a good thing that it happened. We're stronger and happier together now,' Vicky said tranquilly. 'Don't overlook the possibility that it might be the same for you and Michael.'

'I won't,' Marcelle promised.

She did not tell anyone about Hannah and Michael. It was only partly, as Michael had guessed, out of pride. More, it was that what interested her was herself and what was happening within her own head. She allowed herself not to think about Michael, and by extension Hannah, and was interested to find that to do so was even quite comfortable.

Janice's concern for her expressed itself as solicitude.

'Are you lonely?' Janice worried. 'You can always come over to us, you know. Or call any time. What about the weekends? Perhaps we could go somewhere with the kids next weekend, for a break? Andrew and I would both like that.'

This was almost the essence of what Marcelle did not want. She murmured something about the children seeing Michael at the weekends. The mention of the children diverted Janice, as always.

'Are they all right?'

'They seem to be. Clinging, and anxious, but also stoical in a way.'

'That's the most painful part, isn't it, what it does to the children?'

Knowing how she idolized her two boys, Marcelle thought

that for Janice it probably would be the worst part. But with her new clear sight, her own view was that children elsewhere in the world, in Sarajevo or the horn of Africa, were suffering far greater pains. Jonathan and Daisy would probably survive the separation of parents who loved them but could not, for the moment, be sure that they loved each other. She did not tell Janice that she felt this.

On this Sunday morning Marcelle lay in her bath for a long time, letting these thoughts and their offshoots revolve in her head. The water cooled, and the Beethoven tape reached its end. She did not bother to stretch out her hand to change it over. The silence of the house settled around her, an unmatched luxury. The thought of kindly Janice and Andrew, and a noisy weekend of all their children in some borrowed or rented house, made her smile once, briefly.

When the coolness of the water became uncomfortable, Marcelle stood up and briskly towelled herself. She noted the prickle of stubble on her shins with a passing frown. In the bathroom cupboard she found a forgotten bottle of body lotion, and she tipped glistening pools of it into her cupped hand and rubbed it into her legs and knees and elbows. Then she left the bath unscoured, and wandered back into her bedroom. She had spread the Sunday papers out on top of the crumpled covers. The pillows still held the dent of her head. Instead of reprimanding her with its dishevelment, the bed openly invited her.

Marcelle slipped under the covers.

As she lay there, with the newspapers crackling faintly beneath her shoulder, a memory stirred.

Marcelle found herself thinking of a single weekend, years ago, when she was a girl. A weekend she had spent in bed with a boy, a student, whom she had not known particularly well but had been fiercely attracted to. It was not that her tidy room recalled his grimy bedsitter or his stiff and becrumbed sheets in any way. It was perhaps the angle of the light, and the newspaper beneath her, and some sensation within herself. That weekend had been Marcelle's proper introduction to sex. On Monday morning she had got up and gone home. She had seen the boy around after that, but she had not felt any particular interest in repeating the experience, nor had he asked her to. Perhaps they had both felt that it had been enough, and complete, in itself.

It was a long time since she had thought of it, Marcelle realized.

In response to the memory, she slid her fingers over the lotioned skin of her thigh, and dipped them between her legs. She began to stroke herself.

The thought of Jimmy in the mossy shadows of the Ransomes' garden came back to her. Jimmy's rejection had added another layer to the sediment of misery within her, but now the sediment was draining away. It ran out, faster and faster, and the clear water of anger swirled in its place. She was angry with Jimmy, and his silky tongue and devious ways, a good hot-centred anger, but she was also careless of him. She forgot about him, and the garden.

Marcelle knew that she was good. Very good and right and strong, and happy *now*. She came quickly, and pleasurably. She lay for a while in the silence, enjoying the weight of her limbs and the slow, sidling trickle of her thoughts, and then she did the same thing again, this time laughing as she came.

Afterwards, flagrantly at twelve-thirty on a Sunday morning, Marcelle fell asleep.

Eighteen

The little silk and satin dresses hung in their spotlit niches at La Couture, but it was as if the light that shone on them had changed in some way, losing its rosy glow. When the women gathered in the shop one afternoon in July, it seemed to Star that the pretty, frivolous clothes belonged to another era, had become almost historical costumes. She wandered along a rail, touching the velvet bodices and silky tiers of cloth with the tips of her fingers.

'Try the gold one,' Hannah suggested, from behind her desk. 'It would suit you.'

'I haven't got the money,' Star said. Or at least she did not want to spend the money that she did have on buying clothes like these. She had different intentions.

'Nobody has the money. Unfortunately,' Hannah said.

Vicky and Janice were sitting on one of the overstuffed sofas, drinking the coffee that Hannah had poured for them. It was the last afternoon before the school holidays began. There were no customers in the shop to disturb their talk.

Janice looked round. 'Business will pick up again in the autumn. Andrew says it is the same in the construction trade. As soon as interest rates come down, everything will start to move again.'

'Maybe.'

Beyond the shop windows, the tourists were passing up and down Southgate, under the municipal hanging baskets planted with geraniums and lobelia. The weather was windy and changeable, and most of the visitors were wearing pastel-coloured anoraks over their summer clothes.

In past seasons Hannah might have sold an occasional item to a tourist, but the majority of her customers had always been local women, established Grafton and county wives whom she knew well and bought for individually because she understood what they wanted. But this summer they had not come in for their Ascot clothes or their holiday evening wear. The taut suits and the tan-enhancing loose white draperies still hung in their places on the overcrowded rails.

Hannah understood the circumstances perfectly well.

Some of the women were practising small economies, buying a new hat instead of a complete outfit, for the same reasons that their husbands' Mercedes were now two or three years old instead of brand new.

But other customers, many more of them, did not come because of Darcy. When the news was first in the papers there had been a flurry of sightseers who came in to commiserate and whisper afterwards, but none of them had bought and none of them had come back. There was no particular reason why women should prefer not to buy their party dresses from the wife of a man accused of theft, forgery and false accounting, but Hannah imagined that she would probably have made the same choice herself, if she had had a choice to make.

Perhaps La Couture could have survived one setback or the other, but not both. Her takings in the last weeks had dropped almost to nothing.

'But I don't think I'll be here to see the upturn when it comes. If it ever does,' Hannah said.

She walked away from her desk to a niche where a red and white polka-dotted afternoon dress postured coquettishly against the wall, waiting for its saucer hat and net veil and its afternoon of champagne and speeches in some flower-scented wedding marquee. Only it was quite clear that none of these tributes would now be forthcoming. Hannah deftly unpinned the dress from its anchorage, and the empty folds collapsed in her arms.

The pins and tucks in the back of it that had held the tidy outline were revealed, and it seemed that there was a dusty silhouette left on the wall.

'Is it as bad as that?' Janice asked.

Hannah held up the limp frock, then let it drop in a heap.

'Yes.'

'Oh, Hannah.' Janice's face flushed with her distress.

Star had been gazing out at the passers-by. The view was entirely familiar to her, but she was often aware now that she was looking at Grafton afresh, to preserve it in her mind's eye.

'What will you do?' she asked Hannah.

'Do?'

The women drew closer to Hannah. They felt as if they were under siege, embattled within the labyrinths of their uncertain friendships while the walls of established rituals crumbled away and left them exposed.

Janice was afraid, as she had been on the evening of the Ransomes' barbecue. She could not pinpoint the fear; it evaporated when she tried to confront it only to condense again at the periphery of her inner landscape, a thick, dark cloud of anxiety. It made her want to hurry home to secure her children and her husband, in case the erosion she could see around her had begun to nibble there too. Only she knew that if she voiced her fears Andrew would robustly dismiss them.

'I shall close it,' Hannah said decisively. 'It's only a shop.'

'No, it's much more than that,' Vicky said. 'It's what you did. You made it.'

They acknowledged this between them.

'Even so I can't keep it on at a loss. We can't afford it.'

It was strange for them to hear Hannah, the rich man's wife, admitting as much.

'What are you going to do?'

It was Vicky who asked this time.

Hannah understood that the women wanted to know more than what she planned to do with the shop. She thought of Darcy at home at Wilton, alternately animated by the preparation of his case or, more often these days, sunk into uncommunicative silence. She thought of Michael, too, remembering the morning they had spent together at the fashion house showroom looking at the autumn collection. The hemlines had been calf-length, and Hannah loved short skirts. She had felt her interest detach itself from the clothes paraded in front of her, and curiously that detachment now seemed to extend to Michael himself.

'Oh, I'll stick by Darcy, of course. Wait it out, whatever it is.'

She meant the trial, and afterwards, if Darcy had to go to prison.

Janice nodded. Vicky was thinking that Darcy would need all of Hannah's support. She remembered the childishness that their intimacy had uncovered in him, and how disconcerting and finally unappealing she had found it. Her eyes met Hannah's, and she saw the glimmer of a challenge in the other woman's stare. Hannah was vulnerable, for all the armour of her chic dark vendeuse's suit, but she was also steely in her determination.

'I admire you,' Vicky said softly. 'Darcy is very lucky.'

They stared at each other for a moment longer. Vicky's eyes were the first to drop. She would have liked to reach out to Hannah and hug her, but something in the armour held her away.

Star had abruptly turned her back again, to the window and the view of the shoppers in Southgate.

'Yes,' Hannah agreed. 'Isn't he? Do you think the role of stalwart little woman becomes me?'

It was not a question that seemed to require an answer; none of the others tried to supply one. Hannah said in the same even voice, 'I suppose I'd better do something about these clothes.'

She went to another niche and unpinned a second dress. This one was golden-yellow with big black buttons, like shining eyes. On impulse she held it out to Vicky.

'Come on. Put it on. Let's see what it looks like.'

Vicky glanced from the dress to Hannah.

'Put it *on*? With my hips?'

'Don't be such a killjoy. Try it, the colour's right.'

Hannah's face had lightened. She went to the rails and lifted an armful of clothes. 'Let's dress up. We might as well have some fun. Here, Janice, this number's made for you.'

'Darling Hannah, it's orange.'

'Marigold. Doesn't madam care for marigold?'

Star turned back from the window. She was smiling, too.

'Give me the gold one, then,' she ordered. 'And the harlequin suit, as well. I've had my eye on that for weeks.'

Vicky disappeared into the tented changing room and came out in the yellow dress. Hannah regarded her, head on one side.

'Mmm. Needs jewellery. Big earrings. Hang on.' She unlocked a glass-topped display table and held out a fistful of glitter. 'Try that. Next?'

Janice swayed forward, half-tripping in the orange sheath.

'Long gloves,' Hannah pronounced. 'Black suede ones. Over there. Star? There, didn't I tell you the gold one was perfect?'

The women were laughing now. Vicky hitched a taffeta ball dress off one of the rails and held it up, cinching the waist with her forearm and posing for the others.

'I've always fancied myself in one of these.'

'Now's your chance.'

'Vicky, those earrings are a masterpiece.'

'Can you zip me up?'

'Try this on top of that dress.'

They dived in and out of the changing room and the sofas began to disappear under a froth of discarded clothes as more outlandish outfits were put together. They giggled like children raiding their mother's wardrobe as Hannah egged them on, pulling open cupboards and drawers and producing accessories like a magician.

'I've always wanted to do this in here,' Star sighed happily. 'It's like being let loose in a grown-up toyshop.'

They came together in their borrowed magnificence and posed in front of the full-length mirrors. Their dazzle reflected back at them. They had forgotten the windy, mundane afternoon outside.

'My God, we look like the Supremes,' Vicky said.

'My Supremes,' Hannah agreed.

This had become the right way to let go of her shop, by making a voluptuous game of it. She felt a surge of affection for the women and the bright, fragile reflections of their different identities in her unsold clothes.

Star pirouetted slowly in her column of gold.

'I want you to buy that dress,' Hannah told her. 'I'll let you have it at cost. And look.' She unpinned a heap of gold and crystal from a velvet cushion. 'I'll throw in the earrings for nothing.'

Star wound her long bare arm around Hannah's shoulder and held her.

'You are a consummate saleswoman. I give in. I'll take the dress and the earrings, and I'll have to find a whole new way of life to go with them.'

'Why not?'

'Why not, after all?' Star murmured. But Hannah wasn't listening.

'Wait a minute.' She found another velvet cushion. 'These are for Janice and Vicky. A present, one each, to wear on your summer holidays.'

They were more earrings, a pair of gold seashells and a pair of silver starfish.

The Ransomes and the Frosts were taking neighbouring houses beside the sea for part of the summer. The Cleggs would be staying at Wilton instead of making their usual trip to Greece. Darcy had had to surrender his passport to the police.

They smiled at each other in the mirror. Vicky did reach out to Hannah now. She put one hand on her arm.

'I wish you and Darcy were coming on holiday too,' she said. 'I wish it could be the same as it used to be.'

'I know,' Hannah said, acknowledging the apology and the truth together.

Suddenly, for all of them, the years of their friendships and the parties and celebrations seemed precious and fleeting. They had thought that these things were as immutable as the couples themselves, and they had not properly appreciated them until the disintegration was under way.

The women became serious again, and they noticed the incongruity of their exotic clothes. Janice slowly unpeeled her long suede gloves.

'Oh, Hannah, I'm sorry. If only there was something . . .'

She made a gesture of helplessness with the glove, the empty fingers flapping loose.

'Andrew stood half the bail, didn't he? What more could we ask?'

Hannah did not want to cry, but she found that she was close to it. She was reminded of a day, a lunch at Janice's, when she had said something clumsy to Nina, and Nina had sat at the table and cried. Hadn't that also been to do with loss, and the necessity of concealing it?

The shop bell tinkled behind them as the door opened. Hannah and the women looked round and saw Darcy. He seemed large in this feminine enclave, and faintly unkempt. His hair was longer than he usually wore it, and his clothes appeared as if he might have put them on without considering whether the various items matched.

'Am I interrupting?' he called.

'Not at all. Come and see,' Hannah answered. She recomposed her face. Darcy should not see any threat of tears. 'What do you think?'

Darcy whistled. He slid between the women, big hands touching a bare shoulder, the curve of a hip. Carefully he gave exactly the same due to Vicky as to the others.

Star was reminded of how Darcy had once been, proprietorial amongst them, the couples and not just the wives. He was going through the same motions now, determined not to surrender his mastery.

'For me? How did you know I was coming?' he joked, a shade too loudly.

'Women's intuition.'

Obediently they joked back, adopting a kind of awkward flirtatiousness, revealing not for the first time since his arrest that they did not know quite how to treat him.

When the three women had retreated into the changing cubicles in search of their own clothes, Darcy said to Hannah,

'I wondered where you were.'

'You knew I was here,' she said quietly, replacing the discarded dresses on their hangers.

'I wanted to see you.'

It was the truth. The polished, reproachful silence of Wilton had become intolerable, and he had found himself sitting in the pointless expanse of his study and wishing for his wife. He had gone straight out to his car and driven into Grafton.

'It's all right,' Hannah said, as she did to Laura and Freddie.

She put down the coat hangers and held out her arms to him. Darcy went to her, shuffling a little, his confusion momentarily evident to both of them. Hannah patted his shoulder, looking beyond him as if she could see what might be coming.

Her thoughts slid to Michael and then surprisingly away again, to Marcelle. She wished that Marcelle could have been here this afternoon, with Vicky, in the same unspoken forgiving way as it had been with Vicky. The recognition made her wonder sadly what it was she had been doing or hoping to find with Michael Wickham. The evening they had spent here in the shop seemed a long, long time ago; the reflections in these mirrors might have belonged to someone else.

When she considered it, Hannah was not quite sure that she even liked Michael, let alone as much as she liked Marcelle.

Hannah rested her hands on Darcy's shoulders, then briskly shook them as if to force him upright.

'Come on,' she whispered.

Darcy felt a tired admiration for her strength, and at the same time he did what she told him, jerking his head up before the women could see his weakness.

Star emerged from her curtained tent with the gold dress shimmering in her hands.

'You are having it, aren't you?' Hannah insisted.

'I'd better pay for it before I change my mind.'

Hannah led the way to her desk.

'She's done it again, has she?' Darcy joked. 'What a saleswoman. I should put her to work on my reputation, don't you think?'

Hannah said nothing. Her blonde head was bent as she wrote out the bill for Star.

When the dress was in its dark blue bag Vicky and Janice and Star hovered with the Cleggs in the shop doorway. It was time to meet the children from school. The term was over. In a day or so the Frosts and the Ransomes would be on their way to Cornwall for the summer holiday.

Darcy made an elaborate round of kisses and goodbyes. He was like some overbearing master of ceremonies, dismissing them at the end of a performance.

'It's only three weeks,' Janice protested. She felt the cobweb of fear shiver over her skin again.

'Jimmy will be here,' Star said. 'We haven't planned anything.'

'Jimmy, my boy.' Darcy nodded heartily but vaguely, leaving them almost wondering if he remembered who Jimmy was.

The women kissed each other, murmuring their assurances. They left Darcy and Hannah and walked away down Southgate, between the slow surges of shoppers and visitors. At the corner, where Star would turn in a different direction, they stopped to look at the oblique view across the cathedral green to the west front. The contractors were removing a section of scaffolding, permitting a glimpse of pale, bare stone.

'Aren't you and Jimmy going away?' Vicky asked Star.

A scaffolding pole was thrown down, the crash minutely delayed by the distance.

Star was still looking across the green as she answered, 'I don't know. I don't know at all. I've resigned, you see. I'm not going back to school next term. And I haven't any idea what I'm going to do instead, so don't ask me that.'

Janice and Vicky glanced at each other. Everything was changing, sliding out of the old alignments.

'Is it a good thing?' Janice ventured.

Star's sudden smile flashed at them like a beacon. She stood up straight, and the blue bag swung from her shoulder.

'Who can tell? It seems like a good thing now. I feel' – she pointed across the green – 'cleaned up, like the old saints and martyrs. Peeled of the old layers, porous and ready for the new rain to fall on me. It might sting a bit, of course. And the nights might feel colder without the coat of grime. But I've done it anyway. I just have to decide what to do next. Wish me luck?'

When they did so, she thanked them with a touch of her old irony. Then she hoisted the dress bag again and strode away.

Nina liked Grafton at the height of summer. She liked the way it seemed to belong to her, with everyone she knew away on holiday, and she was happy to share the city with the tide of tourists that washed across the green beneath her windows. She worked in her studio, with the pinnacles of the cathedral floating in the sky over her head, and in the afternoons she went for long walks in the green lanes and fields surrounding the town, as she had done in the first weeks before she knew Gordon,

Her only regular visitor was Barney Clegg.

One afternoon at the beginning of August Nina drove Barney out of town in the red Mercedes. It was a warm day, with a faint haze of cloud, and the air was heavy and still. Nina followed the road that led up into the low hills until they found a picnic spot that overlooked the valley and Grafton in the distance. Barney lifted the picnic basket out of the car. It was a wicker hamper, fitted inside with plates and recesses for cutlery and bottles, given to Nina by Patrick. Barney watched in admiration as she unpacked champagne and brioches and raspberries.

'I always thought picnics meant banana sandwiches and warm Pepsi and sand.'

'That doesn't sound much like Darcy.'

'No, but Darcy never took us on picnics. I went with other people's parents.'

Nina handed him a champagne flute and they clinked the glasses together.

'Now you know different. I'm glad it was me who showed you.'

'Are you?'

Nina was wearing her hair tied back at the nape of her neck. Her face was bare and her skin was transparent in the clear light. She looked her age today. Barney leaned forward and kissed her, tasting the specks of moisture on her upper lip. When he drew back, uncertainly, he saw how her eyes sharpened. But she only said, 'Yes. I'm glad of everything that has happened between us. Are you hungry? Stupid question.'

Barney was always hungry. The quantities of food that he consumed had become one of their shared jokes. They ate their picnic sitting companionably side by side, knees drawn up, gazing out over the valley. Nina always liked to think that this view of Grafton, shrouded in the haze of distance and heat, had not changed much since medieval times. She half closed her eyes, eliminating the sprawl of industry and housing that skirted the edge of the city, and the cathedral shimmered for her in the midst of its protective huddle of buildings.

The light grew bruised and purplish as she watched. There was a threat of thunder in the air. Nina felt hot and languid, drowsily uncurled with the effects of the champagne. She let her head drop gently to one side, to rest on Barney's shoulder. He didn't move, either closer or away from her.

'What is it?' she asked, breaking a silence.

'I need to talk to you.'

'Talk.'

'What do you want to happen?'

She could feel that he was awkward, holding a little artificial space between them. The awkwardness was uncomfortable.

She answered, 'Oh, I want everyone to have enough to eat, some dignity, the opportunity of happiness.'

'Don't try to make a joke out of it.'

'That wasn't a joke, Barney.'

'All right. Thanks for your world view. What do you want to happen between you and me?'

While she thought, Nina took his hand. It was dirt-ingrained from his summer gardening jobs. There were coarse blond hairs on the back of it and the thumb crooked inwards.

'I want what we have had. No more than that. Is that a fair answer?'

'Only partly. You say what we have had, but does that mean you want it to go on? Or not?'

Gently, Nina said, 'I see. Shall we say that I don't want it to end, but I know that it can't go on for very long?'

She felt a small but distinct pinch of sadness that was amplified by her loneliness beyond its proper significance, and also a murmur of relief and an affection for Barney that kindled a secondary distinctly physical reaction.

'Is this important now, today?' she asked, sorry that the afternoon's languor should be disturbed.

'I failed my exams,' Barney said flatly. 'Not a great surprise, of course. I'm not going back to college next term. There isn't much point, and I don't want to, because of this thing happening to Darcy. I feel I ought to be here, around the place like some kind of support for the twins, and Hannah and the kids as well, if I'm needed.'

'But?'

'Yeah, but.' Barney disengaged his hand, resting his chin on his fist. 'I want to be somewhere else as well. I've been offered a job by the father of a guy I know. Some landscape work, labouring really, in Australia. Perth. I want to go for a year, travel to some other places on the way back. The kind of thing everyone does.'

'Yes, I see.'

He was very young, Nina thought. She felt ancient in comparison, but she could remember how the smooth surface of youthful self-preoccupation could be ruffled by notions of duty and responsibility. Poor Barney.

'I should go, if I were you. There isn't much you can really do here, is there? Your father's case might not even come to court for another eighteen months.'

'I still feel as though I have these responsibilities. Even though I had to shuffle Lucy off on to you and Patrick.'

Lucy was still in London, staying with Patrick. They had struck up a friendship, genuine for all its external improbability. Patrick had promised Lucy that he would help her to find a job.

Nina stroked Barney's bent head. His hair was thick and floppy and she combed her fingers through it, as she had done before when she held him in her arms. The memory came back to her, regret and a sense of reprieve neatly twisting together with her growing awareness that what she wanted, this minute, was for them both to take off their clothes and lie down on the grass. The afternoon had grown very heavy.

'Do you feel responsible for me?'

'Kind of.'

She sat up, moving away from him. 'Please don't. I don't want you to.'

'Is that the truth?' He was looking at her now. This was what he had hoped to negotiate, evidently.

'What else?'

Barney stood. He stuck his fists in the pockets of his jeans and walked slowly around the car. When he came back to the point where he had started he drew Nina to her feet, settling his big hands on her hips.

'You're great, you know?'

Nina gave no sign of her amusement. He was so large and good-natured and transparent. 'Thank you,' she said solemnly. 'I think the same of you.'

'You really think I should go to Oz?'

'I do.'

Barney grinned, at last. 'Yeah. Perhaps I will. But not yet.'

He edged a step or two backwards, holding her until he felt the bonnet of the Mercedes behind him.

'This car,' he muttered.

'Don't you like it?' She didn't care what Barney thought of it. The car belonged to Gordon, the windy day of the car show-room, the motel room on the motorway.

'What about the environment?' he asked in the faintly prissy way of his generation.

'I tell you what – I'll sell it.'

'But not yet,' Barney repeated. He leant back, sitting on the sweep of the bonnet, his feet hooked on the bumper, conscious of the appeal of this posture. He drew Nina closer, catching her between his knees. Smiling back at him, willing to enter into this game, Nina unfastened the buckle of his belt. As she undid the jeans buttons one by one, she saw the first fat drops of rain splinter into scarlet starbursts on the shining paint.

'Are you afraid of getting wet?' Barney murmured against her throat.

'Try me.'

She didn't want him to talk any more. The differences between the spoken and unspoken Barney were becoming too apparent.

The rain grew heavier as they kissed, but it was warm, oily rain that slid over the car and over their upturned faces. Nina licked a trickle of it from the corner of her mouth. She unbuttoned her shirt that was beginning to stick to her skin in the downpour and bared her shoulders. Barney knelt down in the wet grass to take off her shoes. The rain drummed a jungle rhythm on the roof of the car.

Barney gathered up their discarded clothes and bundled them into the shelter inside. Then they stood up, pressed together, with the wetness of their skin making a slick seal between them. When they kissed again, greedily now, they felt that they were enclosed within a grey vertically washed world that contained no one but themselves.

Nina had begun to remind herself that she was too old and too sober to be cavorting naked in a thunderstorm with a blond boy, and had started to formulate the laughing, tactful evasions in her head. But then she thought, why should I be too old for this, or for anything else, if that isn't what I feel?

Suddenly there was a view down the long tunnel of the past that made her feel dizzy.

The years of her marriage shrank, peeling away before her eyes and diminishing to a mute, one-sided tribute that she had made to Richard, and to Richard's work and needs and opinions, whilst her own cares and concerns had been sidelined. Even her brief affair with Gordon might only have been what Gordon chose to take and then to reject, whilst her own part had been to offer herself for the taking and then to accept his withdrawal, as if it had been no more than her due.

She had made a life of this meekness, Nina thought, and she had assumed that she was happy.

But now, with this extraordinary and disorientating shift of perspective, she wondered if it had not been happiness but the colourless security of acquiescence.

If it had been, and she could not tell for sure because of the distorting glass of distance, and the blurring rain, and the absurdity of finding herself here like this with Barney; but if it had been so, then she didn't want it to be so any longer.

Nina felt something shrivel and crack.

It was as if her old, thickened skin split and fell away in harmless shreds to reveal a new one. Like the cathedral statues, except it was the rain and her nakedness that regenerated her. She felt free, neither lonely nor apologetic, and airily intoxicated by her freedom.

Nina lay back on the bonnet of the car. The curved length of it was warm and smooth under her back, and the rain plastered her hair to her cheeks and pattered on her belly and her eyelids. She spread her arms and then her legs, like a sacrifice.

Barney mumbled, 'That's quite a turn-on.'

Nina briefly opened her eyes. 'Good,' she said simply. Only she knew that she was making this offering not to Barney, but to herself.

He was heavy on top of her, and warm, sheltering her from the rain that had grown cold and sharp. Their bodies slithered together and Nina heard the tiny resonances of the complaining metal as it dented under their weight.

Briefly they found a rhythm that connected with the rain.

Once the sky split with a livid wire of lightning. Then Nina's fingers dug into the smooth muscle of the boy's back as she moved beyond him, without him, to an illuminated compact sphere of her own devising. He tasted her mouth curving in a smile and he glanced down at her, puzzled, ready to be reassured but unable to see into her closed eyes.

Nina's fingers curled into fists and her hips lifted as she came, quickly, with a protesting echo from the dimples of distorted steel.

Then she lay still, entranced by the taste of rain and the rub of smooth paintwork and skin and the rumble of distant thunder and the sound of the boy's panting breath against her ear, all of these knitting together to make the shell of her private sphere, within which she was perfectly contained herself, as neatly as a baby folded inside the womb.

Barney lay with his heavy head resting on her shoulder, and she moved the tips of her fingers gently down the groove of his spine, as she had done on the first morning.

'Are you cold?' he asked her.

'No. Very warm, and pleased with us.'

'Yeah. Not bad, eh?'

Not bad, Nina echoed to herself. *Much better than not bad.*

Barney slid away from her, brought his shirt from the car and tried ineffectually to rub them both dry with it. It was still raining, but the air was lighter and there was a wash of clear light in the sky beyond Grafton.

The inside of the car was a warm, leather-scented bubble that misted over with their breath as they struggled into their clothes. When they were more or less dressed again Barney grinned at her.

'That was a bit of a first for me.'

'The rain, or the car bonnet?'

'The two together, actually.'

'Ah. Me too, as it happens.'

The admission did not betray anything more, Nina thought. Nothing more was necessary.

As she drove home the sun came out. Barney glanced sideways at her.

'Why are you smiling so beautifully?'

She told him the truth. 'Because I'm happy.'

Michael took the children to Cornwall for ten days. They were staying near the Frosts and the Ransomes, because Marcelle and he had agreed that it would be good for Jonathan and Daisy to spend this time with their father, and it was hoped that the company of the other children might help to make their mother's absence less apparent.

Marcelle stayed on alone in Grafton. The Pond School was closed for August; there was not even the distraction of a holiday course for executive wives for her to teach. She moved carefully through a succession of solitary days. Without Janice and Vicky and their tactful visits she felt unfounded, as if she had become less than flesh and blood, but the same isolation also made her much more clearly aware of herself, defined, instead of some extension of her husband and children and their friends.

She read the occasional newspaper reports about Darcy. She had heard that Darcy and Hannah were immured at Wilton, and once or twice she imagined herself driving the familiar route to call on them. It did not seem such an improbability, because she no longer felt any animosity towards Hannah. The knot of anger and grief and bitterness that weighed inside her was twisted around Michael himself.

For exactly a week after the children's departure with Michael, she saw nobody and hardly emerged from the alarming, fascinating quiet of the house. The weather stayed cool and cloudy; even the garden seemed threateningly overlooked by neighbouring windows although she knew that most of the houses were empty, the occupants away in Corfu or Tuscany. She thought of the labyrinthine longings and subterfuges of these family holidays, couples and children confronting one another without the buffers of routine, and felt no particular awareness of her own loss. There was, rather, a sense of the confused buzz of domesticity that had surrounded her, and the sharp, clear silence that she now inhabited in its absence.

She was not unhappy in this time, although she could never quite recapture the pleasure and release of her solitary Sunday.

On the evening of the seventh day Marcelle was sitting in a wicker chair in the garden, in a corner that was made secluded by a projecting wall of the house. There was a row of earthenware pots beside her, planted with a colony of alpines and saxifrages that she had weeded and tidied earlier in the day. The neat little whorls and rosettes of leaves were unassertively pleasing against their collars of gravel. When the bell rang, Marcelle realized that she had been sitting staring at the pots for a long time, with a book lying unopened on her lap.

She thought at first, confusedly, that it was the telephone ringing. The children, perhaps, with the day's news, or Michael with some message. Then she realized that it was the door. She stood up stiffly, glancing down at her clothes that she had given no thought to for a week, and then went obediently to answer the summons.

Jimmy Rose stood on the step.

'Is this entirely unwelcome? Only say if it is, and I will beat a retreat. Not hasty, but quite orderly.'

She knew from the yellowish creases at the side of his mouth as much as from the ornate phrases that Jimmy had been drinking. He was not drunk yet, but on the way to it. She looked at him dispassionately, as if he were unknown to her.

'It isn't unwelcome.' Her voice felt rusty from disuse. 'Come in.'

In the tidy kitchen, from behind the jug of white nicotiana that she had left on the counter-top, Marcelle asked, 'Would you like a drink?'

Jimmy had been out to lunch with his bank manager. This was a regular enough arrangement, at which in the past, after a routine reference to Jimmy's company account, they had always moved on to more congenial discussions of local politics and businesses and their golf games and, over a last drink, whatever

401

titbit of gossip they had heard about their shared acquaintances. Today, however, although the man had been no less cordial than usual, he had reminded Jimmy that his business account was overdrawn substantially beyond the agreed loan limit. No one understood better than he, of course, that in the present climate it was not easy, but he believed that it would not be in Jimmy's own best interest for further credit to be extended by the bank.

Jimmy had nodded, his fork cutting through the pastry of some dish he did not want. Every mouthful he took tasted like chalk, and he needed a long swallow of wine to wash the paste out of his mouth. Business showed signs of revival, he said. He was confident that by the autumn the picture would be different.

The manager pursed his small mouth. He did not press the subject, but neither did he agree to stay for the brandy that Jimmy suggested and definitely wanted.

After they had shaken hands and the man had left, Jimmy sat on his own and ordered one anyway. He drank it too quickly, and then had to go back to the office. The afternoon yawned around him, and at five o'clock he abruptly left and walked the skein of Grafton's medieval streets until he reached an unfashionable pub at the edge of the old cattle market. The bar was empty, but in his depressed state it seemed to be haunted by hollow-eyed cattle-drovers in greasy jerkins, and rank with the smell of animals. He sat at a smeared table and drank two and a half pints of beer with the television blinking over his head. When he could not face any more beer he stood up, with no idea where to go except that he did not want it to be home. He thought of Marcelle.

In her kitchen, he said, 'Scotch. Thanks. Aren't you having one?'

'Just some wine, I think.'

Marcelle produced glasses and bottles. Jimmy kept his eye on the whisky, and folded his fingers around his tumbler as soon as it was offered. The spirit cleared a fiery space in his heavy stomach, making him think that all would be well.

'Are you hungry?'

'Not really. Lunch with the bank manager. The usual crap.'

He felt angry now, properly angry with the man. Through the swirls of his indignation he understood that Marcelle was suggesting something, and without bothering to decipher what it was he followed her. Then a moment later he found himself sitting in the garden, in a sheltered corner with a surprising pool of westerly sun spilling on to some fussy little plants in flowerpots at his feet. It was quiet, except for birds singing in the trees.

Marcelle was gazing at him. She was calm and neat, with her brown hair shiny, not unlike some glossy little hen bird herself. She was better off without Michael, probably. Much better. Anyone could have predicted that.

Jimmy let his head fall back against the chair cushion. There was a comfortable creak of wicker. It had been a long day. He was too tired to be angry any longer. The sun felt pleasantly warm on his face, like a woman's soothing fingers.

'You look nice,' he said to Marcelle. 'You look much better.'

'I am better. Funny, isn't it?'

He did not much want to talk about Marcelle's problems. He had enough of his own. But it was good to be sitting here with her. When had that other time been, in someone else's garden, when he had had to discourage her? That had been because of Lucy. He felt a swell of regret for the loss of her, and then with a determined jerk Jimmy sat upright. There was no point in thinking any more about that.

He leaned forward and put his hand on Marcelle's bare leg, stroking with the tips of his fingers. Her skin was soft. He was deciding that he would salvage something from the dismal day. A pleasant prospect began softly to unravel in his mind.

Marcelle leaned forward too. He could smell her clean hair, and see her unimproved eyelashes and the tiny shreds of dryish skin on her lower lip. Recollections of her body in a bikini from beaches and picnics were superimposed with his imaginings, as he undressed her in his mind. Jimmy thought that he would kiss her. He swallowed a belch as he shuffled himself into position.

Her fingers snapped around his wrist and dropped his hand back in his own lap.

He didn't understand what she was doing, so he wheedled, 'Mar, come on. Just a kiss. We know each other, don't we?'

'Yes, we do.'

'Why not, then? I thought you wanted to.'

The whisky on top of the beer had tipped him over the edge into being drunk. He had an erection and he wondered how long he could keep it if Marcelle was going to insist on persuasion. Renewed irritation fretted at the margins of his consciousness.

'No, that's where you're wrong. I don't want to, Jimmy, not with you. Not a bit.'

He looked down at his feet, at the empty glass he had carefully put down beside his chair, the flowerpots, with a sense of the soft, rosy moments he had anticipated flaking away and vanishing to expose a tinny and monotonous substratum, the reality of his life. His shoes were dusty, he noticed, and there were cracks in the leather across the toes.

'Why?' he managed to ask. Not that he wanted to hear the answer. 'We're both lonely tonight, aren't we?' It was obvious, and mawkish, but it was some of the truth that he suddenly wanted to confess. He did feel lonely.

Marcelle appeared to consider. She was remembering how she had felt beautiful, for an instant, in the Ransomes' dark garden before Jimmy had rebuffed her and anger had finally burned up her humiliation.

She let herself taste the satisfaction of the moment before she told him, 'I've been here on my own, you know, for a whole week. Only me in the house. But I'm not that lonely. You can do a lot of thinking in a week, and one of the things I've thought about is doing what I want. Or not nearly so much of what I don't want.

'And I've just realized, only just, that you fall into the category of what I don't want. Do you think you can turn up here, because Michael's gone, and I'll lie down for you without a word? I don't want to kiss you, and I don't want to go to bed with you, although I might once have done.'

She was smiling, Jimmy noticed, a beatific smile that stirred the irritation in his blood in sluggish, nauseating waves.

'I don't want you to touch me, not the way you do to all of us in corners at parties. It's a bit too indiscriminate to be flattering. I don't like the way you treat Star, or the way you whisper everyone's secrets. I don't like the way you smell of the pub tonight.'

She hesitated, then put her hand up, half covering her mouth, as if the old Marcelle was alarmed by the discovery of this new one, and was afraid that she might go on spilling out more.

Jimmy stood up, unsteady against the wicker chair. Whisky fumed in his head.

'Silly bitch,' he whispered.

He raised his hand and examined the opened palm, then clenched his fist and swiped out with it, needing to hit something to vent his rage. His fist struck the wall of the house and pain juddered up his arm to his elbow. When he looked down at the curled fingers he saw blood springing in the creases. Marcelle was fixed in her seat. At least she wasn't smiling any longer.

Jimmy kicked his glass aside, and heard it ring and then smash on the flagstones. He made his way uncertainly back through the house, slamming the front door behind him. He found his car, after a search along those parked down the road, and drove home with his throbbing fist curled in his lap.

Marcelle sat where he had left her. Even the birds seemed to have stopped singing. After a while the silence began to be oppressive. She went inside and wandered through the quiet rooms, and saw how over-neat and unoccupied they seemed.

The scene with Jimmy had broken a kind of spell. She wanted to see the children, and to talk to Michael, and hold all of them because they belonged to her. As soon as the realization came to her it intensified. The house was only a shell, but she was not so empty herself. She almost ran to the telephone. There were three days of the holiday left. If she set out now, she could be in Cornwall long before bedtime.

Michael answered the telephone.

'You sound different,' he said.

'Michael, I want to come down there. I don't know why I'm here on my own without you. Can I come?'

There was only a second's silence. 'Yes,' he said. 'Yes, come.'

Star watched through the window as Jimmy parked the car. When he slammed the door a loop of seat belt caught in it so that it wouldn't lock, but he flung himself away from it without trying to put it right. Star felt a thread break inside her.

The front door opened and then shut, and Jimmy came into the house. She stood where she was, waiting, until he came into the room. He walked past her to sit down on the worn sofa. He glared up at her then, with his shoulders hunched and his hands hanging down between his knees. The scent of aggression came off him, and his anger shone in red points in his eyes. Star thought she knew what was coming.

'Why are you looking like that?' he demanded.

'Like what?'

'You know how. Like a saint at a bad smell.'

'You said it, not me. How much have you had to drink?'

He took his wrist in one hand. His face contorted. 'Not fucking enough. Not. Nearly. Christ, stop staring at me, will you?'

Star didn't move. Jimmy got to his feet and came across the room.

'Don't touch me again,' she warned him. She saw the blood on his hand. 'What have you done? *Don't touch me* –'

There was a series of pictures in her head, like a slide show, only they were not happy images. Jimmy had not hit her very many times, but she could see each occasion as clearly as if it had just happened. She had collaborated with him, she knew that, in keeping these pictures hidden. Although the scenes were shameful they were not dark in her head; rather they were illuminated by the harsh white light of anger. The light hurt her, in anticipation of the violence.

Jimmy hesitated. They stood in the middle of their living

room, with the evidence of their shared life crowding around them. Star knew every detail too intimately, and felt herself float free from all of it.

'I wasn't going to touch you,' Jimmy mumbled. He glanced down at his fist. 'I hit a wall. At Marcelle's.' The aggression leaked out of him. His eyes were dull now.

Star was watching him. She began to nod. There was nothing that connected her to this room, in spite of its familiarity, nor to the man in the pictures in her head. She had known this for a long time, and understood that she had been waiting for the minute that had just come.

This, then, was how it ended.

She was still nodding slowly, confirming it for herself. The end came neither banging nor whimpering, but in silence as they looked at one another, with their furniture and books and photographs as mute witnesses.

'I'm going,' Star said at last.

Jimmy held out the good hand, but he was standing too far away.

'Going where?'

She saw his confusion, but dispassionately, because it didn't belong to her any longer.

'Nowhere in particular. Just not to be here. I'll take some things from upstairs. I'll call you, when . . . when we have to arrange the rest.'

Star went upstairs. She packed a few clothes in a bag, taking the shirts and underclothes out of drawers without examining them. She felt no more for the room than she would have done for a hotel bedroom.

When she came down again Jimmy was sitting in his usual chair in the living room, with his face turned towards the window.

'I'll call,' she said again, but he did not look round. Star went out of the front door carrying her bag. She walked across the town to the cathedral green, to Nina's house in Dean's Row.

*

The two women sat opposite each other in the upstairs drawing room. Star had drunk two glasses of wine, but she had refused Nina's offers of something to eat.

'You are lucky to live with this view,' Star murmured. The unveiled statues floated ethereally in the dusk. The bare room and Nina's company were like a quiet full stop at the end of the day's sentence. 'Was she pregnant?' Star asked. 'The Clegg girl?'

'Yes.'

'That must have been hard for her. Is she all right?'

'I think so. My friend Patrick has adopted her.'

'I knew about her and Jimmy. And the others, of course. Going back, over the years.'

Nina said what she could, which was not much, and prepared to listen.

'I'm not going home again,' Star told her.

'What do you want to do?'

Star looked into her glass, and then smiled. 'This isn't a bad start. Thank you for taking me in.'

'I'm glad to have you here. It has been lonely lately.'

That was the truth. There had been no disagreement with Barney, but since the picnic he had stopped turning up in his gardener's overalls on the way home from a day's work. Nina poured more wine.

'Do you remember in February, when we first got to know each other, when everyone seemed to be away skiing? We walked across the bridge to the school. It felt as though we were the only people in Grafton.'

'Yes,' Star said softly. 'I rather liked that. It's the same this evening. Do you feel that?'

They sat and gazed out at the glimmering stonework as the light faded and softened it. New layers of understanding seemed to shift and settle between them.

'What will Jimmy do tonight?'

'He'll sit where I left him, with a glass and a bottle. In the end he'll fall asleep. Lying sideways on the sofa, with his knees drawn up and his hands folded between them.'

The intimacy that this betrayed touched Nina with sadness. Husbands and wives knew each other so well, she thought, through all the unbeautiful accretions of habit and routine.

'Don't you want to go back?'

'No, I won't go back.' Star did not betray a tremor of doubt. 'He wouldn't notice if I was there or not.'

There was a flicker, and a wash of light filled the room. Star and Nina blinked at each other, momentarily dazzled by the brightness. Then they turned again towards the windows. The cathedral front was blazing with golden light that turned the greenish summer twilight into darkness. The pale and naked stone reflected in their eyes.

'I didn't know,' Nina murmured. 'Gordon said it would be a whole year before they lit it up again.'

The mention of Gordon was like a further acknowledgement of intimacy between them. Nina never spoke of him to anyone.

They left their chairs and went to stand side by side at the window. Dark attendants were busy with the buttresses of lights at the edge of the green. The women watched, and then looked up once more at the miraculous ranks of reborn saints and angels. The hands and faces and folds of fabric were sharp again, as if centuries had been struck away.

Star put her arm around Nina's shoulder, and they stood silenced by the glory of it.

Then, with another blink, the lights were doused. The darkness seemed impenetrable as the brilliance burned in their eyes.

'They must have been testing them,' Nina said.

'For our benefit, then,' Star asserted. 'I'm glad we saw it like this.'

Nina wanted to celebrate the moment.

'I think we need some more wine. I'll go and get it as soon as I can see again.'

They drank the wine, and talked, but neither of them wanted to eat. It was late when they went upstairs to the room above Nina's, with the same view of the dim green from a different angle through smaller windows. There were bare oak boards here, and a wrought-iron bed with a white cover. Nina turned the cover down, then went to release the shutters from their cases.

'Leave the windows so I can see out in the night,' Star said. She was sitting on the edge of the bed, appearing suddenly unsure of herself in the unfamiliar room. Nina remembered that Gordon had liked the shutters downstairs left open, too. The links seemed to shiver, and catch her again. She sat down beside Star and took her hand.

'Will you be comfortable?' she asked.

There was only one light in the room, a small shaded bulb on the night table. There were strong shadows across the other woman's face, revealing unfamiliar planes and hollows that were startlingly bleached of gender.

Star did not answer. Instead she leaned forward and put her mouth against Nina's, and with the tip of her tongue she made a tiny question mark against her lip.

Nina sat still, with the beginning of the kiss in her bones.

Then, not knowing whether the shiver she felt was relief or regret, she felt herself draw back. There was a hair's-breadth of space between them, and then a hand-span.

'I'm sorry,' she said humbly.

'It's all right. It helps to know, don't you think?'

'I don't think I know anything.'

'Barney Clegg, is it?'

There was something so droll in this that they began to laugh. Their laughter broke up around them, filling the room and dispelling the confusion.

'Yes. But no, not in the way you think.'

Or not even in the way I think, Nina realized, admitting a bizarre possibility to herself for the very first time.

'I see,' Star said mockingly. And then, 'Go on, go to bed now.'

From the doorway, Nina said, 'You can stay for as long as you want. Whatever you need, whatever you like.'

'Thank you,' Star said, with the shadows momentarily and mysteriously bleaching her face again.

Nineteen

It was past midnight when Marcelle reached the rented house on the Cornish coast. She had lost her way twice in the lanes leading to the cove, and she was tired as well as hesitant as she negotiated the last mile of sandy track.

Her headlights picked out a low hedge and the windblown humps of trees, and then the little group of houses at the end of the track. The keel of an upended dinghy made a pale blur in the lee of one of the houses. There was only one light showing, a yellowish square that thickened the darkness around it. Marcelle located Michael's car, and eased her own into the space next to it. Before her headlights flicked off she saw sailboards propped against a low wall, and a wetsuit like a peeled skin left out to dry. She stepped out of the car, stretching to ease her cramped muscles, with her nervous breathing making an irregular flutter in her throat.

The sea air filled her lungs, and she heard invisible surf washing on the beach. At once there came memories of a dozen seaside holidays, with her children and from her own childhood, all of them dissolving into one solution of salt and waves and sunlight.

Now that she was here, she did not think of family holidays in the way she had done back in Grafton, when she was excluded from the conspiracy of this one. Rather the associations gave her a powerful sense of continuity, of the importance of such memories for Michael and herself, to be handed on to the children and to their children in turn. She was a mother, the truth could not be obliterated even if she wished it, and her family dues could not be as simply denied or withheld as she had imagined in her solitude in Grafton.

Another rectangle of yellow sliced through the salt darkness as a door opened in the house with the light. Marcelle made out Michael's silhouette within it. She walked through a sandy rut to a gate, and then up a concrete path towards the door. Michael stood back to let her into the light.

There was a living room with standard holiday-let pine furniture, and red and russet rough-weave curtains left open at the window. The room reminded Marcelle of the chalet at Méribel, and so of Michael elated in the snow and Hannah in her silvery suit.

She blinked in the brightness, uncertain of how she should be now that she had gained her objective and reached the place.

'How was the drive?' Michael asked.

'Long. Uneventful, except at the end when I got lost.'

'Jon and Daisy will be glad you're here.'

'Where are they sleeping?'

Michael pointed to the ceiling.

'I'll go and see them, shall I?'

There was a small room with the door left ajar so that light from the landing made a narrow bar across the floor. Daisy would still not settle down in the dark. Marcelle crossed softly to the bunk beds, and inhaled the warmth of sleeping children. Jonathan slept as he always did, with the covers pulled defensively over his head. Daisy lay on her back with her arms and legs flung out. Marcelle drew the blanket up to cover her shoulders and the child turned in her sleep, mumbling some lost words. Then she opened her eyes, and immediately her face lit into a smile. She lifted her arm and crooked it around Marcelle's neck as her mother bent over her in the confined space.

'Good,' Daisy said distinctly. Then she retreated into sleep again.

Marcelle felt a lurch of unmitigated love for her children that tangled her innards.

Michael was sitting at a drop-leaf table against the drawn curtains when she came back downstairs. There was food on the table, bread and fruit and cold ham, and a bottle of wine.

'Have you eaten?'

'No. I'm not very hungry. But thank you for this.'

He poured the wine and Marcelle gratefully took the glass that he handed her. After her week of solitude these little attentions seemed exotic. She was surprised by the nervous uncertainty that made her breath taut in her throat, because his presence was entirely natural and familiar to her. They were on holiday, in a rented cottage beside the sea, as they had been a dozen times before. It was hard to remember that they had separated, unless she concentrated on the recollection.

They talked a bit about the children, and the other families, and Marcelle listened to the small pieces of news that Michael had to relate. She drank her wine, watching his face and trying to see behind it.

'Why did you decide to come now, tonight?' he asked her, at last.

Marcelle told him about Jimmy's visit.

She described it exactly, but in dry, colourless language, as if it had happened a long time ago. Even so, she could hear that her words fitted into circles, closing links that had gaped open before. Hannah and me, she could hear Michael thinking, Jimmy and you, Nina and Gordon. This is what happens, at our age. These needs are admitted. We are shamed by them, but we cannot deny that they exist.

The easiness of his assumption pricked her, but she let it go, understanding that they had inched closer for it.

Michael said, 'But I don't understand. Why did what happened with Jimmy make you want to come down here, to us?'

'I went inside, after he had gone, and walked through the rooms. Everything was very tidy, exactly how I wanted it, nothing like the house is when Jon and Daisy are at home. I had spent a week putting it in order.'

413

'I can imagine.' He laughed, then, and for a second she saw the man she had married. She laughed with him, in surprised accord.

'I realized that I didn't like it. It was empty, and it made me think of you all here without me.'

Michael heard her take a sharp breath, filling her lungs for some effort of expression. It made her seem birdlike, a fragile but determined creature. He thought then that he did love her, but that somewhere on their complicated journey together he had forgotten how to acknowledge as much.

'I could hear the silence, and I missed the comfort of being a family. I had thought that being on my own made me clear, and defined, and I liked the feeling of that. But at the same time I was so solitary that by the end I was wondering if I really existed. Jimmy didn't exactly confirm anything for me.' She spread out her fingers, as if checking her own corporeality. 'In the end, I came simply because I wanted to.'

It was important, she understood, to admit to her own wishes.

'I'm glad it was what you wanted.'

Michael left his place and walked around the table so that he stood behind her chair. He put his hands on her shoulders. The ridges of scapulae and clavicles felt prominent, barely covered by her thin skin. Different from the silky layers of Hannah; different but also the same, womanly. Michael bowed his head so his cheek rested against his wife's head.

'What about me?' he asked.

Marcelle felt a ripple of amusement, but she concealed her smile. Some of the bitterness that she had knotted around Michael was unravelling.

'I wanted to see you.'

'I'm glad,' he said quietly.

Marcelle slipped from under the weight of his hands, and stood up to face him. She leaned forward, so her head touched his shoulder.

It was not a resolution, she knew. It was a long way from that, even. But it was something, a small exchange of faith.

*

The next day the weather turned warm and clear, as if to welcome Marcelle.

There were delighted greetings from the Frosts and the Ransomes when they arrived and found her having breakfast.

'We missed you,' Andrew said, for all of them.

The three families went to the beach, and made their encampment of windbreaks and folding chairs and watersports equipment amongst the other families. Marcelle contentedly sat in a deck-chair and looked at the children in the sea. Helen Ransome slept in her pushchair with a little white frilled sunshade tilted over her head. Small additions were made to the geological strata of Marcelle's memories. That was the year that happened. *I remember that year.* She realized with relief that this moment, now, was not an ending but a continuation.

'Are you all right?' Vicky and Janice found opportunities to murmur to her. 'Is everything all right again?'

'I don't know,' Marcelle told them truthfully. 'Maybe.' She watched Michael wading into the surf with Toby Frost's boogie board. He looked like a stork, with his elongated legs striking arrows through the foam. Some of her anger with him had gone, partly replaced by a kind of tolerance that seemed to be forming like new skin under an old scab. In the night they had lain side by side, just touching, comfortable with that without attempting anything more. Marcelle had listened as Michael's breathing slowed and deepened. She was tired, too, and it had seemed natural, even luxurious, to lie and listen to her husband sleeping with the rustle of the waves in the distance.

It was a happy day on the beach. The adult happiness affected the children. They played generously and uncombatively together, although Jonathan and Daisy kept referring back to Marcelle as if they were afraid that she might disappear. At the end of the afternoon, when it grew cooler and it was time to leave, they clamoured for more.

'Let's have supper together,' Jonathan begged. 'Can't we, since Mum's here?'

'Why not?' Janice was pleased and plump in her candy-striped shorts. 'We can scrape something together at our place. Everyone come to us.'

The Frosts' holiday house was further along the headland, set a little back from the coastal cliffs in a sheltered hollow. The families congregated in the garden, where wooden pub benches were drawn up against a rough slatted table amidst a jumble of sandy towels and discarded flip-flops. For the adults it was pleasantly relaxed and sluttish to leave the day's lumber and sit in the late sun drinking beer and talking. The children swept into the house in search of crisps and Coca-Cola and then out again, on to the headland. Andrew fussed over the barbecue until the smell of charcoal smoke drifted into the air. Everyone had pink patches on their bare arms and flushed cheeks from the sun. Michael and Marcelle sat together on one of the wooden benches.

'It's like long ago,' Vicky said. 'Being here like this.'

The couples agreed, knowing she meant that it only seemed so long since they had been together in this uncomplicated way.

Janice brought out more bottles and they changed from beer to wine, relaxed because there were only beach paths to be negotiated on the way back to their own beds. The sky faded from blue to pearl grey and then, for an instant, to glimmering eau-de-nil.

The children were rounded up from their games and everyone crowded to the table. The smaller ones were tired now and the first quarrels broke out, but the parents were loose with wine and they officiated good-humouredly until the food was eaten. Marcelle propped her chin on her hand. She felt comfortable with the evening's gossip and drink, and with the undemanding reverberations of friendship. She found that she was smiling. All her joints seemed unpinned; it would be a big effort to stand when the time came.

The sky darkened until they couldn't see beyond the unkempt summer garden. Andrew brought out some candles from the house, and stood them in empty jam jars so the flames burned upright. At once, the visible world contracted to a golden circle around the table. The children ran in and out of it, their voices coming back from beyond the margins.

'Bed for my lot,' Gordon called. 'Mary? Alice? I'll take them, Vicky. You stay if you like.'

'I would quite like,' Vicky admitted. 'Only I seem to have had a lot to drink already.'

'We're on holiday,' Andrew insisted, pouring more wine.

Gordon went away down the track that led to the other house. He was carrying Helen asleep in his arms, and the other two girls held on to his legs as they negotiated the steep path.

The group around the table heard Mary protesting, 'It's not fair, Daisy's staying up,' and the beginning of Gordon's answer, until the receding voices were absorbed by the still air.

'Shall we go too?' Michael asked Marcelle. His arm was around her shoulder, and she dropped her head to rest against it.

'Not yet.'

'Not yet,' Daisy echoed. 'We want to play.' She was elated to be left to stay up with the Frost boys and Jonathan.

'Just half an hour,' Michael said. It was completely dark now. Toby Frost, the leader, was announcing the rules of some game from beyond the garden wall.

'Wait for me,' Daisy shouted to the boys. There was a sugary thud as someone jumped off a low wall into the coarse grass, and the sound of running footsteps. They heard William counting, and then singing something, his chorister's voice very clear and high in the silence. After that there was only the sound of the waves, and the talk around the cluttered table. Andrew leaned over one of the jam jars to stick a fresh candle into the melted ruins of the old one and for a moment his face was grotesquely lit from below, like a Hallowe'en mask.

Vicky lifted her drink and tilted it to her nose.

'Here's to all of us,' she said.

They drank, echoing the toast after clinking their glasses.

They were reminded of the dozens of other evenings that they had spent together, the Christmases and the summer barbecues and the other landmarks of the year, and separately they felt the absence of the Cleggs and the Roses with an unspoken shiver that made them draw closer together and begin to talk of the plans for another season. They were laughing, with their heads close together in the candlelight, slightly drunk with wine and good humour and sea air.

There was a small, bitten crescent of moon hanging low in the sky.

'It's a beautiful night,' Marcelle whispered. 'Listen to the waves.'

The surf was clearly audible now, as if some volume control had been turned up. The sound of it seemed to emphasize the silence that overlaid it. There were no voices, no running feet.

'How long have the kids been gone?' someone asked.

They listened again. There was nothing except the sound of the waves.

'Did they say where they were going?'

'I didn't see which way they went.'

Andrew stood up abruptly, jogging the table so the candle flames wavered. 'They won't be far away. But I'll wander down to the beach and find them. It's time they were heading for bed.'

They listened to his footsteps swishing along the beach path.

'I'll make some coffee,' Janice said into the silence.

She was carrying out the loaded tray when they heard Andrew coming back again.

'Any sign of them?'

'They're not on the beach.'

'How long have they been gone?'

'It must be half an hour. Perhaps a bit longer.'

'You said half an hour, Michael.'

'I know what I said.'

'We'd better go and find them. Mike, you go over the headland that way. I'll do the opposite direction.'

'What about us? What do you want us to do?' Janice asked. There was a panicky note in her voice. 'What have we been *doing* sitting here while they were getting lost?'

'All right, Jan. Stay here. Michael and I will find them.'

After the two men had gone, the women sat at the table with the debris of the evening around them. Marcelle began to pile the dirty plates. She had lost coordination and the rattle and clink of the cutlery sounded unnaturally loud and domestic in the thick silence. They were straining their ears for different sounds. Vicky put her arm around Janice's shoulders and found that she was shaking.

'You're cold. Have you got a jumper?'

'In there, somewhere.'

Marcelle went to look for it. The light in the kitchen was over-bright and harsh, and as she hunted clumsily for Janice's sweater she realized how much she had had to drink. Her mouth was dry and there were queasy flutters of fear buckling her diaphragm. She discovered the sweater over the back of a chair and carried it out into the garden. She was remembering how she had gone upstairs to look at the children last night, and the way that Daisy's face had broken into a smile of delight even though she was fast asleep. '*Please,*' she found herself whispering.

Janice was standing at the end of the garden, gazing over the wall into the dark. She took the jumper from Marcelle, but didn't put it on.

'Something has happened,' she muttered. 'I know it has.'

They waited, and the minutes slid past in silence. At first they had been able to hear Andrew and Michael calling the children, but now there was nothing.

'How long since they went?'

'Ten minutes. Perhaps a quarter of an hour.'

'*Where are they?*'

After another moment Vicky turned her head sharply. 'Listen. What's that?'

It was the sound of running feet. They heard them thudding and slithering on the grass, and then two small figures appeared. It was Jonathan and Daisy. *Thank God*, Marcelle thought. Their faces were little white patches emerging from the blackness straight ahead of the house. Neither Andrew nor Michael had gone the right way.

Marcelle began to run, with Vicky and Janice at her heels. The children came at them full tilt. Marcelle's relief evaporated as they came closer. Both of the children were sobbing for breath and Daisy was stumbling with exhaustion.

'William's fallen,' Jonathan cried.

There was a long, terrible second while he gasped for air, and the children clung on to Marcelle. A minute ago, she thought wildly, everything was all right. We were sitting here drinking wine and laughing, and now that easiness has gone . . .

Janice's eyes and mouth rounded into dark holes of shock and fear. Her hands went up to her cheeks.

'Where, Jon?' Vicky insisted. 'Where has he fallen?'

'The cliffs. He was climbing up and he fell on the rocks. Toby's trying to get down to him. He told us to run for Andrew and Dad.'

Janice's head was wobbling, but she was already heading in the direction that Jon had pointed.

It was Vicky who took charge. 'Marcelle, phone for help. Stay here with Daisy, tell the men what's happened when they come back. Jon, you'll have to show us where he is.'

She turned and ran after Janice, with Jonathan scrambling beside her.

Daisy was weeping. Tears ran down her face.

'William's hurt,' she blurted out. 'He wasn't moving. Where's Daddy?'

'Looking for you.'

Marcelle seized her hand and propelled her back to the house. She wasted seconds because she had no idea where the telephone was, and when she found it she cursed her unfamiliarity with the place as she struggled to describe where the accident had happened. When she hung up she turned to look at Daisy's blotchy, terrified face.

'Help's coming. What happened?'

The child began to cry again. 'We went to the beach, and

we came back the other way. There's a path up the side, the side of the cliffs, it's steep but it's much quicker because we knew we were going to be late and you'd be angry, and then William said he could climb straight up the rocks anyway, and we watched him and he got more than halfway only we could see it was harder than he thought, and then he kind of grabbed at something that stuck out and it broke and he fell.'

'Oh, Daisy.'

Marcelle sank down on to a kitchen chair and held the child against her, hands cupping her head as if she would at least keep this one safe.

'We shouldn't have let you go off like that in the dark.' There was no sound except the sea. 'I wish Daddy would come.'

Toby was waiting at the foot of the cliff, crouched on the rocks beside his brother. He was trembling. It did not look so steep or so high from down here. He thought that William should have been able to do the climb easily. The waves were very loud. William was lying so still, with his eyes closed. He had rolled, rather than falling straight down.

Toby could hear the phrases in his head, broken pieces of explanation, mixed with incoherent begging prayers. He was afraid to touch. Afraid to do anything. There was black blood on William's forehead, and his hair was wet with it.

If only they would come. Jon was a good runner, wasn't he? They must have found their way back by now . . .

Toby could not even tell if William was breathing. He was afraid of the stillness.

There, was that voices? He looked up. Above him, thirty or forty feet up, he saw the glimmer of faces. It was his mother, at last, with Vicky and Jon.

'Please come,' he called to them. He was giving way, now that they were here.

Then he heard his father's voice, shouting, away to the left.

'*Andrew!*'

That was his mother. The sound of her panic increased his own.

'Help us!' Toby screamed. William did not move.

Marcelle and Daisy sat in the kitchen, waiting. There was a clock on the wall with red numerals and thin red hands, and each sweep of the second hand seemed to last for ever.

When the garden gate creaked they leapt up and ran to the window. It was Vicky, with Jonathan. Jonathan was crying too, and the two children met in the kitchen and huddled together.

'Michael and Andrew are there. Is the ambulance coming?'

'Yes. Yes, it's coming. It must be ten or twelve minutes since I rang.'

'I'll ring again. Mike says they'll need a rescue crew.'

When she came back from the telephone the two women gazed helplessly at each other over the heads of the children.

'What has happened?' Marcelle whispered.

Vicky shook her head warningly, the corners of her mouth turned down. Marcelle closed her eyes, but when she opened them again the kitchen and the clock and the fierce brightness were unchanged. The electric hum of kitchen appliances was hostile, trapping them in some minefield of fear and inaction. The barbecue supper seemed a long time ago, part of some other life to which they had now forfeited rights of access.

'Will William be all right?' Daisy asked.

'I hope so,' Marcelle said.

'Look.' Jonathan pointed to the window that faced away from the sea. There were revolving blue lights bumping down the lane.

William was carried from the rocks in a rescue stretcher, with Michael stooped beside him. The stretcher was loaded into the ambulance at the clifftop. Michael and Janice went in it, and the journey over the headland began in reverse. A police car brought Toby and Andrew back to the house. The women and Daisy and

Jonathan were still waiting in the kitchen with the clock-hands sweeping impervious circles above them.

'How is he?'

Andrew shrugged. 'I don't know. He has head injuries. I'm going to follow on to the hospital.'

'I want to come,' Toby said. His set mouth and jaw made him look mulish, the expression at odds with the fearful pallor of his face.

'No. Stay here with Marcelle and Vicky.'

Andrew drove away in the wake of the ambulance. The police and the rescue team had gone, and the darkness and drumming of the surf seemed to those who were left to possess the house. It was long ago that they had sat in the light of the setting sun, imagining that they were the possessors.

The women made hot drinks for the children and persuaded them to go to bed, Jonathan in William's bunk above Toby, and Daisy in Janice and Andrew's double bed. Toby was shivering and the three of them protested dully that they could not sleep, but they did so, collapsing quickly into oblivion as if escaping from the night. Marcelle sat downstairs at the kitchen table, trying not to listen to Vicky in the next room murmuring to Gordon on the telephone.

She thought of the election party, when Michael had gone to the hospital with Darcy after his heart attack and she had sat like this at Janice's table, waiting to find the strength to go home alone. Why had that seemed to cost so much? The memory of Michael and Hannah, of Hannah with the tiny ruff of mud and grass around the tips of her stiletto heels, and her own shock and disbelief, was diminished now, pressed into near-insignificance by the fresh, hideous perspective of this evening.

If only William is all right, she tried to bargain, *if only he is all right, how different then shall we all be, knowing what we know now?*

Marcelle fitted her cold hands together, palm to palm, feeling a guilty pressure of gratitude that her own children were safe. She also thought of Michael, as she had not done for a long time, as a doctor. Michael could do something other than sit. Her

423

admiration for him came awkwardly, because she was not practised with it, but it came, refilling an empty space inside her.

Vicky sat down opposite her. She stretched out one hand and put it over Marcelle's.

'What can we do?' Marcelle said.

'Pray, I suppose.'

They sat in silence, listening.

In the small hours of the morning Michael returned. They saw at once that there was no good news. Marcelle stood up and went to him, aware that she was clumsy about how to take care of him after the night he had spent.

Michael said, without preamble, 'A blood clot has formed under the site of the skull fracture. They will have to operate to remove it. The plan at the moment, unless his condition deteriorates, is to do it some time tomorrow.'

'How bad is he?' Vicky asked.

'Fifty-fifty.'

A weight of silence seeped through the room. The flakes of it were heavy, silting up under the cheery pine furniture, deadening their small, bewildered movements. Michael sat down at the table, eyes closed, pinching the bridge of his nose between his fingers.

'Poor little William,' Vicky whispered.

'What about Andrew and Janice?'

'They're in a side room. Those red hospital chairs, plastic beakers of tea. I've seen it so often, the parents waiting, looking up at you when you come in with the notes, as if you're God instead of some surgeon, with . . .' Michael stopped and hid his face from them.

With his own pain, Marcelle silently completed the sentence for him, *and no better answers than anyone else.*

'It was terrible to see them sitting like that,' Michael said, without lifting his face from his hands.

Marcelle got up from her place. She stood behind him and his hands came up, grasping her wrists, holding her there.

'I should go back to Gordon,' Vicky said, at last.

The Wickhams sprang apart, as if they had forgotten her. Vicky did not think of it then, but afterwards that momentary oblivion shone with a tiny point of pale, hopeful light.

Michael saw Vicky home down the path that Gordon had taken, seemingly days ago. When he came back Marcelle was already in bed. He undressed quickly, dropping his clothes haphazardly, and slid under the covers on the opposite side. Daisy lay between them, her mouth slightly open and her breath thickened with sleep. They both turned inwards, knowing and loving the shape of her and fearing the fragility of the smooth limbs and the skull under the floss of fine hair, as they feared for Andrew and Janice's child in his hospital bed.

Outside it was already growing light.

The operation to remove the blood clot from William's brain took place the next morning. Janice came back in the late afternoon with the news that he was stable, although he had not regained consciousness. Bruised pouches of tiredness had swollen out of the skin beneath her eyes. Toby clung to her and she tried to reassure him that it had been an accident, that it was no one's fault.

The children were given their supper at the same table in the garden. By their own unspoken agreement they left the place that William had occupied the night before empty for him, as if he might suddenly materialize in the midst of the meal.

In spite of the difference in their ages the children seemed to draw together, finding a common ground in their anxiety and in their sober self-importance at discovering themselves to be a part of this emergency. They ate quietly, passing each other the ketchup, slyly demonstrating their good behaviour because they knew that they were watched.

While Janice tried to sleep for an hour, the four remaining adults looked over the row of diminishing heads, from Toby to Alice, through the kitchen window. The parents felt the contrasting tension of their own responsibilities, dividing them as well as linking them, invisible fine threads tangled in the air. They were heavy with the thought that they had been drinking wine and laughing in the garden when William fell, and the knowledge isolated them and drew them together also.

Marcelle was drying plates, polishing them over and over with a tea cloth.

'When he does regain consciousness, is he likely to be damaged?'

Michael said, 'I don't know. I don't suppose that they do, either. But it must be a possibility, even if it is no more than that.'

She did not stop her slow circling with the cloth, gazing out at the same time through the checked curtains to the children at the table.

'Is it our fault?'

It would be Marcelle who articulated the question, Michael thought. She was the quickest to draw blame to herself. But he considered this as a matter of fact, not as a judgement.

'It can't be undone, whether it is anyone's fault or not.'

It was Gordon who answered her. He made a gesture that drew them into a net that they swam in together.

Vicky looked up from feeding Helen, who was perched in a high chair device that fixed to the edge of the melamine-topped table. The baby's face was joyfully smeared with apricot pudding. Gordon had not been there, he had not been in the garden when the older children vanished, but he included himself in the net. She smiled at him, knowing that she loved him.

'Gordon is right,' she said to Marcelle.

Overhead they heard the floor creak. Janice was getting up. This time nobody needed to articulate what they felt, the steady reverberation of friendship.

Janice went back to the hospital, to wait with Andrew.

Two more nights and days passed, and when the end of the holiday came William's condition was unchanged.

The families reloaded their estate cars and headed back to Grafton with the late-August traffic. Andrew and Janice had agreed that they would take it in turns to stay near the hospital, so one of them would be near to William when he regained consciousness.

September came, and the leaves of the chestnut trees in the Bishop's Garden began to reveal mottled veins and margins of brown. In the colder early mornings the river meadows were overlaid with a faint breath of mist, and the cathedral bells rang flatter in the damp air. The city streets emptied as the tide of visitors receded, and ordinary business revived again after the summer's suspension.

The couples waited sombrely for news from the Frosts. When they saw each other it was in quiet pairs, as if they were chastened by the year's happenings. William still lay in a coma.

Star lived with Nina in the Dean's Row house, although she was making preparations to go abroad. Her negotiations with Jimmy were oddly formal and polite, as if they had never known each other well.

Nina herself was restless. She finished a project for her publisher, and could not settle on a new one. She went for long walks, asking herself as she trudged over the fields questions about her future that appeared to have no logical answers. It was only partly enjoyable, now, to have Star's company. She also longed for solitude, as if that would enable her to think more clearly.

One late afternoon she was crossing the green under a whitish, autumnal sky when she found herself slowing and then stopping to look up at the west front. The entire façade had now emerged from the scaffolding, and the medieval statues mounted row on row between their golden pillars to the pinnacles of the towers. She stood for a long time, admiring the exuberance of the ancient masons' work, and the careful homage of the conservationists. Then she turned and, for no particular reason, went into the cathedral through the west porch. She had not been inside it for a long time, but the ecclesiastical smell, and the echoes of footsteps and murmuring voices, seemed as familiar as

427

the inside of her own home. She walked a little way down the nave and then slipped into a seat, and sat facing the high altar with her hands quietly folded in her lap.

It had not been her intention to come to Evensong, but she had only been in her place for a few moments when she noticed that the front two or three rows in the distance were occupied by a handful of people. The organ began to play, and the rounded notes softly filled her head. There was a flutter of surplices as the clergy and the double line of choristers took their places in the quire. The soprano voices rose in the day's anthem.

It was only then, with her mind busy with other things, that Nina noticed the man kneeling diagonally across the aisle from her. He lifted his head after a moment and sat to listen to the singing, and she saw that it was Gordon. He was in his business clothes, and there was a briefcase on the seat beside him.

Nina sat, stood and knelt with the rest of the tiny congregation. Enclosed in the great, dim space she felt a touch of happiness, as she had done here once before, with Gordon.

When the service ended the organist began a voluntary. With the peal of music Gordon left his place and came to sit beside her. It was a very long time, Nina realized, since they had been alone together, and yet no time at all.

'I saw you come in,' Gordon said. 'You appeared sad.'

He did not tell her that the brightness of her hair had seemed to bleed into the air around her pale face, and that he had wanted at once to come to her.

Nina smiled. 'I'm not sad. I suppose I was thinking. I didn't know you liked Evensong.'

'I was at a conservation meeting.' His fingers rested on his briefcase. 'And then I realized that it was the right time. I wanted to offer up some thanks.'

'For?'

'You haven't heard? William Frost has regained consciousness. He had been showing some signs of improvement, and this morning he opened his eyes. Janice was with him. He said hello, and asked where Andrew was.'

The organ voluntary and the choristers' anthem rang in Nina's head. An association stirred in her, and then she thought of the nativity play and William with his father's features and his mother's expression singing amongst the choirboys. The carols and the chapter house and the scent of Christmas had recalled her own childhood. And she had seen Vicky holding the white bundle of her new baby.

Impulsively she reached for Gordon's hand, and he took hers and held it between his own.

'How wonderful. How very, very good. Does that mean he will be all right?'

'Andrew didn't stay long enough to tell me very much. He drove off down there almost at once. But I should think the chances must be good, wouldn't you?'

Nina nodded. Her head was light and her hand felt warm in Gordon's.

'Yes. I'm so pleased for them. It's the best thing I've heard for a long time.'

Gordon had been praying, she remembered. She would have liked to kneel down to offer her own confused and inarticulate thanks, for William and also for her own riddle which now, suddenly and without any warning, revealed to her its clear and happy solution as if it had never been a riddle at all.

'Do you have to go anywhere right now?' Gordon's face was so close to hers she could see the little flecks of colour in his eyes.

'No.'

'Should we go and have a drink, or something?'

Nina thought of her house and Star, and the unacknowledged association between Star and Gordon and herself, and then of the bar at the Eagle.

'Not a drink. A walk, if you'd like that?'

'Yes. Shall we go?'

They stood up, and when they stepped out into the aisle he tucked her hand under his arm. They walked slowly, looking up and ahead of them, as if they had just been married.

Gordon drove them out of Grafton through the lanes that led

towards Wilton. He parked his car in a gateway and they took a footpath that climbed away across a sloping field to a low ridge crowned with trees. They walked comfortably side by side, up the shallow gradient, between bramble clumps weighted with blackberries. Gordon answered Nina's questions about the summer holiday, and about Vicky and his children, and the next phase of the conservation work.

When they came into the belt of ancient oak and beech trees that ran along the top of the ridge their conversation faltered. The layers of leaves underfoot muffled their steps, and the canopy overhead was filled with the crackle of homing birds. They walked on in silence, between the huge tree pillars in the dim space, reminded of the cathedral and the first evening they had spent together.

They reached the other side of the tree belt but they hesitated within the margins of it, as if they were reluctant to leave its shelter. The wood seemed noisy with the wind and birds and the movements of the branches. They stood together gazing out in the direction of Wilton Manor, although the house itself was hidden from view.

'Have you seen Darcy or Hannah?' Gordon asked.

'No, not recently. I don't see much of anyone, except Star, of course.'

'I'm sorry,' Gordon said at last.

'For my not seeing anyone?'

'You know I didn't mean that.'

'Yes,' Nina agreed. She stood a little in front of him and to one side, with her face turned away. She wished now that she had not suggested this walk, although similar scenes had sometimes presented themselves in her imagination. She did not know what to say, and she felt that they had become uncomfortable together.

'I'm sorry for the way I behaved, although not for what happened,' Gordon said. 'Why won't you look at me?'

She did turn her head then. They looked full at each other for a moment, and then Gordon took a step through the leaves so that he reached her and held her. They stood with their faces close together, listening to the sound of one another's breathing. Their mouths did not touch, and then Nina looked past him, down the slope of ground towards Wilton.

'I can't think of any way that anything could have happened differently between us,' Gordon said. 'But I've wished that it might, over and over again, as if wishing enough could change anything.'

This was not an attempt at justification, or an apology, but a statement of simple truth. Nina understood that he had wanted to tell her as much, and she felt her discomfort fall away.

'I wished too,' she said softly. 'Although it doesn't make any difference, as you say.'

He held her tighter, with his fingers knotting in her hair. Nina closed her eyes for an instant and then opened them to see the bars of cloud low on the horizon and the shadows between the trees.

'What about you?' Gordon asked.

'I don't know. Not for sure, anyway. But I have begun to think that I should leave Grafton and go back to live in London. I've been here for nearly a year. I have a feeling that the cycle should be completed, and then abandoned.'

'Is that what it was, a cycle?' Gordon wondered aloud. 'All the things that have happened this year, beginning with when you came?'

'Does that mean you think my coming here caused these things to happen?'

His arms tightened around her.

'No. Only that you were the catalyst. I think that when people like us have been married for a number of years, when our children have been born and begun to grow and our circles of friends are in place, we let ourselves imagine that these things are immutable. Time passes, and if there is no particularly piercing joy, well, there is no sharp pain, either. Then something happens, or someone like you appears, and the balance shifts. Everything that had once seemed clear and secure is revealed to be something else. To be blurred, and precarious.'

'Perhaps that is true,' Nina said. 'Perhaps. And now what happens?'

'Some of the balance will be regained, and some will not. And there will be different perspectives for everyone.'

'Including you and me?'

'Yes. Perhaps for us most of all, because of what might have been.'

Nina nodded, a little sadly.

Gordon let his hands drop and she stepped away from him, lifting her hair from her face and knotting it behind her head. He felt that the gesture fixed her back within herself, cutting him off from her.

They listened to the birds for a minute longer, and then they began to walk again, retracing their steps through the band of trees towards the open slope of hillside.

'When do you suppose you will leave?' he asked her, unwilling to hear the answer.

Nina walked briskly, with her hands pushed into the pockets of her jacket.

'I don't know. Once Star has gone off to America, once I have found somewhere to live. In a month or so, maybe.' She shrugged, and her dismissiveness hurt him.

'We shall miss you.'

'Only a bit. And then the equilibrium will be restored.'

She saw his face then, and put her arm through his, so they walked as they had done down the cathedral aisle.

'Now you are looking sad.'

'And you are happy,' Gordon realized.

'I am all right,' Nina said sagely.

She might have told him her secret, but she did not. Nina was certain that she was pregnant, and there was the added certainty that had come to her in the cathedral, that she wanted the baby more than anything.

Barney's baby, but not Barney's: her own.

Twenty

Star was wearing the gold dress from La Couture, and the earrings that Hannah had given her.

She checked her reflection in the small mirror in Nina's upstairs bedroom, trying to see her own face as if it were a stranger's. But the features remained familiar, obstinate. Star stood back again, and then acknowledged with a flicker of amusement that it was absurd to be dressed up like this for a dinner *à trois* in Nina's kitchen.

It was the involuntary amusement that did make her seem different, just for a second.

Star turned her back. Her suitcases lay on the bed, almost ready to close. There was a plane ticket to Portland, Oregon, in a folder beside them. Tonight was her last evening in Grafton; tomorrow she was flying to visit her sister in the States. She did not know exactly how long she would stay; or where she would go when her sister's hospitality was exhausted. The uncertainty was exhilarating rather than alarming.

Nina had insisted that there must be a celebration of her last night in England.

'Who shall we invite?' they had asked each other.

They rejected the Grafton couples two by two, although they both knew without saying as much that they would have welcomed Gordon alone, for the proper evening *à trois* that they would now never share. In the end they had settled for themselves and, laughing a little at the idea, Barney Clegg.

Star went down the stairs to the kitchen. She had enjoyed her stay in Nina's tall, bare house, and the freedom it had given her. Separation from Jimmy had convinced her that she would never go back to him.

Nina was cooking. She had dressed up for the evening, too, in black lace and velvet. She whistled at the sight of Star.

'You look wonderful.'

Star had not seen it herself, but it was the truth. The old, inimical look had gone and a faint flush of excitement warmed her cheeks. She twirled to show off the dress.

'I'm glad Hannah made me buy it. But aren't we rather done up with nowhere to go?'

'Not at all. We have got everywhere to go, and tonight is only the start. Drink this.'

Nina gave her a glass of champagne. Star came to peer over Nina's shoulder at the contents of the saucepans. The gold dress swished behind her.

'Smells good. Barney will be happy.'

'Barney's always happy,' Nina laughed.

The black velvet dress left her back bare. Star looked at the freckles on Nina's shoulders, and the tender points where they ran together and coalesced into faint blotches. She reached out and stroked the discolourations with the tip of a finger.

Nina was used to these odd, oblique caresses. She had grown to like the intimacy that they implied, and the way that intimacy was partly undefined, and although she had half wished for solitude she knew that the house would seem cold and pre-dictable when Star was finally gone.

'I shall miss you,' she said.

'I will miss you too,' Star answered.

She leaned forward and kissed Nina, her lips just touching the corner of her mouth. Then, with the same grave attention, she rubbed away the tiny lipstick mark that was left.

The doorbell rang.

'It's the boy,' Star grinned, and went to let him in.

'Oh, God,' Barney wailed when he saw them. He was wearing

434

jeans and a sweater, and he carried two bottles of champagne in the crook of his arm. 'Why didn't you tell me?'

'Tell you what?' Nina asked innocently, relieving him of the bottles.

'That I should be wearing Dad's cowboy DJ or something.'

The women laughed. There was a hint of conspiracy between them that made Barney see them for an instant as two halves of a whole that excluded him.

'If we had wanted Darcy and his dinner suit we would have asked him,' Star said.

'I'm flattered that it was me who was invited.'

'So you should be. Shouldn't he, Star?' Nina smiled. She filled three glasses and lifted her own. 'Bon voyage,' she wished each of them simply. In another week Barney would be on his way to Australia.

They toasted each other.

'You are beautiful,' Barney said truthfully, when he had downed his drink. 'Both of you.'

He felt rather in awe of them, and of their faintly distant, definitely female collusion. It was as if he had been taken up for an interval and was now being returned, gently but firmly, to his own generation. This might have been disconcerting, if the champagne and the smell of food had not lifted his spirits. Barney reminded himself that he was looking forward to his own adventures as well as to an honourable release from the anxiety at Wilton. He was also relieved that his affair with Nina had come to a blameless end. He did not want to hurt anyone, nor had he any intention of being hurt himself.

Nina serenely filled his glass again. They would enjoy their evening, as they had enjoyed their summer together. It had been a lucky affair.

'Shall we eat?' she asked, nodding to the table. It was laid with her best linen and glasses, and the candles were lit. Barney drew back the chairs for each of them.

It became a good evening, when the champagne took hold and blurred their differences. That they were each on the point

435

of separate departures made a bond between them, and they each determined that this goodbye should be a benign one. Nina and Star gently drew Barney into their conspiracy, alternately teasing him and flattering him and then offering some proper revelation of themselves so that he relaxed and accepted his role of diligent squire to their glittery black-and-gold partnership.

He also drank a great deal, thawing in this feminine warmth. By midnight he could not do much more than sit at his end of the table, smiling and blinking and offering his benevolent assent to the women's talk.

At length Nina said, 'Barney, you can't drive home. Leave your car here, and I'll call you a cab.'

'Can't I stay with you?'

He flung out his arm and caught her as she passed his chair. He held her and pressed his face against the smooth velvet folds of her dress, sighing with pleasure.

'I'm a happy drunk, aren't I? Don't cause aaaa-any trouble?'

Nina stroked his hair. 'None. But you'd better go home tonight. I'll telephone for you.'

But she was barely back in her seat before there was a heavy knocking at the front door.

'Da-daah!' Barney saluted. He stood up, not very steadily.

The women glanced at each other. 'I'll go,' Nina murmured. It was Jimmy.

'I'd like to see Star,' he said reasonably. 'To say goodbye, or whatever else needs to be said.'

'Is she expecting you?'

Jimmy looked much as he always did. If he had been drinking it was difficult to detect, as it always was with Jimmy. But Star had told Nina enough to make her wary.

'Is she *expecting* me? What are you, the maid or something? No, she's not expecting me to turn up at this moment, we don't have an *appointment*, but I'd like to see her. She's there, isn't she?'

His voice grew perceptibly louder. Nina stood back. 'You'd better come in, then.'

Jimmy followed her down the stairs to the kitchen.

436

Barney was leaning one shoulder against a cupboard with his huge hands knitted around a cup of coffee. Star was standing, too. The candles burning on the table behind her outlined her dress with a secondary rim of gold. Jimmy gazed at her, and at Barney, and the empty wine glasses and the comfortable detritus of the evening.

'I didn't know it was a party. I'm sorry.'

No one spoke for a long moment, although Star stared directly at him with her head held up.

And then Jimmy made a sudden swinging movement towards Star. It was a lunge at her that was so uncontrolled and so indecipherable in its intention that Nina called out '*No, Jimmy!*' and Barney collected himself sufficiently to threaten some counter-attack, spilling much of his coffee on the way. Jimmy shook him off without a glance.

Star held her hand out to Jimmy. She caught him by the wrist so that he didn't blunder against her. But there was as much support in her holding as there was self-defence.

'What's happening?' Barney mumbled.

'It's all right,' Star said coolly. 'Everything is all right.'

'Is it? Would you say that?' Jimmy's face was twisted on one side, as if with the beginning of a paralysis.

To the surprise of the other two, still waiting ready to defend her, Star put her arm around his shoulder. She stooped from her greater height to reach his level. She guided Jimmy to Barney's chair at the table, and helped him to sit down.

There was another knock at the front door.

'This'll be your cab,' Nina told Barney.

'I'm not leaving you with *him*, here, if he . . .'

Jimmy ignored him. He was sitting at the table with his head in his hands, with Star at his side.

'Say good night, Barney,' Nina warned.

To her relief he did as he was told. Upstairs, with the taxi waiting, he mumbled to Nina, 'I'll call you. Before I go, you know? Perhaps come by, if that's . . . I'm pissed, that's the trouble. I'm going to miss you, and this . . .' He pointed upwards, at the house.

'I know,' she said gently.

'Will you be okay? With Jimmy?'

She promised him, 'We shall be quite okay.'

He kissed her clumsily. 'Well then. Thanks for . . . you know. All of it. And for being you. Most of all that.'

'Thank you too. For more than you realize,' Nina added.

Barney climbed into the car. He turned back, sentimentally, for a last glimpse of her through the rear window, but the house had already swallowed her up.

Nina waited in the hallway, listening. She could hear low voices, nothing more. She hesitated for a minute longer, and then went thoughtfully up the stairs to her bedroom.

'I've never seen that dress before,' Jimmy was saying.

The skirt of it fell around his feet in rich folds. He thought it made his wife look beautiful, medieval, but he could also only see this metamorphosis of Star's as a sign of her freedom. She had escaped from their narrow chrysalis, wriggled away from it and unfolded a pair of miraculous wings. He was left behind, flightless. He felt his own weight pulling him down into solitude.

'What time do you leave?'

She told him, and they talked about the mechanics of her journey, and the routine plans she had made for the first days of her stay. The neutral exchanges manoeuvred them towards the thickets of what remained to be said.

'Have you put the house on the market?'

Jimmy nodded. 'The agents weren't very encouraging. There isn't a lot of demand for three-bedroomed estate houses in a poor state of repair, would you believe.'

'But we need to try, don't we?'

Half of the unloved house was hers. It was her chance of independence, where the walls and windows had once represented the exact opposite.

'Do we?'

His face had grown sharper and lost its healthy animal cunning. The lopsided twist was partly an uncertain smile, and partly a sneer that denied it. His mouth slackened, so that both the smile and the sneer faded. He seemed dull and confused, and almost frightened.

'Don't go,' Jimmy begged.

When Star said nothing he began to talk faster, mumbling at her, 'I don't want you to leave. I'd give anything for you to come home. It could be made different, if we both wanted it to be. I know I haven't been all that great to you, but if I promised something . . . Christ, I don't even know what, but to try what you wanted, whatever that is, then we might be better, mightn't we? Could we not at least try that much, instead of letting our lives fade out into nothing. Like this, this defeated whisper we are now?'

He ran his fingers through his gingery hair so it stood up in a barnyard crest, such a familiar gesture.

Star touched his arm. 'Stop,' she said.

'Stop what?'

'This. The speech. I can't come back, Jim. I don't want to. I want to do what I'm doing.'

He looked full at her then, surprised, and she saw that even this last moment had been a performance for an audience of one. He had expected that she would come back; the idea that she could truly abandon him must have been unthinkable. She was touched with unruly pity.

Jimmy said slowly, 'Jesus. You're brutal, aren't you?'

She considered the accusation. 'I suppose. If I have to be.'

His mouth hung open. Then he rubbed it cruelly with the back of his hand, and gazed down at the faint glisten of spittle on the sandy skin.

'That's it, then? Is it?'

She said nothing, wanting to spare him that much. In the warm, rustling and ticking space of Nina's kitchen they sat side by side, listening to the dry seconds running out between them.

At last, Jimmy stood up.

'I'll be in touch with you at Jane's if there is any news about the house.'

'Thank you.' Jane was Star's sister in Oregon.

He waited for a moment more, but there was nothing else. Star sat with her head bent and heard him go up the stairs to Nina's front door, and let himself out of the house. She was wondering, fearing, if even now she might have capitulated.

She sat for what seemed a long time after that, until the cold wrapped around her bare shoulders and made her shiver. Then she went upstairs and knocked on Nina's bedroom door.

'Come in,' Nina said at once. She had been lying in the dark.

'Don't turn the light on,' Star begged. When she found her way to the edge of the bed and sat down, Nina's warm hand touched her arm.

'You are so cold. Get in under here.'

There was a rustle as Star unzipped her gold dress and laid it over a chair. Her heel tips clicked on the oak boards as she discarded her shoes. Then she unfolded her stiff legs and arms, carefully, into the warmth of Nina's bed.

'Have you been crying?'

'A bit.'

'What did he say?'

Star looked up into the darkness. 'Oh. The usual things.'

'And what did you say?'

There was a brief silence. And then Star laughed, a little spurt of laughter that was still on the edge of tears. 'None of the usual things. Not much.'

'And now he's gone?'

'Yes.'

They lay quietly. Star felt her limbs warming again. Nina's hand moved, then found hers and held it.

'And is that all right?'

Star answered, 'I wasn't sure, for a minute. There seems so much in a marriage to dismantle, and then the time comes and it suddenly looks small in retrospect, almost insignificant for the effort and pain that have been spent on it. There is a kind of pity and sadness that comes and you think, perhaps we should rescue it. But I don't believe there can be or should be a salvage operation for us. So it is all right, in its way. I suppose Jimmy'll see that too, in the end.'

She was thinking of him sitting at the table downstairs, with his hair rubbed up into spikes, and in her sad sympathy she was grateful for Nina's affection and the warmth of her hand.

Star added, 'Thank you for the celebration this evening. I'm glad it happened here.'

Nina smiled. 'Me too.'

'Barney Clegg,' Star mused. It was both a summing up and a dismissal, although kindly enough.

'Yeah. Star, may I tell you something I haven't told anyone else?'

'Ah. You're going to marry him?'

It was Nina's turn to laugh. It was a low, amused chuckle with an edge of triumph.

'No. But I am pregnant.'

'Barney's?'

'Yes, but no. Mine.'

Star took a moment to absorb this. Then she said with generosity, 'I'm very pleased. I think that's wonderful.'

'So do I,' Nina whispered.

Star turned on her side, to face her in the darkness. Then she slid her hand to Nina and over the ridge of her hip to splay her fingers across the soft pocket of flesh.

'It's only eleven weeks.'

'But I think I can just feel something.'

'Just, perhaps.'

'What are you going to do?'

'I've been thinking, planning it. Move back to London, probably. I can't stay in Grafton, can I? I'll sell this house, buy another close to the park or the Heath, near to schools, where other people with children live.'

The possibilities multiplied ahead of her, daunting and inviting.

'You are lucky,' Star told her. 'A baby. Think what it will be like.'

They drew closer, so their faces were almost touching.

'I am thinking,' Nina said drowsily.

They were both tired. Soon, they fell asleep.

In the last week of October the Frosts telephoned the other couples, and Jimmy, to invite them for Hallowe'en.

'It's not a big do,' Janice insisted. 'Not like last year. It will be just us, for a drink and some supper. But I think we should do it. You will come, won't you?'

The couples and Jimmy agreed that they would. No one suggested to anyone else that they should feel like survivors.

When the night came, the Wickham children and Mary and Alice Ransome wanted to go trick-or-treating with the Frost boys. The ghost costumes and skeleton masks were found, and the luminous gel and plastic talons, and the children dressed up. They streamed out into the smoky night, with Andrew and Michael in discreet attendance. While they were gone, Janice put on her best black dress, noting that it hung a little looser on her than it had done the year before, and turned her attention to preparing the dinner. Marcelle sat in the kitchen with her.

'Can't I do anything?' she asked.

'Nothing,' Janice said firmly. 'Not this time.'

They knew that they were comfortable with one another again.

Michael was at home once more and Janice did not any longer ask if Marcelle was all right, and Marcelle could see for herself that Janice had softened with gratitude for William's recovery. They had fallen back into the pattern of making wry, humorous acknowledgement to one another that they were wives and mothers, and that these conditions were eternally imperfect. But there were also other pieces now, made clearer within this unspectacular domestic mosaic, that were concerned with relief, and near-satisfaction, and the small triumph of having preserved this much of the picture of their lives, this far, at least.

The meat was put into the oven to roast, and the table was laid ready for another evening.

'Let's hope they'll be back soon,' Janice sighed, looking at her watch.

'Shouldn't bank on it,' Marcelle said cheerfully.

The Ransome girls were to spend the night at Wilton with Freddie and Laura. The Cleggs' new au pair, Zoë, who had replaced Mandy at the beginning of another school year, had already arrived to collect them before the front door banged open again. The children poured back into the kitchen, bringing the cold air with them. Their ghoul make-up was smeared with sugar and they brandished the bags of sweets that their threats had extracted.

'We dropped an egg and a pile of flour on the Watkins' step,' Toby shouted. The kitchen surged with children and noise.

Zoë was already rounding up the Ransome girls with antipodean authority. 'Mrs Clegg says they'll be on their way as soon as we get back,' she told Janice.

'Good. Andrew, did you let them dump stuff on the Watkins' front step?'

Andrew was taking beers out of the refrigerator. He gave one to Michael and opened one for himself.

'Nothing to do with me.'

'Ma, it's *Hallowe'en.*'

Daisy and Jonathan were staying the night with the Frost boys. The tide of children began to ebb upstairs. Watching them go, Janice thought, It's the same, and I was afraid that it would never be. The sameness, shaded with the summer's difference, seemed entirely blessed.

Only William hovered in the wake of the others. His face was hidden behind a luminous fright mask, and his head was covered with a black hood.

'Take them off, Will.'

He did as he was told. His face was revealed as moon-pale, and there was a big, livid patch at the side of his skull where the hair had not yet regrown to hide his scar. Janice went to him and touched his shoulder. She wanted to lock him in her arms and cradle his head, although she would not permit herself this

443

demonstration. In any case William ducked away, out of her reach.

'I'm all right, Mum.'

'I know, I know.'

He was only partly all right, she understood that, because the spectre of his own mortality had left William with the legacy of fear. A tentative child who watched from the margins had emerged from the hospital bed in place of the younger William. And yet, as if in temporary compensation for the loss of his confidence, Janice's own nameless fear had disappeared. The summer's weight of anxiety had lifted, replaced by a sense of deliverance and renewed strength. In her relief she felt that the currents between the couples, even the superficial patterns of their lives, were no longer awry. Relief made her want to sweep up the friends and absorb them into her own happiness. She had been determined that this evening must take place so it could be set at the opposite end of the year, to close off the months that were now past.

William went away to join the other children. Janice took off her apron and reached for the glass of wine that Andrew had set down for her.

Jimmy was the next to arrive. He gave both Janice and Marcelle identical greetings, a kiss on the cheek and an arm appreciatively snaking around their hips. They let him feel, Marcelle as gracefully as Janice, but the frisson that Jimmy once induced had died away. Without Star Jimmy seemed deflated, smaller, touched with sadness. The women humoured him kindly with their responses and it occurred to Marcelle that the men had always humoured Jimmy, in their different way. He had never been a real threat, she thought, except to Star herself.

The Ransomes brought champagne, once Darcy's prerogative. Vicky submitted to Jimmy in her turn. She had lost weight and showed it off in a narrow calf-length dress and high-heeled suede ankle boots, and Jimmy's hands smoothed greedily over her behind as he kissed her.

Gordon was thinking of Vicky a year ago, flushed and

mountainous in her white maternity dress, and then of the coloured lights that had revolved over Nina's hair. He had crossed the cathedral green earlier in the evening, not because he needed to but because the house in Dean's Row drew him to it. There had been no lights showing in any of the windows and he had loitered like a boy, amongst the trick-or-treaters, wondering where Nina was.

The couples hovered in the kitchen, drinking champagne, waiting for the Cleggs. Jimmy was boisterous, his voice rising and chopping through the surges of talk. The Cleggs were three-quarters of an hour late but they appeared at last, with Darcy in Hannah's wake. He was thinner too, much thinner than he had been, but his face was not a healthy colour and there was loose skin in folds under his jaw.

'What are we celebrating?' Darcy asked, seeing the champagne. 'Birth or marriage? Or some other life event?'

There was a small silence before Gordon said, 'We could celebrate the cathedral, perhaps. The work on the west front's complete. And we heard today that there is the possibility of more funds from English Heritage, which means we could renew –'

Darcy interrupted, 'Is anyone as tired of the bloody cathedral as I am? As if there were nothing else in Grafton worthy of love or money?'

Vicky stood beside Darcy. She wanted to protect him from his own impatience, and deflect unwelcome attention from it. Hannah was talking to Janice at the other side of the room.

'I'm tired of it too. Gordon's always there . . .' Vicky said.

Andrew passed between them, pouring champagne.

'We could spend a few grand restoring my place instead,' Jimmy joked. 'Then some poor sod might think of buying it and Star can get to Mexico. Or wherever it is she wants to go.'

'Is that what she's planning?' Marcelle asked.

'Yeah. Good luck to her,' Jimmy pronounced.

Marcelle would have talked about how he was without Star, and tried to discern what their separation meant for him, but his bare-faced flippancy rebuffed her.

445

Janice summoned them to the table.

Once they would have taken their places without thinking about it, well practised at neatly alternating themselves, but now that their number was uneven they found themselves hesitating. In the end Jimmy sat between Hannah and Vicky, leaving Gordon and Andrew together at the end of the table.

Janice said, 'I should have asked an extra woman, shouldn't I?'

'Nina, perhaps?' Jimmy goaded.

The invisible and silent threads of anxiety shivered around the table, but Vicky gave no sign of having heard anything. Her even flow of talk never faltered, and her smooth face was animated as she leaned across to make some point to Hannah. Gordon's dark head involuntarily lifted, just for an instant, at the sound of Nina's name.

'Perhaps not,' Janice murmured.

'Don't worry on my account. I am as happy as could be right where I am,' Jimmy told her, putting his arm around Hannah's shoulders.

Hannah had faded. She seemed less voluptuous than simply plump, and her hair and her make-up and clothes were dimmer and more perfunctory in their design. The other couples had seen little of the Cleggs over the summer, although Hannah had been generous in offering whatever help she could to Janice while William was in hospital.

Hannah sat, with the unwelcome weight of Jimmy's arm pressing on her.

She was thinking with a touch of weariness that this evening was the same as a score of others, for all the complicated dances of the last year. She glanced over at Michael, diagonally distant, as far away from her as he could be. The confusion over the placing had left him sitting next to Marcelle, and Hannah noted that that was appropriate. Michael was Marcelle's husband, and she felt nothing more for him than that. The nimbus of desirability that had surrounded him had entirely faded; it was surprising even to recall their meetings in the tented secrecy of the shop, to remember that he had left his home and staked himself out in the chipboard confines of the hospital flat.

Had he done that for her, or against Marcelle?

Hannah's thoughts skidded away from the riddle. She was tired, and the speculation seemed not worth the effort. There were other concerns now, concerns that were no more welcome than thoughts of the dead business between herself and Michael, but simply more pressing.

La Couture was closed, and Hannah was trying to sell her lease on the premises. The money would help, although the mysterious wellsprings of Darcy's income seemed not to have dried up entirely. But although the Southgate location was prime, there had been no serious interest in it. There were not many new enterprises budding in Grafton at the moment.

Without the shop, Hannah knew, all she had was Darcy.

She looked at him and he raised his eyes to hers at once. The wine in his glass was almost untouched. She was strict with him about what he ate and drank and he had begun to be obedient, to please her. He suffered from outbursts of pointless anger or bitterness, but mostly he was docile, like Freddie. Hannah had determined that Darcy would stand trial, and that she would help him and support him as far as it was possible to go. It was the only way, she believed, to salvage something of their lives. That was how she regarded it now, as salvage, but she was determined to preserve what she could. There was not much energy left over from that for anything else.

Yes, an evening like scores of others.

She had a sense of similar occasions, also the same, waiting ahead of her. In time Jimmy would introduce someone new – or a series of new women, bimbos, Hannah reflected with malice, smiling at Jimmy as he withdrew his arm at last, and in the end one of them would become permanent – but she did not believe that any newcomer would have the impact Nina had done. Not that it had been Nina's arrival alone. It had been the time, and the unvoiced and unanswered needs ticking away within them, that had also been to blame. And then it had shaken down again, all the disorder except for Darcy's and her own, and returned to the end point of this evening.

Hannah glanced at Darcy again.

Was this what she wanted to salvage? And then, if not this, what else was there? She bent her head, and with the tines of her fork traced parallel lines on the white linen of Janice's tablecloth.

Jimmy patted the back of her hand, and Hannah ignored him.

After her lemon soufflé had been praised, and eaten and praised again, Janice leaned forward to look at them collected around her table.

'I have got something to say,' she announced.

Her expression declared that it was serious, and they fell silent one by one in amusement or uneasy expectation.

'I know you think I'm sentimental,' Janice began, bright-eyed.

The murmurs around the table were teasing, but affectionate.

'And that I've had a couple of glasses of wine, as usual.'

There was some patient laughter, as they waited.

'But I want to say this because I know it is important. I want to thank you for being here this summer. You made Andrew and me feel that we were surrounded with love and care when William had his accident, and it helped us both, and it made me feel grateful even when I was my most afraid. When I thought he might die. Even then, do you know?

'I'm not as good at expressing myself as Darcy, or Vicky, or any of you, really, I know that. I only seem able to talk like this when I've had a couple of drinks. But I feel so happy tonight, and so lucky, and I want you to be part of it with me. I wanted us to be here together. It's not just because of William, although what happened to William made me see things I hadn't looked at properly before.

'We are lucky, you know, even though it has been such a year. We're friends, all of us, and we love each other, and that friendship is what is truly valuable. I want to hold it, and keep it.'

At the beginning, they had sat, not meeting each other's eyes. But this naive speech of Janice's in its happy honesty touched something in each of them.

448

Andrew looked across at her, separated from him as she was by the length of the table. He had been relieved, up until now, that the evening had been civilized and that the awkward undercurrents had stayed tidily submerged. He would have advised Janice to keep quiet, but even though she had done the opposite he knew that he was pleased.

Marcelle was watching Hannah, who had been staring unseeingly at her hands folded on the tablecloth. Then, without warning, Hannah looked up too. They regarded each other, expressionlessly at first and then with the ghost of an exchanged smile.

'I only wanted to say that.' Janice smiled at them. There were tears in her eyes. 'There's no use expecting eloquence from me, is there? I love you all, and I said once before that our friendship is what we work for, as much as we work for our children, and that's what we should keep in our minds.' She sniffed, and then rubbed her cheek. 'Oh, look at me. I'm going to have to stop, aren't I? Before I really start.'

She took the clean handkerchief that Michael held out to her and buried her face in it.

There was a second's silence, while embarrassment and the temptation to laugh quivered amongst them.

But then Darcy began to clap. It was a big, hollow sound, unidentifiable as irony or assent. After two or three ringing claps that fractured the silence, the others joined in and there was a patter of hands as they applauded Janice. It was real applause. Awkwardly they smiled at each other.

'Bravo,' Michael murmured to her.

'We love you too, Jan,' Jimmy called.

Nina was in London, at a party.

She had come with Patrick. The host was the architect she had met at a Hampstead lunch, almost a year ago, when she had run away from Grafton and the threat of Gordon. They had walked across Hampstead Heath, the architect had asked her to have lunch with him and she had declined the invitation. This evening he seemed pleased to see her when she threaded her way in Patrick's wake through the crowded room.

The architect's house was in north London, a red brick semi-detached villa on a hill that looked across a dipping vista of windows and rooftops towards Alexandra Palace perched on its higher hill. There were blond wood floors and minimalist furniture and large modern paintings. It was a metropolitan evening, familiar to Nina in a dozen respects; she could never have mistaken this setting for Grafton.

'Now, who do you know, apart from Patrick? Or who would you like to meet?' the architect asked her, with the tips of his fingers resting on her arm.

Nina gazed at the room, at the heads and shoulders and décolletages and the moving lipsticked mouths and gesticulating hands, and smiled. She did not have any qualms about coming back to this. Not much had changed in a year; not much, and everything.

'We seem to know quite a lot of people in common already.'

It was true. There were at least a dozen acquaintances of hers in the thick of the crowd. There were even Lucy and Cathy Clegg, also invited along by Patrick. The twins were now out of their Lycra mini-skirts and into seventies revival crochet and flares. Patrick had helped Lucy to find a job in a gallery, and Cathy was cooking in a wholefood café in Covent Garden. The girls waved at Nina from across the room. They were wearing their long hair dead straight, and parted in the middle.

'You know those two? Aren't they great?'

'I do know them, as a matter of fact,' Nina murmured.

The architect steered her into a group containing a pair of psychotherapists, a journalist and a painter.

'I'll be back,' he promised her.

Nina guessed that he would. He was not unattractive, and it occurred to her that one or two brief love affairs might approximately blur the truth of her baby's paternity. She smiled again as the conversation drew her in. She rather liked this new, determined version of herself.

The groups of party guests rotated, and coalesced, and split apart again.

Food appeared and was eaten, and the noise level rose. The Clegg girls confided to her that living in London was a thousand times better than Grafton, and that Patrick had been totally, amazingly kind to them. Nina passed from group to group, listening to news and gossip. Late in the evening, as the crowd began to thin, Nina found that she was tired from standing, and she slipped into an empty corner of the architect's long black sofa. The rest of it was occupied by a man in jeans, and a woman who was partly hidden from Nina's view by the man.

'Shall I get some coffee?' she heard the man ask. Then he stood up and Nina was left on the sofa with the woman. Nina became aware that she was being stared at, and she turned her head.

The woman said, 'I'm Miranda French.'

She was younger than Nina, perhaps thirty or so. She had dark red hair like Nina's, pulled back into a short plait with a puff of frizzed fringe over her forehead, dark red lipstick that made her mouth look almost black, and thin, straight eyebrows with pronounced wings that bracketed her dark eyes. Her stare made Nina uncomfortable. There was something else about her too, an air of faintly threatening intensity that might only have been the result of too much to drink.

'Nina Cort,' Nina offered.

'I know. You are a friend of Darcy Clegg's, aren't you? And those are his daughters?'

'Yes. How do you know Darcy?'

The woman gestured dismissively. 'Oh, I worked with him, years ago. Bad news all this, isn't it?'

They talked stiltedly for a moment about Darcy and the press coverage and the trial for which a date was yet to be set. Miranda French kept her eyes fixed on Nina's face, and Nina felt a shiver of premonitory discomfort that made her want to get up and leave the woman behind, anywhere that was out of her sight. She was rehearsing the move in her head when she saw with dismay

451

that Miranda's eyes were full of tears. The woman blinked, and the first tears overflowed over the spikes of her lower lashes.

'You don't know who I am, do you?' she whispered.

'No, I don't.' Nina could hear the slow circulation of blood in the echo chambers of her own ears.

'Why should you?' She leaned forward and Nina resisted the longing to move away, out of her reach. 'But I loved him. I was his lover.'

Stupidly, Nina shook her head.

'His lover? Darcy's?'

The woman said, forming the syllables carefully with her dark lips, 'Richard's.'

The party noise did not falter. Nina heard it like waves crashing around her.

'Richard was my husband.'

Miranda's shoulders were shaking. She had begun to sob, pressing the palms of her hands against her cheeks. Nina became coldly aware that the nearest people were turning to look at them.

'Do you think I don't know he was your husband? Oh, Richard took good care that you shouldn't find out about us, he was always careful of you. You were to be protected, always. But *I* was his lover. I was there with him.'

'Where were you with him?' Nina asked, her face stiff.

'In Norfolk at the cottage that week. I only left him that morning. I was the last person to see him. He came out into the lane to wave to me when I drove away.'

Nina saw in her mind's eye the apple tree, and the path beneath it, and the cottage behind. When she arrived with Patrick, Richard's body had been carried inside.

'How long?' She did not want to ask, to hear any more, but she could not help herself.

'Two years.' The other woman's mouth was stretched and her lipstick bled into the creases at the corners of it, and her eyes were streaming with glassy tears.

There were people staring curiously at them both. For Nina

452

the important thing became the need to limit this damage. She must get away from here at once, and from the people, and the woman herself.

'Here we are,' she heard someone say. It was the man in jeans, carrying a cup in each hand.

'Excuse me,' Nina said clearly. She managed to stand up, and make her legs begin to move, pushing herself between the knots of people who cut her off from the door. She did not see Patrick, or the architect. There were people on the stairs but she climbed past them with her fingers floating over the banister. Her coat was in the heap on a bed in one of the rooms. She put it on, turning up the collar as if it would protect her. Then she retraced her steps, hurrying with her head bent, praying that she might get away without even Patrick seeing her.

Outside in the safety of the darkness she stood gasping for breath as if she had been running. The sky was clear above the orange varnish of the street lights, and the air was cold.

It took her a moment to remember where she was, and longer to recall that her car was parked in the parallel street. When she found the Mercedes she sat huddled inside it, staring unseeingly along the bonnet at the lines of tidy houses that spread down the hill.

The image that kept recurring to her was of the red-haired woman, Miranda, driving away from the cottage and Richard standing in the lane to wave. He had always done that for Nina too, come out to wave her off.

Nina's hands were locked on the steering wheel. A couple passed, walking along the pavement with their arms around each other's waists, and they glanced back to look at her in the car. The intrusion made her turn the key in the ignition and begin to drive, without any idea of where she was going.

Two years. She thought of the times with Richard that the span of their last two years contained, which holidays and which birthdays, and tried to remember if there had been any change, any one moment when he had become less her husband than another woman's lover. She could not think of any. Richard had always been the same, and that made her feel even more duped and disorientated.

She kept on driving, through a maze of unfamiliar streets. She saw the lurid light of an all-night filling station, and stopped for petrol. From the call box beside the forecourt she dialled Patrick's number, and was surprised to hear his answering machine. The party seemed to belong to some remote time; it was bizarre to think that Patrick was probably still there. She left a non-committal message to say that she was fine, but would not be back that night.

She drove on, thinking about Richard and the long thread of their marriage, not just the last two years.

The familiarity of the Mercedes, the mechanical depend-ability of it, was oddly comforting. After a time she saw signs for the motorway and followed them towards the orange-lit ribbon of it in the distance. It was a relief, when she swept into the fast traffic, not to have to stop at lights and make the arbitrary decisions of whether to turn left or right. The rhythm of driving soothed her, and the sharp shock of what she had heard began to subside. She felt sad and weighty, all her senses dulled.

The road carried her on in an arc around London and then, without thinking about it, she took the westbound link that led away from the city towards Grafton. Once out into the country the blaze of oncoming headlights out of the darkness grew hypnotic. Nina realized that she was tired, that her eyes were heavy. She knew it would be easy to let her eyes close, and to take her hands off the wheel, letting them fall into her lap. She would let go altogether, let everything go. Her head nodded once and her eyelids drooped.

Then she jerked herself upright. Fear and self-disgust icily trickled down her back.

She opened the window and let the cold air rush into her face. She groped for the controls of the radio and filled the car with loud music. She was shivering, partly from cold and partly with the horror of what she had almost willed to happen.

There was the baby. Not Richard's, but her own. And there

454

were the other cars, in front of her and behind her, with their invisible occupants behind the eyes of oncoming light.

Nina remembered how, in the time after Richard's death, she had begun to long for her friends to interrupt their loving sympathy and tell her that he was gone and she was still alive, and that she must get on with living her life. She thought now, Anyway, that is what I have done.

She had gone on living, some of the time competently and at other times handicapped by loss, and resentful of it. There had been Gordon and Barney and her friendship with Star and the Grafton couples, and her work, and soon there would be her child. She would go on living, whatever truths sprang out of the past to ambush her.

The realization that she was glad of it came to her with a curl of happiness.

She thought back to her love affair with Gordon. The pain and the delight of it remained with her. She had not condemned Gordon then or now for what he had made Vicky suffer. How could she have done? And so how then could she condemn Richard, whose life was over, and who would never be able to tell her the truth?

Nina groped towards the beginning of understanding, that she might be angry with him, and that she might also be jealous and saddened, but she could not judge him for what he had done, for what was in the past and irretrievable. She felt the first lick of sympathy, too, unwilling as yet, for the weeping red-haired woman.

As she drove on, heading westwards, she was thinking about secrets and betrayal, and the Grafton couples, and the delicate private equilibrium of marriage.

After another hour she was growing drowsy again. The clock in the glow of the instrument panel told her that it was three a.m. At the next junction Nina turned off the motorway and took a road at random, following it through a village and on out into a patch of open country. When her headlights picked out a wide grass verge she swung the car off the road and switched off the engine. In the darkness she tilted back her seat and wrapped her coat tightly around her. Her thoughts stilled and faded and she fell asleep.

It was daylight when she woke. The rising sun shone straight into her eyes, and she was stiff and very cold. The grass in front of the car was touched with the glitter of frost.

Nina drove slowly back to the village she had passed through in the middle of the night. When she saw the name, she realized that she was only twenty miles from Grafton. There was a country road that she could take, and the road would lead her directly past Wilton Manor.

It was half-past nine when Nina turned in at the driveway of the Cleggs' house. The sun was melting the frost on the grass and Darcy was out in his Sunday morning gardening clothes raking up leaves from the gravel.

Nina climbed out of the car, chilled and bedraggled in her party clothes, her body aching from the cold and the long night.

'Nina? Nina, are you all right?'

There were holes in the elbows of Darcy's jersey; Nina had never seen him look less than immaculate.

'Yes. More or less, I think. I was at a Hallowe'en party in London, and I slept in the car on the way down.'

Darcy held her hand. Nina was surprised to see the concern in his face. 'You are so cold. Come on, come in the house. Hannah's taken Freddie for a riding lesson, but I can manage to make you coffee and some breakfast.'

The big kitchen was warm and seemed infinitely welcoming. Nina sat at the table, drinking the hot coffee that Darcy gave her. Laura ran through the room in her nightdress, and Darcy caught her and sat her at the table.

'Eat your breakfast,' he ordered her. He smiled at Nina, a little defiantly. 'The house seems very quiet, with Barney and the twins gone.'

'Yes, it must do.'

'We were at a Hallowe'en party last night too, at Andrew and Janice's.'

'How was everyone?'

He glanced at her. 'The same, more or less, except for Jimmy. Janice had a few drinks and made a speech about friendship. It almost made me cry, as a matter of fact. I must be getting sentimental.'

'I don't think it's sentimental to value friendship, is it?'

Again, he looked sharply at her. 'Perhaps not. Are you hungry?'

Nina realized that she was ravenous.

Darcy made her scrambled eggs, and she ate them gratefully.

When she had finished eating, and Laura had run away to look for Zoë, Darcy asked her, 'What is it, Nina?'

'I wanted to ask you something. May I?'

He gestured. 'Why not? I've plenty of time.'

She began without hesitation. 'I met a woman at the party last night, a woman called Miranda French. She told me that she knew you. And she also told me that she was my husband's lover. Did you know about it?'

'Yes,' Darcy said. He opened a drawer and took out a packet of small cigars. He lit one, and inhaled deeply. 'These are utterly forbidden. Yes, I knew Miranda well before I married Hannah. I heard about her, and Richard's death, and then I forgot about it. I remembered again after I met you, and I realized you were his wife.'

'You never told me.'

Darcy asked gently, 'Why would I want to hurt you?'

No, Nina thought, he would not want that any more than she had wanted to hurt Vicky, or unwittingly to set off the reverberations through the quiet world of the smiling, handsome couples. Richard had not wanted to hurt her, either. Her security with him up until the day of his death was evidence of that.

'We're all guilty, aren't we?' Nina said aloud, unthinkingly.

Darcy laughed, and for a moment he became the big, confident man she had met a year ago.

'No doubt of that,' he answered, drawing on his cigar. 'Guilty as hell.'

Nina looked at her watch. She wanted to be gone before Hannah came back.

'Thank you for my breakfast,' she said.

'Don't go sleeping in your car beside the road any more. It's dangerous.'

'I won't.'

He walked out with her to the Mercedes. Before she stepped into it Darcy held her arm.

'Were you careful with my Barney?'

It was the first intimation Darcy had given of knowing anything about it. Nina gazed levelly back at him.

'I was. I promise I was.'

He nodded, and then kissed her cheek before he stood back to let her go. As she drove away Nina saw him watching with his arm raised, waving her off.

Nina thought she would collect a few more of her possessions, and then drive back to London. She found the house in Dean's Row silent and cold, with the ashes of the last fire she had lit lying in the drawing room grate. She went to the window, and stood for a long time looking at the west front of the cathedral and the golden tiers of restored saints and martyrs and archangels.

The vision of regeneration and renewal was deeply pleasing.

Then Nina folded the old shutters smoothly across the window again. She fitted the catch into its secure socket, closing the November sunlight out of the cold room.